Love from Italy

AN OMNIBUS

A Note from the Author

All three novels in this collection are set in the north-east region of Italy known as Friuli (or Friuli-Venezia Guilia), including the beautiful sinking city of Venice.

I was actually born in Casarsa Della Delizia, in Friuli – the place Marco escapes to in *The Mystery Of Carmen* – which is a ninety-minute train ride from Venice via Mestre. Casarsa was once a humble farming community where daughters were often sent away at the age of 10 to work for the rich. Now it is a wealthy small town whose rooftops gleam with solar panels.

The late poet and filmmaker Pier Paolo Pasolini once wrote that his time in Friuli, briefly as a teacher, was one of the 'most beautiful years of my life', admiring its many customs and dialects.

He wrote of Casarsa's 16th century houses: 'They display the soft blues and blackish tones of some crude Renaissance painter . . .'. He recalled the boys and old men of the local choir . . . 'their hair combed, by Catholic tradition, with a part on one side and a forelock standing up over their wooden and irregular faces.'

All three novels are set in the 1950s – a time for me of romantic ideals and new possibilities – and I have drawn on the ways and some of the strange stories of the Friuli people.

If you believe in love, my stories are for you, wherever you are.

Giovanna Bozzer, 2000

Love from Italy

AN OMNIBUS

Three romantic sagas set in the 1950s

The Mechanic
The Ghost of Valentino
The Mystery of Carmen

Giovanna Bozzer

EQUINOX PUBLISHING LTD

This edition printed by Equinox Publishing Ltd,
Edgware House, 389 Burnt Oak Broadway,
Edgware, Middlesex HA8 5TX, UK.
E-mail: Volliver@hotmail.com

A CIP catalogue record for this book is available from the
British Library.

ISBN 1 903644 00 3

Typeset by Palimpsest Book Production Limited,
Polmont, Stirlingshire

Printed in Great Britain by Omnia Books Limited, Glasgow

Cover picture: Rudolph Valentino taken from The Sheik. Grateful
acknowledgement to Paramount Pictures.
Cover design: Gareth Bouch

To my mother,
Santa Bozzer

The Mechanic

'Hey, Lorenzo!'

It was my mother shouting up from the foot of the stairs.

'Are you up yet? Your breakfast is ready!'

I heard her in a dream and now I rolled off my pillows awake – 'I'll be down in ten minutes,' I moaned loudly.

I threw the bedclothes onto the floor. If I didn't do that at this precise moment I'd never get up at all.

I'd just doze on until my mother crowed up again.

I ran to the bathroom, knocked a soap container to the floor – which I didn't pick up – and stamped about flat-footedly so that they knew downstairs I was up.

'Every morning's the same,' scolded my mother as I entered the kitchen a few minutes later. 'Noise, noise, noise. It sounds like an earthquake in the ceiling—'

'How can you have an earthquake in the ceiling?' I asked, rubbing my eyes.

'Don't try to be clever. It's a wonder you don't fall through the floor to your breakfast. If only you went to bed early at night it wouldn't be such a rush in the morning.'

She placed a warm plate on the table in front of me. That was her bait. She knew I would never leave the table till I'd eaten. So now I was caught in her net, she'd begin her other routine which was to wail about my life and tell me what I should be doing with it . . .

'Lorenzo,' she'd say, juggling spitting pans at the cooker, 'you're twenty-eight years old and you've still not settled down yet. I feel sorry for poor Luisa – you've not even proposed to her yet—'

And while she talked on automatic she'd bring the frying pan, spitting fat, to my side – I leant away to avoid staining spots on my clothes – and scraped prosciutto omelette onto my plate.

I'd watch the flesh on her arms and chin wobble as she lunged at pan and plate with the spatula.

'It's time you grew up!' she'd conclude, as she did every other morning, noon and night, throwing the spatula into the empty pan when she was done.

She was plump and tall in her middle years, and still had the lustrous black hair and bright coal eyes of the Friuli people, so close to Venice . . .

Oh yes, my father, I almost forgot him. He sat opposite me every morning and we'd grunt at each other by way of conversation . . .

Today she said, 'It's a year since you and Luisa started going out.' She stood over me, peering down at my munching head with her arms folded.

'Leave him alone Elsa,' groaned my father reading a newspaper – 'At least when he's eating. He's got his garage to think about, not some wife.'

'I don't mean to nag him,' she said, as if I had left the room, 'but I do worry about him.'

'Why, mamma?' I asked looking up. 'I will marry Luisa when the time is right.'

For the first time that morning I looked at her full in the face. She was still beautiful, but for her plumpness. She had this habit of saying everything with a surprised expression on her face and a shriek in her voice, as if what she said had just occurred to her that very morning.

A stranger might think she had awoken with fresh thoughts. But really her script hadn't changed in months – once upon a time she learned that repetition gets you results eventually.

'Eh, mamma,' I said with a smile, 'when are you going to lose some weight?'

She was annoyed by that – 'Don't you be cheeky – you're not so old that I can't still give you a wallop – when are you going to settle down with Luisa?'

I had upset her so I kissed her on the cheek. 'I have to go now,' I said rushing out.

It all sounds like an ordinary morning, just another day in a predictable life. But it was not to be . . .

I stepped into my van and drove to my garage a mile down the road. Yes, I was, and am, a car mechanic.

I had just started up my own business. Some people thought I was mad to work for myself. Why not? I like to work at my own pace, not be answerable to anyone – except the bank manager. If I was as good as some people thought I was, I knew I had a little empire on my hands.

I planned to expand it one day. I didn't want to live hand–to–mouth like my family, or live off the land.

My mother always said I was born under a car – 'I don't know who you take after,' she'd say. Well, I found a living there, under the car.

But that particular day, which had started in its normal way, would be like no other. It would be a turning point. Maybe life had wanted to test me. I had always stuck to what I wanted in life. *I'd* decide when I married. *I'd* choose my career.

But how far was I prepared to strike out on my own against other people's expectations? Would I be prepared to break the rules in matters of love? I wasn't asking such questions *then*. I wouldn't have thought of them.

All I ever really thought about was my garage . . .

That morning I was to be found . . . under a car. Sometimes I felt like a robot doctor. 'Pass the scalpel. Pass the wrench.' I had no nurse then. Or rather, I had no assistant – I couldn't afford one, and in any case the workload was not that heavy.

I had always been fascinated by broken down cars. To begin with you had no idea what was wrong with them, or where to start with the repair. Time passed in a blur as you fiddled with pipes and caps, searching for the problem. Each car was a new challenge, each day held new adventures . . .

Everything was in place. My life, then, seemed like the workings of a car. Pull the ignition and the fan belt turned. All perfectly logical, straightforward.

There was nothing complicated about a car, once you had read the manual.

But *this* morning would be anything but logical . . .

So I was lying under a car. Working. Oil was dribbling onto my overalls . . . nothing complicated . . .

I heard a car pull into the garage – another customer.

Good, I thought in the murk of the undercarriage. More business.

With a push of my legs I wheeled myself out into the daylight.

I looked up and there she was. Someone you'd never expect to see in a place like this . . . a very beautiful, very glamorous woman, looking very alarmed.

Alarmed by the sight of oily me probably.

Her long blonde hair seemed to fall like a waterfall over the length of her slender body, and her wonderful scent immediately made me ashamed of my grease and rags.

Her alarmed expression passed in a moment. Then her face lit up in a huge, friendly smile – perhaps she was amused by this greasy man in his overalls who had emerged from the ground like a mole . . .

I was captivated by her startling green eyes. Silently I struggled to my feet, feeling grubby in her perfect presence.

She broke the silence: she said there was something wrong with her car – would I take a look at it?

'I'd be very grateful if you could do it within the hour,' she said gently, still smiling. 'I have a very important business matter to attend to.'

'Depends what's wrong with it,' I said, gruffly. 'I'll see what I can do.'

Ordinarily I would have kept the car over for a day as I had other repairs. But those green eyes . . . and that red . . . car of hers . . . and in any case it all added up to a lot of money – I was a shrewd businessman even then.

I opened the bonnet and was knocked back by a wave of heat from the engine. 'It'll have to cool,' I said, 'it'll take a few minutes.'

She stood on the spot.

I felt her gaze.

'Have you done this job for long?' she asked.

It was more than a time-filling question: there was true interest in her voice. Something in her familiar, easy manner pleased me. Maybe I was flattered at that moment by her attention.

'For some time,' I said. 'I used to work for a garage – then I decided to set up my own business.'

'Very enterprising,' she said with a fixed look and a smile. 'You must have given your wife a shock – it's risky working for yourself.'

Even I knew she was asking me if was married.

'I'm not married – not likely to be yet.'

The engine creaked and clicked as it cooled and I opened the water tank.

'I'm married,' she said, as I sunk under the bonnet.

'Yes.'

'To an old man. He has a bad heart. So I have to run the business for him.'

'What sort of business?'

'Well,' she said, drawing closer to the bonnet, 'it's to do with doll making.'

I pulled up from the engine and our eyes met once again. My heart was racing. I knew she had caught me. My impulse was to ask her out – but how could I? How many other times had I been turned on by a pretty face?

But her elegant clothes. And my filthy overalls. The two were not made for each other. I always had some sense. I was never the dreamer or mad optimist.

Still, the impulse wouldn't budge: how would she react if I did attempt to date her?

I don't believe in mind-reading or any of that nonsense but at that very moment she said to me:

'Would you like to have a drink with me tomorrow evening?'

She doesn't waste time, I thought to myself. I think I blushed, maybe because I feared she'd read my thoughts. I was stuck for words. Normally I like to do the running, but with this one I knew instinctively that I had to forget the rules, and my dirty overalls.

'Yeah,' I stuttered. 'It'd be nice to see you . . .'

There was nothing much wrong with her car that cold water couldn't put right. As she got in I wondered if I really would see her again.

She turned the ignition key.

She shut the door.

And unwound the window.

'What's your name?' she asked.

'Lorenzo Viardy.'

'I'm Anna Gilli.'

'That's a lovely name – Anna.'

'I'm glad you like it. I'll meet you here tomorrow night then.'

'I'll be here.'

With that she drove off.

I threw down a spanner and rested against a drum. What was that all about? I asked myself. Am I dreaming? Why would a rich and beautiful woman be interested in me? She didn't appear to mind my oily appearance.

If Anna wasn't a dream, certainly the rest of the day passed in one. That is until Luisa called at the garage at five in the afternoon as she usually did.

Our habit was to disappear inside and make love on a bed chair just beyond my little office. Today I wasn't in the mood. I was quiet, and almost resented her being there. Luisa asked me if there was anything wrong.

It wasn't like me not to want to make love.

'You don't seem very pleased to see me – or am I imagining things?' she said.

'Of course I am happy to see you,' I said, preoccupying myself with something that could have waited. 'But today's been a bad day – I just want to go straight home.'

Poor Luisa. This was the first time we'd not gone into the back of the garage. She was a pretty brunette with dark brown eyes – not very tall, certainly shorter than my mother – and a slim frame.

She looked upset, not so much because I was not going to make love to her but because she sensed I was miles away from her. And she told me so.

'Come on Luisa, I'll take you home – I'll feel better tomorrow.'

In the car we had nothing to say to each other. I racked my mind for something to talk about. I could scarcely believe that one brief meeting with a stranger could alter me so much.

When we arrived at her family's home she asked me if I was taking her out that night.

'Sorry Luisa. I'd like to but I have something important to discuss with Piero.'

'What about tomorrow then?'

'I can't. I have a business thing to sort out – I will call you Luisa.'

She was sulking now – in some ways she was still a child, and I was her first love. I think.

As she turned to step out of the car, she asked, 'Have you grown tired of me?'

She didn't look at me. I don't think she could bear to hear my answer.

'Of course not,' I said, touching her shoulder.

She was not reassured.

Then I drove home, only a quarter of a mile away. Suddenly I felt very happy, free and renewed. I bounced into our small garden which my mother kept so well; and indoors I started to sing *Come Prima*, which was a very popular song then.

'And why are you so full of the joys?' a voice asked from the back of the house. My mother's.

'I just feel I want to sing,' I shouted.

Anna had already entered my soul and I knew her not at all. I couldn't possibly tell my mother.

She would have said I was the biggest idiot and worse besides.

★   ★   ★

The next morning Luisa was waiting for me outside the house as I left for the garage.

'What are you doing here Luisa – why didn't you call in?' I said, throwing some tools into the back of my car.

'I didn't want to,' she said with petulance. 'And if I had your mother would have only asked me what I was doing here so early in the morning.'

I ignored her words – 'Take you to work?' I said casually.

'No. I just want to talk to you Lorenzo.'

'What about?'

'For the first time since we started going out I feel unhappy. I love you very much but suddenly I don't know you any more.'

I faced her – 'What's the problem?'

'I don't know . . . you've changed—'

'You're not sulking about last night? Or about tonight, because I'm too busy?'

Tears streamed down poor Luisa's cheeks.

'Come on Luisa,' I said embracing her, wondering whether my mother might be watching us from the kitchen. 'There's no need to cry.'

'I'm sorry Lorenzo. I just want to hear you say you love me.'

'Of course I do.'

I did not like myself for lying to her. I just wanted her to stop crying so that I could get to work and think about Anna.

I kissed Luisa gently on the lips – 'I have to be going now. I've got a lot to do in the garage but I can run you to work first.'

This time she nodded silently.

Before I dropped her off I said I'd call her soon.

'I hope you will Lorenzo,' she said with a bit of edge in her voice.

11

But it wasn't Luisa I was thinking of as I entered my garage. My mind was full of Anna's long blonde hair framing her perfect oval face, and the light from her emerald eyes. I wasn't sure what was happening to me. There was this battle inside me ... yes, I was scared of my feelings for her ... I loved Luisa too ... I had sort of planned to marry her ... eventually ... but now I wasn't so sure.

I really didn't know what to do.

The next evening I prepared to meet Anna. I got out my best suit.

In the mirror I couldn't help admire myself – I didn't think I was being vain then: I admired my dark eyes and contrasted them with Anna's green.

My father always said I had my mother's good looks – when she was younger.

At the garage I waited for her ...

And waited.

But she never turned up. I was so disappointed and miserable. It had been too much to expect, and it was too early to return home so I decided to go some place for a drink, and I got drunk that night.

Under the influence I began to suspect she had played a little joke on me. Why would a woman in her position take any serious notice of me?

I was just a plain mechanic. I lived in a different world from hers.

But I also knew in my heart that there were no rules about what you ought to feel for another person, whatever their class. Love just happened.

I could have got in touch with Luisa in the next few days but I wasn't in the right mood to see her, not just yet. I needed to sort myself out. Days, weeks, passed; poor Luisa.

12

She looked so solemn when she finally called at the garage.

'*Ciao*, Lorenzo,' she said one day. 'It's been ages since we've seen each other – I thought I'd make a move and come and see you. I want to know what's happening. Are you bored with me?'

I raised my head from a car engine – 'Of course not, but I've a lot on my mind at the moment.'

'Shall we go somewhere tonight so we can talk about what's bothering you?'

'Sure,' I said, thinking that it was unlikely I'd see Anna again. 'I'll pick you up at seven-thirty.'

Luisa smiled for the first time. I sensed her relief. And before she left I kissed her on the lips.

After she'd gone I slipped under a car I was servicing. I remember thinking that I'd do another hour's work before going home. I was so deep in thought that I didn't hear a car pull in.

But a voice broke my trance.

In a flash I had slid out into the light and was on my feet. There Anna stood gazing at me.

She was as beautiful as I remembered her, and all my first feelings for her – replaced since with anger and confusion – were stirred to life in a moment.

Once again her green eyes blinded me.

'I am very sorry,' she started. 'I didn't mean to stand you up – the night we were supposed to meet. But I had some trouble with my husband, he wasn't at all well. He had one of his attacks.'

'What's wrong with him?' I asked, taking her word as gospel and forgetting my own pain.

'One day I'll tell you all about him.'

'What about the following days – why didn't you let me know – you could have. I heard nothing.'

13

Anna approached me – 'Will you forgive me then Lorenzo?'

'I don't know you . . . what's to forgive?'

'Are you free tonight?'

'No.' I couldn't let Luisa down again. 'Why do you ask?'

'It's the birthday of one of my friends today and she's giving a party tonight and I'd like you to come with me.'

It was her eyes which were really doing the talking. I couldn't resist them.

'All right, Anna,' I said coolly, almost unable to control my excitement. 'I'll come with you – but it means cancelling my other plans.'

'Are they not important?'

'No. Where's the party?'

'In Venice, and my friends are very nice.'

'Are they rich?'

'Yes!' she said, with sudden slight irritation. 'Why do you ask Lorenzo?'

'It's just I'm not used to mixing with rich people – I don't want to let you down.'

Anna's eyes widened with surprise – as if I had said something very odd.

'A bright man like you should not fear anybody,' she said with real feeling. 'It does not matter what class you belong to. You have to learn to stand up for yourself – like I had to!'

Now it was my turn to be surprised. She was quite vehement, fiery – the opposite to the warm side I'd only seen so far.

'What do you mean Anna?'

'I'll tell you one day when we get to know each other a bit better. Believe me, darling, there's nothing special about my friends. And when you meet them you'll agree.'

14

She called me darling! I must admit that her words rallied my confidence. She had spoken with true feeling – she was clearly strong, full of character.

'So we meet here tonight?' she asked.

'Yes, here – at eight? And I want you to have my phone number in case you can't make it.'

'All right darling, eight it is,' she said, taking the crumpled piece of paper I'd written my number on.

She leaned forward and for the first time kissed me softly on the lips, which set my heart pounding. I was too nervous to respond.

Then she drove off.

My God! That woman had done something to me, though I could only mumble and gibber to myself what that might be. I couldn't even find the words in my own head to describe all the deep blinding feelings I felt for Anna.

I now had a problem. What would I say to Luisa, having promised to take her out? And would Anna really contact me if she couldn't make it?

I decided if she let me down I'd never see her again.

On my way home I spotted my friend Piero in the street and stopped the car.

'*Ciao*!' he cried. 'You finished work?'

'Yes – I'm off home now.'

'What about a drink?'

'I can't – I've got a lot to do.'

'So, what about the weekend? We can go cycling in the country with the girls and have some fun in the fields – well?'

Piero seemed so young at that moment though we were of the same age – friends since childhood. He was shorter than me, very dark, olive-skinned . . .

'No. Luisa is too serious for any fun in the fields.'

15

'Come on,' he said grinning, 'you're losing your sense of humour – I was only joking!'

'I can't make the weekend.'

Piero was always the sharp one, never missed a trick – and he was direct. He asked me straight out, 'Are you still going serious with Luisa then?'

I stuttered a bit – 'I . . . think I am.'

Back home.

The delicious aroma of tomato sauce for the pasta. I see my mother now. Leaning over the cooker, hot and bothered, more because of her weight than the steam rising from the pot.

She turned to me – 'Eh, Luisa called, it's her day off – she seemed very happy. Have you proposed to her Lorenzo?'

I threw up my eyes. 'Please mamma, not again. How about some spaghetti.'

'You'll have to wait for your father,' she bellowed. 'He should be back soon.'

I went into the living room to write a little note to Luisa. I thought up some flimsy excuse for not seeing her that night. Later, after dinner, I callously posted it on my way back to the garage to pick up Anna.

I got to the garage a bit early and lay on the bedchair nervously wondering if Anna would turn up. At eight precisely my green-eyed lady made her entrance in her red car.

'*Ciao* Lorenzo,' she shouted. 'You see – I have not let you down!'

She got out of the car – 'How handsome you look tonight.' I was greatly flattered.

'And you look fabulous.'

I recall she was wearing a silk green dress to match her

16

eyes which was pinched at the waist to show off her hips. The perfect shape. For the first time she wore her hair up – though I preferred it worn down.

I couldn't help but take her in my arms and kiss her passionately. I remember now her trembling slightly but responding to me. At that moment I knew she meant more to me than anyone I'd ever known.

A little later we drove to Venice and left the car near the city railway station. We ignored the gondolas (priced for the tourists) and took a simple motor boat up the Grand Canal.

The waters turned our trip into an adventure, a mystery trip for me. Even to Italians who live on the outskirts of Venice, the city is a place of romance and glamour. We passed hordes of foreign visitors drinking coffee and sipping liqueurs in open cafes along the waterways – the rest of the world, so near to my little life.

We arrived at the flat of Anna's friend a little after nine. It was larger than I expected, elegantly furnished, with much marble and many mirrors. Several couples with drinks in hand stood talking in the living room . . . light music serenaded them . . .

A couple appeared from nowhere to greet us, Lucinda and Dino. I was treated as an immediate friend because of Anna. Everyone was very friendly and ordinary as she had said they would be.

The drinking however changed the mood of the evening. At one point I wanted some water and Anna pointed the way to the kitchen. Just as I about to enter – the door was ajar – I was stopped by talking within. It was Lucinda and Dino.

'Well, Anna has taken a lover,' she was saying, 'and he's so handsome.'

'Can you blame her?' he replied.

'With that nut case husband of hers she can't have much of a life. I do feel sorry for her. He just uses her.'

'They don't even sleep together — I bet.'

I was embarrassed, I didn't want to hear more. I knocked gently on the door and opened it wider — 'May I come in?'

'Is it you Lorenzo?' Lucinda said, turning to face me. 'Come in. Have you been there long?' she asked with a grin.

'Er, no . . .' Perhaps something about my sheepish manner suggested I had been eavesdropping. I didn't feel spontaneous.

'Enjoying yourself?' asked Dino.

'Very much — I just want some water.'

The music had been turned up by the time I returned to the party, so had the voices. Anna waltzed over to me — 'Are Lucinda and Dino in the kitchen?'

At that moment the pair reappeared, Dino bearing a beautiful birthday cake with — I was told — twenty-four candles aflame. A great 'wow!' filled the room and then the singing of Happy Birthday to Lucinda.

She blew out all the candles with a few puffs. Anna's friends were like children. Their money made them playful, bold, whimsical. Someone opened bottles of Spumante. I didn't want to drink too much — I had no intention of sleeping there the night. Everyone drank without thought, Anna included.

Then I heard a woman say aloud to another how dishy Anna's friend was, as if were deaf, or a moron.

'I wonder what he does for a living?' she asked.

'I bet he's a boxer,' said her friend.

'He's a big boy!'

'Whatever he does I wouldn't mind spending the night with him.'

Then they cackled like a couple of hens, spilling Spumante all over the place.

I was tempted to say something but before I could say a word I was astonished to see one of the girls take off her shoes, mount a table, and do the rumba. Everyone surrounded her clapping with the music. One by one they all threw out their hips.

Then Dino put on some Oriental sounding music. Anna did a belly dance with much whooping from the rest – I longed for her to take off her tight dress, she was good.

I caught her as she lost her balance at the end. Just as I carried her out of the room, one of the women said to me, 'You're just like Tarzan! Why don't you carry me off after you've dropped off Anna in your tree house!'

So that's what they thought of me. The men laughed – I would never have tolerated my girlfriend saying that to another man.

The party had got out of hand, it was too much for me. I wondered if any of them would remember anything tomorrow morning . . .

Then the doorbell rang – Anna was still in my arms, semi-conscious. Everyone continued dancing and screaming, so I carefully lay Anna down on the floor in the hallway and answered the door.

The caller was a little fat man, completely bald like Benito Mussolini, staring up at me as if I were some sort of dumb animal.

'Good evening,' he said quietly. 'My name is Signor Gilli. I'd like to see my wife Anna.'

I was so amazed by his arrival that I jabbered a bit. For some reason I told him my name.

'So you are the young man Anna tells me about. I am very pleased to meet you Lorenzo and thank you for accompanying my wife.'

If the party had not left me speechless then his words did. Why had Anna told him of me? — what had she said to him? I said he'd better come in.

Anna was still sprawled in the hallway — 'I see Anna has had quite a few drinks,' Signor Gilli said flatly, without surprise.

He peered up at me. 'But you will get her home safely, won't you Lorenzo. I shall not stop. I just wanted to say hello to Anna.'

I wondered to myself why he didn't just take her himself.

Anna had now stirred to her husband's voice and was struggling to her feet. She gazed blearily at him, saying 'What are you doing here Ottavio? I thought you didn't feel very well.'

'I am not well,' he replied quickly, 'I am just here out of curiosity.'

'Oh yes — and what have you sniffed out?'

'That you are in good hands with Lorenzo.'

I assumed he thought me some sort of idiot. Or he was naive. Or he was the nut case Lucinda described him as.

Everyone seemed to be talking about me as if I were not present.

'Take good care of her,' Signor Gilli said to me as he passed out the door. 'Goodbye.'

I couldn't resist a chuckle at his fastidious little hand movements.

Anna had perked up a bit and was now arranging her hair in her compact mirror.

I said, 'I think it's time to go home.'

She looked at me — 'We don't have to. We could sleep here like the rest.'

I couldn't fathom her attitude. Her husband would be

expecting me to return her. I didn't say this. Instead I told her that I was leaving now – 'And you're coming with me whether you like it or not!'

Anna smiled, indulgently, and seemed to relax. 'Very well darling, as you wish.'

As she stepped forward she tripped, and for the second time that night I managed to catch her before she did herself an injury.

I opened the door to the living room where everyone was spread out on the floor, flattened by Spumante. Everyone that is but Lucinda and her boyfriend, in bed together I guessed. There was no one to say goodnight to.

In the car I asked Anna to give me the directions to her home – 'If you're sober enough.'

Anna reacted sharply to that. 'I may have had a bit too much to drink,' she said, 'but I'm sober all right!'

And she was right. Forty minutes later we drew up along the two black wrought iron gates to her home.

'Do you have your keys to get in?' I asked.

'Of course,' she said. 'In my handbag.' Without warning she threw her arms around my neck – 'Would you like to spend the night with me, Lorenzo? Home with me?'

I was astonished she could ask me that, I thought, what with her husband more than likely waiting up for her, judging by the lights streaming from rooms.

'Come Anna,' I said, gently disentangling her arms, 'I am going to take you up to the door.'

Her huge villa stood some distance from the gates. I half expected her husband to meet us but all was very quiet. I helped Anna unlock the door – 'Can you make it in?' I whispered.

'Of course I can manage,' she said petulantly. 'I'll be all right.' She snuggled against me. 'I want you to kiss me before you go Lorenzo.'

'Not here. I'll have to use your car to get home – I'll return it sometime tomorrow.'

I drove back to the garage where I left her car, and then drove home in my van. It was two in the morning when I got in. All was quiet thank God. It wouldn't have surprised me if my mother had waited up for me with her rolling pin – no, I joke. She was a good soul really but like all Italian mothers she worried too much – even though I was twenty-eight!

In bed I kept thinking of the events of the evening, thinking about Anna, her odd husband, their wealth. It is strange how money affects people's conduct. I don't say all rich people are the same but money alters the usual rules of life.

I tried to compare Luisa and Anna: there was more to contrast. Luisa was untouched by life while Anna . . . well, she seemed to know everything. I felt the urgency of seeing her; I would have to see her again soon. And what of poor neglected Luisa?

Then I was lost in sleep.

I planned to take Anna's car later next day. At about eleven that morning Signor Gilli phoned me to tell me that he would send somebody to collect the car.

'How is Anna?' I asked.

'She is still in bed,' he said neutrally. 'I don't think she is feeling that good after last night.' To my surprise he then said, 'Lorenzo, how would you like to come here for supper tomorrow night?'

I didn't know what to think. What was the old man up to, this rich man? I decided there and then that I must talk to Anna first. I told Signor Gilli that I would think about it.

Later in the afternoon Anna phoned. '*Ciao* Lorenzo.' She sounded bleary. 'How are you?'

'I'm fine,' I said. 'Are you feeling better?'

'Yes much better. Did my husband tell you that I was unwell?'

'Yes. Anna, he's odd.'

'Odd? I told you before not to pay too much attention to him—'

'But he has invited me to supper tomorrow night. I don't understand what's wrong with him—'

I had expected her to be disturbed by this news. But she remained calm. 'Do come to supper Lorenzo.'

'I'll be there because it's you I want to see Anna.'

'Good. I'm already looking forward to seeing you again my darling and I'll think only of you till then.'

'And I'll be thinking of you.'

But the truth is I was not happy with this strange set-up. For no sensible reason I suddenly thought of Luisa – I should go see her. I needed to be with someone I understood. I knew I'd find sanity with her. Of course it was wrong of me to be so selfish. I didn't love her the same way as before . . . but I still wanted to see her.

I called on her after supper. Her father met me at the door.

'Oh!' he said with sarcasm, 'It's Lorenzo. What can I do for you?'

I told him I wanted to see Luisa.

'She's not here,' he said, scratching his naked chest matted with grey hair. 'She has gone to the pictures with a friend. And where have you been lately?'

Foolishly I asked, 'What do you mean by that?'

He snarled at me, jabbing his forefinger at me threat-eningly, 'You know damn well what I am talking about Lorenzo. You don't realise what you are doing to my daughter. It's about time you made up your mind about her and stopped stringing her along!'

23

I held my breath for a moment and then told him to mind his own business.

'My daughter is my business!' he roared. 'You forget we're talking about my daughter!'

Luisa's mother came to the door, drawn by his shouting, wanting to know what was going on.

'Nothing!' I said to them before leaving.

In the car I couldn't help thinking I would have said the same if my daughter was being treated so badly by a bastard like me. I parked outside a local taverna where I knew Piero might be.

And he was. He was talking to somebody at a table.

I placed a hand on his shoulder – 'Hello!'

He turned and looked up – 'So, what wind blew you in?'

'A strong one.'

He laughed. He always laughed easily. He lost his temper easily. I remember his grin and how quickly he could lose it.

I bought a drink and sat with him. His friend had moved to another table – I suspected Piero had asked him to leave us.

'Have you seen Luisa recently?' he asked. 'Or have you got tired of her? What's wrong with you? You haven't been yourself lately.' Before I could answer he added, 'I'm your best friend – tell me what's bothering you.'

I sipped my liqueur. I told him I had a lot on my mind. It was not easy to talk about.

'It would do you good to open up,' he said.

This was the old Piero who at school had always chivvied me to join in, his dark fast eyes full of mischief, always pressing me to do something.

'Are you worried about your business?'

'Not really.' I said.

'Come on then. Tell me!'

It was hopeless to resist.

I confessed about Anna and her eccentric husband and about my lies to Luisa and how I didn't like myself for all this.

When I finished he said, 'Listen Lorenzo, Anna is a married woman with a basketcase of a husband. What future have you with her? You're wasting your time. She's rich – to her you're just this toy, a good looking toy to show off to her friends, like a new car.'

'You're wrong. It's not like that. We love each other.'

'Open your eyes!' he said harshly, his face instantly stern and mature under the black waves of his hair. 'Even if she feels something for you, how long will it last with a spoilt bitch like that?'

'Better if I go,' I said rising. 'I can't listen to this.'

'OK you go – but if you want some good advice – make up with Luisa. She's good for you!'

I walked out and said not another word in case I lost my temper.

In the warm evening air I wondered for a moment if he was right. But what had being right or wrong to do with anything? I was certain I loved Anna, that's all that mattered. Commonsense would simply ruin everything and force me to go against my nature.

The next day Piero phoned me at the garage, asking if we could meet up. I asked him why. I didn't want any more lectures.

'I was going to suggest something. Course, I don't know how you will take it.'

'So, say what you want to say then.'

'I can't,' he said. 'It would take too long to explain.'

I relented. It would be good to see him again if he could control his tongue. We arranged to meet later that evening after Anna's.

25

However, Piero was not the only person taking a keen interest in my life. My mother had not been pleased to learn I would not be having dinner at home. When I got in from work at six she called me from the kitchen, and as usual she came straight to the point.

'What has happened, Lorenzo? Luisa was here today and she tells me you're not going out with her anymore.'

'Well, mamma,' I started, putting down my tool bag, 'it's true I've not seen much of her lately. I need to sort myself out – what I feel for her.'

'Better that you do!' she said as she stirred the soup. Her frantic little movements over the pot shook her head – I could tell she was trying to hold her temper. 'What a pity if you and Luisa don't get together.' Then in a dramatic gesture she smacked the wooden spoon down on the stove and looked at me hard – 'Have you someone else?'

Nothing infuriated my mother more than a mystery but I felt I couldn't tell her about Anna.

'If I have found someone else there's nothing you can do about it,' I said.

'I just hope you know what you are doing Lorenzo.'

At that moment my father walked in, thank God. Mamma instantly shut up.

Past seven I left for Anna's. This would be a bizarre date, I knew, with her husband in attendance. I arrived about twenty minutes later. Anna's husband answered the door, much to my surprise. I had expected a servant. He was well turned out in a white jacket and black trousers, his head polished.

Quite a contrast to my casual clothes – but I knew I looked good in them.

'Ah, hello Lorenzo,' he said without a smile. 'It is nice to see you again.'

26

'Thank you Signor Gilli—'

'Ottavio. You should call me Ottavio.'

He seemed normal, in control of himself, except for the flatness of his voice and blankness of expression. He led me silently along a marble-floored hallway, hung with portraits, to a large dining room where Anna was seated at the table fiddling with the arrangement – the flowers I think.

When she saw me she got up in a rush and put her hands to my face – 'Darling, how handsome you look.'

I blushed a little at her intimacy. Yet when I glanced at Ottavio he was smiling broadly, as if we were a couple of kids at a birthday party.

It was yet another strange thing about him. He didn't seem to mind how Anna and I conducted ourselves in front of him. Another husband would have shot me for the way I looked at Anna.

She shimmered spectacularly in a startling white dress – to match Ottavio's jacket.

There was little small talk. We sat down and food was served.

'You have a beautiful home,' I said to them both.

'I am glad you like it,' Ottavio said. He looked at Anna and she gave him a half-smile. It was difficult to tell whether it was affectionate or sneering.

'And how long have you been a car mechanic?' he asked.

'Six years.'

'And you enjoy it?'

'I do, very much. With a bit of luck I hope to expand it before long.'

'And have you other ambitions Lorenzo?'

'I . . . I don't know what you mean. That's my ambition.'

To my alarm Anna snapped at him – 'Have you finished questioning Lorenzo? It's none of your business – questioning him like that!'

'My dear,' responded Ottavio submissively, 'I didn't mean to be intrusive or overly personal.'

With a spoon at his lips he appeared so humbled that I felt I had to say I appreciated his interest: 'You can ask me whatever you wish.'

As I said this he put down his spoon and began to rub his head with one hand and pull at one of his ears with the other.

Anna threw her napkin on the table.

'Ottavio, you're feeling unwell!' she shouted.

Without hesitation he got up and apologised. I couldn't help feeling sorry for the poor devil. Anna was about to follow him out the room but I asked her not to – 'Wouldn't it be better if you left him alone,' I said. 'You should have better ways with him and not humiliate him. He's not well.'

Anna shrugged her shoulders and returned to the table. 'Sometimes he really annoys me,' she said quietly.

'I don't think he was saying anything out of place. He was just trying to make conversation. I don't see why you got so irritated.'

She leaned over and placed her hands on mine – 'I know I am not the most tolerant of people. Forgive me darling.' Then she smiled wildly. 'Come Lorenzo, I want to show you the garden.'

'But we haven't finished supper.'

Anna wasn't concerned. She grabbed my arm and pulled me to the door. 'Let's see the garden before it gets dark.'

It was not so much a garden as a field in bloom, a wonderful rainbow of colours, broken up by large fruit trees. I inhaled and felt great peace.

'This,' I said, 'is like the Garden of Eden.'

She laughed, 'And we are Adam and Eve?'

As we strolled along a narrow rosewalk Anna told me a little more about herself.

'I have not always been rich, not till I met Ottavio. He's been rich since birth. He was a widower when I met him. My life has been much harder than his. From my early teens I had to work full-time to support myself. And in the evenings I studied at secretarial school. I passed and ended up in Ottavio's company. After only one week he proposed to me.'

'But he's so much older than you . . .'

'Old enough to be my grandfather. He's sixty-seven now, and I'm a spring chicken twenty-seven.'

'Forty years difference!' I said, horrified. 'How could you marry someone so much older?'

'I didn't think twice about marrying him at all. Age was irrelevant. I only thought about all that money he's got. I guessed I'd be secure for life.'

'Is that really why you married him?' I was alarmed at her honesty − or hard-heartedness.

'Yes,' she replied simply, with no apology.

'Didn't you think you should love him?'

'The money was a more important issue − at the time. I never thought about love!'

'And you think about it now?'

Her green eyes worked their old trick on me again. 'Yes, darling. All the time.' She turned away. 'I could have just been another secretary and supported myself. But that wasn't enough for me.'

'So how does it feel now? You have everything but love.'

'But I have you darling, and you are my real love.'

I had longed to hear her say this. Such were my feelings

29

for her that, for my sake at least, I couldn't have continued the relationship on just a casual basis . . .

I felt I had to say, 'You can't have both Anna. Me and Ottavio. You have got to choose – one without the other.'

'I don't know what you mean Lorenzo—'

I was about to say more when I was stopped by a rustling in a nearby bush at the end of the rosewalk.

I spun round.

There was definite movement, an animal maybe; certainly no breeze, as the air was still. Then I heard it scurry off behind other bushes.

'Who's there?' I shouted out.

'Who do you think?' said Anna. 'Nothing but my little fat man of a husband.'

'It can't be.'

'It's him, yes, yes. Remember the birthday party? He turned up then to see what was going on – and one of these days I am going to lock him up!'

'Would you?'

'You bet I would!'

I was troubled by her attitude to him and by the thought that he must have overheard what she had said about his money.

'Don't you think you treat him badly?' I said.

'But he's like a little boy!'

After that we walked back to the house. There, back in the dining room, was Ottavio, seated at the table (now cleared by the servants), reading a newspaper.

Anna giggled at him, 'How did you get back here so soon? We saw you behind the bushes and don't deny it.'

He was calm. 'I don't deny it. I just happened to be passing on the other path.'

It was all very intriguing, the odd game this couple

played. It was still puzzling why he had invited me to supper.

He turned to me – 'Would you like a drink?'

I said I was about to leave and thanked him for the evening.

'Don't go just yet,' Anna persisted. 'Have a drink with us.'

'Sorry. I have to be going. I have to check something at the garage.' It was an excuse.

'Very well then. I'll walk you down to the gate.'

Before I left Ottavio said, 'It has been a pleasure to have you here, Lorenzo. You are like a breath of fresh air.'

Out at the gate I asked Anna what he meant by that.

'God knows!' she said loudly. 'He just says things as they occur to him in his sick little mind.'

She softened her tone, 'I want to see you tomorrow night. We didn't have a chance to be alone tonight.'

I put my arms around her, holding her gently for a moment and I kissed her. For all I knew Ottavio was at the window spying on us. Right then I was even more certain that I loved her. But what future did we have? 'What would your husband say if he knew about us?'

'Nothing.'

'Isn't that strange? Unless he's stopped loving you.'

'I run the business for him and perhaps now that's all that matters to him.'

I found that hard to believe – that business could be put before love.

'I'll see you tomorrow night,' I said, and I kissed her again. How I wanted to stay with her.

It was just past ten – still time to catch Piero for a drink and find out what he wanted to say to me. When I got to the taverna he wasn't there – impatient as ever.

An early night then.

Back home my mother was still up with her knitting needles.

'What are you doing home so early?' she asked.

Before I could answer she put down whatever it was she was knitting and produced a letter.

'Here, since you're here, I got this – it's from Argentina, from your aunt.'

I didn't feel like reading it. 'You tell me what it says. Is she all right?'

'She's OK. She's coming over to stay for a while with your uncle and maybe Graziella. It's years since I've seen Carla. You were twelve when she was here last.'

Graziella is my cousin.

'I suppose I shall have to sleep at the garage.'

'I'm afraid so Lorenzo. There just isn't enough space for us all in this house. You don't mind Lorenzo?'

'Of course not,' I said, thinking of Anna and our possible nights together. 'The garage is not so bad for sleep.'

The next day Luisa phoned me at work. She wanted to see me. It was her day off. Could we meet at the bar near the railway station? Reluctantly I agreed. She was already there when I arrived at one. Somehow she looked different, thinner maybe.

'*Ciao*!' I said too brightly. When our eyes met I felt embarrassed, probably guilty. 'Want a drink?'

'Just a cappuccino.'

After a pause she looked at me – 'Have you anything to say to me?'

'Depends what you want to hear Luisa.'

'Don't you think you owe me an explanation—'

'Here, there's your coffee.'

'Don't you owe me an explanation for the way you have discarded me.' There was fury in her dark eyes.

'Calm down Luisa. I did try to see you the other night but you had gone to the pictures.'

'All right, I am here now.'

I had never seen her so angry. I was tempted to tell her about Anna but, no, Luisa would have made a scene. I didn't want that.

'Listen,' I said, 'I'll explain to you why I have kept away from you. It's because I need time to myself. I'm not sure anymore what my feelings for you are – try to understand Luisa.'

'But it's been weeks since I have seen you properly. Don't you think you've had enough time to decide what you intend to do.'

'No, I need more time.'

She took up the spoon and played with the cappuccino froth. 'I will give you more time Lorenzo provided you're honest enough to tell me that there's nobody else.'

The tortures women inflict! I couldn't tell her of Anna. So I lied, 'I haven't found anyone else.'

Shortly afterwards I returned to the garage. I justified my lie on the grounds of Luisa's temperament. She would have become sick had I told her the truth. Like the rest of her family she was very temperamental. Anything she didn't want to hear would make her hysterical.

On the other hand I knew she loved me and that made things worse for her – and for me.

Mid-afternoon a tan-coloured car pulled into the garage. Good, another customer I thought. But it was Ottavio. What the hell did he want?

He wound down the window. 'Sorry if I'm interrupting your work Lorenzo, I know how busy you are but I have come to apologise for last night. You must think Anna and I an odd couple.'

He was a mind-reader. I sort of guffawed to make light

of his remark – 'All marriages are the same,' I said. 'It's none of my business – but tell me Ottavio, why did you invite me round? – a humble car mechanic?' I added with a smile.

He seemed to take breath for an answer, winded perhaps by my direct approach. 'A friendship is a friendship Lorenzo,' he said after one very deep breath. 'What has your occupation to do with it? I have a great regard for you – I think you are the most sane person I have ever met.'

Once again I found myself nonplussed by Ottavio. I wanted to ask him what he was talking about, but instead I thanked him for his kind comment – 'Now I must get on with my work.'

'Surely. And I must be going to meet Anna – don't forget to visit again – sometime.'

Well, I had to laugh. How could someone other than a fool not have noticed that Anna and I were in love? Perhaps he had decided to close his eyes, I pondered. He must have noticed something. How did a fool like that get to run a big business?

Then I remembered Anna ran it. What a life she had – to be married to him and his work.

Early that evening Anna arrived to pick me up as planned. She was not her usual ebullient self, but very quiet. 'You look pensive, Anna.'

'Sorry darling,' she said with a weariness. She undid her scarf. 'It's Ottavio again, that son-of-a-bitch.'

'What's he done now?'

'He came to collect me from work but when he got there I was still holding a business meeting. He just barged in. Of course we had a row when we got home.'

I couldn't imagine Ottavio rowing with anyone.

'I don't know what's wrong with him,' she continued,

'but he seems to have got worse lately. He goes everywhere where I go. He's getting me down.'

I held and kissed her. 'Something has to be done about him,' I said.

I got into the car and we drove off with Anna at the wheel. I asked her if she had considered leaving Ottavio.

'Sometimes,' she said, 'but I know I will never leave him.'

I was shocked to hear these words, expressed so simply and casually. She really meant it. She would never leave him.

'So I'm just another man to you,' I said. 'Someone to play with?'

At that she pushed her foot down on the accelerator.

'Slow down!' I demanded.

But she ignored me as we sped faster and faster.

I shouted, 'Slow down – you'll kill us both!'

We were doing a hundred miles an hour.

'You're not worried about death!' she bawled above the din of the car. 'After all, if we die we can go up together to the land of the fairies!'

I shouted and shouted to her to slow down. Then in desperation I lifted my right leg over the gear box and kicked her foot off the pedal and grabbed the wheel.

At that she seemed to come to her senses and she gently braked the car. We parked by the roadside.

She apologised over and over again.

'What good is an apology,' I said furiously. 'You could have killed us. What came over you?'

'I don't know,' she said holding her head. 'Maybe it's because I had a bad day.'

'I think I'll take you back. There's no point going anywhere tonight after this.'

We exchanged places and I drove back to her home in silence. I walked with her to the gates. She told me to take her car — she'd collect it tomorrow.

I said, 'No, I'll catch a taxi at the station.'

'As you wish,' she said sadly. 'I'm sorry for tonight but when I'm upset I'm not very good company. Believe me darling, I do love you.'

'I love you to.'

On my way to the taxi rank I worried more about the risk she'd taken with the car. What was that about the land of the 'fairies'? Was Ottavio driving her insane? I couldn't understand why she would *not* want to leave him. What was the point of money if it was the only thing that kept two people together?

Love and money.

I could only give her all my love. If that was not enough for her — well, what future for us?

I recalled Piero's words — I hadn't rung him — perhaps he was right: I was wasting my time with Anna. Like some younger brother I felt the need to see him.

I caught a taxi to his usual taverna. To my relief he was there, laughing with a group of people. I envied him for the first time. He was content with his girlfriend — no complications.

I had been reasonably happy with Luisa until Anna came into my life.

I winked at Piero when I caught his eye and he came over — 'So where were you the other night?' he said. 'What are you doing here?'

'To see you. I need to talk about something.'

'So, what's happened now?' We sat at a table. 'I thought you might be with Anna,' he added. 'Has she given you up already?'

'No, nothing like that.'

I told him what had happened – her speeding like a maniac.

'Good, God,' he said, 'you must stop seeing her – she sounds unstable to me.'

'Not her!' I said. I signalled to the landlord to bring over two liqueurs. 'It's her husband who's crazy. And he's driving her mad!'

For a change Piero gave up his bullying ways and tried to reason with me.

'That maybe so,' he said, 'but that doesn't explain her driving like that – you could be in the mortuary now! And if she has troubles with her husband why should you get involved in their squabbles? I'm going to tell you again Lorenzo, forget about her. Go back to Luisa. You may think you don't love Luisa anymore but you'll be surprised if you try again with her.'

Poor Piero. Life was so easy for him. It was such a simple thing for him to say. Once my life was as straightforward as a car engine . . .

I told him I loved Anna and if I could help her in anyway I would.

He threw the liqueur down his throat with a toss of his head – I could never do that – and said, 'Have it your own way Lorenzo. And don't turn to me when you're in trouble.'

'I just wish you'd understand a bit more – so, anyway, what did you want to say to me the other night?'

'Ah yes,' he said, waving for more drink. 'I did have a suggestion to make.'

And what a suggestion!

He advised me to visit a clairvoyant.

'She'll help you,' he said. 'I know for a fact that other people have gone to this woman and they're much happier afterwards.'

I couldn't believe it. Why would a good Catholic boy like him want to go to a witch? Suddenly I couldn't decide who was the maddest – Ottavio, Anna or Piero.

'Have you seen this clairvoyant?' I asked.

'No, I don't think I need to. Someone pointed her out to me in the street the other day.'

'What does she look like?'

'Just like anyone else walking in the street – no broomsticks!' We laughed. 'Try her – she might give you something to think about.'

No point pretending I wasn't tempted. I had nothing to lose. If nothing else it would be a laugh – 'Could you make an appointment for me?'

Piero laughed again – 'It's always me! OK – if it'll bring you to your senses. I'll phone you with the time and date. She works just off the Piazza San Marco.'

'Is that legal?' I asked naively.

'"Is it legal?"' he echoed in a mocking voice. 'You should visit the piazza sometime. It's not just clairvoyants doing business round there.'

Before I left I told him about my relatives from Argentina coming to stay.

'Any daughters?' Piero asked.

'Just the one – Graziella.'

'I might come round to see her if she's the right age.'

'She must be under twenty – I'm not even sure she's coming over. Besides, you've already got a girlfriend – or do you want to stray like me?'

He just smiled.

The following day I phoned Anna. Her maid told me she was out.

'Is Signor Gilli there then? I'd like to speak to him.'

'If he's in who should I say is calling?'

38

'Just say Lorenzo.'

I could hear her walk quickly away. A few moments later she returned: 'I am sorry. He is out.'

'Can you tell me how Signora Gilli is?'

'She was unwell last night but she seemed fine this morning.'

I said goodbye and put down the phone.

Two hours after that call Anna herself turned up at the garage in a taxi. She looked her more usual self, full of life, sparkling, as if nothing had happened last night.

I told her I'd phoned her place – 'Did you darling? I haven't been home yet. I had to attend to some business matters. Then on impulse I thought I'd come here.'

She kissed me on the lips. 'I want to apologise for last night. Am I forgiven?'

'I forgive you – only if you promise never to do such a stupid thing again. We could have been killed.'

'Shall we hide away in the garage?' she said. 'I feel the need to kiss you.'

'So do I – but I can't, I'm too busy, and I'll mess up your dress with my overalls. I've got to finish a car tonight – it's being collected tomorrow.'

She giggled. 'All right – I'll see you tonight.'

She walked to her car but then turned before she reached it, as if she had just remembered something – 'Can't you get someone to help you here – an apprentice or assistant?'

'Not till I make more money.'

'Well, I'll see about that.'

'What do you mean?'

'I'll let you know,' she sang, and then jumped into her car. But I wasn't prepared to let her go. I playfully leapt in front of the car and placed my hands on the bonnet.

'Best if I tell you now,' I shouted above the noise of the

39

engine, 'from now on I'll be sitting behind that wheel of yours when we go out together – if you don't like that then we'll go out in my van!'

She shot her head out of the car, and laughed – 'So, you don't trust me anymore!'

'It'll be for the best.'

She laughed again – 'You win darling. My car will be at your disposal.'

Back home my mother said Graziella would definitely be coming to stay. My uncle and aunt would be sleeping in my room, and I'd have to clean out the small storage room and buy a bedchair for my niece.

'So where do I put all this rubbish to give little Graziella her nice little room?' I said pointing at sacks of odds and sods. 'Don't worry about me – sleeping in the garage.' I was teasing my mother, of course.

She sensed I was in a good mood so she chose this moment to get serious.

'You haven't got another girlfriend, have you?'

'If I have what's it to you?'

'Never mind!' she snapped, knowing I'd say nothing.

For a few minutes I thought Anna had stood me up again on our evening date. Just when I was about to give up on her she roared into the garage.

'Sorry I'm a bit late,' she said breezily. 'I was on the phone to one of my managers about a business matter.'

'Why the long dress? We're not going anywhere special, are we?' I asked, with my arms around her waist.

'I like to dress up for you Lorenzo. I know *you* will appreciate anything I put on.'

'Just about,' I said with a smile.

But her mood suddenly changed.

40

Green eyes ablaze, she said, 'Are you trying to tell me what I should wear?'

I was surprised by her new tone . . . 'Of course not Anna . . . I just thought . . . come on, let's not spoil tonight.'

With that we got into her car and drove off.

However she hadn't finished.

'You know Lorenzo, if any other man tried to tell me what to wear I'd scratch his eyes out – but from you I can take it – just about.'

'What's so different about me?' I asked calmly.

Her mood was softening I felt.

'You're different because you stand up to me. I admire you! I've always had my own way with men!'

'Including your husband?'

She pulled off her scarf and let it flutter in the wind. She giggled – 'Oh Ottavio – he's not even a man!'

She shouted at the top of her voice – 'He's nothing but a fat lump!'

'If you loved him you wouldn't speak about him in that way. It's a pity he's not man enough to throw you over his lap and spank you like a child.'

She laughed. 'Would you do that to me Lorenzo?'

'Sure. I'd want respect from a woman if she was my wife.'

'Well,' she said, giggling, 'I worship at your feet, you are a god! and I love you very much.'

'Oh yes, but even with me you try it on.'

'Do I?' she squealed, excited.

'Definitely.' I decided to get serious . . . 'Anna, why stay with Ottavio? There's no love between you – it can't be just because he provides you with what you want.'

'That's about it,' she said quickly, more serious now.

'And what about me? Where do I fit into your life? You

must realise we can't go on like this forever. Something has to happen before long.'

That quieted her. She tied back her scarf. For a few minutes she said nothing, clearly thinking.

Finally she said, 'Of course you are right Lorenzo, I do think about us, and if Ottavio gave me half the business I would leave him tomorrow.'

'I doubt he'd ever give you that.'

'I could fight for it. Women have to fight for everything in this country – we'll get no help from the Pope! I could fight and I'd get my half.'

I spotted a roadside taverna and decided to pull in – 'Let's have a drink,' I said.

Anna turned heads the moment we entered the drinking house. There were many infuriating sounds of admiration – or lust.

'What a beauty we got here,' I heard one man say. I said to him, 'You can look but don't touch.'

There was laughter at that.

'Jealous?' Anna said playfully as she took a seat.

'Perhaps I am.'

After an hour I suggested we return to my garage.

'Good idea,' she said. 'Then we can be alone at last.'

As we drove back we knew we'd make love – I drove almost as fast as she had the other night.

The moment the garage door was shut we fell on each other passionately, our hands rushing over each other's body as if we were newly-weds.

But just as I began to unbutton her dress we were stopped by an awful scratching sound from a side window, as if a claw were being run across the glass. We both looked up at once but could see nothing at the window – I was shaken and angry.

I stormed outside to catch the peeping tom and give

42

him a belting. But no one was to be seen. When I returned to the garage Anna had buttoned herself up – all passion gone.

'I bet it was Ottavio,' she said bitterly. 'He would do anything to stop us loving each other.'

'Don't be silly—'

'I'm not! He followed us for sure. He knows what's going on between us.'

With hindsight I should have credited Ottavio with the intelligence to work out the situation, but at the time I took him to be a simpleton who by some lucky quirk had ended up Anna's husband.

'He knows all right,' Anna continued. 'You don't know how cunning my little fat man is. He has done so many strange things to me. You don't know him as I do.'

'Maybe not. It's better if I take you home now – and then you can sort out your life with your husband, if you want to continue with me.'

'Don't put pressure on me Lorenzo,' she said, facing me. 'Give me time – if you really love me.'

'I'll give you time Anna . . . Don't say anything to him about tonight when you get home – pretend nothing has happened. We have to sort something out. What I can't understand is why he is so nice to me.'

'That's his way. Lunatics are full of cunning, they think of everything—'

'It doesn't make sense . . .' I took Anna in my arms again and kissed her neck gently . . . 'Shall we forget about your old man and take up where we left off?'

Before she could answer I had a sudden thought. I broke away and blanked out the window with an oily old cloth. There was just the one window in the garage – 'Whatever's out there is gone now I'm sure,' I said.

Then we kissed again and undressed each other and

I led her to the back of the garage to my bedchair where we made love and spent our first wonderful night together.

The next morning at seven she rose and said she had to go – 'I'm sorry darling,' she said. 'I love you so much Lorenzo. I'm so happy. If only I could slip into your pocket and stay with you all day . . .'

'I'll ask my mother to open up my pockets.'

She laughed.

'And,' I added, 'you know what you have to do if you want to be with me all the time.'

I got out of the bedchair and took her face in my hands – 'Maybe I haven't the money to offer you but you have my love. I'm the only man who has loved you. If you trust me Anna I can make something of this garage – I feel confident—'

'I do trust you Lorenzo. I know your business will grow and grow – sooner than you think perhaps—' She had a languid expression.

'How beautiful you are,' I said.

'I want to help you Lorenzo. I have money of my own . . .'

'Please Anna, let me do things my way, with my own hands.'

'Why do you have to allow your pride to stand in the way? It would be so much easier for you if you allowed me to help you. At least think about it.'

'I have already,' I said.

Anna was now quite cool: 'I will persuade Ottavio to give me my part of the business. I have been married to him seven years – it's time I had my dues.'

'Why did he leave you to deal with his business?'

'Why, do you think I'm the little woman who should

stay at home?' she said, almost sneering. 'It's simple, I do a better job than he does. And besides, even he knows he's not quite right in the head.'

I didn't like her talking about him like that. Even in a bad marriage I thought there should be basic respect. I felt we had said enough.

'Cup of coffee before you go?' I asked.

'Thank you darling. That will be very nice.'

As we sipped I told her that it was only a question of months before I could afford to employ a hand to help with the repairs.

She said, 'Well if you change your mind remember my offer. I'm more than happy to help you.'

She put down her cup – she hardly touched her drink – and kissed me. 'See you soon my love,' she said, 'I'll phone you.'

I took hold of her as if it were our last moment together of all time. Doubts always surfaced just as she was about to leave me – I loved her so much I was almost superstitious that I'd never see her again.

When she had driven off I left for breakfast with the family. Predictably my mother wanted to know where I had been all night – and who with. I told her I had been to a party and it was so late when it ended that I slept at the garage so as not to disturb her – 'Anymore news from Argentina?' I asked.

I had hardly noticed by father in his vest at the breakfast table.

He answered, 'Yes, they'll be here any day now – it'll be good for your mother to see her sister again.'

I took my place at the table. 'So, who did you take out last night Lorenzo?' asked mamma.

It was pointless playing word games with her.

I said plainly, 'A lovely lady I think the world of.'

45

'What about Luisa? I hope you haven't forgotten about her.'

'I'll see her soon,' I said, buttering toast, 'and I will explain everything to her. But I'm telling you now – I will never marry her.'

My father munched on, unconcerned by my news.

But mamma was predictably upset. She'd set her heart on Luisa for me. It had been almost an arranged marriage in her imagination.

'Who is this other woman?' she demanded to know.

I couldn't very well tell her that Anna was a married woman with a rich lunatic for a husband. So I just said that the 'other woman' was a nice girl, and – 'I love her very much.'

This was too much for my mother. She raised her arms in shock. She may have been secretly pleased at the prospect of me settling down at long last, but she couldn't stand not knowing who my intended was. First, she would have to approve the woman of my life.

But not this time.

In defeat she said, 'I just hope you know what you're doing.'

Meanwhile my father munched on.

The moment I got to the garage the phone rang. Could it be Anna? A customer?

It was Piero.

'*Ciao* Lorenzo! I tried to phone you earlier. What happened to you?'

'I had a late night,' I said.

'Sure you did! Who is she? What have you been up to?'

I ignored his questions and asked him what he had been up to. It was his turn to ignore me – 'Hey,' he started, 'I saw

46

Luisa last night. She looked very unhappy. She said she still loves you Lorenzo – you should do something about it!'

'Yeah, yeah – I am going to see her.'

'I've made your appointment with the psychic. If you're still interested, it's this Saturday afternoon at three.'

I couldn't believe I was going along with this but I said OK and he gave me the woman's address.

He said, 'Remember to call me at the taverna after you've seen her. I want to know what she says.'

Around lunchtime I spotted Ottavio approaching the garage. For the first time I felt unnerved by him. He must have known I had spent the night with his wife.

'Lorenzo,' he shouted out, not seeing me at first. I was standing in my tiny office. 'It's Ottavio Gilli – I hope this is not the wrong time to call but I want to talk to you.'

'What about?' I shouted back. I was wiping my hands now.

'Anna. She has accused me of spying on you both last night.'

I came out onto the main floor.

'Believe me,' he continued, 'I was at home sorting out some business papers but she always thinks the worst.'

He was like a little boy who runs back to daddy full of excuses. Even if what he said was true, why would he come to me of all people to explain himself? Shouldn't he be asking me what I was doing with his wife?

He looked so pathetic that I decided on the spot that it was time to end all the nonsense.

'Look Ottavio, this is not the time or the place to discuss it. But now you're here I have to tell you that I am in love with Anna. And I'm going to take her away from you.'

My heart was thumping at my own words. I wasn't thinking. But Ottavio's reaction was hardly what I expected.

'I know what is going on between you and Anna,' he said. 'I also know that she will never leave me for you Lorenzo. Not because she loves me but because she has too much to lose.'

He looked around the garage – 'You have nothing to offer her,' he added.

I could have strangled the life out of him for saying that.

I shouted, 'I have more to offer her than all your money. What kind of man are you? You knew what was going on between Anna and me and you invited me into your house.'

'I would like to explain many things to you Lorenzo. In spite of what has happened I still respect you because you are a completely honest person and perhaps a little naive, if you don't mind me saying so.'

'You'll soon see I am not all that naive!'

'You're confused then.'

'Certainly by you!'

'I am sorry Lorenzo that you seem so angry. I would like to tell you of many things but, as you say, this is not the right time.'

He turned and was out of my garage without another word.

I drove off in my van to cool down. What a wimp Ottavio seemed to me, and a creep – he had all the cunning of a manipulative weakling. Now I understood why Anna treated him with such contempt, and how such a man could drive you mad.

In my simple life I had never encountered such a complex personality. I was furious that he had called me naive.

Back home there was a letter waiting for me – I guessed

from Luisa. In fact it was from her mother – Luisa was unwell. 'She wants to see you as soon as possible,' she wrote.

I didn't want another confrontation with her father but it would look bad if I ignored her. I didn't mention it to my mother – she would only say it was all my fault, of course.

After lunch I called on Luisa, and thank God her father wasn't there.

'What's wrong with Luisa,' I asked her mother, Signora Vincente, at the door.

'I don't know,' she said, 'all I know is she's losing weight and she's asking for you Lorenzo.'

She didn't seem angry with me, she was almost pleasant even. Had she called for the doctor?

'Yes, but he won't come till tomorrow morning.'

I went upstairs to Luisa's bedroom. I gently opened the door. It was dark – the curtains were drawn. There she lay, her eyes shut. I was struck at how gaunt her face was in the light from the door. I whispered her name. Her eyes opened immediately. She smiled at me.

'*Ciao* Lorenzo. It's nice to see you. It seems such a long time . . . I hope you don't mind coming.'

'Of course not.' I entered the room but left the door open so I could see her.

She said, 'I thought that if I did not see you before I died, I'd die in misery.'

'Don't be so silly,' I said crouching down. 'You've a long time to go before you die.'

I took her hand and held it. 'I can't stay long – I'll call again and stay longer. But only if you promise not to talk about dying.'

She smiled weakly. 'Thanks Lorenzo for coming – I feel a bit better already.'

'Try to rest Luisa – too much talk will tire you.'

How guilty I felt as I drove back to the garage. It passed my mind that she had made herself ill to force me back – but, still, she did look very ill: I was anxious to know what was wrong with her.

As I parked outside the garage I noticed Anna's red car opposite. In a trice she shot her head out the window – 'Lorenzo, darling, I was waiting for you. I thought you would never come back!'

'I was making a sick call,' I said gruffly.

'Who's ill? A relative?'

'No, an ex-girlfriend. I was going to marry her before I met you,' I said for all to hear.

'Well!' Anna was astonished, her eyes suddenly as round as saucers. 'This is news to me.'

I hadn't discussed Luisa with her.

'I am sorry for her,' she said with real feeling, walking over the road towards me. 'Are you still fond of her Lorenzo?'

'In a way I am. But it's all over – although not for her.'

'What are you going to do darling?'

'What can I do? I can only hope she gets over this.'

'And all because of me,' she said to herself, a little surprised. 'What's she like, Luisa?'

We began to make for the garage. 'She's a pretty girl, wonderful in many ways. For a while I thought I was in love with her and I seriously planned to marry her – but that wasn't to be . . . Come on Anna, come in and have a strong black coffee with me – you'd like one, yes?'

'Yes, I would.'

Inside we kissed.

I asked, 'So what are you doing here at this time of day?'

'I have a three o'clock appointment.'

'Yes. What about?'

'A little business I have to attend to.'

I didn't believe her for some reason. She was hiding something. But at that moment I didn't want to know her secret. Already I was learning that she needed her own life – she would tell me things, or not, as the mood took her.

I poured coffee as I told her my other news, of Ottavio's visit. 'I feel like part of the family – with all these visits from the Gillis,' I laughed.

Anna was furious. 'That little runt – one of his games, running to you. I suppose he told you I accused him of creeping around here last night. He just wants to embarrass us. I suppose you were kind to him.'

'No, I wasn't very sympathetic, in fact I was rude, though not without provocation.'

'He didn't say anything to me.'

'Maybe what I said was too painful—'

'What did you say?'

'I told him I wanted you.'

'You *actually* told him?' she asked, spellbound. 'You told him!' Then she laughed to herself.

'You're not angry then?'

'Angry?' She laughed more. 'That'll teach him. How did he take it? Was he upset?'

'No. He said he knew about us.'

'I told you he did.'

'He said you would never leave him. He was so certain of that. He said you did not love him, but his wealth was more important to you – which is true.'

'I have been honest with you Lorenzo. I told you his money means a lot to me. You can't blame me for wanting a share of his business – a business I have made even more

51

successful. After all I've worked very hard – I am not going to let him end up with everything when I leave him.'

'I understand that,' I said.

In the back of my mind was still a worry – our future hinged on money, and I resented that.

She embraced me and rested her head on my chest – 'I love you Lorenzo, I have never felt like this for any other man. I ask you only to trust me.'

'I love you too, so very much.'

I kissed her lips, her beautiful lips, and her hair . . .

Abruptly she broke away and said – 'I must go now or I shall miss my appointment. I'll see you here tonight?'

'I'll be here.'

As she started the car she said, 'Don't take any notice of Ottavio. He's a phoney.'

Only when her car was just a dot in the distance did I realise how sad she had been with me. Her laughter was joyless, hollow. She had not told me something, something that perhaps had nothing to do with Ottavio.

It was an instinctive feeling. Experience had taught me never to ignore it.

Back home my mother asked me, 'What do you know about Luisa?'

'What about her? What has happened to her?'

'She is very ill. They had to call a doctor because she had a very bad turn.'

I told her I knew she was unwell and that I had seen her lunchtime.

'So why didn't you say something to me?' she shouted.

'I don't want you making a fuss mamma.'

'At least you had the decency to go see the poor girl. What's really wrong with her?'

'I don't know yet.'

After I changed I visited Luisa again. This time her father answered the door. I expected another fight, but his wife appeared at his side just before either one of us had a chance to say anything.

'Luisa's asleep,' she said.

'May I see her for a minute?'

'I think better not in case she wakes up. It's nice of you to call again Lorenzo. She seemed to get worse this afternoon.'

'Did the doctor examine her?'

'He couldn't find anything physically wrong. He thinks it's nervous stress, and she needs lots of sleep.'

Signor Vincente said calmly, 'I want to talk to you about Luisa. I shan't keep you very long.'

His wife disappeared back into the house – obviously they had planned this.

'I know,' he said, scratching his stubbly chin, 'that I was short with you the other day, but Luisa went through a bad time when you stopped seeing her. I don't blame you, but I'd be grateful if you would come and visit her till she recovers – it would help her very much.'

I was touched by his words. 'I'd come and see her anyway. I'm still very fond of her.'

'I know that Lorenzo. It's not your fault. I know feelings can come and go. One minute you love. The next minute – pfff!'

I had not not thought Luisa's father the philosopher. Or was it all a trick to get me and Luisa back together?

Anna failed to turn up for our date that evening. There was no call. Nothing. I despaired. I had given Luisa up for what?

In the morning we received another letter from Argentina.

53

They'd be with us in three days' time. But my mother was more preoccupied with Luisa.

'Poor girl,' she said, 'it's not to do with you, is it?'

I wasn't in the best of moods – 'Don't say that, I'm not to blame.'

To our surprise my father – perhaps sensing we might argue – said firmly, 'He is not to blame.'

Later that morning Anna phoned the garage to apologise.

'What's the point of apologising?' I shouted. 'Not even a message!'

'Please forgive me Lorenzo. I had a terrible time with Ottavio, trying to talk to him about my share of the business.' She did sound exhausted, strained.

'What has all that to do with me?'

'He put me in a bad mood and I locked myself in the bedroom.'

'And I suppose Ottavio locked himself in his bedroom!'

'Please don't be like that. Can we meet tomorrow night?'

I felt frustrated. Everything depended on her moods.

'Can't make it – I'm visiting Luisa,' I said childishly, hoping to make her jealous.

'How is she?' She sounded truly concerned, not jealous. What an actress!

'Still very unwell.'

'Can I see you after you've seen her?'

'That's not possible.'

I wanted her punished. She had to learn I was not another Ottavio who would excuse her bad behaviour. Just thinking of Ottavio hardened my attitude. The weaker he was the stronger I must be – otherwise our relationship could never survive.

'So when will we see each other Lorenzo?'

'When you're next in the mood Anna.'

Anna, unpredictable as ever, remained calm and cool. 'Lorenzo, you give me a call when you want me.'

'Sure, I will,' I said without conviction. But by then she'd put the phone down.

After supper I went to the taverna to see Piero for a chat.

'So how's everything?' he asked.

'Hopeless! Did you know about Luisa being unwell?'

'She looked very thin last time I saw her.'

'I went to her home—'

'So her old man didn't throw you out, eh?' Piero laughed.

His bright good mood irritated me: 'Not at all. He was OK with me.'

'Oh!' he said, exaggerating his surprise. 'And don't forget your appointment with the medium tomorrow. The spirits watch everything we do! She'll be a great help to you Lorenzo—'

'I can't see what help she can give me.'

'You're still going aren't you? It took a lot of trouble setting up—'

'Yes, I'm going!' I snapped.

'After you've seen her you'll feel different.'

'Well, I'm looking forward to a day off in Venice at least, doing nothing.'

'The city of lovers . . .'

'Shut up! I can't remember the last time I had a day off from work. I've been getting really tired lately.'

'It's not work that's making you tired,' laughed Piero. 'You're trying to run away from something, aren't you Lorenzo? Come on, you can tell your old friend.'

'Can't you be serious about anything? I don't know what to do. The more I think about it the more confused I get.'

'If life with Anna is not plain sailing then jump overboard, that's my view.'

Piero will never know how close I came to hitting him.

'I love Anna!' I said earnestly.

He raised his glass – 'It'd be simpler if you just returned to Luisa.'

'Simpler? You really do believe in life after death!'

Piero shook his head in mock disgust.

'And what about you?' I said, trying to put him on the spot. 'When are you going to marry?'

He rolled his head a bit, his eyes too. This was his way of telling me I must be nuts.

'Maybe next year,' he said. 'Maybe not.'

The moment I got home my mother shouted out she wanted to talk to me.

'A young woman came here tonight,' she said, hands on hips in the kitchen. 'She was asking after you. A blonde with clothes worth more than I spend on food in a year!'

I was stunned that Anna had the nerve to come to my home.

My mother asked, 'Who is she?'

'What did she want?'

'I told her you weren't here, and she was very pushy. She wanted to know where you were. I told her I had no idea. So, who is she?'

'She's my girlfriend.'

'*Madonna*! Are you mad? She looks very rich, the way she dresses. And was that a wedding ring I saw on her finger? Is she married?' The expression on mamma's face: it was as if I had told her I was pregnant.

'Yes she's married.' I couldn't lie.

My poor mother! She wanted to know how this disaster

could have happened, had she led me on, how I thought it could work – 'Take my word for it, Lorenzo. It will never work out. And what about her husband? Oh God, the scandal!'

I sat at the kitchen table. 'Please mother, we love each other. We're taking it one step at a time. We're planning our future together.'

'You have no future,' she shouted, her little fists tightly bunched. 'No future for you with this adulterous woman!'

I couldn't help half-smiling at that. 'I don't want to discuss it. I am going to Venice tomorrow, and I'm spending the day there.'

'Are you taking that woman?'

'No. I have a little business to sort out.'

First thing the next morning I checked the garage. I had four cars to see to, but they could wait. I looked long and hard at those four cars and imagined forty-four of them: that's how many I'd have by the time I had expanded the business, I dreamt.

Then to Venice. It had been years since I had a full day in Venice. As a boy I had played hide and seek with friends down its maze of ancient, narrow walkways and bridges . . . Now my adult eyes noticed the green slime-encrusted watermarks gradually creeping up old brick walls; Venice really was sinking . . . Still, there were many beautiful foreign women to see, students too, brought to Venezia by Canaletto prints . . .

'Lorenzo! Lorenzo!'

I knew the voice. I turned on a bridge to see a mass of red hair flying in all directions. It was Lucinda, Anna's friend – carrying what looked like a small shopping bag.

'Can I help you with that?' I said.

She laughed. 'No need — I can just about manage lingerie! What are you doing in Venice?'

'I'm just seeing someone at three. I like to walk around.'

'It's good to see you again,' she said taking out a headscarf from her coat pocket.

'And you — fancy some fries in the Piazzo San Marco?'

'Fries! That's a great idea,' she said. 'We can pretend to be tourists and confuse the waiters.'

We were all mad about fries — or chips — at that time, something the British and Americans had brought to Italy during the War. As we took our seats at a restaurant she said, 'God knows what you thought of us at my party. We drank so much. I'm going to have another party, a birthday party for Dino. You must come with Anna. How are you two? You're still seeing her aren't you?'

'Yes, yes,' I replied, glancing at my plate. 'But of course there's her husband . . . I wonder if we, Anna and I, have a future.'

Lucinda made a face, as if to say: Don't ask me. Then she asked, 'Do you think she's in love with you?'

'Well, I'm sure . . . that's an odd question.'

'I only ask because I'm not sure she can leave Ottavio.'

'Doesn't she confide in you?'

'Yes, she tells me some things,' Lucinda said carefully, 'but I don't feel she tells me a lot about herself.'

For some reason her words dulled my appetite. What secrets did Anna have that she couldn't share them even with a close friend?

'You're not eating, Lorenzo. What's up?' she said. 'I hope I've not upset you . . . To be honest I don't really understand her and her weird husband.'

I got up to leave and put some money on the table — 'Sorry I have to go—'

She put her hand on mine — 'Lorenzo, I really like you

58

– maybe I'm wrong – the things I've said about Anna. We can't always know even our best friends. Do please sit down. You should stay at least until I've finished.'

'OK. But let's not discuss Anna.'

'I give you my word,' she giggled. 'But you can't stop me talking about you.'

'Sorry?' I asked picking at my side salad.

'That I find you extremely handsome and very charming – I'm forward, aren't I. If I were Anna I wouldn't give you time to think twice!'

I'm sure my face did heat up a bit, like a schoolboy's. She was so direct she made Anna seem shy. I was flattered, naturally.

I could only say, 'What would Dino say if he were here now?'

'My fiancé is simply very rich. A good catch. And if I had a choice in these matters I'd go for someone like you Lorenzo.'

'How can you give your life away just for money?' I was thinking of Anna too.

'Money is not important in itself,' she replied, amused by my disapproval. 'But what it buys. I'm not even that concerned about having a husband. You know, if I knew you wanted me I would leave Dino for you. Or at least sleep with you.'

I couldn't believe my ears. This was new to me – treating people like items in a shop.

I said, 'Well, now you've got that out of your system, I think I've got to go.'

She pulled a pleading face. But she knew I wasn't tempted, so she smiled playfully, as if to say she'd been kidding. I felt sure her heart would remain unbroken.

'In any case I will be late for my appointment,' I said.

'And may I ask who the lucky person is?'

59

'That's my secret,' I winked.

We walked out into the square of San Marco. For the first time I noticed the astrological signs on a clock-face next to the church. We kissed each other goodbye – just as friends.

I watched tourists throwing bread to the pigeons, a child chased one in circles. Then I headed north to the home of the psychic.

On the way I thought more of Lucinda. Wealth had spoilt her, she seemed too liberated to me. I only hoped her next party wouldn't turn into a Roman orgy. I imagined her in a past-life as Messalina, the sex-crazed wife of the Emperor Claudius . . .

I spotted a tortoiseshell silk scarf in a street-market and bought it for my mother.

The staircase walls leading up to the medium's apartment on the first floor were very damp. Centuries of stagnant canal water had seeped into the brickwork, filling the air with a musty odour. The Borgias themselves must have known this building . . . Somehow it had withstood time and the sea . . .

A rather plump, very ordinary looking woman answered the door. I had expected a bony vision in veils, something mystical: instead she looked just like any other old woman in black clothes who lurked in the back streets of Venice with her washing basket.

'*Si*, I am Signora Lugano, come in,' she said crisply.

She told me to sit opposite her and to give her a personal object to hold. For a moment I thought she was asking for her fee – 'No,' she explained. 'I work by holding a personal possession like keys. It's all in the vibrations, know what those are? I work by psychometry. An object please.'

I gave her my watch, and glimpsed round at the gloomy

room. Here again I had expected exotic things: silk curtains, sparkling crystals, animal heads. Instead it was dominated by a dark cocktail cabinet and a suite of green chairs. There were family photos everywhere . . . it all seemed very simple, normal.

What little light there was seemed to glow from the polished floor, as if the floor itself hummed with spirit life.

Hell? My heart thumped a bit, I didn't know what to expect . . .

She stroked the watch, played with it in her hands, I hoped the strap wouldn't break . . . 'Movement, I feel movement, I am in a car – do you have a car?'

'Yes.' I coughed.

'Watch the car – get it checked. Cars, cars, cars—'

'I run a garage—'

'Sshhh! Don't tell me anything,' she snapped. 'Just answer yes or no. I pick up a triangle! What's this triangle then?'

'Triangle?'

'Three people.'

I thought quickly. Four people I would say. Me, Anna, Luisa, Ottavio. Perhaps she meant three people plus me – '*Three* people?' I queried.

'Three people, yes: the eternal triangle. And mental illness. I can't see clearly if it's a man or woman. This mental illness. Perhaps you know of this?'

I was still wondering whether she meant four people. I blurted, 'I don't know for certain . . . but I'll bear it in mind.'

'In your work I see an offer from a man and he will give you the opportunity to expand your business. I feel it coming very close.'

I couldn't but think she was just a mind-reader: I had thought of business expansion before I left for Venice—

61

'Mental illness, watch it—'

I thought of Ottavio, a definite loony. She told me other things, things known only to me and my family; and I left her modest home impressed yet confused.

Nothing she said had made precise sense yet I was certain she told me more than Piero might have been able to tell her about my life. Signora Lugano was no help on my love life.

When I'd asked her if I should continue to see Anna, she said simply, 'Ah, well I mustn't live your life.'

But I was glad I had seen her. At least I was lucky in business.

Back at the garage I phoned Anna. The maid told me she wasn't in. 'Nor Signor Gilli,' she added unnecessarily. I didn't like her attitude.

The moment I put down the phone it rang. Surely not Anna. It was Piero – 'I thought you'd be back by now,' he said chirpily. 'How did it go with the witch?'

'Oh, she gave me this warning for a friend,' I said, 'this friend with the initial P. She warned me that if this friend called P doesn't watch out he will get his girlfriend in trouble and will have to marry her! I think the P is you, Piero.'

'Oh yeah yeah,' he laughed. 'Now you'll have to tell me what she really said over a drink tonight.'

I didn't want him to know too much, or maybe I didn't want him to know how little there was to tell, so I said I'd call him later.

Certainly Signora Lugano had failed to predict one very big surprise when I got home. There in the kitchen, chatting away with my mother, was Anna.

Both turned to me at once. My mother had her startled-eye expression—

'Anna. What are you doing here?' I said, not disguising my amazement.

'I had to settle a little business and I thought it was time to pay a visit to your lovely mother while I was passing this way.' Anna gazed at her – 'She has been very sweet to me. She made me a very nice coffee.'

I had no illusions about what my 'sweet' mother was really thinking.

'I didn't see your car parked outside,' I said.

'It's round the corner.'

'Shall we go – I'd like to talk to you.'

'Oh, OK – is that for me?'

She had noticed the small package in my hand: the silk scarf.

'No, er – for you mother.' I handed it to her. Poor mother. She didn't know what to say.

Anna jumped into my car and started up. 'Mind if I drive Lorenzo. So what's this mysterious visit to Venice?' she asked. 'I did try to phone you. That's why I came to your mother's. Of course I expected to find you there. I hope you didn't mind darling.'

'Course not,' I lied. 'How did you know where I lived?'

'Oh, I followed you one day—'

'You didn't have to do that Anna – I'd have given you my address, you only had to ask . . . I wanted to prepare my mother . . . about you.'

'I think she approves of me,' she said, making light of it all. 'But now I have met her I see no reason why I shouldn't visit her again. What a nice woman she is – I can see who you take after Lorenzo. She could be the mother I never had – so what were you up to today?'

'I went to Venice – I met Lucinda by chance. We had something to eat in one of the tourist places—'

63

'What! Well, lucky Lucinda!' shouted Anna, and the car shuddered. She couldn't contain her anger. '*I* could have spent the day with you Lorenzo in Venice. I do hope you sent Lucinda my love.'

'You don't have to worry about Lucinda, she was just friendly, and I had to see someone in the afternoon. It would have been very boring for you – I am glad I was alone in fact. I did miss you though.'

Anna gave a long, heavy sigh. She said, 'Sorry – no wonder you get angry with me. You're not cross are you?'

'How could I be angry with you for long.' I put my hand on her shoulder as she drove.

Then I thought of our last conversation on the phone, how bad tempered it had been. So I said, 'Look, I just want to say . . . in future let me know when you can't keep a date. I feel an idiot being stood up, and it hurts.'

'I'm sorry darling,' she said in a baby voice. 'I promise I won't let you down again – I always think of you.' Then her voice became serious: 'I do love you, truly.'

She stopped the car in a layby. We embraced and exchanged soft kisses and for a few moments I forgot everything – work, Luisa, my family, my business, Ottavio . . .

Back on the road we were warm, quiet. But a sudden thought cooled me. I remembered my Argentinian relatives were due tomorrow. I told Anna.

'For how long?' she asked. 'Will it make any difference to us?' She seemed alarmed again.

'Not much, they're staying just four weeks. I'll have to entertain my cousin Graziella some evenings I suppose – we can still see each other.'

'That's a relief. You make me feel so good when you say nice things to me Lorenzo. When are you coming again for supper?'

'I'll have to see.'

'I'll invite Dino and Lucinda – they can sit on Ottavio if he plays up like last time.'

I laughed – thinking of outrageous Lucinda. We were approaching my local bar to the right and I had a sudden impulse to show Anna off.

'Come on,' I said, 'Let's have a drink here.'

Without a word she turned into its courtyard. As we entered the taverna a dozen amazed familiar faces turned our way, before the nodding and winking. The natives were impressed.

I spotted Piero at the bar talking to a stranger.

'Wait here a moment,' I said to Anna.

I had barely got within feet of him when he sensed my presence and turned to face me – 'Lorenzo!' he shouted, typically. 'I'd given up on you!'

'Sorry, I'm with Anna tonight – she's over there.'

Lorenzo looked over to the entrance and wolf whistled, almost silencing the taverna for a moment. 'Is *that* your trouble?'

'That's Anna, and she's mine.'

'Ow-wow! I can see why you're tired!'

I escorted Anna over to the bar. In a moment Piero had taken her hand and was planting a crop of kisses on it. Gallant Piero. Then she surprised us both.

'Thank you Piero,' she said, 'would you like another drink?'

His eyes boggled. In all his life I don't think Piero had ever been offered a drink by a woman. Any girls he brought to the bar were chained to a table all evening while he hovered around the bar. He laughed, which meant he was embarrassed.

'Well, why not?' he said. 'How can I refuse such a lovely lady.'

He had just the one drink with us before leaving. 'Eh,

Lorenzo,' he said with a wink, 'I'd like to see you sometime soon and ask you something – you know what I mean.'

When he had left Anna said, 'What a nice *ragazzo* Piero is. He knows his way round women. Do you two share girlfriends Lorenzo?'

It was my turn to laugh. 'You have a twisted mind, Anna.'

'I saw that wink of his – what are you two plotting?'

'Nothing! It's just business.'

In the car I thought of the Argentinians again . . . 'You know I'll have to sleep in the garage,' I told her. 'Your boyfriend will have to sleep with broken cars and his toolbox – there's not enough room in the house for us all – the family need my room.'

'But darling,' she said gently, 'I have plenty of room, I could accommodate you. And I'd be so happy to have you near me – Ottavio wouldn't mind.'

'I don't think that'd be a good idea.'

'Don't be so proud. Please come and stay.'

'It wouldn't be right – it has nothing to do with me being proud. Look, Ottavio wouldn't like it.'

'What do you know?' she said sharply. 'I know he's peculiar but in his way he likes you Lorenzo. It won't be very nice sleeping in that garage of yours. And as for that bedchair – it's OK to make love on for the odd night, nothing else.'

The way she said it: I had to laugh.

'The bedchair is just fine,' I said. 'I'll still have meals at home. But thanks for the offer. As I lie in my silly bedchair I shall think of all the comforts of your home I'm missing – including you.'

I dropped her off round the corner from my home where she had left her car and I watched her drive off.

Would Ottavio wonder where she had been this evening? The psychic had mentioned a lunatic. If nothing else he was soft-witted to let Anna out at all hours.

In bed I could only imagine the situation at Anna's if I moved in as her lover-lodger. Ottavio would be lurking in hallways at night listening for suspicious creaks or moans, crouched on all fours in front of the keyhole to see if Anna was in my bed.

Then there'd be their constant bickering, all those domestic skirmishes ending up with Anna screaming at him. I could do without all that.

She had to be some kind of saint to put up with him, a martyr. Soon she must decide what she really wanted – sanity or the asylum.

I rose early. In the kitchen my mother was preparing the welcoming feast for our relatives.

'Mamma,' I greeted her, 'you're working too hard. There's plenty of time yet – they're not due till mid-day.'

'Oh, and you're the expert, are you? I'm not just boiling eggs. I have so many things to prepare.'

'Well, while you're doing that I want to talk to you.'

'Oh, yes,' she a said little sarcastically.

'Anna – what did you think?'

She opened the water tap to fill a pot and drown out my words. Above the roar she shouted, 'You've picked the wrong moment to talk.'

I shouted back, 'So when's the right moment?'

'Can't you see I'm busy.' At that moment she turned off the tap.

'Don't get so excited mamma. I can see you're busy. We'll forget it for now.'

I heard a sound behind me – my father was shuffling in.

'What's going on here,' he grumbled. 'All that shouting, the vases were rattling.'

'Nothing's going on,' said my mother, lifting the now heavy water-laden pot onto the stove. 'It must be your brains rattling!'

'There's nothing wrong with my brains.'

A row was in the offing – there always was a row when relatives were due – so I suggested to my father he go back to bed.

'Oh no you don't,' said my mother. 'When you've both had your breakfast I want you both to clear off. Eh, and you,' she snapped at father, 'go wash your ears, then maybe you'll hear better.'

I left the two of them to do battle and made my way to Luisa's. I was surprised and pleased to find her up and about.

'I do feel better,' she said gently.

'Where's your mother?'

'Out shopping.'

She waved me into the house, and trailed a scent of fresh rose, a reminder to me of happier times.

'So how is your love life, Lorenzo, with the beautiful Anna?'

I couldn't tell whether she was mocking me: her voice was just a murmur, her manner calm; too calm. Then it occurred to me: how did she know about Anna?

'Who's been talking then?'

'Mamma spotted you with a woman in your car, and Piero told her who she was. He said you were sleeping with this Anna.'

'Piero should mind his own business. I would have told you about her.'

'But you didn't.'

For some reason I told her that I loved Anna. Perhaps I

68

thought that such a confession might make Luisa feel better if she knew she had lost me to love rather than a passing infatuation.

But I didn't know women. I didn't know people!

I expected hysterics, a scratched face at least, but Luisa remained calm, as if she were still under a sedative.

'Would you like a coffee, Lorenzo? It's still hot.'

'That would be nice.'

I followed her into the kitchen and caught a whiff of her rose again.

As she poured she said, 'Spending all that time in bed gave me time to think. I think I can understand others, and myself, a bit better now. That's why I'm not angry with you. When I found out about Anna at least I understood what had been going on. Is it true she's married?'

I couldn't lie. Better to hear it from me than bloody Piero. 'But,' I added, 'we're planning to be together.'

'I also hear she's rich.' Luisa passed me my coffee. 'How do you plan to keep her in the grand style she's accustomed to?'

'I'll worry about that later,' I said irritably. 'I am sure I'll manage.'

'Look Lorenzo, shall we remain friends? I won't ask anymore questions about Anna. I know it's none of my business.'

'Of course we can remain friends,' I said touching her hand, 'I don't want any bad feeling between us. Why don't you come over sometime this week. My relatives from Argentina are coming today.'

'I'd love to meet them,' Luisa said excitedly, no longer calm.

'Will you be well enough?'

'I feel better already.'

I left Luisa's for home. Half way there I saw Piero

walking hand-in-hand along the street with his latest girlfriend. I drew the car up to them and lowered the window.

'Wo! Lover boy,' he shouted. 'Where did you crawl out from?'

'I've just come from Luisa's.'

'So you've two on the go now.' His girlfriend giggled.

'Eh, why did you tell Luisa's mother about Anna? What kind of friend are you? It should have come from me.'

Piero rested his hands on the car top and placed his head in the lion's jaw of the open window. 'Now don't go accusing me. I can explain what happened—'

'I can't stop now Piero, forget about it. Just remember we've both got secrets, eh?'

He backed away and I drove off. I'd let him stew a bit in his guilt before I forgave him.

I had only been back home a few minutes when a taxi pulled up outside.

Suddenly my mother was shouting, 'They've arrived, they're here!' over and over again (I hoped my father had cleaned his ears out by now).

My main hope was that Graziella didn't look like a horse – since I'd be expected to keep her amused and take her out.

Early signs weren't good. From my bedroom window I saw a very tall, slim middle-aged woman rush towards my mother, and the two embraced and kissed – that must be her sister, Aunt Carla.

If Graziella was anything like her mother I'd have to get a pair of stilts.

Worse was to come.

Behind her was a male giant, the tallest, fattest man I'd ever seen in my life: the taxi swayed as he struggled out of it and landed feet first onto *terra firma*. My Uncle Alberto.

But God was on my side. Not quite as tall as her mother, but tall all the same, was a younger woman behind my uncle – my cousin Graziella.

Now she was a beauty.

Long black hair, the darkest eyes – Piero would be panting. I knew I'd be proud to take her out and show her off.

I should explain that many, many Italians had emigrated to the Americas since the Twenties in search of work and a new life.

My aunt had moved to Argentina with her new (and hopefully thinner) husband when I was about eight.

Our three guests were now in the kitchen and my father was pouring wine as my dear mother dabbed at her streaming eyes.

'Oh,' cried my aunt, 'you're not Lorenzo, are you? You're so good looking, oh—' She embraced me, then felt my shoulders and arms. 'Oh, he's well filled out, Irma.' she said to my mother. 'He takes after his mother – when she was young!'

No one ever said I looked like my father. Not much was registering on his smiling face. I think he often switched off into a fantasy world, like today for example, standing against the sink next to my huge uncle and getting slowly blotto as he worked his way through the bottle.

Graziella was shy, sweet, overwhelmed by all the emotion. As for my Uncle Alberto, he could possibly be a problem.

This was confirmed at our first lunch. Not content to slurp his soup and suck his pasta he denounced Italy as a corrupt nation.

'A young man like you Lorenzo should come to Argentina – you'd be running your own empire by now.'

71

My mother gave him a hard look at the prospect of losing her precious son.

'Italy – it's all Mafia,' he said. 'You set up a company – you have to waste profits on protection, as the Mafia call it. You want to bury your wife – you have to ask the Mafia. Mafia, all is Mafia—'

'Who wants to bury his wife?' asked my aunt who'd lost none of her high-pitched local Friuli accent.

He replied, 'I'm just saying, if you wanted to bury your wife, you'd have to get a Mafia undertaker—'

'And if I wanted to bury you,' my aunt interrupted, 'I'd have to get a Mafia removals firm to cart you off!'

All of us laughed at that, even my uncle, whose jowls wobbled like a beached whale's belly.

Then at the end of the meal, when he had plucked every last bread roll, and sprinkled the last of the mozzarella on the final strands of the spaghetti al luovo, he suddenly took in a very deep breath, held both fat hands to his belly to steady himself, and let out the longest, loudest, most revolting belch I'd ever heard.

My mother and father were so stunned by his appalling manners that they seemed frozen, not sure where to look.

Graziella and her mother were used to this display as neither flinched or attempted to apologise.

Instead my aunt said to my mother, 'Come on, I'll help with the dishes.'

'No. Go upstairs and rest. Lorenzo can help me clear up.'

'And I'm off to bed,' growled my sleepy uncle.

My bed, in fact.

It was wonderful to see my mother so completely happy with all the family around her. No matter how much more work their visit created, she was ecstatic.

'You must be feeling tired,' I said to her 'All this preparing, cooking . . .'

'A little, but it's worth it. Perhaps Graziella will find someone nice here. Make sure you look after her.'

'Of course,' I said, picking up a dry cloth. Now I saw my moment to discuss something else. 'Mamma, can we talk about Anna? Did she say anything when she was here . . . ?'

To my relief she didn't lose her temper. I think the presence of her sister had mellowed her . . . for the moment.

'What did we talk about now . . . ?' my mother said almost to herself, scratching at a pan in the basin. 'She said she was in love with you, she said she didn't mind you had no money, she thought you were the most intelligent man she'd ever met, and honest with it. I was honest with her. I told her I did not approve of my son being with a married woman. I worry about you Lorenzo,' she added, looking up at me now.

'Why did you have to say that to her?'

'Because I see no future for you and her.'

'Let me worry about that.'

'Sure, you're far too old to take any notice of me. But you take a good look at her Lorenzo,' she said, shaking a knife at me. 'There is something very odd about that woman.'

'What do you mean?'

She remained quiet for a moment. Perhaps she was wondering whether it was wise to speak her mind and risk a row and disturb the slumbering family upstairs.

'Don't you . . .' she started. 'Don't you think she's a bit strange? I sensed it. She's like a bomb. She could go off any minute. She was too nice. Does she think I am some fool peasant woman? Maybe I am a peasant woman but I'm no

73

fool – and why did she come here uninvited? Didn't you think that was strange?'

The tension building up in me made me laugh a bit. She passed me a wet dish to dry.

'Mamma, you and your imagination.'

'No. I sense these things. Here, are you going to dry those glasses,' she said pointing at the draining board, 'or are you waiting for the wind to work on them!'

That was a good moment, I decided, to change the subject.

Towards dusk I had a chance to talk with Graziella who, when out of earshot of her parents, was light and chatty – very girlish.

'So, you have a boyfriend in Argentina?' I teased. 'You won't be left alone for long in Italy.'

She laughed, blushed a bit, and threw her long dark hair back from her face with small head movements.

'What if I show you the sights tonight, we can have a drink or a dance . . .'

'Oh, yes,' she said excitedly. 'I want to learn all the Italian dances.'

'How old are you now Graziella?'

'Nearly eighteen,' she giggled.

'That's good. So you won't have to stick to orange juice. Eh, you speak good Italian. Not bad for an Argentinian!'

'I'm not Argentinian. We always speak Italian indoors.'

From the landing upstairs someone shouted, 'Stop flirting with Lorenzo!'

It was Aunt Carla who'd been eavesdropping. Then we heard her laugh.

'I taught Graziella Italian from the age of two,' she added.

'That's the best age,' I shouted up the stairs.

Graziella popped upstairs to get ready.

'She's a good girl,' my aunt said when she came down. Then she raised an eyebrow at me . . . 'But I wonder if you're a good boy . . .'

At that moment the doorbell rang. I heard my father mumble something to the caller, he was still a bit drunk.

Then I heard another voice – I recognised it immediately. Anna's.

I felt immediate annoyance. My main fear was she'd kick up a fuss in front of my family if I said the wrong thing; or even if she caught sight of Graziella.

I rushed to the door and shooed my father away. 'What are you doing here Anna?'

'Just passing through. You don't mind, do you Lorenzo?'

She was wearing a shocking mid-length strapless green dress, showing off her beautiful, naked, shoulders. Just the sort of look to enrage my prudish mother. I could hear the family whispering and giggling behind me.

'*Buona sera a tutti*,' shouted Anna to them, giving them all a tiny wave.

I suspected Anna was checking up on me. Or Graziella. But before I could say another word my mother had pushed me aside and invited Anna in.

Uncle Alberto had finally risen from the bed – even then I wondered if he had cratered the mattress – and now gazed at Anna, in all her emerald beauty, with the eyes of a rutting bull.

To add to my woe Graziella chose this moment to make her entrance in a glistening red dress. She looked fantastic.

'My, how very beautiful you are,' Anna said. 'And who are you?'

'Lorenzo's cousin Graziella,' broke in my mother, sensing trouble.

'What a wonderful contrast, the red of the dress with your lovely black hair,' said Anna. 'If I didn't know better I'd say you're ready for a night on the town.'

After more pleasantries – with the family exchanging glances, wondering who Anna was – I took her gently by the arm and led her to a corner of the living room.

'So where are you off tonight dressed like that?' I asked her.

'Nowhere special. But since I'm here now you can ask me out.'

Her normally green eyes seemed dark with suppressed anger.

'I'd like to Anna,' I whispered, 'but I've already promised to take Graziella out for the evening, it's her first night here.'

Just then Graziella, who was a lot more shrewd and mature than I'd given her credit for, came up to us and said, 'Why don't the three of us go out together?'

For once God – or at least Graziella – was on my side. What a brilliant solution! 'Great idea,' I said. 'We'll all have a great time.'

My mother looked appalled, but then so did Anna who for once was speechless. At last they had something in common!

Outside, ten minutes later, I was just about to unlock my van when Anna said, 'We can't go in that Lorenzo.' She turned to Graziella: 'We're all dressed up and he wants to drive up in his truck. Honestly! Men haven't a clue, have they. Come on, we're all going in my car.'

With that she looped her arm in my cousin's and marched off.

'What a car!' squealed Graziella. 'Let's do a hundred.'

'Two hundred when I'm driving,' Anna said.

She had not complained about my van before.

'And where are you taking us Lorenzo?' she asked, shaking the car keys.

'There's an open-air dance by the river – and *I'll* drive.'

She didn't argue.

The evening was warm, almost sultry. Beautiful colours played on the water's surface along with a white full moon. People everywhere were dancing, or strolling arm-in-arm, revelling in love. Graziella was happy to sip her wine.

Anna knocked hers back as if it were Russian vodka.

'Excuse me, ' she said loudly, rising from the table, 'while I get another drink.'

Soon enough bottles of wine and spirits were being brought to our table by a waiter – 'From the lady at the bar,' he muttered, nodding at Anna.

She returned with a fresh glass of wine in her hand.

'Why did you order all this?' I asked. 'Go easy. I don't want a repeat performance of Lucinda and Dino!'

'Oh, what's he worried about?' Anna bellowed, attracting some attention. 'I'll be OK.'

She gave Graziella, who sat quietly watching us, a maternal smile – 'These men,' Anna added, 'they worry over anything, don't they?'

'Graziella,' I broke in, 'would you like to dance?'

She jumped up without a thought – 'Yes, yes!' – leaving Anna to her distillery.

Graziella was a great mover, just like her cousin of course, but I suspected she was up to a little mischief in her constant over-the-shoulder glances at Anna. She could do any dance – the rumba, foxtrot, old style two-step.

During a quiet number Graziella whispered in my ear, 'Is Anna your girlfriend?'

'Not much longer at this rate.'

'I ask because there's a man sitting with her. Maybe he's chatting her up.'

I turned to look and nearly tripped on Graziella's leg at what I saw. Anna's new 'admirer' at our table was Ottavio.

'Are you all right Lorenzo?' asked Graziella, now parted from me on the dance floor.

'Yes.'

'Do you know that man with Anna?'

'Yes. That's her idiot husband.'

Graziella's face broke out in a wicked smile. 'But he looks so old,' she said viciously. 'And he's bald! Does he know?'

'Yes,' I said, 'we have an arrangement. Ottavio is a eunuch!'

Graziella gave a little shriek. She had heard nothing like it in Argentina.

As we hurried off the floor she said to me, 'How could you have an affair with a married woman Lorenzo? And she's rich. How long can it last?'

'You sound just like my mother, Graziella. Don't criticise me.'

'I didn't mean to, I'm sorry.'

Anna and Ottavio looked up at us together as we approached the table.

'Ah, Lorenzo,' began Ottavio, 'and who is your very charming friend?'

'Good evening, Ottavio. Meet Graziella, my cousin from Argentina. Graziella, meet Signor Gilli; or Ottavio to his friends.'

She just nodded to him and then, to my relief, asked him boldly for a dance. Ottavio looked slightly alarmed, revealing his crooked tombstone teeth . . . 'My dancing legs are not what they were.'

'They never were, Ottavio,' slurred Anna above the music. The hooch had already hit her brain.

'As I said, my dancing legs are not what they were. But on the other hand I can't very well refuse such a charming lady.'

Anna laughed and waved her husband off – 'Go on, go on . . . lose some weight!'

In turmoil I sat next to Anna.

'That cousin of yours,' she said, 'she'll go far having the nerve to ask that old fool for a dance.'

'What's he doing here? You're drinking too much. How did he know where to find us?'

'Followed us of course. That's what I have to live with.'

On the floor Graziella and Ottavio made quite a pair of dancing love birds: she nearly a head taller than he, whose shiny head gleamed just under her chin.

'I'll have to watch him—' I said seriously.

'Your cousin is perfectly safe. Besides, she knows how to take care of herself. Ottavio's passed it.'

'You sure Anna? He's got enough stamina to chase after you. He's full of surprises. And you're drunk. I said no more repeat performances—'

Anna groaned loudly – 'You big mamma's boy! Go on, have a drink, it'll do you good.'

In a flash of temper I picked up her bourbon and threw it into the river.

She screamed, 'Lorenzo, what the hell are you doing!'

'You've had enough for tonight. And I'm tired of your old man following us everywhere.'

She leaned across the table – 'The only way to stop him is to throw *him* into the river!'

'I may just do that Anna. Why did you come tonight? I told you my relatives were coming. I had to keep my promise to take Graziella out, and—'

'—and I've spoilt it for you,' she finished.

'Now Ottavio turns up. I can imagine what Graziella will be telling the rest of the family.'

Anna softened her tone in an instant: 'I'm so sorry,' she said, oddly stroking my eyebrows, 'but if I don't see you I get very lonely.'

'Don't do that,' I snapped. 'Ottavio will see us.'

'Please pour me another drink, darling.'

'No way Anna! No more drink. I'm going to take you home soon.'

On the dance floor Ottavio now looked ripe for a coronary, all red and heaving. His legs were beginning to buckle. Graziella spotted me waving her over. She grabbed hold of Ottavio by the arm, acting as his crutch in the struggle back to our table.

He collapsed into the chair – 'Phew! Let me get my breath. Your beautiful cousin, Lorenzo, she can dance.'

Anna banged her glass on the table. 'Ottavio! I am surprised your trousers didn't drop down during the rumba! What a sight! Everyone would have jumped into the river.'

'You have been drinking too much, my dear,' he said, showing a bit of spirit for a change. Then turning to Graziella he continued, 'You know, my body is not that bad, except I am a bit overweight. But look at poor Anna here. She could do with a few extra pounds. One day her clothes will slide off her and she'll be arrested for indecency.'

'You're such a silly man,' said Anna, raising her voice again. 'Who do you think you're kidding?'

While Anna railed on, Graziella giggled, amused and bewildered. I whispered to her, 'Do you mind if we go home now?'

'Not at all.'

We helped Anna to her feet as she continued her tirade. Before we put her in the backseat of her car, Ottavio said to me, 'Lorenzo, I would be very pleased if you and Graziella came for supper one evening next week.'

'You certainly choose your moments, Ottavio. I'll call you—'

'Oh yes,' purred Anna, over-sweetly, 'do come to supper, *both* of you.'

Then, unable to control herself, she flashed her splendid eyes on Ottavio and screamed, 'You son-of-a-bitch! What the hell is it with you? You follow me everywhere. What have you to say for yourself?'

'I wish you would be quiet,' Ottavio responded strictly, 'and not embarrass us in front of friends.'

Just as he turned away to say something to Graziella and me, Anna raised her right leg and kicked out at him, booting him in his rear. Ottavio's arms were thrown out by the force of the blow and he stumbled forward catching his balance. He turned to face Anna, his face flushed with fury.

'Get her out of my sight!' he roared.

I grabbed hold of Anna and rushed her into the car – I was as certain Ottavio would hit her as amazed by his show of anger. He was not entirely the passive fool I'd taken him for.

Graziella put a comforting hand on Ottavio's shoulder.

In the car I attempted to give Anna a talking to. 'You have behaved disgustingly tonight. You should be totally ashamed—'

'So you're taking his side are you,' she shouted.

'I'm not taking anyone's side – you're drunk and you've made a fool of yourself in public.'

'You mean I have not conducted myself as a *lady*!'

'Exactly what I mean.'

81

'I'll remember that Lorenzo,' she snarled.

I drove her back home, Ottavio behind us with Graziella in his own car. After we'd dropped her off Graziella said, 'Wow! What an evening. That was brilliant. I think there's something wrong with Anna – don't you think?'

'There's nothing wrong with *her*, it's her husband – he follows her, and she can't hold her drink. She becomes a different person. Alcohol affects some people like that.'

'But why does she go on at him like that?'

'The truth is she can't stand him.'

'How terrible to live with someone you detest.'

'That's why Anna behaves that way. It turns her head, the frustration . . .'

'So why doesn't she just leave him?'

'It's not as simple as that—' Of course, Graziella was right: why didn't she leave him?

'Sorry Lorenzo, but I don't know what to think of Anna – not my business anyway.'

'That's right. And don't tell the family about tonight. They wouldn't understand.'

'You must love her a lot . . .' said Graziella.

'I do. We love each other. We can't live without each other. She'll leave her husband.'

Back home, all was quiet; a sign I was trusted with Graziella. I took off for the garage bedchair.

I can remember thinking on that ride back that maybe it would be best to finish with Anna – for *her* sake. Our affair was putting great pressure of her. Why would she want to risk her lifestyle and security for me? We were both trying to rush things. We had both got caught in a fantasy. Ottavio was the reality.

Certainly another night like tonight would finish us . . .

But you think that night was over? No such luck. As I drove into my garage forecourt I glimpsed a strange creature in my headlights. For a moment I thought it was some kind of spirit – sent by the Venice psychic Signora Lugano.

But no. It was Anna, waiting for me.

I threw the car door open. 'What the hell are you doing here?' I shouted.

'Be quiet Lorenzo, you'll wake the neighbourhood. I called a taxi the moment you left.'

'Where's Ottavio?'

'Who cares? In bed I suppose.'

'You should be in bed too after all the drink you've had.'

'I know I drank too much but I knew what I was doing, and I came to say sorry darling, for my dreadful behaviour.' She had already wrapped her arms round my neck. I could smell coffee on her breath . . .

I said, 'I just wish you would drink less.'

'I know. I will try.'

We entered the garage and I flicked the light switch.

'Did Ottavio follow you here?' I asked.

'I'm sure he didn't this time. I told him that if he did I wouldn't be responsible for my actions.'

'So, he *does* know you're here . . .'

'Well,' she said slowly, 'I had to warn him. And you know what he said? He said he couldn't care less what I get up to.'

I held her by the waist. 'How long do we have to go on like this?' I said, tired, but suddenly happy she was here.

'Not much longer *cara*.'

She gently held my head and kissed me on the lips. She knew I couldn't resist.

We undressed and and slipped into my uncomfortable

83

bedchair. Neither of us complained. The evening fiasco was suddenly forgotten.

In the morning she got up early and dressed quickly. 'Are you still thinking of moving out and getting a flat?' I recall asking her.

'Yes, it won't be long, darling. Just trust me.'

After the taxi had collected her I slipped back home for breakfast.

Everyone was up and at the breakfast table when I arrived – except Graziella.

'She's still in bed,' said my uncle. 'She must still be tired after last night.' Then, his mouth churning with food, he leered over me, 'Who was that gorgeous blonde?'

'Alberto!' shouted my aunt.

'That was my girlfriend, uncle.'

'You're the lucky one! No wonder you don't come to Argentina. I wouldn't, in your shoes.'

My aunt gave him a sharp dig in ribs with her elbow. 'Take no notice of him Lorenzo,' she said. 'he's all talk and no do.'

My uncle licked marmalade off his plump fingers like a cat washing its paws, and added, 'I'd go after something like Anna.'

His wife gave him a dismissive wave of the hand – 'Pphhh! All talk!'

'You've got a wife and daughter to think about Alberto,' said my mother sternly, who'd been quieter than usual. 'That should be enough for you!'

I thought she was over-reacting a bit. Perhaps she was thinking of Anna too, a married woman. My uncle said nothing. Instead he gulped down his coffee, making sounds like a gurgling plug-hole.

'Here, Lorenzo, your breakfast,' my mother said.

'A minute mamma. I want to clean up.'

Before I could get to the bathroom my uncle asked how I had got on with Graziella last night.

'Great,' I lied. 'we had a great time.'

Later in the morning Piero called at the garage. 'Eh, Valentino! So what did the medium really say then?'

'You never give up, do you. Not telling more tales to Luisa's mother I hope.'

'Come on Lorenzo. Forgive and forget.'

'The medium? I was impressed. There's something in it.' Then I fibbed, 'But she told me to tell no one what she said. It would be bad luck if I blabbed.'

'You can't even tell Piero, your old friend? I don't believe you.'

'I need all the luck I can get! I'll tell you one day – I promise.'

'By the way,' he said, helping himself to coffee, 'last night your Anna popped into the taverna. I was at the bar and she gave me a little wave, then rushed out.'

'Last night? Yes, I saw her . . .'

'It's love sickness, Lorenzo. All my women are love sick for me,' he laughed. 'Anna doesn't know where she is with you, what with Luisa—'

'But I don't know where I am with her!' I said. 'She never gives me a straight answer to anything.'

'She's insecure, like most women. The more beautiful, the more insecure! How well do you know her Lorenzo, besides her having a husband?'

Piero for a moment was no longer the fool, but the wise man. He had a point. I didn't know Anna at all.

'Then it's time,' he added, 'to get to know her better. Sit her down and talk. See where it gets you. She's a person.'

85

'Eh! I'm no virgin who doesn't know about relationships, y'know—'

Piero laughed and threw an oily rag in my face—

'Eh!' I added, 'I'm not new to all this. Anna is a mystery, not some simple girl you can pick up over a drink.'

'Find a simple girl Lorenzo. You're simple!'

I threw the rag back in his face.

'Anna just tells me what she wants me to know, and nothing else. I don't want to lose her.'

We babbled on till a car turned into the garage – my relatives.

Uncle Alberto wrestled out of the driver's seat with a lot of groaning and gasping – 'Thought we'd surprise you Lorenzo. I hired the car – gives us more freedom. I want to see some old faces and places.'

I had dreaded having to introduce Piero to Graziella – it had to happen I suppose – and the moment they met I saw mutual attraction. Or trouble, in a word.

Meanwhile uncle was sniffing round my garage, kicking the odd wheel and squinting at engine parts on my bench. 'Not bad Lorenzo, not bad. You're the right age to develop this little gold mine. What are your plans?'

'I want to expand. But I need cash. I need a bigger garage to handle more work. Trainee mechanics to give me time to develop things.'

'That shouldn't be a problem for a good mechanic and businessman like you – you coming over to the house tonight?'

I nodded.

'Good,' he barked. 'We'll talk over a glass of wine. We'll talk business—'

'What do you mean uncle?'

'Can't talk now,' he said, lumbering back to his car. 'I'll see you tonight.'

Piero hadn't wasted time. I overheard him asking Graziella if he could take her out for a drink one evening. 'That'd be very nice,' she said.

Piero wore his silly dazed expression as the family drove off. 'That cousin of yours,' he said, 'she's very beautiful. You don't mind if I take her out?'

'I thought you had a girlfriend already. Who was that girl you were walking with the other day?'

'My mother!'

'Piero, we're talking about my cousin, so watch it.'

'Just a drink with Graziella! I'll be proud to have her by my side. And that uncle of yours – eh, you'll have to sell the garage to feed him! What's he like?'

'Don't know yet – except we're all on rations to keep his belly full.'

Piero laughed, how easily he did.

'Fancy some lunch back home?' I suggested.

'Thanks, but I'm seeing someone at the Piccoli – see you later.'

Back home my mother said Luisa had called hoping to meet the Argentinians. I barely listened to this minor news. My head was full of what my uncle had said, that he wanted to discuss business ... I felt vaguely excited ...

'So I invited her to supper, Lorenzo – make sure you're here. She still looks thin, poor girl, but she says she's better.'

Later in the afternoon I called Anna. As usual the maid was curt.

'Signora Gilli is unwell. I had to call for the doctor this morning.'

None of this surprised me. The drink, the hysteria, the

midnight visit – hardly any sleep – we should both be in hospital.

'Hello, Lorenzo—' It was Ottavio on the line now. 'Don't worry about Anna, it's nothing serious. Just those drinking habits of hers. When she gets the taste she doesn't know when to stop.'

'Does she have a drink problem?' I asked.

'Oh no, no, nothing like that. It's her, her—' he was searching for the right word – 'her metabolism. Are you and your delightful cousin coming to supper? I don't think we settled on a date. What a lovely soul Graziella is, and very intelligent.'

I was irritated by his little endearments, his dainty courtesy. 'Thanks Ottavio,' I said dismissively, 'I'll phone you tomorrow – I need to talk to Graziella.'

The fool must have known that Anna spent the night with me, yet he still invited me to supper. Perhaps he'd given up. He would let Anna live her own life provided she ran his business . . .

That didn't sound right to me, though. The day would come when I faced Ottavio and asked him what his marriage meant to him . . . perhaps Piero was right. I was simple!

Around five that afternoon Anna phoned me back. I was under the car, and just got to the phone in time. Call it telepathy, but I was certain it was Anna—

'*Cara*,' she said in a low voice, 'I am much better now – it's so sweet of you to ask after me.'

'Did Ottavio tell you I called?'

'No, my maid.'

'A doctor was called – it must have been serious—'

'It was nothing, I just felt queasy—'

'Well you've made a speedy recovery by the sound of it.'

'The doctor said I shouldn't drink for a while – but then doctors feel obliged to say something when they can't find anything wrong—'

'I think the doctor is right. You should listen to him, and not try to convince me you're all right.'

'I'm not trying to convince you of anything, darling,' she said, unruffled. 'I know you'll see through me, any case.' She giggled.

'But does Ottavio see through you, Anna? You've got away with it up till now – but only because he puts his business before you. That suits him. It doesn't suit me.'

She paused for a moment.

'Lorenzo, are you coming this week, for supper?'

'I think I will – if you promise not to touch the booze.'

'Oh, am I not allowed even one little drink, just one glass of wine for my digestive system—?' her voice faded away pitifully, playfully; as if she might die without her one glass of wine.

I had to laugh at her performance. 'Not one glass,' I insisted.

'How can you be so hard?'

'This is silly talk, Anna. I must go now, I have a car to finish.'

A short while later I delivered the repaired car to its owner. As I made my way back to the garage on foot I heard a car horn behind me. For one dread moment I thought it might be Anna on another Lorenzo expedition. Thankfully it was my relatives. 'Hop in then Lorenzo,' shouted my uncle.

I got into the back with Graziella. She was full of excitement for Italy – 'What a beautiful country—'

'You've seen nothing yet,' said my uncle. 'Next week

we're off to Rome for four days. Train might be quicker. Come with us Lorenzo – it'll do you good.'

If only I could just take time off like that . . . with all the work I had on. Still, I said I'd think about it.

'You have to find time for leisure,' he said. 'And if you want time with your ravishing blonde, all the better.'

My aunt tut-tutted – 'Shut up Alberto.'

Over her shoulder she said to me, 'Your uncle's in love with the pretty lady.' Then she threw up her eyes.

Graziella whispered to me, 'Don't take any notice – my father's full of air.' And she laughed.

I was relieved Luisa didn't turn up for supper. I suppose she expected me to collect her; but it would have been embarrassing having to try to explain to the family who she was, what with Anna still fresh in all their minds.

Afterwards my uncle suggested we go for a drink. I decided not to take him to the Piccoli – too noisy, and Piero might be there – but to a quieter one just outside town.

On arrival he made straight for the bar.

'So,' he said pouring the wine, 'like I said this morning, your garage interests me. I can see you running a larger concern altogether. You don't want to spend the rest of your life dodging brake fluid—'

'I agree uncle. I need cash.'

'You need cash, I know. So I have a proposition. How would you like to go into partnership with me? Together we can expand the business, get in labour. I have cash to help you, and I've a sharp eye for a good earner. I can see you take your work seriously – you don't allow a pretty blonde to stop you working.'

He rummaged in his pocket for his cotton hanky and

mopped his face. I'd noticed back home how easily he sweated after the first gulp of the vino.

Would he live long enough, I wondered to myself, to benefit from his investment?

'I don't know what to say uncle. I had always planned to be my own boss—'

'You'd still run the show of course,' he continued. 'I'll be safely back in Argentina, waiting to count all my money! All entrepreneurs need a cash investment to get off the ground. Big companies have shareholders. You can have me instead. We can't all choose how to do things – at least I'm family, and I'll be far away. Of course I'd expect a return. I'm not offering this out of love! Think about it. You won't regret it.'

I felt it was an honest offer. For the first time I liked my uncle. He knew the world, how it ran . . . 'Let me think about it,' I said.

'Good! You think about it.' He got up and returned with two huge tumblers of scotch – 'chasers for the wine.'

After he'd settled his huge bulk on the stool again he asked me whether I was thinking of marriage. 'How serious are you about this beautiful Anna. If she's rich she could be a partner in the business too!'

I said what he wanted to hear: 'I'm in no hurry to marry. There's plenty of time.'

'Good for you. Before I went to Argentina I had no money and I was already married. With hard work, determination and a bit of luck I succeeded. I was one of the first to see that money could be made in haulage.'

'Why all these years before you came to see us then?'

He mopped his face again – 'I know, I know. I made my little fortune over the years, it took time, and I was busy. Now we have a wonderful big house. I would like you to come and see us when you feel more settled in your business.'

'When I have built my empire, you mean?'

'Don't leave that decision of yours too long Lorenzo. You're a good mechanic but don't waste your time with little things or else each day will end up like yesterday. Little bills for little jobs, and before you know it you have six kids.'

I wouldn't be rushed for a decision. I didn't want to be carried by dreams or fantasies: I would think it all through.

I'd check out my uncle for reliability.

I'd get my mother to talk to her sister.

You couldn't trust anyone.

'No word from Luisa,' my mother said back home. 'She must be ill again. Lorenzo, go see the poor girl. It's not like her.'

'I'll try to see her tomorrow, mamma.'

That evening I found a note from Anna pinned to my garage door – for anyone to see.

It read: 'This is just to say how much I love you. I shall call in the morning – I have to pass your way on business. I want to see you, I hope you don't mind, I won't keep you long. Love Anna XX.'

When she hadn't turned up by eleven the next morning I called her home.

'La Signora Gilli is at the doctors,' announced the maid, as if it were a social call.

'Why? Can you tell me?'

'That's a private matter,' she said coldly. 'You'll have to ask her yourself.'

'I will!' I hung up.

I couldn't concentrate on work, I forgot all about Luisa.

Perhaps Anna did have a drink problem, or something more serious. Could she be pregnant?

I phoned again at the end of the day.

'La Signora Gilli has had to attend an important business meeting,' the maid announced pompously.

'Did you tell her I called?'

'I did.'

'And?'

'Well, I passed your message to her.'

'She said nothing?'

'I just pass messages on, Signor Viardi. Signora Gilli will be in contact when she's ready, I'm sure. Would you like to leave another message with me? I shall be only too pleased to pass it on.'

I would have sacked her on the spot had I the power to. Little lap dogs like her are worse than snobs, yap-yapping at all strangers.

'No message, thank you,' I said.

I felt crushed. I was worried about Anna's health, disappointed by her treatment of me – after all her promises. She hadn't confided her problem in me. She didn't trust me.

But then how could she when we hardly ever saw each other? We were still strangers, strangers in love.

We would remain strangers while she remained with Ottavio.

I waited a little longer for her to call. But nothing.

At the door I could hear much laughter from within. My uncle, aunt and Graziella had brought much needed life to the house.

Then I recognised another voice – Luisa's. The moment I entered she cried hello and sprang over and kissed me on the cheek, her eyes blazing with life.

'Well Lorenzo,' said Uncle Alberto, holding a glass of

wine, 'how many more ex-girlfriends have you got hidden away who are as pretty as this one?'

Luisa giggled, I blushed.

'Thank you uncle,' I said, 'for your tact!'

'What a lovely sweet creature you are,' he roared to Luisa.

Standing together they looked like the elephant and the mouse.

'Oh yes, a delightful creature,' echoed my aunt who clearly thought her more suitable than Anna.

My mother came in with more wine glasses: 'I'm always telling Lorenzo that Luisa is the wife for him.'

Graziella, beautiful in a long white dress, raised her eyebrows at me.

Then to everyone's surprise my father, who had become almost totally mute in my uncle's presence, suddenly piped up: 'Leave the poor boy alone. He's a big boy now, old enough to decide for himself.'

'Thank you papa!' I said.

As more drinks were poured I asked Luisa, 'Are you well now?'

'Much better,' she said quietly.

After that all I could say was that I had to get washed and changed – 'Supper will be in half an hour,' shouted my mother behind me.

Just as I reached the top of the staircase I was stopped by knocks on the front door.

I groaned to myself.

I knew those impatient sharp raps, I recognised them as Anna's.

Before I was half way down the stairs my uncle had got to the door.

'Anna! Lorenzo, it's Anna—'

I leapt into the hallway but not before the rest of the

family had positioned themselves for a full view of our visitor. Anna was dressed in a dazzling canary yellow dress, off-the-shoulder, and far too revealing for family taste.

'Lorenzo, I'm so sorry I couldn't make today,' she said from the door, as if no one else were present.

My uncle didn't bother to disguise his glee at my embarrassment. 'Come in Anna,' he bawled, 'we were just about to start dinner. Why don't you join us? Irma, that will be all right won't it . . . ?'

My mother said nothing, and my aunt seemed about to say something.

'Well,' said Anna hesitantly, 'I don't want . . . Lorenzo can we talk for a—'

'Nonsense!' bellowed my uncle. 'Come on in! Luisa, you don't mind do you? I don't mind – we'd love you to stay.'

Anna was less hesitant the moment she heard Luisa's name.

'Well, perhaps I'll stay for the first course,' she said. 'Is that OK Lorenzo?'

What could I say? Either my uncle was a complete idiot or a mischief-maker. I suspected mischief.

'Of course, Anna come in.'

Luisa stood calm, giving no sign of her inner feelings. 'Are you going to introduce us Lorenzo?' she asked quickly.

'Oh *you're* Luisa,' cried Anna before I could say another word, holding out her hand, and for two seconds I imagined they might become sisters.

Then, gazing at Luisa's informal cardigan, Anna said, 'If only I'd known I'd be at a family get-together I wouldn't have come so, well, over-dressed!'

In the corner of my eye I saw my mother raise her arms in silent fury to my aunt. I knew I should have stayed at the garage.

95

The atmosphere in the house had been jolly. Now it was tense. Unaware of, or indifferent to, the trouble he had caused, my uncle escorted Anna to the table, looking as if he'd devour her with the *antipasti*.

'You'd be a beauty queen in Argentina,' uncle said to Anna. 'Your face'd be on advertising hoardings all over the cities.'

She smiled up at him – 'Would it? And what would I advertise do you think?'

'Well, you could advertise my company – I own a haulage company, you know.'

'Haulage? *Madonna*! Would I have to pose on a mountain of scrap metal?'

Very hilarious – at least my uncle thought so. I was certain Luisa would strike out at Anna at more provocation. If not Luisa, then my aunt.

Anna stayed for the entire dinner as I'd expected. When the family had warmed up a little, Anna turned to me and said, 'What a hectic day I've had, please forgive me for not showing up but I was just too busy, even to call you.'

I didn't want a scene so I told her not to worry. She made no mention of a medical appointment. It took all my self-control not to ask her all the questions in my head. I should be furious with her . . . I turned to Luisa on my other side – 'Are you all right?' I asked.

'Fine.'

'So you've met everybody now.'

'I certainly have.' Then she whispered, 'I can see why you're attracted to Anna.'

'That's a silly thing to say,' I whispered back.

'She's very beautiful.'

'I didn't fall for her looks.'

'You must have—'

Luisa was stopped by a shocking sound – one of uncle's

unrestrained, shameless belches. Among the many we had witnessed this was the loudest and most disgusting.

'Alberto! You shouldn't eat so fast,' said my mother.

'That was an extraordinary sound,' said Anna to uncle, as if he had said something witty. 'You know, you're going to have to lose some weight or you'll go pop one day.'

'I know I'm fat,' uncle said, enjoying Anna's direct, unstuffy ways, 'but I love food – particularly when it's cooked so well. But you're too thin Anna – just a scrap of a girl. Isn't she Luisa?'

Luisa just smiled weakly. Anna had to have the last word: 'Thin people live longest Alberto. It's a medical fact.'

After dinner I offered to walk Luisa home. 'No Lorenzo, it's only a few minutes – you stay and keep Anna company.'

I knew Anna would expect me to see her home. Before we left she thanked my mother for a wonderful supper.

'Let's all go for a drink,' said uncle. But I think aunt gave him a painful kick under the table judging by the pained expression on his face. 'Not tonight,' I said. 'perhaps tomorrow.'

In the car Anna was relaxed – she had jumped in the driving seat, knowing I hated being her passenger. 'What a lovely family you have Lorenzo. I wonder if you realise how lucky you are.'

I had another question in mind. 'Anna, why did you see your doctor today?'

'Who told you that?'

'Your maid.'

'My darling, she told you that?' Then she brightened up and became excited – 'Well of course I didn't tell her why I went to the doctor. It was for a business reason.'

'What business reason? Who goes to their doctor for a business reason? What are you hiding Anna?'

Vehemently she denied hiding anything and accused me of being hysterical.

'No, Anna, you're hiding something. What business reason? What kind of doctor did you see?'

'Oh Lorenzo. I saw the doctor for a check-up just to renew the life insurance. I'm worth a lot of money, you know. If I had known you would make such a fuss I'd have taken you with me.' She put her hand on my shoulder . . . 'Then you could have come behind the screen with me. There's nothing wrong with me – unless you'd like me to make something up so you can feel happier.'

All that worry – over life insurance! But this didn't explain her failure to turn up after she'd promised.

'I didn't promise to see you Lorenzo. I simply said I might be round sometime in the morning as I was passing through. It wasn't a date, we hadn't agreed anything . . .'

I felt so deflated that I stopped arguing. She hadn't written that she *might* call into the garage, she'd said she *would*; but what the hell.

She now talked sensibly: 'Stop this nonsense Lorenzo. I want to know if you're coming to supper on Saturday at seven – with Graziella of course. If you don't bring her, Ottavio will have nothing to do but cry in his soup. You know what he said this morning? That Graziella was the only person who treats him with respect.' Anna cackled wickedly. 'I mean Graziella is still just a child and Ottavio is flattered by a child's good manners – pathetic. She is very sweet, I know, and has winning ways, but ten years of adult life will knock that out of her.'

'That's very cynical,' I said sullenly. 'Why should she have to change at all?'

'That depends on who she ends up with. Men always

ruin women. Perhaps Graziella will meet someone like Ottavio. God help her.'

Ottavio! Ottavio! Always in our thoughts, always haunting our conversation. I wanted to talk about essential things – 'Have you spoken to Ottavio about your share of the business, about breaking up the business and coming to live with me?'

She seemed to take a deep breath before replying, 'Of course I've talked to him—'

'Then why the hell didn't you tell me? When did you talk to him?'

'Why are you yelling? There's nothing to report except he won't agree to give me my share of the business. Of course he wanted to know why and so I told him – that I wanted to be with you.'

'We should talk to him together. You could sue him—'

'Don't be ridiculous! Why is everything so simple to you? He owns the business. I shall work on Ottavio my own way. It'll take time, I'll wear him down.'

I was exasperated by her attitude, by the fact that my life hinged on her actions and decisions.

'I feel so uncertain about us Anna. We can't go on much longer like this.'

'Come now darling,' she said, changing her tone again. 'It's not all that bad. It all takes time to prepare, to think about. A deal with Ottavio is not going to be easy. After all, I'm his main asset!' She stopped the car by the roadside and turned to me: 'Just remember one thing: you are the man I want to be with.'

Her words lifted my mood momentarily. I truly believed her, and at that moment thought again of my uncle's offer of a business partnership.

That was the solution to our problems.

If I accepted his offer then Anna and I could live

together in some comfort: she wouldn't need to worry about Ottavio and his bloody business. I told her of my uncle's plan.

Her reaction was unexpected: 'That's really wonderful . . .' she began. Then she added, 'But that changes nothing for me. I want my share of Ottavio's business, I built it, I'll get my share if I have to kill him.'

My patience snapped. I grabbed her by the shoulders and began shaking her – 'You are a selfish, spoilt bitch,' I shouted. 'Your only concern is money. You and your husband are made for each other—'

As I saw it, I was ready to sacrifice my independence to have her, while all she could think about was scoring points against Ottavio.

Anna glared at me for half a minute – coldly, furiously. I'm sure she wanted me dead at that moment. Then she said, 'Finished now, Lorenzo?'

Before I could say another word she started up the car, reversed it, and shouted, 'Back to your mother's!'

I had never known anyone drive so fast and recklessly as she did on that journey, forcing at least two local cyclists off the road and into hedgerows. I knew if I tried to stop her we'd crash into something.

She skidded to a halt a few metres down from my home and screamed, 'Get out of my car and get lost!'

'With pleasure, Signora Gilli,' I said, trembling a little.

I had barely shut the door and her car screeched off with a great roar, leaving smoking rubber marks on the road. I was completely astonished by her behaviour, certain that at any moment I would hear the terrible sounds of a collision and then she'd be lost forever.

I couldn't believe that I had said or done anything that justified this treatment.

She had to have it all, and her own way, I knew that

much. She wanted me, Ottavio, the business, everything.

But I knew something else. She wouldn't have it all with me.

Stunned, I forgot for a moment that I was sleeping at the garage and, by force of habit, entered the house. My mother and aunt, in the thick of conversation in the kitchen, didn't notice me at first.

'Where's the rest of the family?' I said interrupting them.

'In bed,' my mother said, drying some cutlery. 'What happened to you? You look pale.'

My aunt smirked. 'Looks as if he's seen a ghost,' she said.

'I'm surprised you've come back here,' my mother chipped in. 'Not going to the garage then?'

I felt like a little boy again, all these silly queries and remarks.

'I just returned to get something,' I lied. 'Excuse me, but I need some sleep.'

They giggled as I pretended to collect something from the living room before shutting the door behind me.

I slept well at the garage but awoke exhausted. My dreams were full of gunshots and cannon fire. It felt like the War all over again.

Around midday Ottavio drove into the garage. I sighed heavily.

'Hello Lorenzo,' he shouted, stepping out of his car.

'I'm very busy so make it short Ottavio.'

He seemed untroubled by my off-handedness. 'I shan't keep you long,' he replied brightly.

'Is it so important it won't keep?'

'It could be important. I want to know if you'll be bringing Graziella for supper. This Saturday?'

101

I wiped my hands with a soiled rag: 'Fine. You came this way just to ask me that? You could have phoned. I've already told Anna we'll be coming.'

I had already decided I'd still go – just to see what Anna would do next.

'I only wanted it confirmed,' he said climbing back into his car.

'Well now you have your answer.' Then I teased him: 'Say, Ottavio, have you set your heart on my cousin?'

'Good God!' he said, taking my question seriously. 'I'm old enough to be her grandfather. What's wrong with you today Lorenzo? I know you saw Anna last night because she returned home in an awful mood. She was muttering the most terrible things . . . I take it that you two must have had a row or something—'

You'd think the fool was talking about his daughter, and not in fact his wife. He knew I was sleeping with her. He now knew that Anna and I wanted to be together.

I crouched down to his level as he sat in the driver's seat and said, 'What is wrong with you Ottavio? Are you a man? I think you've got a problem. Don't you feel any jealousy? Don't you care?'

Any other man I knew would have tried to kill me for saying these things. Ottavio just half-smiled and said, 'I'm passed caring about what Anna gets up to. She can do what she likes so long as I have peace and quiet. Besides, at my time of life one gets tired running after someone who couldn't care less for me. Maybe Anna never did love me and maybe she is only happy when she is with you Lorenzo – but she's still with me. And I have no intention of helping either of you by putting my business at risk. I will not be paying her off so you can set up your love nest. No, you two stay as you are. I'm happy with that.'

I could scarcely believe it. He was giving Anna and I

his blessing to continue our relationship – that's if we still had a relationship.

'You don't mind me being with your wife – everyone knowing?'

He just made a face and shrugged his shoulders.

'What kind of husband are you?'

'Anna works for me. She is not a business partner or shareholder. She's my special employee. If she wants to live with you I won't stop her. But she goes without a penny and of course she would cease to work for me if she left.'

'Your business would be nothing without her. She's worked hard for you—'

'Lorenzo, she chose to take care of my business. I agreed to give her something to do. I let her do it. That doesn't mean she now owns my company or has a claim on it.'

'You're a spiteful, vindictive old man—'

'I have no wish to spite anyone. I have good reason not to give her anything and perhaps one day, when you are calmer and more mature, I shall tell you what that reason is.'

I demanded to know the reason – I accused him of inventing some sort of mystery to excuse his meanness – all the while forgetting that it was his wife I wanted to take from him.

'I must leave you now,' he said gently. 'I mustn't keep you from your work. See you Saturday.'

He wound up the window and carefully reversed out of the garage.

It was all a game to the old bastard, torturing Anna and teasing me.

He had nothing to lose.

At around one that day I returned home for a bite to eat

and noticed Anna's car parked outside. Something flipped in my belly at the thought of seeing her so soon after our row, but excitement was mixed with irritation at Anna's craftiness.

She couldn't face me eye-to-eye at the garage so she hoped to win me over by making charming small-talk with my mother. Why couldn't people just be straightforward?

But I was wrong. Anna wasn't in the house, only my mother. The rest of the family were out.

'You're late for lunch,' said my mother, turning over a potato and vegetable omelette in the pan. 'Where have you been?'

'I'm not that late. I've a lot on – has Anna been here?'

'Not that I've noticed. Maybe she's hiding in the larder trying to fatten herself up for you!'

I laughed and gave her a kiss on the cheek.

She added, 'I've not seen her since last night – poor Luisa – you must go apologise to her and tell Anna not to turn up like that again.'

'It's odd. Anna's car's parked outside.'

My mother joined me at the window – 'Are you sure?' she asked.

'Of course I'm sure. She must be around somewhere.'

As I filled our glasses with wine I told her that we'd had a minor tiff, nothing important. I didn't want to give her more ammunition against Anna.

'What sort of tiff?' she kept on repeating.

'Just nothing!'

'About her husband – eh?'

'No.'

'Lorenzo, I have to say something. I am sure there is something wrong with that girl.'

'You already said that before.'

'So I'm saying it again. There's something not right with her. Haven't you noticed?'

'For God's sake, not again mamma. There's nothing unusual about her except she's a bit insecure and she likes good clothes. She's used to a different life.'

She sipped her wine as she gazed at me thoughtfully. 'Look Lorenzo, maybe I'm wrong. I don't want to upset you.'

'Let's talk about something else. I want to ask you something about Uncle Alberto. The other night he offered to come into partnership with me, he wants to put money into the garage so we can all be millionaires!'

She was astonished. 'Alberto never said anything to me, nor did Carla. What are you going to do?'

'Has he really got the money? I'll need a lot of money for expansion.'

'He's got the money all right. How much do you think it's cost them to fly from Argentina? He's even offered to pay for us to visit them. Take my advice – accept his offer. Alberto was always good with money. He wouldn't have made that offer unless he was sure there was something in it for him. You'll never get another chance like this.'

Her words lightened my mood. My mother was thinking of me and I was thinking of Anna.

'I've got to think about it a bit more,' I said.

That evening I looked up at my pretty cousin and said, 'Eh, Graziella, your boyfriend Ottavio wants to know if you can make Saturday for supper.'

She flung a cushion at me—

'Graziella!' cried my mother. 'I hope you can stitch. Who's this Ottavio?'

'Anna's *husband*!' shouted Graziella.

'Oh *Madonna*!' my mother squealed, waving her arms with the shame of it.

Graziella sat beside me on the settee. 'This Saturday? I think I can make that.'

'He called round at the garage just so's he might see you.'

'Stop lying. He's too old and he's too odd-looking – and, unlike some I could mention, I avoid married people!'

'Oh!'

'That's a wise girl,' shouted my mother who was now in another room. Then she came through with a shocked expression on her face – 'Lorenzo, you mean to say, you talk to this Ottavio? Does he know about you and his wife?'

'Sure. He's encouraging us. He's going to be my best man at our wedding!'

My mother crossed herself and said *Madonna*! several times . . . 'What wicked times we live in when a husband encourages his wife's adultery . . . Lorenzo, go to Don Alfonso and confess yourself!'

Graziella and I just laughed.

'I only want to see their house,' said my cousin. 'See if it's as good as ours back home. Will I have to wear something special?'

'No. Just a sock in your mouth.'

'Seriously!'

'Just something nice but not too competitive.'

Uncle Alberto waddled into the room, yawning and stretching – looking nothing like the dynamic tycoon of Argentina.

'Lorenzo,' he barked, 'what are you doing tonight?'

'I've made no plans uncle. Why?'

'Thought I'd like to try this Osteria Piccoli I keep hearing about – one of your haunts I believe. For a drink.'

'OK.'

★   ★   ★

106

Eight-thirty in the evening and Anna's car was still parked outside. It was like a sentry watching my movements.

I went out to double-check it really was her car. You could never be too certain, I deluded myself. Straight away I saw her white jacket carelessly thrown on the backseat.

As I peered about I felt someone walk up behind me.

'What are you looking for Lorenzo?' It was my uncle.

'It's Anna's car. I'm puzzled why it's here – I haven't seen her today.'

'That's strange.'

'I'll phone her home from the garage and find out where she is. It won't take a few minutes.'

There was no answer. Not even Anna's maid this time to put me in my place.

'Come on then uncle, let's go to the Piccoli.'

We lumbered into the backroom of the taverna and ordered drinks.

'So young man,' began my uncle, 'have you thought about my business proposition – or is your head full of Anna?'

'Strange,' I said, 'but if you'd asked me a few hours earlier I wouldn't have been sure. Now I know what to do. I'd like to accept your offer and go into partnership with you.'

He banged the table as he roared approval, ordered two bourbons and gave me a hug. Uncle did nothing by half measures, and I was beginning to like him more for that.

'You won't regret this,' he said with total certainty, which gave me confidence. 'This is the first day of the rest of your life. We will drink to our new enterprise.'

And with that we threw back our heads and ordered more.

'Like I said before, me and the family are going to

Rome next week – come with us. Get to know me more.'

'I think I know you already, uncle. I'd like to come but I'm behind with work.'

'I like that! You and I – we're very alike. I too put work first. When we return from Rome the two of us will go on a shopping expedition. We will find larger premises – a garage for dozens of cars. We will settle all the paperwork before I return to Argentina. I'm a stickler for these things. If it's not in writing people break agreements; that's what I learned in haulage, and it's the same in all other types of business. No, you won't regret this. This is a joint investment – and I'm the one who's really taking the risk!'

That little speech of his told me a lot about Uncle Alberto. If he couldn't even trust his own nephew with a verbal agreement, I certainly couldn't trust him. I knew then I'd have to read the small print of whatever deal we struck.

'I will do my best uncle.'

'I know you will. You're an excellent mechanic and you've a good head. But I have to get something off my chest. Never let any woman distract you from your work, and that Anna – well, I'm a simple plain-speaking man – that Anna of yours, she's a classic maneater, if you know what I mean. You'll have to watch that firecracker, oh yes, I know the signs.'

I had no idea uncle was an expert on firecrackers and maneaters, or knew of their 'signs'. To look at him I'd say he knew more about pork chops. I'd have to be firm with my new partner.

'Anna is my business, uncle, not yours. You don't know anything about her – so how can you judge her as you do? I'd appreciate it if you didn't criticise her.'

Uncle's eyebrows shot up – 'I am sorry Lorenzo, I didn't mean to upset you. I didn't realise she meant that much to you. I mean I had affairs before I married—'

Fortunately he read my face before he said anything worse. He laughed to relieve the sudden slight tension, 'Come on now,' he said. 'We'll go home now and tell the family our good news.'

As we made for the door Piero walked in with his girlfriend Rosita.

My uncle took her hand and said, 'My, my, now *you* are a little firecracker.'

Piero put his hand on uncle's shoulder – 'Watch this man Rosita. He's looking for a younger wife.'

'Oh I am,' said uncle, 'someone I can whisk back to Argentina. Come on Lorenzo, buy more drinks for our guests.'

So we started all over again at the Piccoli. I pulled Piero to one side to talk about the mystery of Anna's car.

'Ah! I thought that was Anna's car,' he said. 'I passed by your place around two this afternoon. I assumed she was in with you.'

Rosita's hand was now somewhere near uncle's lips. 'You look like a Rosita,' he was saying. 'All Rositas are brunette, have white teeth and wear red silk blouses.'

'And you look like an Alberto,' she said giggling.

'And what do Albertos look like, my Rosita?'

'Like you.'

Gales of mindless laughter followed that.

Then he said: 'Oh yes, you're a Rosita. You girls, you come in thinner models these days. There's no flesh on you.'

'No,' interrupted Piero, 'you have enough for two.'

Uncle laughed at that as well, and gave Piero what I thought was a slightly less friendly slap on the back.

'Careful uncle,' I said, 'Piero used to box at school and he's very jealous of his girlfriends.'

'*Girlfriends?*' queried Rosita.

'I mean in the past,' I added quickly.

A hour later uncle and I had arrived back home. Anna's car was no longer parked outside. I asked my mother if she'd seen who drove it away.

'I don't spend my life staring out the window,' she said tartly.

'You do if the neighbours are rowing.'

'I've better things to do. Who puts the dinner on your plate?'

Graziella, who was seated at a window, laughed at my mother's reply.

She came over to me and said, 'I wasn't going to say anything to Aunt Irma but I saw Anna take the car away. I thought about saying hello to her but she disappeared very quickly.'

'Did she look this way?'

'No – she seemed in a hurry. I was surprised she didn't call in. You must have fallen out.'

My mother, her hearing bat-sharp as usual, rushed up to us – 'You should have told me Graziella. Lorenzo, why didn't Anna call in?'

'Not that it's anyone's business,' I almost shouted to the lot of them, 'but Anna and I did have an argument last night.'

Now my aunt joined in – 'Don't you think she's behaving oddly, parking her car out there all day.'

'If it is odd then that's my business,' I said.

'Quite right,' said uncle, who had learned fast. 'This is Lorenzo's affair – I mean, er, business – and we mustn't interfere. Graziella, you shouldn't sit by windows.'

'Only cats sit by windows,' said my mother.

My uncle roared, 'I wasn't thinking of cats!'

All this talk only served to revive my worries about Anna.

I couldn't deny to myself that her behaviour was, at least, designed to attract attention. But there might be a good, rational reason for what happened today. It was too easy to jump to wrong conclusions now that everyone had decided she was eccentric.

I thought up a dozen possible alternative explanations . . .

The next day I phoned Anna.

'*Pronto*, the Gilli residence.' It was the maid.

'Hello, it's Lorenzo. I'd like to speak to la Signora Gilli.'

'*Si, momento.*'

I could hear the clack of her shoes, then muffled talking; the sounds of conspiracy, I imagined.

'Hello.' It was Ottavio on the line. 'What can I do for you Lorenzo?'

'I phoned to find out if Anna is all right.'

'So far as I know. Did you think she was ill?'

'I only ask because she left her car outside my house yesterday and didn't call in. That doesn't make sense, does it?'

Ottavio was silent for a few seconds. I was about to rouse him with a *pronto*! when he said, 'Lorenzo, you mustn't take too much notice of Anna, she's only trying to play games. She's looking for attention, like a child, but I'm sure you can cope with this.'

He then chuckled, which enraged me.

'What's there to laugh about?' I shouted. 'How could any decent man talk about his wife like that?'

'You have to understand, Lorenzo, that I am practised in Anna's funny little ways. She can't help herself the way

111

she is. As her husband I learned a long time ago that I have to live my own life or else I'd spend all my time playing up to her nonsense. I make the most of a bad job.'

'Then let her go. She doesn't want you.'

'I know. But she will stay with me and my money. No matter how much your love, my money will win. I take it we are still on for Saturday?'

I slammed the phone down, churning with violent thoughts. Now I fully realised how much I had underestimated Ottavio. He was openly teasing me, almost challenging me to fight his money. Far from being the spineless wimp, he was a cold monster set on entertaining himself at my expense.

I wondered again how Anna could have brought herself to marry such a man. What did their marriage tell me about Anna?

Angry, depressed, I turned from the phone in my small, cluttered office to face the familiar garage scene of jacked-up cars and lonely tyres – my friends for the day.

I picked up my toolbox and prepared to toil. As Uncle Alberto would say, I was the good mechanic.

Later in the morning, much to my surprise, Lucinda phoned me.

'Hello, handsome,' she drawled in her deep voice. My stomach fell in disappointment.

I'd hoped it was Anna.

She added, 'And what are you doing with yourself?'

I was in no mood for seduction scenes.

'Well, what do you imagine I'm doing?' I said. 'Earning my daily bread, unlike some.'

'Oooooh! We are in a mood! You don't mind me calling do you? We're still friends I hope . . .'

'How did you get hold of my number Lucinda?'

'Anna of course. I just heard you've given her the push. I couldn't believe it so I thought I'd like to hear it from the horse's mouth. Poor Anna, she's terribly, terribly upset—'

'It's not like that – anyway who told you that?'

'That would be telling—'

'Then mind your own business Lucinda.'

'Don't be like that Lorenzo. I like you and I'm fond of Anna and now I feel sorry for her.'

'You don't feel sorry for her—'

'OK, well if you don't believe me Lorenzo . . . but Anna didn't know how lucky she was—'

Lucinda then listed my virtues including my honesty and my greatness as a man. I began to suspect she was making of fun of me, yet the more rude I was the more she persisted.

'Lucinda, I'm not really in the mood for this right now. I don't know who told you I'd given Anna the push, but that's not true – and that's from the horse's mouth.'

She ignored this and instead asked me when I was likely to be in Venice again. Not for a long time I said, it was fit only for tourists.

'Oh Lorenzo, but I live in Venice and I'm not a tourist. By the way, are you going to Anna's on Saturday?'

'Yes, but only because I promised my cousin that I'd take her.'

'Don't be like that Lorenzo. I heard about your cousin – Graziella, yes? I am certain you won't be able to stay away from Anna for long. She loves you, you know.'

Though Lucinda irritated me, her words suddenly cheered me; gave me hope . . . 'I love her too but I can't go along with whatever she wants. She's never going to leave Ottavio—'

I heard a long sigh . . . 'You're so open Lorenzo, there's

113

no side to you. I admire that. What a contrast you are to that fat little Ottavio—'

'I have to go Lucinda, I'm very busy.'

'I'll let you go then. And don't forget Dino's birthday party next week.'

'We'll talk at Anna's.'

What a day that was.

To equal my inner turmoil, the atmosphere in the garage had turned tropical by mid-afternoon, even with all the doors open.

No siesta for me.

The sweet smell of frangipani from outside drew me into a short daydream with Anna. It was as if nature herself were trying to seduce me from my work.

At one point I thought I'd collapse in the heat and went and lay down in the back, with a bottle of cold water resting on my forehead.

There, fatigued, miserable, boiling, I dozed. In fact I slept for a couple of hours.

In a dream I thought I heard my name being called . . . no, it wasn't a dream . . . someone in the garage was crying out, 'Lorenzo!'

As I came to, there in the office doorway, stood the giant silhouette of my Uncle Alberto. How he laughed at his hardworking nephew.

'What are you doing down there Lorenzo?'

I struggled onto my feet and rubbed my eyes – 'The heat, I thought I'd rest awhile.'

To my surprise and pleasure he suggested I call it a day and return home with him.

'No,' I said, 'I have a few things more to do. It'll cool a bit soon – you're back early.'

'We changed our plans and then I thought I'd see what

Lorenzo is up to.' He gave me a wink. 'And I hear you're taking Graziella to Anna's place tomorrow night. She's very excited. I take it I am not invited! I wouldn't mind seeing that luscious Anna again – only joking . . . I'm just having a bit of fun with you, Lorenzo.'

Maybe he was, but I sensed he was also trying to find out if I was hooked on Anna – testing how much his investment might be put at risk by the 'maneater'. Uncle was clever like that.

Jokes and laughter were his way of dealing with the world and getting information.

'And tell me Lorenzo,' he said after a pause, 'did you find out why Anna left her car outside the house – you don't mind me asking?'

I shook my head. 'I haven't had a chance to talk to her yet.' I was keen to change the subject.

'She does do odd things, doesn't she?' he said more serious now.

'What do you mean uncle?'

He was sitting on a stool which creaked worryingly under his immense weight – 'I know it's none of my business, but I don't think I have to explain what I mean. She's not . . . ordinary, I'll say that for her . . .' Then he gave me a broad smile – 'But enough of that. I'll see you later Lorenzo.'

He got up and left me to my work and in no doubt as to what he thought of my lady love.

Uncle better tread carefully. His money gave him no right to tell me how to live my life.

I made up for my dozing by working till eight. The car I'd worked on had to be delivered that evening so I took off my overalls and tidied myself up.

I was about to drive off when a red sport's car curved

into my forecourt, blocking my way. It had to be Anna. How was I supposed to react to her?

I had no idea.

I was certain she had got Lucinda to call me and say I had finished with Anna to see what I would say . . .

First her long legs, then her beautiful blonde head. I wanted to make love with her there on the ground.

Her green eyes, sometimes dark when she was in a fury, were now red – or at least red-rimmed, and sad. She shut the car door gently, and we gazed at each other awkwardly for several moments.

I broke the silence. 'What are you doing here Anna?'

She stepped forward. 'I had to see you Lorenzo. I know everything is my fault and that I've been terrible to you but I'm here now . . . I want us to be happy again.'

Her few words disappointed me. She was saying we should pick up where we left off. No mention of something new, like leaving that toad husband of hers.

'What's the point Anna? We're getting nowhere. Then next time you'll throw me out of your car like a dog – and into a river if we happen to be passing one.'

She rested her body against my car and crossed her arms. 'I don't know what to say . . . I don't mean to do these things to you Lorenzo.'

'The point is you do them and nothing makes sense. Nothing you do or say makes much sense. We can't just carry on. I've told you before I'm not Ottavio. You can treat him the way you do and get away with it, but not me. You keep trying to pretend I'm Ottavio. I can take so much, then that's it.'

She shivered and bowed her head as if to cry. 'Do you still love me?' she asked quietly.

'Yes, I do Anna. But enough is enough. Think about the way things have gone up to now . . .'

Eyes shut, she clasped her head and slid her hands from the temples, pulling her tumble of blonde hair into a ponytail before letting it fall back into its natural style.

She was wrapped in thought, self-absorbed, thinking of something new to say, I imagined. How much I wanted to hear her say she would live with me.

I knew that if she could not bring herself to say that *now* she never would.

Instead she asked: 'Are you coming tomorrow night?'

'That's already arranged so don't ask again. But after tomorrow we must not see each other – or at least for a while, so we can both think things over—'

'How can you say that? How can you do this to me? You're everything to me—'

'It's not something we can discuss. That's how I feel. I have waited patiently for you Anna but in the end Ottavio and his business are more important to you. Ottavio will never give you what you want; you know that, and you're not prepared to face it—'

'You've been talking to him again.'

'Yes. I wanted to know why you'd parked your car outside my home.'

'Why not? I had a business matter to attend to and it was easy to remember where I had left the car.'

'So why didn't you call in – afterwards at least?'

'I didn't have time – I had to rush home—'

'There you go again. Making a mystery out of nothing. What business did you have that would bring you to my neighbourhood? It's always the same. Your business, your schedule, strange appointments. You're always on the run!'

'So what did Ottavio have to say?' she asked coldly.

'That you were just playing games – he's right. You're like a child.'

'That fool. And of course you two are suddenly friends,' she said sarcastically.

'Of course you're playing games, it's obvious. He said about your marriage – he was making the best of a bad job.'

She said nothing to that.

'Whatever happens from now on,' I continued, 'is because I decided it.'

She turned slowly away and walked to her car.

'I see,' she said, talking into space, 'I get the message, it's clear as crystal. You are cruel—'

I couldn't hear the rest. She was murmuring more to herself, and my heart and head were pounding with the drama of not knowing what she might do next.

It would have been so easy to call her back and start the game again. But thank God I didn't give into her as Ottavio would have done, as he did in all things except one – for his own sick reasons.

As she got into her car I convinced myself I was doing her a favour. I was her last chance to escape her own self-made prison of fake security with her fake husband.

She would go away and think my words through and see the light.

She quickly reversed the car out, then shot off in her usual crazy style. Her reckless driving was as much fury as a tactic to worry me about her safety – she knew me so well – but I prayed all the same for her life and for her to return to me.

I was gambling she would see sense. If nothing else Anna would make me a devout Catholic!

I felt that I had made the most important decision of my life, more important than going into partnership with my uncle, or anything else.

To live my life on my terms.

Yet the day was still not done. Life must continue, which that evening meant delivering my customer's car . . .

On the way I spotted Luisa walking alone in the warm dusk. She resembled a celestial creature with the fireflies playing above her.

It was as if fate, having brought me Anna and her torments, now revealed to me Luisa and her peace. Our relationship had never been any trouble. I don't think I'd given it a second's thought. It just happened.

Maybe that was the secret of a happy life.

Just to see Luisa relaxed me. She still looked very thin in her simple floral dress – I sounded the car horn and she turned and smiled.

'What are you up to?' I shouted out of the window.

'Oh, I've finished work. I'm feeling much better—'

'That's great – want a lift? Come on.'

'That would be nice.'

She jumped in and as we rode along she told me she'd returned to work a few days earlier.

'You never said anything the other night.' I was thinking of our disastrous family supper and Anna's arrival. She obviously didn't wish to talk about it because she changed the subject and asked me how life was treating me.

'Well, I've had my ups and downs,' I replied in one long sigh.

'I'm sorry to hear that,' she said genuinely.

An impulse suddenly took me – 'What are you doing tonight Luisa?'

'Nothing. I'm still waiting for someone to take me out.'

'And what would you say if I asked you – as a friend?'

'You really mean that, Lorenzo?'

'Course. If I didn't I wouldn't ask.'

119

She giggled. 'I'd be very happy to go out with you. As a friend!'

We arranged to meet later. I delivered the car, and back home uncle announced he was taking the family out for a drink.

'Join us after your supper,' he said jovially.

'Thanks but—' Then I whispered that I was taking Luisa out tonight. 'Not a word to my mother or else she'll assume I'm back with Luisa, and before you know it she's talking about grandchildren again.'

Uncle never lacked for entertainment during his stay. Now he laughed again – 'And what about Anna?' he said, not whispering.

'Quiet. It's a long story.'

'Well, tell me to mind my own business but I think you'll be better off with Luisa. You'll see this for yourself Lorenzo.'

Still whispering, or trying to, I said, 'What have you against Anna? You know nothing about her—'

'She's a married woman, what are you going to do with a married woman? I always go by first impressions, I'm not clever, I go by what I see and rarely am I wrong.'

Uncle was now talking at his usual volume which would have suited a town meeting.

'A level-headed fellow like you,' he added, 'needs someone like Luisa to keep you happy.'

His good sense irritated me – how I hated the voice of experience! 'Thank you for your wise words, uncle.'

'You'll thank me for it one day,' he said, registering my sarcasm.

'Next time I want to see a fortune-teller I'll consult you instead.'

He looked away with a knowing smile. He'd seen, heard and done it all before.

★   ★   ★

120

After supper I washed, dressed, and collected Luisa.

She stood waiting in her doorway flanked by her smiling, waving parents who clearly thought this was a reunion. No chance, but this wasn't the moment to put them straight.

Still, Luisa did look very pretty in her blue dress patterned with little white flowers. I liked the way she had taken to drawing her hair behind her ears, making her look older, more sophisticated.

Her scent, her sweetness, reminded me vividly of why I had found her so attractive in the early days.

And that set me wondering, as she trotted down the steps towards me: why can't we just fall in love with those who best suit us?

I said, 'Fabulous, you look great.'

'Thank you,' she said, glowing with happiness.

I suggested we drive into Venice – 'There's a great place there where we can dance.'

She clapped her approval—

'And if it's full,' I added, 'we can go to the Osteria Sebastione.'

'Wherever you want to go, I go!'

How easy it was to please Luisa, everything so free of hassle. After the complications of Anna I was just happy to be with someone who was simply happy being with me.

'Tonight,' I declared, 'we will enjoy ourselves!'

So who was I kidding? I could think of nothing but Anna, and what we had said to each other that afternoon, and the terrible prospect of never seeing her again.

I must have been silent less than a minute when Luisa interrupted my thoughts—

'Are you all right Lorenzo?' Her tone told me I had not been listening to her as she talked about her day.

'Is there something on your mind?' she asked.

I shrugged my shoulders. 'I don't want to talk about it now, Luisa. Come on, let's enjoy ourselves.'

'You might feel better if you got it out of your system,' she said, her eyes full moons of compassion. She seemed so much more grown up since the time we first courted. Ridiculously, the thought hit home that she was no longer a girl.

'No questions tonight!' I said, smiling. 'We don't want to spoil the evening.'

'I didn't mean to pry – but remember you can talk to me about anything.'

I gave her a wink. How much I wanted to love her.

In Venice Luisa said she'd prefer we walk to the dance hall rather than take the vaporetto. It was a fabulous, warm evening, the air fresh for once and full of the giggles and garbled intimacies of strolling couples from other countries.

Venice was a park of shared happiness – despite the straw-hatted gondoliers on the canal whose voices could be heard protesting at a speeding motor launch, rocking their romantic passengers. Lights sparkled on the waters, everything was in constant movement, a city relaxed but never resting . . .

Not thinking, I put my arm on Luisa's shoulders, drawing her closer to me.

She looked up at me for a moment, a little in surprise, then with affection. So many times I had seen that look. And each time I had felt a slight pang of guilt that she was giving more of herself than I could ever.

Along a tourist market, a street artist offered to draw caricatures of us for 500 lire.

'Go on,' said Luisa. 'Then you can give it to me as a keepsake.'

'No,' I said, 'you're the beautiful one.'

Luisa giggled.

'You're both beautiful,' said the young bearded artist, a student I guessed. 'But I shall make you both ugly!'

We laughed and moved on.

'What a love market Venice is – I hadn't quite realised,' said Luisa.

I liked that phrase, 'love market'. I told her of my sudden fantasy of shopkeepers selling parcels of romantic dreams and being paid in kisses.

'What a madman you are,' she said. 'You're a real romantic—'

'Would I bring you here if I weren't?' I joked.

At some point in the evening I began to notice Luisa peering over her shoulder and growing quieter.

'What's up?' I said finally.

'I don't suppose you've noticed but I think someone is following us – since we left the car. Maybe I'm imagining it.'

I turned to face the crowds – 'Who would want to follow us?' I asked. 'We aren't spies. You should have been a detective, Luisa.'

'There!' said Luisa pointing. 'That man – he's pretending to look at the boats.'

I looked and looked – I wasn't sure whom she meant, what with people crossing our view. I didn't recognise the man.

I said, 'Whoever he is he's probably going our way . . .'

'I'm not so sure,' Luisa said. 'He stops when we do.'

The dance hall, was as I feared, packed. We squeezed in, tried to find some space, but it was impossible. In any

123

case I liked lots of room to move around, so we went to the Osteria Sebastione—

'Not as lively, is it?' I said. At least we had seats and a table.

'It's not your fault. It's nice here – so long as I'm with you—'

Multi-coloured lights shone down on us, making mini-rainbows on our flesh, in the glasses, against the gloss walls.

On those walls hung ghost-white Venetian masks. The lights, the vibrancy of the people, the swiftness of time – it was a dazzling moment (just a moment) and my heart wished for . . . Anna.

I drank bourbon, Luisa a good wine – in fact she gulped it down and I encouraged her to drink more. At least if we were dancing we would have had an excuse to touch each other, to be very close.

Now we had to rely on the alcohol.

Which failed us. While we'd walked, the scenery, the people, had given us things to talk about. But now seated in this bar our conversation dried up a bit, despite Luisa's best efforts.

My mind was numb, I couldn't think—

'Lorenzo!' Her voice had a new urgency. 'That man I was talking about, who I thought was following us – he's here on the other side of the bar.'

I yawned and said, 'You've been drinking too much Luisa, you can't see clearly anymore.'

'I'm sure it's him,' she persisted.

I scanned the bar – I'd had a few drinks myself – and, yes, I had to admit the guy she'd pointed out in the street was here now, sipping a tiny liqueur.

'I'm going to ask him what he wants,' I said, to break the tedium.

'Careful Lorenzo,' said Luisa. 'maybe I'm wrong.'

'No. I want to know what he wants. Maybe he's after my body,' I joked.

Luisa got up after me – 'Don't go Lorenzo. He maybe a nutcase. I wish I never said anything now.'

My mind was set. I wanted words—

'Excuse me,' I said, tapping him on the shoulder. 'Are you following us? What do you want?'

He was a smallish man, middle-aged . . . he smiled faintly – 'I don't know you, Signore,' he said. 'Sure you've got the right man?'

'My girlfriend noticed you following us – from the car park.'

'Not me,' he said. 'Why would I want to follow you – I don't know you. You drunk?'

Luisa joined us and held my arm.

'You his girlfriend?' he asked. 'You want to take your boyfriend home and sober him up.'

I felt like hitting him there and then, whether he was following us or not. I didn't like his insolence. Or maybe that was the drink.

'Come on Lorenzo—' started Luisa.

'You after my girlfriend?' I demanded to know, determined to make trouble.

He smirked – 'Why would I? There are plenty of pretty girls around.'

I grabbed his lapel – 'You after my body then – you're wasting your time if you're after my body.'

People around us had begun to notice the fracas—

He brushed my hand away and made a rapid getaway through the crowd. He hadn't even finished his drink. I decided to let him go.

'Come on Lorenzo, it's getting late,' said Luisa. 'Time to go home.'

The fresh air, cooler now in the darkness, brought life back to my head.

'I just hope your mother doesn't see you drunk,' said Luisa.

'What if she does! There was something odd about that guy in the bar.'

'I blame myself,' said Luisa, ignoring me.

'You've been drinking too. Your mother will blame me . . .'

'I've not had that much,' she lied. 'Anyway you're not to blame and don't worry about my mother. She'll be in bed by now.'

She scratched something off my collar. 'Besides,' she added, 'I am in no hurry to go home. I would like to go back to the garage with you Lorenzo – like the old times. Don't worry. I know where I stand with you. I have no illusions about us getting together again. I know what you feel for Anna.'

I wrapped my arms around her and said, 'You don't know what you're saying – the wine's gone to your head. I'm going to take you home before we do something we both regret.'

Luisa stroked the back of head. 'I wouldn't regret anything. I still love you Lorenzo and always will.'

'You can do better than me, Luisa. One day you will meet someone very special—'

'I've met him already—'

'No Luisa.'

We parted and walked back to the car. We barely spoke a word as night lights flashed by.

I watched Luisa to her door – 'Thank you Lorenzo for a lovely evening' – and made for the garage and its charmless bedchair.

The crickets were more restful tonight, their sound

replaced by the trickling of shallow streams that ran through the town from the very distant Dolomites.

I had been tempted to go to bed with Luisa.

Now I was proud that I'd done the honourable thing and avoided another round of pain. My life's ambition would be neither to love nor hate anyone, but live in a state of total passivity – like my father.

To be a blissful statue . . .

As I searched my pockets for the garage keys in the night gloom, my eye was caught by the red tip of a cigarette in a car parked on the opposite side of the road.

I couldn't see who was in it . . . perhaps after the encounter with a suspected spy I was feeling paranoid . . .

I stepped unsteadily towards the stranger's car, but as I did so it roared to life and was off.

Half way down the road a pale street light betrayed it – it looked like Anna's car. So Anna was following me now as well as strangers in Venice, as well as Ottavio.

Or perhaps it was Ottavio in the car . . .

I laughed to myself and collapsed into the bedchair and dreamt of cats' eyes gleaming in coal bunkers.

The next morning my head felt as if it had been weighed down in a coal bunker. The garage walls shuddered. The phone rang.

It was Luisa. 'Lorenzo, I have to ask you,' she said seriously, 'but did I sleep with you in the garage last night?'

'Of course not,' I snapped, 'I took you straight home. Don't you remember?'

'*Madonna*! I hardly remember anything. I've never drunk so much. I remember being followed.'

'Luisa – go back to bed. I'll talk to you later.'

My new dread was Anna's supper party in the evening. I half planned to stagger back home and collapse in

Graziella's arms and tell her I was dying — we couldn't possibly go to Anna's after all.

But no. Graziella would never believe (or forgive) me . . .

Back home I pushed away the breakfast. 'Just black coffee, mamma.'

'You look terrible Lorenzo,' she scolded, 'where were you last night?'

'A party, I drank a bit too much.'

'Did you go with anyone?'

'Just me!'

Later I returned to the garage for a couple or more hours but soon gave up and snoozed.

Back at the house Graziella seemed to be trying on three different party costumes at once — 'What do you think, mamma? The yellow? The white?'

'Don't overdress,' I said.

'I'm not!' she said. She skipped over to me like a child. 'I'm really looking forward to tonight Lorenzo. What do you think will happen?'

'We'll eat soup, Graziella—'

'I can't imagine Anna eating anything—'

'That's enough of that,' said my mother.

My aunt entered the room with a black gown draped over her arm — 'Why don't you wear this Graziella?'

'What?' Graziella squeaked in horror. 'That's so old-fashioned. It's a funeral dress.'

To make her point she hummed the Funeral March.

My aunt laughed — 'Stupid girl. Dresses like this are above fashion. They're timeless. You'll beg me to let you wear it one day.'

'At your funeral mamma!'

My mother was horrified — 'Graziella!'

'All this squawking,' I said, raising my voice. 'Graziella,

wear the red dress, for God's sake. You look great in
it.'

'No way am I going to wear the same dress Anna saw
me last time. Do I really look good in it?'

'Fabulous!'

I took hours washing, shaving, dressing, and slowly the
tiredness left me.

I'd wear nothing grand, just casuals.

When I finally emerged in the living room Graziella
was waiting for me, not in her stunning red dress but in
her stunning, if not blinding, white one with the frilled
hemline.

'That'll do,' I said.

'Is that the best you can say?'

'Graziella, you are a vision in white.'

'A vision!' repeated Uncle Alberto who had placed his
hands on his daughter's waist. 'Keep an eye on this one,' he
said to me, 'make sure she doesn't get up to anything.'

'I shall keep an eye on Lorenzo!' said Graziella.

'Don't worry uncle,' I said. 'I'm the only one in danger
where we're off to tonight.'

To make some sort of point to Anna I decided to use the
van to get to the party. Graziella didn't seem to mind – 'It'll
look odd parked outside their villa, though,' she said.

'That's the idea,' I replied.

We arrived before eight. I rang the gate bell and more
than a minute later someone strode onto the front terrace
and approached the gate.

'Who's that – the butler?' whispered Graziella.

I squinted – 'No, someone called Dino – a friend of
Anna's.'

I was surprised that Ottavio had not been the first to
greet us.

'And who is this beautiful young lady?' Dino asked, gazing at Graziella.

After the introductions he closed the gate behind us as we drove up the drive.

'Quite impressive – for Italy,' said Graziella, taking in the dimensions of the Gilli's white villa and its two marble female forms holding up the porch.

'Just wait till you get inside,' I said. 'You can't imagine it.'

I wanted Graziella to be a little impressed if only to show her that a simple mechanic could hook the lady of the palazzo.

As we entered we were greeted by Lucinda swathed in a flock of ostrich feathers.

'At last,' she drawled in her throaty voice, 'I get to meet your cousin, Lorenzo. I've heard so much about you – Graziella, isn't it? And it's lovely seeing you too, Lorenzo.'

To my embarrassment she kissed me on both cheeks and then on the tip of my nose.

The four of us together strolled into the Gilli's vast drawing room with its fat and sumptuous sofas upholstered in red, ocean-size oil paintings of roly-poly naked women, and other decadent excesses.

Graziella could not contain her awe – 'And the floor is marble too,' she muttered. 'And the chandelier – it looks like a huge fountain. All this red. It's violent!'

Ottavio and Anna were nowhere to be seen. I turned to Lucinda – 'So where are our hosts?'

'Well, Ottavio is on the phone for some reason but he keeps holding up his fingers at me to say he'll join us soon.'

'And Anna?' asked Graziella.

'Who knows, darling. Waiting in the wings to make

the big entrance. That'll boost her confidence, though she always looks splendid.'

'And the staff?' my cousin asked. 'Dino had to answer the door.'

'Well he has to earn his keep!' she giggled, putting her hand in his. 'I think all the staff are in the kitchen. It's best to take things as they come at *la casa* Gilli . . .'

I was unsettled by Lucinda's mocking tone – Anna deserved at least respect – but I let it pass for the moment.

Ottavio was the first to appear. His eyes immediately alighted and blazed on Graziella, shaving years off his face in renewed vigour.

'What a joy to see you both,' he said not looking at me at all.

Graziella loved the attention – 'You look terribly elegant Signor Gilli—'

'Ottavio!' he corrected.

'Very handsome,' she added.

That must have been a first for Ottavio – to be called handsome. But to be fair, the old man looked distinguished in his dark dinner jacket and purple bowtie – and with his polished head.

To add to the suave effect his belly was miraculously flattened, thanks to a corset, well concealed by his waistcoat.

In the background Dino and Lucinda could be heard giggling – at Ottavio or something else I was uncertain.

'I am so pleased you could come Graziella—' he said.

At that moment there was a cough and we all held our breath as Anna did indeed make her grand entrance, in her long emerald dress with a white wool sash, her glorious blonde hair piled up and adding nearly a foot to her height.

We gave her a brief applause punctuated with bravos! from Lucinda. Anna's eyes darted about here and there, making her seem slightly unconfident.

Servants in white livery appeared from nowhere and were helped by Ottavio with the drinks.

Anna walked straight up to me and kissed me on the cheek. A stranger might have assumed she was my wife judging by the way she had positioned herself by my side, holding my arm and gazing into my eyes.

'Darling, how fabulous you look,' she said.

I tugged at my jacket sleeve – 'I should have hired a dinner suit – I thought this was going to be informal.'

'Who cares,' she replied, 'you look modern – not like a waxworks!' She threw an angry glance at Ottavio.

Anna had never been relaxed at the best of times, but tonight she appeared to me a lot more nervous if not jittery. I felt no connection with her, blocked out—

'You weren't outside the garage last night by any chance?' I asked.

Now her eyes turned angry on me – 'Do you think I have nothing better to do than loiter about the streets at night? You flatter yourself!'

I felt crushed by her brutal and sudden change of mood.

The maid announced that dinner was ready.

Without a word, but with a new smile, Anna coiled an arm round mine again and led me forward, behind Dino and Lucinda, with Ottavio and Graziella at the front, each couple linked at the arm.

The dining room was blinding in cut-glass crystal and silver.

'Bravo! Bravo!' cried Lucinda once again, oddly I thought.

Graziella asked Ottavio why the table trimmings – such as the napkins and the candles – were all red.

'Because red matches red,' Anna answered for him, smiling benevolently. 'Red reminds me I am alive.'

Ignoring Anna, Ottavio pulled out a chair, beckoning Graziella to sit by his right side, Lucinda to his left. I had never seen him so animated as he was that night with my cousin, taking up her hand and kissing it, while she giggled and flirted. Uncle Alberto would have been proud of her.

Of course I knew the evening would be a likely disaster. But I had hoped that the presence of her friends Dino and Lucinda would at least restrain Anna's drinking. Had I been Ottavio I'd have forbidden her one drop, but we had hardly sat down and she announced her intention to toast everyone of her guests—

'First Graziella – come on everybody,' she exhorted by waving her hands, 'a toast to Graziella, a visitor from Argentina; may she enjoy her stay and learn the art of living a long and profitable life from us Italians. *Salute!*'

We raised our glasses and sipped while Anna quaffed her wine in one greedy gulp.

'And Lucinda,' Anna said, refilling her glass, 'may she settle down with one man instead of running after the tourists in Venice!'

'I don't,' screamed Lucinda, laughing with Dino—

And on Anna went, toasting Dino for being a rich idler, and me for the good luck I would need to expand my business – 'But first he needs to find a good reliable wife to make his breakfast!'

She slurred, 'And finally,' emptying the bottle, 'a toast to me – for having to put up with *that* over there!'

As she threw up her glass to Ottavio, wine slopped everywhere on the table.

'That's enough,' I said to her, 'you've drunk enough already—'

'Let go of my arm and don't tell me what to do,' she said through clenched teeth. 'You give me indigestion!'

So ridiculous was this remark that both Graziella and Lucinda collapsed in giggles.

'You're giving *me* indigestion,' I shouted. 'Stop making a spectacle of yourself.'

'Let go of my arm – you're hurting me.'

I would have left there and then but for Lucinda who seemed to calm Anna by oddly stroking her shoulder – 'Come now, Anna,' she cooed, 'there's no need for that.' A couple of servants mopped up the spilt wine while Ottavio signalled to another two to serve the soup.

I felt my old contempt for him again. He had done nothing to restrain his wife during her outburst. He wasn't even prepared to save his own dinner party guests the embarrassment of witnessing her bad behaviour.

Anna wasn't calm for long. In an attempt to lighten the mood Lucinda turned to Ottavio, still laughing from something Graziella had whispered to him, and said tactlessly, 'You're enjoying yourself – you need to meet more young people!'

Ottavio smiled.

'He's only making a fool of himself,' said Anna, stirred to life.

Here we go again, I thought.

'Anna,' he said softly, 'it would be better if you went and lay down next door.'

I was certain she would throw her soup at him but to everyone's relief she held her tongue and just scowled at him.

In fact she was silent during the main course, content to ignore the food and guzzle a bottle of Chianti by herself, so that by the time of dessert we had almost forgotten she was there.

The sight of Ottavio eating fruit and cream set her off again. 'Just look at him,' she blurted to me, pointing at

Ottavio with contempt, 'look at how the old man makes a pig of himself. He hasn't stopped eating and talking since we started.'

Dino covered his face with his hand in a playful gesture of shock.

'That's what people do at dinners, Anna,' I said sharply.

'They don't make pigs of themselves!'

'That's enough!' I barked. 'If you don't behave I shall leave now.'

Anna now lost all self-control.

'All you ever do is criticise me!' she shouted. 'Everything I do is wrong.'

Foolishly I responded, 'You could learn a few lessons in courtesy from Graziella.'

She popped her eyes at me in exaggerated surprise. 'Oh, excuse me!' she wailed. 'And I suppose next you'll be saying I don't treat Ottavio properly – that I could learn a few lessons from Graziella on that score—'

'Tell me Lorenzo,' said Dino, in a mis-timed attempt to calm things, 'how is your business coming along?'

'Very well Dino—'

'Very well, indeed,' echoed Anna. 'But tell Dino where you're going to get the extra money from.'

Ottavio struck the side of his dessert bowl with a spoon for attention – 'That's quite enough Anna!' he said firmly.

'Don't strike the gong at me as if I'm the servants,' she shouted. 'You son-of-a-bitch. You just belt up! I'm talking to Dino.'

How shocked poor Graziella looked at Anna's crazy outburst. In stark contrast to Dino and Lucinda's suppressed cackles. What a joke all this was to them – and what a wonderful scandalous story this evening would make at their own dinner parties.

Ottavio turned to Graziella and whispered something. Her nods infuriated Anna – 'What's going on there?' she demanded to know.

And when she received no answer she picked up her napkin, crumpled it into a ball and threw it at Ottavio, hitting him full in the face before it fell into his dessert bowl.

Anna laughed hysterically. 'Bull's-eye! I only wanted to cover your pigeon head,' she said between sobs. 'Your head's just like a pigeon's – small and ugly!'

I grabbed hold of Anna's hand—

'Let go of me bastard!' she screamed. 'Let go—'

'That's right Lorenzo, hold her there,' Ottavio said calmly.

'Let go! Let go!'

'She'll rest in a minute,' said Ottavio.

Moments later she did cease to struggle. Once again it was as if someone had switched her off at the mains: she was quiet now, inert, her head downcast.

'I am sorry,' said Ottavio briskly to us all. 'Let's go into the next room and have coffee.'

I let my hold slip. I gently took Anna's hand and guided her as if she were a child.

'Are you all right?' I whispered over and over again to her.

She said nothing, moaning a little, peering at me blankly like an idiot.

I felt humiliation for her and exasperation at Ottavio. Why had he left it to me to take care of her for all to see? I wanted to carry her away to a safe place where I could comfort her.

Anna was certainly unstable, that couldn't be denied – I'd seen how drink could turn sweet natures into monsters – but what did Ottavio's conduct say about him, virtually gloating on his wife's disgrace?

Everyone was quiet, sipping coffee, in the next room. I helped Anna to a chair.

The moment I took a step back she struggled to her feet. 'Excuse me,' she said in the quiet, coherent way drunks do when they realise they're drunk, 'I think I will lie down as I feel very tired.'

She walked unsteadily across the room.

I had an instant premonition of what she would do next.

As she passed Ottavio she gave him a sudden, very nasty kick, causing Graziella to shriek.

'Good God, she's mad,' said Dino.

'Anna!' I shouted.

She ignored us all as Ottavio made a face and rubbed his leg.

'You all right Ottavio,' asked Lucinda indifferently. Then not waiting for a reply she added: 'It's just the drink. I've seen this before. She's just had too much to drink. Soon she'll be fine.'

Hypocritical bitch, I thought. This was just an evening's entertainment for her and her spoilt boyfriend.

'Can you walk?' I asked Ottavio, with no sympathy in my voice.

'It'll just bruise. One gets used to this sort of thing.'

I asked him how often this happened but he said he didn't wish to discuss it now . . .

He smiled warmly, paternally, at Graziella who was feeding him compassion with her big, dark eyes.

'Come on, you,' he said to her. 'I'll show you the rest of the house before Anna buries me.'

When they had left, Dino and Lucinda laughed hysterically, shaking their heads in disbelief.

'I've seen it all now,' said Dino.

I asked Lucinda, 'Has Anna always been abusive to Ottavio?'

She poured fresh coffee into her cup – 'It's got worse, no doubt about that. Only when she drinks. The question is: why does she drink in the first place?'

'That marriage is a sham!' said Dino, his first sensible point.

'I'm not so sure about that,' said Lucinda. 'Still we all know about Lorenzo.'

The couple giggled. A silly, superficial couple who felt no concern for Anna's welfare – or Ottavio's for that matter.

Presently, Ottavio and Graziella returned from the tour of the house beautiful. She was in a daze, captivated by the elegance money buys. Ottavio took down a sherry decanter, which for some reason had been placed on a book shelf, and filled five glasses.

'I am very sorry about tonight. Don't think too badly of me and Anna,' he said to us all.

He handed me a glass.

I said, 'It's quite a routine you and Anna have. You should be on the stage.'

He nodded agreement and smiled.

Ottavio was reluctant to let us go that night. His usual calm had given way to a lively restlessness. He insisted I have another drink when I hinted to Graziella that we should be making tracks: it was Graziella he really wanted to stay, maybe because she was – or appeared to be – unspoilt, untouched by the world, yet mature as well.

A fascinating mix to a mixed up rogue like Ottavio.

'I'm old enough to be your grandfather,' he said, passing a finger down the side of her face. 'And glad to be!'

'Don't forget our party, Lorenzo,' cried out Dino as he and Lucinda made their way out. 'And bring Graziella!'

I didn't promise – I said I'd be in touch; in any case Graziella would be in Rome next week.

138

Eventually Ottavio walked us to my van parked in his drive. Countless shooting stars were silently zipping across the sky, a free firework display that held us all in thrall for a long time.

'A miracle,' Ottavio whispered to Graziella. 'The ancient Romans always saw shooting stars as omens—'

'Omens of what?' she asked, hypnotised.

'Of great leaders, their souls, rushing away from earth.'

She giggled at his seriousness.

'Ottavio,' I said, 'sometime soon I'd like a word in private.'

'Of course – is it something important you wish to discuss?'

'Pretty important I'd say – I'll give you a call.'

He smiled, then took my cousin's hand and kissed it. 'My dear,' he said, 'thank you for your company and for giving me a spark of life and I hope to see you again.'

Graziella struck me as slightly embarrassed by his old-fashioned, courtly creepiness—

'Of course you will,' she giggled.

In the van she asked me, to my surprise, 'Do you think there's something wrong with Ottavio?'

'Why? Because you gave him his spark of life, *my dear*?' I teased.

'Be serious! That was the worst party I have ever been to!' she said.

And there I was thinking she had been totally won over by Ottavio.

'He didn't take his eyes off me all evening – I nearly died,' she continued. 'And as for Anna!'

'Careful—'

'She's barking – she's certainly no lady of the manor – and her attitude to Ottavio! I couldn't believe it . . . and shouting like that.' She squealed with laughter. 'I couldn't believe it, it was wonderful. It's not just the drink Lorenzo, there's a screw loose somewhere . . . I'm sorry Lorenzo. I know—'

'Don't be sorry. You're perfectly right,' I said. 'I've just not wanted to face it. When you love someone—'

'I know,' said Graziella.

'How do you know? You're just a babe.'

'No I'm not!' she said crossly. 'I've got a good imagination.'

'Well, Anna's not well, I can see that now, I'll get the truth out of Ottavio if I have to kill him.'

'Oh don't do that, Lorenzo. He could be my sugar daddy!'

'Just you wait till I tell your father.'

'If you do I'll tell him about Anna, screaming and kicking—'

'OK, OK. I surrender! So tell me, Graziella, what did Ottavio say to you on your walk around the house.'

Her light mood quickly disappeared. 'Do I have to?' she asked defensively. Then she changed her mind. 'I suppose I could tell you a few things . . .'

'Mmmm . . .'

'Well,' she started, 'he said he knew all about you and Anna and he said he didn't mind at all.'

'He said that to you?'

Once again I asked myself who was the crazy one: Ottavio or Anna. Or me!

'Yes. He said he didn't mind so long as you kept her happy. Because he could never make her happy – even right from the start.'

'Amazing!'

'He also said I speak very good Italian and that I would make someone a splendid wife.'

'You'd also make a very good priest,' I said. 'To get Ottavio to confess all that rubbish.'

The following Monday I decided, along with my mother, not to visit Rome with the Argentinians. In any case I had some news for dear old Uncle Alberto: I had spotted the perfect site for our new venture.

'The only problem is the price – one million lire.'

He looked appalled. Then he said nonchalantly, 'Is that all? That's about the price I expected. While I'm away get all the details together so we can go for the kill on my return.'

This was Alberto the tycoon talking now. 'And don't worry about the cost so long as you're certain it's what you want. I'm confident that what you want I will want.'

His total faith in me was the best confidence boost anyone could have had.

On the day the family departed for Rome, on the Tuesday, Anna called me at the garage. She wanted to see me.

'I don't think that would be a good idea, Anna. I think we should stick to our agreement not to see each other.'

'I didn't agree to anything,' she said quickly. 'Please, Lorenzo, stop punishing me – I have to see you.'

I was torn by the new pleading tone in her voice, and instantly racked with guilt and misery.

'OK,' I relented. 'But just half an hour at lunchtime.'

'Why not tonight?' she asked, her voice now confident.

'No. Absolutely not—'

'How can you be so cruel Lorenzo—'

'Don't go on Anna – I'll see you lunchtime.'

I had hardly put the receiver down but the phone rang again – this time Lucinda. It was a wonder I got any work done in those days.

'I know you're very busy,' she tinkled in her breathless way, 'but this is to do with Anna. Are you interested?'

'I am busy, but come on, what do you want to tell me. Tell me quick.'

'Well, what a charmer! Anyhow, I think you should know this. Dino met up with an old friend who happens to know quite a lot about Anna. He said that Anna has been on some sort of medication for years, and has been in and out of doctors' surgeries for God knows how long. Apparently because of the drugs she is not supposed to drink at all!'

I was struck by the complete lack of concern in Lucinda's voice, only by her excitement in being the first to tell me the gossip.

Her news threw me into fresh turmoil. If Lucinda was telling the truth then Ottavio wasn't the real problem between Anna and me—

'I don't know what to say,' I said slowly. 'I'll have to think about this.'

'Shocking, isn't it— ?'

'I hope Dino is not telling everyone about last night.'

'Lorenzo!' she said, pretending to be shocked. 'We're Anna's friends. I'm only telling you because you're the only person who might knock some sense into her. I'd love to know what this medication is, and why she has to take it. I mean, Dino's friend said that prescriptions like this are to control a long-term condition. I'd love to know what that is.'

Once again she sounded as if she were gossiping about someone's sex life—

'Well, if you have any other news Lucinda let me know.'

Anna must have confided in someone – this 'Dino's friend', for instance – so why hadn't she confided in me?

What a difference it would have made to our relationship

had she talked to me openly and given me something to *understand*.

Anna turned up at the garage about an hour before lunchtime.

I'd already taken off my overalls and cleaned up – if nothing else, of late, Anna had made me more self-conscious of my appearance.

Even at that moment, as she stepped out of her car, I wondered what she could have possibly seen in me.

She looked tired and drained. Normally her make-up was a meticulous mask, but today the tired eyes were honest, as her drawn expression.

'Thanks for seeing me,' she said simply.

'Come on in.'

She nodded and went into the little back room and sat on the bed chair.

'Have you something to tell me?' I started.

She just gazed down at the floor as she said, 'First, I'm sorry about last night—' Then she broke down in tears.

I sat by her side and put my arm around her.

'What's wrong, Anna? Why are you crying? Is there something you want to tell me?'

She dabbed her eyes with a white linen handkerchief, and I caught a whiff of its sweet rose scent – it was that scent alone which could soften me—

'There are so many things I want to tell you,' she said, 'but I don't know where to start. I'm not sure I'm ready to go into it – particularly now you don't want to see me.'

'And if I say I'll see you again, you'll tell me. Is that it?'

'I don't mean it like that . . . it's just picking the right moment . . .'

'This is the right moment. Why did you want to see me if you don't want to talk to me?'

Without warning she rose from the bedchair and walked out of the room. I called after her – 'Anna! If you leave now . . . it'll be better if we have no more contact.'

As I watched her get into her car I was suddenly so overcome with feeling – of love or sympathy, I am no longer sure, or maybe desperation at the thought of never seeing her again – that I jumped into the car with her, pulled her towards me and kissed her on the lips.

I held her very tight, I said over and over again, 'I love you.' Nonetheless I knew this was somehow a mistake.

She responded by stroking my head, as if I were ill, and passed her lips in little kisses down the side of my head, saying my name over and over again.

When I let go there was still surprise on her face at my change of heart – as surprising to me as to her. 'You really do love me,' she was saying.

'We can still see each other,' I said, 'but you must trust me, you must tell me everything about your life, I must know.'

'You really mean that Lorenzo? We can see each other?'

'But you must talk to me. Think about what I mean to you.'

'I don't have to go. Why don't I stay?' she said.

'Go away and think, Anna. I need to know everything about you. You must decide to trust me.'

'Why don't you just enjoy me—'

'Trust me first.'

The moment she drove off I knew nothing would really change, that she would tell me nothing and I would continue to wonder and question and forgive her.

I thought of my mother's words – she'd said Anna and I had no future – and then I felt I wanted to weep myself, for us, and for me for being so weak.

But of course I didn't cry.

I had a choice, I realised, a choice to live with uncertainty or not.

And with that thought I returned to my work.

Or tried to. For no sooner had Anna left than Piero turned up.

'You look terrible,' he said.

'Thanks.'

'More Anna troubles?'

'What else – next subject!'

'OK. Let's talk about the Piccoli. Let's go for a drink tonight. We can drink and you can talk all you want.'

I didn't have to think about that. 'All right, you've asked me at just the right moment.'

'What's up?' Piero was not insensitive. He knew when to hold fire on the jokes. 'No, don't tell me,' he added quickly. 'Tell me tonight.'

'So what are you doing here?' I asked, forcing a smile.

Luisa was sitting in the kitchen sipping wine with my mother. It was lunchtime.

She looked up, her face glowing with contentment. 'It's my day off. I thought I'd come round and talk to your mother – in fact I'm just leaving.'

'Don't leave on my account—'

'No, have your lunch in peace. I promised my father something. Hope to see you soon . . .'

She spoke the last words almost at whisper level – words she half hoped my mother wouldn't hear. Of course she heard.

'Say you'll see her soon, Lorenzo!' shouted my mother.

'Quiet mamma.' I turned to Luisa – 'I'll call you later.'

I sat down to a vegetable omelette—

'Not like you to drink wine at lunchtime,' said mamma,

not disapproving. 'It's funny not having Carla, Alberto and Graziella in the house. I'll miss them when they go back to Argentina.'

'Well, they've invited you over and it won't be long before you go.'

'The journey would kill me Lorenzo. You just want to see the back of me!—'

'Nothing could kill you mamma. What did Luisa have to say?'

My mother rarely ate with me at lunchtime. But if I was in her good books she would sit at the table and talk. This she did today – I soon discovered why—

'Luisa told me you took her out the other night. I knew you two would get back together.'

I sighed heavily. 'We are not back together mamma. I only took her to Venice—'

But I could see it was hopeless. Mamma wore her told-you-so smile which made her deaf to me.

'And I told Luisa about your Uncle Alberto going into partnership with you – hope you don't mind—'

'Why should I mind?'

'Are you going to take her out again Lorenzo?'

'Mamma! Let me eat in peace. Luisa means nothing to me. And if I take her out that's my business.'

I'm not sure what she thought I had said because she rose from the table with a smug expression on her face, nodding to herself.

'That's my boy,' she said.

'Give me whisky! Whisky!' I shouted like a man dying of thirst. The Piccoli barman – I forget his name now – poured in his usual unhurried style.

It had been a long day. Anna had given me heartache and the lunchtime wine a headache. All I needed now was Piero to give me earache. Still, it was good to see him.

'You stopped shaving?' I asked him as we settled in our seats.

He stroked his face – 'No, but Rosita likes to feel a rough face, if you know what I mean.'

'Filthy devil.'

'You should give women what they want,' he said. 'That's what your trouble is Lorenzo – you never give women what they want. It's easy. You find out what they want and supply it. Luisa – she wants your love and you want this Anna. And this Anna, she just wants your body and you're worried about her husband.' He laughed out loud. 'You were always the same – and you know what will happen? You'll end up with no one!'

What could I say? I smiled indulgently – 'Thank you for your cheery words Piero. What are friends for!'

'And that psychic you saw. You never told me what she said. Have any of her predictions come true yet?'

I'd forgoten about Signora Lugano. Come to think of it she'd foreseen my business development. I recalled she'd spoken of a triangle and mental illness—

'Things are beginning to take shape,' I said cryptically. 'I won't say anything more than that.'

'And where are you with this Anna?'

'Why do you say *this* Anna as if she's from another planet or someplace? I don't know where I am with anything. I'm not sure I know Anna—'

'You're confused,' he broke in. Then, changing the subject – 'But I hear you're going into business with your uncle.'

I shouldn't have been surprised that the news had got around. There was no such thing as a secret in these parts, except what people knew already but called 'secret'.

147

'No, I'm not going to tell you who told me,' he added. 'But if you really want to keep a secret you don't tell your mother. So, at least your work is looking up, that's really good news. Maybe when you've made it big you'll remember your old poor friend Piero and give him a little job. And while you're about it, get some more drinks in.'

I collected our glasses – 'Sure I'll remember you. I'll give you a broom and duster to keep my garages clean.'

When I returned I said to Piero, 'I want to talk to you seriously. When are you marrying Rosita?'

He threw his eyes up in mock despair. He'd heard the question many times before. 'When she's pregnant!' he said.

'No, seriously. No more laughs. Do you intend to marry her?'

It wasn't Rosita who interested me. I wanted to know what he thought he was getting from the relationship. What he had just said about a man giving a woman what she wanted had hit home.

Or maybe the drink had got to my head and I now believed Piero had the answer to love.

He propped his head on his hand. 'What about you and Luisa? You think you've dropped her – things can change.'

'We were talking about you and Rosita.'

'So, anything can happen!' he said, holding out his arms. 'Everyone thought you were going to marry Luisa. Everyone expects me to marry my Rosita. But I'm not so sure. Maybe I'll wait two years before I tie the knot.'

'I thought you gave women what they want—'

'Sex. I'm talking about sex. How do you know Rosita wants to marry me? Did she tell you she wanted to marry me? Eh, maybe I'm waiting for her to propose to me! Did

148

you think of that? Why not? Maybe men want to know if they're wanted. That's it, eh?'

He was grinning, not laughing. Here was my best friend and I had no idea whether he was serious or playing games.

'Don't be a fool all your life Piero—'

'No, I mean it. Everyday you wonder: does she really want me? That's you and Anna, isn't it? That's me and Rosita. I'm waiting for her to decide what she wants. Eh, maybe I'm just joking! You think too much.'

I gave up. The more I tried to get him to talk sense the more he wriggled away. Maybe it was the drink, but he reminded me a little of Ottavio right then, not giving me a straight answer, playing with life . . .

I could forgive Piero. Ottavio was another matter.

I had thought about it long enough. But now it was decided. I would confront Ottavio one more time and force him to talk straight with me about Anna.

Something about that last evening with Piero had made up my mind for me – I had to know my future, I didn't want to muddle along like him, I *knew* Anna wanted me. Ottavio was part of the problem . . .

I phoned Ottavio the next day and we agreed to meet at my garage 7.30 that evening.

I remember he was a bit late – unusual for Ottavio. Anna always said one of the things that irritated her about him was his punctuality. Just when I thought he'd chickened-out in whooshed his black car—

'Lorenzo, I'm so sorry . . . I was held up . . .'

'Don't worry. We've plent of time. Let's go somewhere else, somewhere quiet and have a drink.'

'Fine. Hop in. I know a place in the country.'

So we drove to what he called an *osteria* on the outskirts

of Mestre, close to Venice, but was in fact a hotel. It crossed my mind that he'd chosen a very public respectable place to deter me from breaking his neck.

He ordered a half bottle of bourbon and we settled in one of the cosy rest rooms where elderly couples snoozed and coughed . . .

'I presume this is about Anna,' started Ottavio. He looked tired, old.

'Yes,' I said. 'I want to know what's wrong with her.'

'I am puzzled why you think that anything very particular is "wrong" with her, I—'

'Don't beat about the bush Ottavio. I can see she is unwell. I want to understand what the problem is, and I know you can tell me. I love her, and you have used me because you think I am some simple mechanic who can't think – someone you can laugh at—'

'How wrong you are, Lorenzo,' interrupted Ottavio, leaning forward in his seat. 'I didn't decide that you should fall in love with my wife, or for you to become her lover – indifferent as I am to how she enjoys herself. I only ask she remains my wife. I couldn't have prevented what happened between you and Anna. After all, years ago we ceased to live as man and wife. All that we have in common now is the business. People may say that I use Anna but that is not the case. The truth of the matter is that Anna always wanted to be a very important part of my business, as I explained to you before . . . It was an outlet for her, although she was more adept than I could have imagined . . .'

And on Ottavio went in his reasonable way, not answering my question, talking to me as if I were a child and Anna were his daughter—

'Yes, yes,' I said impatiently, 'you've said all this. So why did you follow us wherever we went if you didn't care?'

150

He paused in mid-sentence, and put down his glass – 'But I had to Lorenzo.' He paused again, as if in two minds to say more . . . 'The thing with Anna . . . is that she can be unstable at times. I worry about her when she's out with other people . . . you've seen for yourself . . . I never know what she is going to do next. And of course alcohol makes matters worse. People think that I'm the cause of her erratic behaviour, and I don't mind if they do – I know you think that – but ordinarily I refuse to discuss this with anyone – her illness—'

I turned cold to hear him say this. I had suspected it but had hoped I was wrong—

'What illness?' I asked.

'I had not planned to tell you Lorenzo. I'm not sure myself what the illness is, it's like schizophrenia, that's as much as I know. She been seeing a psychiatrist for a very long time and there hasn't been a moment when she wasn't on drugs of one sort or another – that's why it was important that she avoided drink—'

'Is that why she was always at the doctor?'

'I wouldn't say she was *always* at the doctor, but yes, recently her condition has got worse. There's not a great deal that can be done. Her mother suffered from the same illness.'

He gulped the last of his drink and re-poured.

'I do know that you love Anna,' he said, 'and believe it or not but I do want her to be happy. She has experienced many happy moments with you, she loves you very much. Maybe I should have warned you earlier – but you wouldn't have believed me, you would have accused me of lying to frighten you off. I'm sure you agree—'

I felt too stunned to respond. I said nothing.

'Well, you wanted to know everything so you must prepare yourself for something else. I said her health is

151

deteriorating very rapidly. She is not going to get better – ever. I should have put her into some sort of hospital years ago. Living with Anna all these years has been a nightmare – and I sometimes wondered whether I would go mad myself trying to protect her—'

'But how could she do her work if she was so ill?'

'Work concentrates her mind. Away from work and she falls apart. I don't understand it myself. That's the way it is. She is my responsibility.'

Part of me couldn't believe what Ottavio was saying: it was a terrible lie, another of his malicious games. I looked for signs in his face of mischief but all I saw was deadly seriousness.

I asked, 'If you don't know what her illness is, how can you be certain she won't recover?'

'I am afraid that is not possible. Every doctor we have consulted says the same. And her mother died of the condition. If there was a cure I would have found it by now.'

I could no longer drink. I'd sought the truth and now I wanted it to go away. God, I prayed, why do these things happen to us? I had not expected this.

'Try to drink a little more, Lorenzo,' he said. 'I'll get another glass—'

The spirit burned its way down my throat like acid. To add to my misery was the realisation that I had been so wrong about Ottavio.

I had called him a wimp, I had accused him of not being a man, in a situation that I probably could not have coped with myself.

When he returned with more bourbon I asked him if he loved Anna. He thought for a long time.

'At the start of our marriage her illness was not apparent. I loved her very much, and still do. It's because I love her . . .' He stopped. 'What wasn't apparent soon became apparent. She started having the sort of temperamental fits you witnessed, and then one day she told me about herself and her mother. I was devastated, as you are now. I had married late in life and had hoped I'd found someone to spend the rest of my life with in happiness. That wasn't to be. But if she concentrated her mind on work she was stable – that was a wonderful discovery. I couldn't let her simply go off with you Lorenzo. While she can work there's a chance of her having more time. Emotional pressure, she can't deal with it. You would only put emotional pressure on her. I have had the time to balance my life with hers – why change it now when her life could end at any moment?'

I didn't argue with him. I knew I never would have been able to deal with her, or make the kind of sacrifices Ottavio had; choosing to bear humiliation for her good.

'Of course,' he continued, 'I had no illusions that she married me for love. To her I was just the money man—'

'Didn't that upset you?'

'I loved her and that was enough for me. I derived much pleasure from giving her the things she always wanted. But for this happiness I've paid a higher price than I could have ever anticipated—'

We were interrupted by the proprietor of the hotel who seemed to know Ottavio well.

'Everything all right gentlemen? Another drink?'

I said to Ottavio – 'Let's leave.'

He agreed and settled the bill.

In the car he talked more.

He cautioned me to be very careful with Anna from now on. I could continue to see her but not to put pressure on her to make a new life with me.

'I know it's what you both want,' he said, 'but think of Anna even if you don't want to think of me.'

'I know, I know,' I said, crushed by what he had told me, by his humanity, and by a growing awareness that some part of my own life had ended.

He said, 'You must not tell her what I have told you.'

'I won't – I will understand—'

'Good,' he said, with some relief. 'I always knew you were a good man – that's why I do not object to your seeing Anna. I regret now that we did not talk earlier. I am sorry for all the trouble I've given you – following you around, and all that nonsense.'

Not thinking, or just speaking my mind in a state of shock, I said, 'I judged you wrong Ottavio—'

'We should be friends Lorenzo. We have Anna in common. I like your cousin Graziella – it is a pleasure to know her.'

He dropped me at the garage and I waved him off.

I wondered whether we would ever talk again – I hoped so.

I wanted to know so much more.

My relations returned from Rome the next day.

Graziella was full of city excitement – 'We went down into the catacombs – oh God Lorenzo, what if you were buried alive!, and we saw the Colosseum, the Vatican and the guards with their funny hats . . .'

I smiled weakly at her brochure descriptions. The last thing on my mind was Rome.

The first thing on my uncle's mind was our partnership. I told him everything was in order and that the seller of our new premises wanted a contract of sale drawn up.

'That's not necessary,' he barked. 'I'll just hand him the money – cash! Then we can haggle a lower price.'

'Uncle! It was you who said everything should be in writing.'

'That's different. You've got a lot to learn about business, boy. You never pay the price asked for. Ever heard of bartering? We'd all be bankrupt if we paid the prices in the shops!'

Whatever. If he had known my true feelings on the matter he would have got the next flight back to Argentina. Now that I knew I had no future with Anna, the garage seemed to be an irrelevence.

What was the point of just accumulating money, work and responsibilities in a loveless life?

But I had come this far with my uncle. Part of me just wanted to see what would happen and perhaps another part of me hoped Ottavio had lied or that Anna would recover, or *something* . . .

The following day I drove my uncle to the garage vendor. He was impressed – 'This is much better than I expected Lorenzo. Now where's this Signor – whatisname?'

'Cavallo, uncle.'

'Cavallo, Cavallo, Cavallo, Cavallo . . .'

'Why are you repeating his name?'

'Trying to memorise it. You can't barter without remembering names. Remember that Lorenzo.'

Uncle's memory didn't fail him for we bought the garage for 100,000 lire less than first agreed.

In the car he said, 'This is an omen, Lorenzo. Our first success. I just know we are going to make so much money. You're very quiet Lorenzo – cat got your tongue?'

'No, no – I'm just amazed at the price,' I lied.

I wanted to see Anna – to tell her she need not worry anymore. She could remain with Ottavio and see me . . .

'And now you must put your little garage up for sale,'

he said, 'and you must inform all your customers of your change of address—'

'Uncle, don't worry. I do know how to run a business.'

The next few days were hectic and took my mind off Anna.

One evening, after dealing with a thousand and one queries from my uncle, she called suppertime at the house, unexpectedly.

Something in me coiled tight at the sight of her – 'Anna, er—'

She looked different, more gentle and relaxed, in her summery long pink dress. Her hair, usually coiffed perfectly, was still wet from washing.

'I called because I saw the sale sign outside the garage,' she said.

'I was about to call to tell you,' I said, tugging at her to come into the house. 'We've found a new garage – I've been really busy with one thing and another. I've had no time—'

'Not even for me?' she said, in a distant, tired voice.

'Come on, come and sit down,' I said.

Uncle Alberto barged into the hallway – 'Anna! Beautiful Anna—'

She gave him a little wave.

'It's all gone too fast,' he said. 'We return to Argentina soon. Our holiday is nearly over.' Then he shrugged quickly. 'But that's life. Everything over so quickly – but don't take any notice – I'm not feeling very bright—'

His words saddened me, they reminded me of my life, and of Anna's.

He took hold of Anna's hands – 'Has he told you I've fixed him up for life? Yes, I've bought him the biggest garage in these parts. Henry Ford himself will come to have his cars repaired.'

Anna laughed lightly—

'And I'll make sure,' said uncle, 'that he hires two assistants—'

Anna turned to me and said, 'I am very happy for you my darling. This is exactly what you needed.'

As I watched uncle beam with self-pride I wanted to say I had nothing anymore, nothing at all—

My mother joined us, her pinny dusted with flour – 'Anna, are you staying?'

I had never known her to be so friendly with Anna.

Before she could answer I took Anna's hand and lied, 'Sorry mamma, I forgot to mention it, but we're going out.'

'Oh! I wish you could stay,' said uncle. 'Both of you.'

'You're not leaving right now uncle,' I said. 'We'll have a big sit-down meal with Anna before you go . . .'

We took Anna's car – 'This is a surprise,' she said. 'I'm not really dressed to eat out. I only really called to know more about your business—'

'Don't worry, you look beautiful. There are so many things we must talk about . . . We can go to some little place to eat – and no alcohol! Agreed?'

I hadn't meant to say that so stridently and for a second I dreaded she might lose her temper. But she was unperturbed. She just nodded her head like a good child.

Then she said: 'We should talk. I want to tell you something about myself, something I should have told you . . .'

A sudden chill froze away my appetite. I knew what she wanted to tell me – I never guessed I would have to hear it again.

We found a small cafe and ordered coffee – 'I'm not hungry, Lorenzo. You eat.'

'I'm not that hungry myself . . . still.'

To please the patron I ordered two simple salads.

Then softly she told me what I knew already. What few hopes I had for our future died there. I couldn't tell her I knew because of my promise to Ottavio, and I couldn't put on a performance of shock, out of respect for Anna.

I sat at the table numb, not knowing what to say or do.

'I know this must be a terrible shock,' she finished.

I went through the ritual of asking her the questions. About the doctors, the medication, her family history, the real likelihood of death.

As she talked and explained I tried to calm myself with the thought that she would not have told me had she not loved me.

But that thought only sharpened the pain – there was no longer any doubt in our relationship.

No doubt that she loved me.

No doubt that we would never share our lives together.

My voice trembled, I took hold of her hands. 'Whatever happens,' I said in fits and starts, 'we love each other – we'll see each other all the time. I won't ask you to leave Ottavio – we'll let things be. I know you'll get better—'

We left the cafe soon afterwards. I remember the patron making a small fuss over the salads we hadn't touched – 'Is there anything wrong?' he asked. 'We never have complaints . . .'

There was disbelief in his eyes as I tried to soothe his hurt feelings. Anna touched him on the shoulder and said, 'We're no longer hungry. We've had some sad news.'

In the car again I gripped her arm as I drove.

'Mind what you're doing,' she murmured. 'Strange. It was always you who warned me to drive carefully.'

'Don't say it like that – as if our lives are over already.'

I stopped the car on a grass bank by the curb. She was quiet, her thoughts elsewhere. Her hair was dry now, straggly and wild. I preferred it that way.

'What's up Anna. Are you feeling all right?'

She didn't answer until I gave her a gentle nudge – 'Anna?'

'I'm just relaxed.'

I said, 'I love you very much. Your illness makes no difference to me. And when you recover – you will recover – we can start a new life together. We'll have lots of money, I'll be able to look after you, Anna.'

She stroked my head – 'Of course we shall be happy. I will do whatever makes you happy . . .'

But in our hearts we knew our time together was nearly done. The injustice of it made me want to scream at the world, to rage and weep—

Anna broke my thoughts: 'Poor Ottavio. He's the one who's had to put up with me all these years. I always tried to blame him for everything, to excuse myself. I think I blamed him . . .'

I had never expected to hear Anna ever speak kindly of Ottavio.

'I love you very much,' she said, 'I am sure you have prolonged my life—'

'Please Anna, don't talk like that. If anyone has given you life, it's Ottavio – '

'He created a nursery for me – I'm not stupid, I know that. He created a nursery to keep me calm. You have given me life—'

'I just know you will be cured,' I said desperately.

She folded her arms around me – 'Let's make love now. Let's make the most of all the time we have together . . .'

'I can't, Anna, not now . . .'

I felt stupidly superstitious for a moment. I thought that

if we did nothing we wouldn't use up the time we had left – so we would have more time together. I couldn't think straight.

I started up the car and drove back to the garage.

There Anna held me again.

'Just think about now,' she said over and over again. 'Just think about now.'

My superstitious fears melted away and we made love for many hours, oblivious of time, of the future.

I gazed into her green eyes and felt I had journeyed to another place where our love was an eternal, indestructible thing – a place where all memories live, where Anna lives for me now.

In the morning, when Anna had left me to return home, I was filled with a new enthusiasm. I would make my new business work for Anna's sake. It had meant to be for us and it would be so.

Nothing – not even death – would change that.

Uncle Alberto could never have guessed at my thoughts – thank God. He was a man possessed by the fear of failure.

We signed contracts, men were hired – I was made to draw up business plans for him to take back to Argentina. There, I imagined, he would pin them to his office wall and rub his hands at the thought of reaping all those rewards as his nephew laboured.

The night before my family's departure I took them all to the Piccoli for a goodbye celebration.

The tears streamed down my mother's face all evening—

'Come on, mamma,' I said. 'Don't cry. It won't be long before you see them again.'

Uncle Alberto heaved himself around on his fragile wood stool and asked me, 'Any regrets going into partnership with me?'

'None,' I said toasting him.

We reminisced, promised, wept and hugged, and at some point at the Piccoli my thoughts returned to Anna.

With the clarity drink sometimes gives the mind I asked myself: how long has she to live?

Each time I saw her would be harder to bear . . .

'Eh! You talking to yourself?' my uncle said to me. 'I heard you say something—'

'What?'

'You said, "She won't be with me much longer". Who do you mean?'

I half-smiled – 'I didn't realise I was talking to myself, it must be the drink.'

'Were you thinking of Anna?'

I looked away – I didn't want to discuss it—

'I'm sorry if things are not working out between you,' he said. 'But you're still very young and time passes. She comes from a different world and she would always give you the runaround – I know the sort.'

My uncle, of course, knew nothing.

And the fact that he did not know Anna at all was a strange comfort to me.

She was my secret, someone priceless and rare; and I thought of Ottavio – the third person in the triangle.

The triangle!

I thought of that psychic in Venice. She had spoken of a triangle . . .

'But forget about all that, Lorenzo,' my uncle was saying. 'We will be in touch with each other once a month and you'll keep me informed of progress and of any problems. If you need anything don't hesitate to ask . . .'

In bed that night I wept.

I cried for what would never be.

Epilogue

Not long after my family's return to Argentina, Anna passed away – much sooner than I ever feared. My last regret is that I did not visit her more in her final weeks. But I could not stand to witness her mental deterioration, the dulling of her green eyes which even now are in my mind as a last terrible memory of her.

That was in 1958, and now is . . . whatever now is.

I am writing many years later. My business prospered as Uncle Alberto was certain it would.

I am, as you may guess, still single.

At my late mother's urgings Luisa and I tried to recapture something which in fact we never had – it was hopeless, we both knew it, and eventually she married someone else.

Piero married his Rosita . . .

The sense that I have been working for both Anna and me has never left me.

She remains a living force in my life.

She lives with me now, is always close, and I dream of what would have been.

The Ghost of Valentino

At the age of 12 I first fell in love with Rudolph Valentino, the 'Great Lover' of the silent screen.

Who was he? I used to ask myself, this man, this star of *The Sheik* and other silent movies. Everyone seemed to speak of him, and gradually as I grew older, I too, became more intrigued, and full of curiosity, about this celluloid object of Latin fascination.

Such was his legend, even in his own lifetime, that his name became part of a domestic language for other things. His name would be used in arguments between couples.

'Who do you think you are – Valentino?', she might say in a temper.

'Ah! Valentino,' he would shout. 'I'm not Valentino.'

I wanted to know the man who could command such awe – was he some kind of god?

One day at my grandfather's – I often popped by for a chat because he was more a friend than anything else – I asked him if he had heard of Valentino, who had died more than thirty years earlier.

'*Mia cara*, Vilma,' he said, 'of course I've heard of him. Who hasn't?'

'But you never go to the cinema . . .'

He laughed. 'Not now maybe . . . People still talk about

him. Perhaps I know more about his life than about some of our neighbours.'

'So what do you know? Tell me everything,' I said with a 12-year-old's teasing smile.

His old eyes rolled up to the ceiling and he stared at nothing in particular for a moment . . . then rubbing his face, he said:

'You wish to test me? Well, to start with, Valentino was the most handsome and charismatic of the silent screen actors. No one could compete with him . . .'

'What's charismatic?'

'It's the ability to attract for no good reason!'

As he spoke on my imagination wandered and grew, and still I wanted to know other things, things hard to articulate . . .

'When Valentino appeared on the screen,' he continued, 'he had this tremendous ability to create romance for women, they would fantasise about him . . .'

It sounded like a dream, I thought, a fairy story.

I asked: 'Will you take me to see a Valentino movie?'

'Sure I will,' he replied. 'They're showing *The Sheik* again soon.'

And of course the day came when he took me and I shall never forget the impression it left on me, on my imagination. From that day on, Valentino preoccupied my thoughts, as I grew into young womanhood. Even now to some extent. He is still there, in my dreams, as . . . charismatic . . . as ever.

Because of him, at the age of 27, I am still single, still my father's 'partner' at his chocolate company, Bertolini's.

My mother never did go out to work, she being a 'lady of leisure', a great party-giver and spender of our chocolate profits.

My father didn't seem to mind what she did so long as she was happy. She was still a beautiful woman, still loved by him.

I have a sister Christina, a few years my junior, yet she was already married with one daughter. We were temperamentally different yet got along reasonably well.

I see myself now in the office, tired, rising from my desk and stepping to the window to rest my eyes. I'd gaze at the people outside, everyone so busy, rushing backwards and forwards.

It was not then a large town so I more or less knew everybody, at least by sight. We lived not far from Venice. One day, at the office window, it suddenly dawned on me with an awful clarity that I would soon be 28 and I was still unmarried, still without children and with no steady boyfriend.

Not that I was short of contenders. Like my mother I was very attractive – though I say so myself – and could have had just about anyone I wanted. Much of my life was spent in disappointing eager men (married or not) with cool rebuffs.

I was still at the window when my father entered the office.

'Vilma, you're in a dream there. Do you see Valentino coming down the street?' he joked.

I turned to him with a smile. 'Papa, I doubt Valentino would visit even if he were raised from his grave.'

'Don't be so sure!'

'He's someone worth dreaming about!'

My father went to the cocktail cabinet and filled two glasses with wine. I always made sure we were well stocked with alcohol for our most valued clients. But, of course, when we were feeling especially exhausted we'd raid the cabinet, and I'd sometimes indulge myself with a scotch.

As I sipped the wine my father remarked, as if reading my mind:

'Soon you're 28.'

It was something I did not wish to hear at that moment, it sounded like a reproach, something stolen from my own fears. I started wondering where all those years had gone. What had I done with my life?

'It's no big deal,' I lied.

I caught him gazing at me oddly as if trying to unravel me. Finally he said, 'I worry about you Vilma. I'd have liked to see you married by now . . .'

I'd heard it all before. I smiled: 'I'm sorry to have disappointed you papa, but that special man has not arrived yet.'

He poured another glass of wine and drank it with one throw of his head. His eyes were half closed, as if trying to control his patience with a child, as he said, 'Vilma, you will never meet anyone while you continue chasing a ghost Valentino.'

This annoyed me . . . 'Please papa, don't interfere with my life. As for Valentino, it's just admiration and what he stood for.'

But my father was not really listening to me, he was familiar with my line. 'I know your grandfather filled your head with romantic notions about the "hero"! I know you still fantasise about this actor to the extent you won't let go. No one can compete with that. No one can enter your life while you dream!'

I grew angry. 'Excuse me papa, but I have a lot of work to do so I'd like you to leave.'

'So have I!' he replied, offended.

He banged his glass down on my desk. Then, changing his mood abruptly, he turned to me on his way out, and said 'By the way, I have found a new sales director—'

'Oh, who?'

'His name is Roberto Donato. He is very good, you shouldn't have difficulties with this one.'

'I should have met him first . . .'

'He is very efficient, he understands how we must move forward. It will be important for you to get to know each other without delay.'

A few days later I was tidying my desk when I looked up with a start to see a man in my office.

'*Buongiorno* Signorina Bertolini,' he said. 'I hope this is a convenient moment to introduce myself. I'm Roberto Donato . . .'

Typically, my father had not thought to make the introductions himself.

The man gazed at me but I think more in fear than anything else, so that I detected nothing indiscreet or presumptuous in his holding my eye.

He had very dark looks. I must admit that for a moment I thought of Valentino. There was just a passing resemblance.

'Please take a seat,' I said briskly. 'I'd soon let you know if it wasn't the right moment,' I added, smiling a little.

To my irritation, my father's words resurfaced in my head even as I spoke. Was I living in a dream? What was wrong about a romantic fantasy? What was so great about so-called 'reality' and all its failings and compromises?

'I believe I have some papers to sign, Signor Donato,' I said.

'Yes I have them here.' He opened a briefcase. 'If you don't agree with my report we can discuss it, of course.'

For the next two hours we discussed company business. Just as he was rising to leave, I asked, 'Fancy a drink?'

'I'd like that very much.'

169

He said it in such a way as to tell me it was my company, not the drink, he preferred.

I poured a scotch and handed it to him.

'I do hope you'll feel part of the family at Bertolini's.'

'I'm sure I will. It's a great company with an even greater future.'

'My father speaks very highly of you.'

He was too practised to register too much pride in his face – 'Thank you, Signorina.'

As he drank his soft dark eyes failed to leave me so that for the first time in our meeting I felt self-conscious. To break the mood I left my seat and moved to the window.

Perhaps my movements were sharper than intended because now he said, 'I hope I've not embarrassed you, Signorina.'

'Not at all,' I replied quickly, to remove any doubt, surprised by his directness. 'Anyway, I think we've said everything for now, so if you'll excuse me . . .'

Roberto rose to his feet without hesitation – 'Before I go I wonder if you would give me the pleasure of having dinner with me tomorrow night.'

I looked at him with undisguised astonishment. Was it now the fashion to date one's superior at the first meeting? For promotional purposes, perhaps? Yet my first instinct was to say yes. But wisely I found myself saying, 'I'm sorry, but I don't have much time for dinner dates. This business keeps me up very late.'

He frowned, a little. 'At least think about it,' he said.

But I was uncompromising. 'There's nothing for me to think about.'

'I will ask again, if I may.' He said it gently so that it didn't sound like a threat, then left my office.

I smiled. 'Business comes first here, Roberto. Mind you deliver on your professional promises first.'

Of course I was tempted. My father would have said: 'Ah, there she goes, sabotaging herself again. All for that dead screen lover Valentino.'

Back home we sat to dinner.

'So, Vilma, what do you think of our new sales director?' my father asked.

'Splendid. He seems to know what he's doing, especially where women are concerned.'

My father almost choked. 'What do you mean by that?' he demanded to know, as he tried to swallow a tube of pasta. 'What are you saying?'

I couldn't help but giggle. 'I just mean, he's a very fast worker as he's already asked me out to dinner.'

My father pulled out the wine cork with a pop. 'Well, he certainly doesn't waste time. Mind you, Vilma, perhaps you need a man like him to shake you up a bit and drag you away from the big lover of the silent movies.'

My mother laughed but had the sense to say, 'Please, Orlando, leave her be. It's her life and she can please herself.'

This annoyed papa. He threw down his napkin once he had mopped up sauce on his tie – 'I will never understand women!—'

'*Mio caro,*' my mother soothed, 'I am sure you understand me . . .' She was joking, I'm sure.

He was so angry he stormed from the table. My mother was not in the least flustered.

She turned to me – 'Vilma, don't get upset about your father's remarks. He thinks he has your best interests at heart. That's one of the ways men try to control women. They're doomed to failure. But even I worry about you sometimes and wonder if you'll ever settle down.'

171

'You mustn't worry, mamma,' I said patiently. 'I am happy with myself.'

My mother picked at some salad – 'But how can you be completely happy when there's no one to share your life with? You'll notice this more as you get older – then you'll understand what your father and I are saying.'

Later in my bedroom I reflected on my parents' words. How do you *decide* to marry? It struck me as ridiculous that something so important could simply be decided. Nor was I going to settle for less just to please my father.

It wasn't as if I had set my heart against a husband.

After all, 27-going-on-28 is not the end of the world.

It was time perhaps to find a place of my own, a nice little flat for now so I could please myself, not having to answer to anyone about how I lived my life.

I lay on my bed and gazed at a framed portrait of Valentino on my bedside table. He gazed slightly away from me, as if to avoid giving me an answer. It was a film poster for *The Four Horsemen of The Apocalypse* showing him in Argentine gaucho costume – his classically Italian oval-shaped and olive smooth face framed by glossy dark hair . . .

It was at these moments, before this portrait, that I could meditate about anything. I explored his face as so many times before, never failing to discover some new feature or pattern – the sensual curve of his lips, a message in his eyes.

What I sensed about him was a hidden naivety – or innocence – a vulnerability in this cold world. I think it was that which completed his charm despite the illusions of his tremendous fame.

I thought of my grandfather and his version of Valentino's life. Not that I believed everything he told me. I could judge for myself. It was Valentino's character, as revealed in his face, which truly enthralled me. He was and is an eternal star, I think, because he could somehow communicate his sensitivity and romanticism via the camera.

Cynics might say actors simply play a role despite their true nature. But Valentino played himself, that was his secret, and he expressed his fantasies on the screen – I suspect because he could not express them in his life.

Perhaps he did not realise this himself. One had only to know his life to understand this. Only by being an actor – by playing a part – could he be himself.

The romance he offered women the world over was a dream, but dreams, I have found, can offer the truest freedom . . .

A knock at the door broke me from my reverie—

'What is it?' I said.

'It's papa.'

'Yes, what do you want?'

'Let me in just for a moment.'

'I am very tired,' I said.

'Please, Vilma. I have something to tell you.'

I relented and let him in.

He respected my space by not coming much beyond the doorway. 'Roberto Donato called,' he said, 'and he asked for you. I told him you had gone to bed. He's clearly interested in you . . .'

'Thank you, papa, for the message. Sounds like he hasn't given up on me.'

To annoy my father I rubbed a speck of dust off Valentino's portrait.

'Why not give him the benefit of the doubt and see what he's made of?'

I sighed . . . 'I may . . . but, papa, I'm going to bed now.'

* * *

On my desk the following morning was a single red rose. I could guess who placed it there, certainly not the cleaner.

I picked up the rose and and admired its sweet, misleading, potent scent.

'Miranda,' I called to my secretary. 'Who put this rose on my desk?'

'Oh, I meant to tell you,' she replied, rushing into my office. 'Signor Donato was here.'

I pretended to be astonished. 'How strange!' I said.

Later in the morning Roberto phoned me. The first thing he asked was whether I liked the rose.

'Sure,' I said. 'We have employed a romantic it seems.'

'There are many things you have yet to discover about me. So will you come out with me?'

'No,' I said matter-of-factly. 'But . . . you can ask me again sometime. And, you never know, maybe I'll say yes.'

Then I hung-up before I could say anything else.

You might think my mind was full of Roberto after that. Not in the least. I was suddenly preoccupied with my grandfather's birthday party and dinner planned that day back home. I hadn't even thought what to get him so I left work early to get to the shops.

My grandfather and I still discussed Valentino. He knew so much about him because his parents had been fans, too.

Back home I asked my mother what she'd bought grandpa. In her usual way she extinguished a cigarette – 'Mia cara, the party is my gift.'

'I've bought him a pair of cuff-links.'

'Oh, let's look . . . oh yes, amber, he loves amber,' she cooed stroking the stones in their gold settings. 'He'll look handsome in those.'

I said, 'It's a good idea throwing him a party for a change. It can't be much fun living alone.'

She sighed, and looked at me with a slightly pitying expression. 'Do you really believe he is always alone?'

'What do you mean, mamma?'

'He's never wanted for company – honestly, Vilma, you have so much to learn. All the beautiful women—'

'Beautiful women?'

'Yes, darling, didn't you know? There's a queue sometimes!'

'What, *girlfriends*? At his age?'

My mother laughed heartily and a little scornfully I thought, a laugh frequently heard at parties all over town.

I added, 'He can't get up to much at his age.'

She raised her eyebrows. 'Don't you believe it! A man like him will always be busy with the ladies – until he kicks the bucket.' She lit up another cigarette.

I was shocked by this revelation, so casually made. I'd always thought of him as a harmless, celibate soul.

'This is really news to me.'

My mother exhaled a cloud of blue smoke, 'Vilma, I remember even as a child he couldn't keep his trousers up. At the first opportunity he would go for it like a goat with any woman he fancied. Of course my mother knew and forgave him. She loved him. And I still love him, too, despite his escapades.'

'But why didn't you tell me before now?'

'Well, I didn't think to . . . and I'm telling you now because I've grown tired of you always speaking of "grandpa" as if he's a saint . . .'

A car pulled in just outside, the gravel stones spitting there usual welcome under the heavy tyres. I peered out

175

the window. It was my grandfather, his tall, slim self looking nothing like his 75 years.

'Is it my father?' mother asked.

I looked at him with eyes afresh as he palmed down the creases in his smart dark suit – 'He looks so youthful,' I said without turning to her.

'So he should! He has lived his life selfishly. The only good thing he did in his life is make lots of money. Certainly he's always been a good provider, I'll say that.'

I was trying to resist disappointment. I had always wondered why my mother was never demonstrative with him, always slightly reserved, whereas with others she was extrovert, uninhibited and open. Suddenly I was no longer sure he deserved his place on my pedestal.

Our maid Maria announced his arrival. He followed soon afterwards. Closer up he looked tired, and we couldn't fail to notice the early stages of a moustache and beard, both still in their stubbly infancy. In the new light shed by my mother he looked, fleetingly, like a dirty old man, my whole view of him altered by her words.

'Ah, the two most beautiful women!' he said. 'My loving family.'

He kissed us both in turn – almost deafening me with a smacker close to my ear.

'Papa,' my mother said, 'I don't think all that facial hair makes you look at all distinguished.'

He gave an indulgent smile, and with mischief in his eyes said, '*Mia figlia*, I can never please you. So the moustache – at least! – stays.'

Minutes later my sister Christina and her husband walked in. Then my father with, to my astonishment, Roberto.

My grandfather sidled up to me and whispered, 'Who's that man? He's certainly not Valentino – but there's something about him . . .'

'Ah, but grandpa, he *is* Valentino. He has reincarnated so that at last we can be together.'

My grandfather laughed with short-breathed gusto – my mother's laugh was similar, rumbustious.

'You really are a rascal Vilma,' he said. 'You like to tease an old man.'

Maria re-entered the room with a large silver tray laden with tall crystal flutes. It was all so odd. This party had hardly been arranged, it had simply happened on my mother's whim earlier that day. A large bottle of champagne exploded in my father's hands and in a moment the flutes were carelessly filled with frothing, fizzing drink.

'So how are you?'

Roberto had slipped to my side. Perhaps it was the first flush of alcohol but I was attracted, not really knowing why or how much.

'So you persuaded my father to bring you.'

'Oh, he invited me. He persuaded me.'

'He did, did he,' I said, glancing at my father across the room.

At seven that evening after the champagne aperitif and blinis the party of eight sat for dinner.

'At my age, what better way to celebrate my birthday than with my family,' grandpa said.

'I'll sit to your right,' mother said to him.

'I prefer not too many people,' he added.

Roberto seemed already part of the family and it was pre-dictable that my matchmaking father would contrive to get us seated next to each other. He did this by simply pointing people to their chairs leaving no room for argument . . .

'Well, papa,' I caught mother saying, 'I expect you'd prefer to be out cavorting than with us.'

Grandpa raised his eyebrows in mock surprise, 'Certainly not.'

'You'll have fewer opportunities with this lot,' she added. There was a new sharpness in her voice, due to the drink. She clearly wanted to annoy her father. But his sense of humour was not lost . . .

'I have plenty of time for other activities,' he said. 'At my age, and with my declining faculties, I have less energy for, er, adventures.'

Roberto and my father laughed though my sister and her husband didn't seem sure how to react, not getting the joke. My mother stayed quiet glaring at her father stonily before taking up her soup spoon.

Some part of me wanted my mother to say more, just to see what happened, but thank God the dinner passed without further incident, grandpa effortlessly entertaining us all with stories. Even my mother had to smile.

He was the first to leave. I put my arm about his waist as we walked to the door.

'Vilma,' he said, 'I haven't seen much of you lately. Let's not lose touch. I'd love us to chat as we used to.'

I looked up at him, still not sure about his beard, 'I'd like that. I promise to see you soon.'

Roberto was reluctant to leave, happily allowing his glass to be refilled . . . my parents had wandered out into the garden to take in the fresh evening air, and leave us alone, I suspected.

'So, are you enjoying being at Bertolini's?' I asked. I couldn't think of anything else to say to him except discuss business.

'It's great . . .' he started, 'but, look, can we talk about us?'

'Us?'

'Yes—'

'I didn't realise there was an "us" to talk about . . .'

'I want to get closer to you – is there a chance?'

I refilled my glass with white wine and rested against the bureau. 'Don't expect too much of me.' I said. 'At the moment I don't want to be close to anyone, not just yet. I want to make that clear.'

'Just give me a little hope—'

'Oh, Roberto—'

'I don't want to pressure you in any way but we could be friends at least – let me take you out one evening so we can get to know each other and start from there.'

I half-smiled, more to myself. I replied, 'I know my father wanted us to be alone. I know he wants us to get together—'

'This has nothing to do with your father—'

'It has for me. I have not decided yet about going out with you. So between us, it's just business, just Bertolini's. I can't start making promises I can't keep or just going along with something . . .'

And as I spoke I could sense his disappointment – 'I don't give up that easily,' he said, 'but you're not giving me much choice but to leave the company. I just need to know if you have any feelings for me at all.'

I was agitated by this attempt at emotional blackmail. Even if I'd had strong feelings for him I would have resented being tested in this way, and to give an answer when I'd made it clear that I didn't know what my feelings were. This was not the right approach towards me.

Suddenly I was put off by his urgency, by his readiness to dump Bertolini's if he couldn't have what he wanted. He'd said he didn't want to pressurise me, so what was he doing now?

So coolly I said, 'I have no particular feelings for you, Roberto, so now you know.'

179

With that he gulped down his drink and left the house.

He didn't leave immediately. Then one day he came into my office and announced he had another job to go to. He explained he could not remain while there was no hope of getting together with me.

'Just one small sign from you Vilma and I will stay,' he concluded.

'You haven't been here for very long,' was all I could summon up. 'But if that's how you feel, there's nothing more I can say, except that I admire you as a colleague.'

His news did sadden me. I didn't want him to go. He was good for the company, I liked him, and at some level was attracted to him. But I didn't want anyone in my life. You see, I couldn't imagine replacing Valentino, certainly not with Roberto, not with any other man I knew. I was saddened to be reminded of this — that Valentino was a reason for not getting closer to someone . . .

You think me foolish? Of course I knew Valentino was part of a dream. Even were he alive he wouldn't have looked at me twice, always surrounded by famous women. I was afraid to wake from my dream . . . I say 'afraid'. Or was I just being true to myself? True to an emotional ideal?

Why settle for Roberto because I feared not surrendering my Valentino dream? Why pretend to have a feeling for fear of being lonely?

Sometime after Roberto had left my office, the phone rang.

'Vilma.' It was my father. 'Why are you allowing Roberto to leave? You do realise that we are about to lose one of our best representatives, and besides, he was a good opportunity for you — he could have made a good husband!'

180

I flared up, 'I am sorry Roberto has decided to leave but mind your own business from now on, papa.'

He paused momentarily, astonished at my anger. Then he blasted, 'Very well, Vilma! If that's what you want. Rest assured I won't interfere with your life ever again – so that you can end up the happy spinster.' He hung-up.

What constantly puzzled me was how he could talk to me in this way. What gave him the right? At that moment I made the decision I'd put off for too long – to leave home at last and get my own flat.

The next day I visited an estate agent.

'To rent or buy?' asked the bald man.

'Rent.'

'A flat you say? On your income you could rent a house.'

'A flat, thank you.'

'A house has more space . . .'

Why was it that men always wanted to change my mind?

'A flat, please,' I repeated.

I kept cool deliberately to annoy him, to make him realise he had no power over me whatsoever.

'Fine,' he said finally, 'a flat.'

A few days later he phoned to say that two flats seemed to suit my requirements. I collected the keys at his office.

The first flat did not impress me. I immediately suspected that the agent had recommended it to spite me for my wilfulness. Even the second was not what I'd asked for, but the furnishings were in good taste and I decided there and then it would do for now.

'Father, I am leaving. I have found a flat not far from here. I shall be moving out immediately.'

He could scarcely believe it. Marrying and leaving was one thing, but simply to leave the parental home unmarried . . . that was a different matter.

'What has come over you, Vilma?' he pleaded. 'Why do you want to live alone? There are plenty of rooms here for us all.'

'It's for the best, papa. It's time I stood on my own two feet . . .'

My mother, eavesdropping in the kitchen, came into the living room and said, 'Orlando, I think Vilma should live alone. She isn't a teenager . . .'

She gave me a comforting smile. I could tell she was quietly elated by my decision, perhaps happy I was showing signs of independence at last.

'Trust you to side with Vilma!' papa shouted. He knew he had lost this battle.

In fact I didn't move out until a few weeks later due to a cock-up by the estate agent. At last I felt such happiness to have my own place. How could I have put this off for so long? I felt free of my father, free of his expectations.

Weeks elapsed – passed my 28th birthday – and I heard nothing more from Roberto. Yet I heard through the grapevine he'd not moved far away. I missed him certainly, missed his interest (or ardour!), I could have been kinder to him. But he would have misinterpreted the slightest interest for love. I think he was more the dreamer than I.

But one thing Roberto had taught me about myself. My resistance to pressure. Through Roberto I had become more aware of my resentment of my father's attempts at control . . .

One day, in my new flat, I decided to visit grandpa . . .

'*Cara* Vilma,' he announced in his affectionate way,

'come and have a glass of wine with an old man. Stay for supper!'

I didn't mind in the least this kind of loving pressure.

The wine cork popped and two glasses were liberally filled . . . 'And how is your mother?' He hadn't forgotten her attitude to him at his birthday party.

'She's fine – still partying!'

'She's just like me, we're so alike she and I. She was a little sarcastic with me at the party, and odd, and indiscreet. I suppose she told you a few things about your naughty grandpa!'

I giggled lightly and held his gaze. I wasn't sure what to say.

'Well, whatever she said, you know, I have been around. In my younger days I was looking more for affection than anything else. Your grandmother, she criticised me like your mother does now. Your grandmother didn't understand me – nor does my daughter.'

What was there to understand? But I said, 'Mother said nothing about you grandpa.'

He smiled broadly, 'Ah! *Mia cara* Vilma, you're just trying to cover up for your mother. I know her better than you think.'

'She said nothing!' I repeated, but with a giveaway smile.

'Sure, I have a few lady friends even now, at 75! Even at 75 you get to feel a bit lonely. I need company like everybody else, and I'll tell you something. I don't have to drag any of my lady friends into this house! They all come voluntarily, and I hear no complaints. There's nothing sordid.'

I didn't pretend not to know what he was talking about. 'Grandpa, you don't have to explain anything. I love talking about life with you . . .'

He placed his strong arm about my shoulders. 'You are the sweetest child, Vilma. How nice you always are to me, I love you for it. Also, you are my best friend – with her own flat at last!'

'Yes, free of family . . .'

'That's good. And what of that fellow Roberto?'

I gently broke away from grandpa's embrace, 'I am not sure.'

'Not sure? I had the impression that he was in love with you, the way he looking at you at the party.'

'Roberto left the company and that's the end of it.'

He was surprised, 'What happened? Why did he leave?'

'He said he could no longer work with me because of his feelings for me . . .'

Grandpa went quiet for a while. Then he said, 'Your father doesn't like me much because he thinks I have twisted your mind over Valentino.'

'That's nonsense, absolutely untrue. I am sorry grandpa, he is wrong about that. I have to sort myself out, to decide what I want in life. No one can help me, not even you.'

He brought the half-full bottle of wine over to me. Perhaps he thought it would loosen my tongue. 'What you have just said, Vilma, is very interesting . . . so what does Roberto mean to you?'

I found it hard to find the words because I wasn't sure myself . . . 'I find him attractive, but – I can only tell you this – I think of Valentino even now, the ideal of a lover . . .'

'Even now you think of the Great Lover?'

'As an ideal . . .'

My grandfather changed expression. 'I will never forget the time I took you to see Valentino in *The Sheik*, that did it! He captured your imagination. I do understand something about him. Women loved him because he

184

expressed so well his own fantasies on the screen. I don't think he understood why he was so adored.'

'Perhaps it was the only way he could express his true feelings – on the screen. Do you think, grandpa, that off the screen this "great lover" was like any other man, craving marriage and children?'

'Of course,' he said, 'you know that – he married twice. But maybe he used all his luck up on the screen because he certainly ran out of luck in life where women were concerned – despite his looks and charisma. He never had any happiness with the women of his choice. Maybe that was the price he paid for his great ambition . . .'

While he talked on I sipped my wine slowly and pondered. I interrupted my grandfather . . .

'There must have been a reason why he was always attracted to the wrong women, two lesbians for heaven's sake.'

He laughed at that. 'How much wine have you had? How do you know they were lesbians?'

'I've read books, heard stories . . .'

'You know, Vilma, the trouble with him was that I don't think he looked at women to love them – not in his life in any case. He looked to see what they could give him. Both his wives were intellectuals, he liked that. He wanted popularity as well as all that artistic respectability which he thought he could get by marrying clever women. That was his dream. They dominated him, and soon he discovered that they had married him for their own reasons, not for love. They loved his fame! But, my dear, like you he wanted happiness, he wanted it all.'

Grandpa never criticised me, but even in my tipisiness I sensed he was trying to tell me something, something I knew myself already.

That romantic dreams can be destructive.

My eyes had grown heavy with wine . . . grandpa giggled. 'Too much vino, Vilma! I have led you astray again.'

He called Clara, his housekeeper. For a moment I thought she had a fat, old twin. But I was seeing double.

The next thing I remember was waking up in another room. I had fallen asleep briefly. Clara stood over me – 'Signorina, are you feeling better now?'

My head throbbed, my mouth felt dry. 'Thank you Clara, I'm OK. Where's my grandfather?'

I had hardly finished talking and he appeared in the doorway.

'So, you have recovered, Vilma. You'll never make an alcoholic! Come and join me for supper.'

It was late. 'I think I'll go now . . .'

'But the night is young,' he persisted. 'You have plenty of time to have supper with me.'

'I have a report to read, I'm afraid . . .'

'Very well,' he said a little crossly.

There was no report to read, I just felt incredibly tired.

How I got home I can't recall even now. My mind was full of Valentino and my grandfather's thoughts.

Back at the flat I was astonished to see all the lights on. Surely I hadn't left them on – it was so unlike me. The other odd thing was the unearthly stillness of the apartment. Even the usual rumble of neighbours was absent. But I was tired, I ate a little supper and showered, switched off the lights and lay in my bed . . .

I dozed out of this world and went to a place where I felt a hand lightly stroking my face.

I woke with a start. Had I dreamt it? I switched on my bedside lamp. As I scanned the room I felt a a rush of air on my cheek, as if someone had blown on it. I was amazed by the sensation, not fearful. I must still be dreaming, or imagining things. There was no one in the room.

I switched off the light after a moment and fell asleep.

At breakfast the next morning I smiled to myself. I must drink less wine. The phone rang. It was papa.

'Vilma, I must talk to with you this morning. I will see you in your office at ten-thirty.'

'What's up?' I said casually.

'I can't explain now.'

Some time later, at eleven I think, my father came to my office. The first thing he did was go to the cocktail cabinet and pour himself a drink – this was unusual even for him, given the hour.

He said, 'I hope you're not going to let me down. I am going to ask you to do something.'

'Er, that depends . . .'

'I want you to go to Milan tomorrow to meet Ruggero Collini.'

'Collini, of Collini's? Whatever for . . . ?'

Collini's was a major rival of ours and Collini himself was something of a self-made tycoon.

'Don't ask too many questions,' my father said snappily. 'You are to stay at his home. I am sure he will be impressed by you. If everything works out we will be doing much business with him – this is a great opportunity for Bertolini's to expand . . .'

'But why me?' I asked. 'Wouldn't it be better if you went?'

'It's important you meet him, someone young and clever, he prefers that. If Roberto were still here I'd have sent him. Besides, I have too much to do here . . .'

He suddenly went pale and passed his hand over his chest. He took a seat.

'Papa, what's wrong?'

He sat down breathing heavily. 'Don't worry Vilma, it's just a touch of indigestion . . .'

'You worried me for a moment. I think you should see a doctor.'

The very mention of the doctor – or 'quack' as he called him – brought colour back to my father's face.

'No more fussing, please.' he said.

'You should drink less, that could be the trouble.'

He got up, apparently fully revived, his old self again, ignoring my advice, but I think grateful for my concern.

'Just make sure you know everything you need to know for Collini,' he said. 'A lot depends on this, Vilma. And if he's persuaded we can do business together, then I will come out to Milan myself to complete the deal.'

The next day I caught the train and had arrived at Milan station by eleven that morning. From there I caught a taxi and was at Collini's home by midday.

On the outskirts of the city the car halted outside a pair of black, gilt-edged wrought iron gates. I had not even rung the bell and I saw a maid trudging towards me on the driveway within.

The gates opened as if my magic, and the maid, who gave me a tiny nod, picked up my case without a word and carried it to the house. I assumed I was meant to follow.

The Collini residence was impressive, if a little osten-tatious, a huge manor house in the English style with ivy sneaking up the south side.

At the front door a woman waited for me . . .

'Signorina Bertolini?' she said. 'Hello'. We shook hands. 'My husband sends his apologies – he was unexpectedly called away but will join us soon.'

She was an elegant woman, blonde, slim and well

tailored in a pink Chanel suit. She wore a bright tartan hairband – but no make-up whatsoever, which I thought odd, particularly in a woman in her forties. Perhaps she wanted to show off her beautiful natural complexion.

She led me into her home. The hallway was lined with portraits, grounded in Italian marble, dominated by a fabulous fountain-like chandelier which threw out reflected sunlight in all directions.

Instead of taking me to my room, or asking me if I wished to use the bathroom, we headed straight for the back conservatory and its potted vegetation. It was like a chic greenhouse with oases of easy-chairs and tables, blazing with red geraniums.

'Would you care for an aperitif?' she asked.

'Thank you.'

While the maid was sent for she talked about her two daughters, both married very young.

I heard the heavy tread of footsteps approaching the conservatory. I imagined the maid must be rather masculine or overweight . . .

'Ah, that must be my husband,' said Signora Collini.

On cue he appeared in the doorway, a tall man, rather handsome. Ruggero Collini had black hair, grey at the temples, and appeared about fifty.

'Hello,' he said casually. 'You must be Signorina Bertolini. I am so sorry I wasn't here to greet you.'

His wife fell silent as he sat opposite me.

Unlike her he was full of effortless charm though I detected a hint of arrogance, a sense of his own power, which grated me slightly.

'So I'll leave you two to it,' his wife said, relieved I guessed that she did not have to play dutiful hostess with me anymore.

189

She bent down to her husband and he kissed her lightly on the cheek.

'So, come,' he said to me. And he led me to another room in the house itself, an office, with a breathtaking view of the gardens. I took in vines heavy with grape and avenues of trees which gave scale to this Eden.

'Is it not a wonderful sight,' he said. 'I forget everything just looking out the window. May I offer you a drink?'

'Your wife sent for the maid—'

'Oh, well, we'd better start again, then. You have to book the maids round here!'

I preferred to get down to business.

'I like that. You don't waste time. But, you know, it is lunchtime and I never skip meals. We will resume later. Yes?'

'I don't mind—'

'No, no, an empty stomach always leads to bad business,' he said, standing close to me, his dark eyes full of unwelcome intimacy.

Lunch was thankfully light and the conversation comparably trivial, his wife quite expert at saying very little at great length. Within an hour we had returned to his office with its faint air of leather and old books . . .

He was quite different now. The serious businessman. I was quite astonished at his knowledge of Bertolini's, and of our shared market.

'The good thing is that Bertolini's and Collini's don't really need each other,' he said. 'But together we can dominate the Italian market and expand across the Alps – two companies combined but independent of each other.'

I opened the document he'd had prepared on our two companies. Yes, it was well prepared and accurate. My father had been wise to send me; he knew I could read balance sheets in an instant and detect flaws or misleading figures intuitively.

Here we sat for a number of hours. I had assumed I would have to persuade Collini into a co-operative venture with his company, but in fact he was already sold on the idea. My impression was that he wanted to know how wised-up Bertolini's was, how ready we were for the 'way forward', as he put it.

'But I can see you are tired,' he said suddenly. 'It's very thoughtless of me. May I call you Vilma? Please call me Ruggero.'

He summoned the maid to take me to my room at long last. 'You will of course dine with us—'

I had already decided that I would return home the next day.

'But you're welcome to stay,' he said eagerly, rising to his feet. 'But look, you must come to my club tonight and meet some of my friends . . .'

Would he have been so amiable with Roberto? He was too attentive, too keen to please me, and I was certainly reluctant to spend a whole evening with him. On the other hand, we were going into business together so I had to make small sacrifices.

'Sure,' I said. 'With Signora Collini?'

'Good God no. I mean, Lina has things to attend to here.'

That was the first time he had referred to her by name. She had forgotten to introduce herself properly.

Over supper he said to her, 'I am taking Vilma to the club. Is that OK with you?'

'Oh really,' she said heavily. 'Do I ever refuse you anything?'

Irritation clouded his face, I imagined, as he replied,

'I'm taking her there to meet some friends. Bertolini's and Collini's will be doing much business together.'

'As opposed to funny business . . . ?'

Ruggero was furious with his wife. He whispered something to her as I broke bread, pretending not to notice discord. What they said to each other I didn't hear. It was a good moment to withdraw and get ready for the evening.

'Enjoy yourself,' she said icily as I left the table.

In my bedroom I giggled to myself. Weren't all marriages the same? Self-indulgent husbands and their bitter wives. That game wasn't for me. That was their dream.

As I dabbed scent behind my ears I dreamt of Valentino having dinner with his wives, gossiping, eating soup . . . no, I couldn't imagine it. I couldn't imagine anything so dull.

At around ten we left the house for his club which, helpfully I discovered, en route, was simply called The Club.

Ruggero was dressed very casually, I had chosen a modest black silk slip.

'You look wonderful,' he said in the back of the car. 'I have so much enjoyed our discussions – I hope we see a lot of each other in the future – it's so important we make friends with the people one does business with, don't you agree?'

'Yes,' I said, gazing out as we passed homes sparkling in twilight, 'provided it's just business.'

He laughed. 'What else? You sound like Lina. Unless you have something else in mind . . .'

Now it was my turn to laugh, at his mischievous audacity. I was old enough to know that laughter could be misinterpreted. So I added, 'My mind is as clear as crystal, Ruggero. With me it's just business.'

He said nothing to that. He ordered the chauffeur to drive faster.

We stopped outside a tall building in the centre of Milan. Ruggero spun out of the car and opened the door for me in the time it took his chauffeur to readjust his cap.

'Here we are, Vilma, welcome to The Club.' He held me gently by the hand and we took the lift to the second floor.

I had not been prepared me for this. I half expected a quiet library-come-drinking club. In fact The Club seemed modelled on something out of Las Vegas. One corridor led to a dimly lit restaurant where shiny faces loomed over trembling candles. Another corridor took you to the casino where pot-bollied men in strained waistcoats threw away small fortunes in plastic chips. Along the third corridor I could hear dance music and see flash light.

We made our way to the dance hall bar.

'So what do think of all this?' he asked, as if he owned the place.

'It's, er . . .'

He gulped down his drink and ordered another – 'I'll make sure you have a good time, we know how to live in Milan!'

'Thank you, but I can't stay long, as you know Ruggero.'

He took his empty glass and stared into it as if inspecting something. 'That's a great pity. Maybe next time you'll let your hair down.'

In fact I was already captivated by the music which put me in the mood to dance, but I said nothing.

'So who have we here tonight?' Ruggero said more to himself. 'Ah, I'll introduce you to that lot over there.'

He almost pulled me over to a group of people and I was astonished to see Roberto with a young woman among them. At first we pretended not to know each other, allowing Ruggero to introduce us.

In a lull Roberto took me aside and said, 'I never expected to see you in a place like this, Vilma.'

But sharp-eyed Ruggero was soon upon is – 'You never said you two knew each other. What's going on here?'

'Roberto worked for Bertolini's until recently,' I explained smoothly.

Ruggero turned to Roberto's pretty blonde companion, Elena, and asked her to dance – 'You don't mind, do you Roberto?'

'But do I mind?' said Elena, teasingly.

Roberto shrugged his shoulders, and the pair headed for the dance floor, but not before she had thrown me a rapid head-to-toe disapproving glance.

Alone together Roberto and I were tongue-tied momentarily. I decided to be provocative.

'So I see you haven't wasted time in finding yourself a replacement,' I smiled.

'So you and Collini, are you an item?'

I laughed. 'Don't be ridiculous. Collini's and Bertolini's are going into business together.'

'That's ambitious. Good luck to both of you then.'

'And good luck to you with young blondie over there. You certainly deserve it.'

'You mean that?'

'Absolutely.'

Roberto offered me a drink. When I refused he asked me to dance . . .

So we danced. The music was slow now. Roberto held me close with his face almost touching mine.

'Vilma, *mia cara*, Elena is not really for me,' he said softly.

'It's not my business,' I replied, 'you don't have to answer to me . . .'

He held me more tightly now . . .

'I wish you wouldn't say that, Vilma. I still think the world of you. I'm just going out with Elena for company. We know where we stand with each other.'

'Don't be so sure, Roberto. Judging by the look of her, she's got other ideas.'

'Are you warning me . . . ?

'I'm just telling you what I see . . .'

I won't lie. I was still aware of the attraction between us, my body soon felt limp in his hands. It was the first time we had been so physically close. I grew a little dizzy on his scent, all mixed up with hypnotic music and seductive wine.

New music was played. Before the spell could be broken he asked me to dance again and I happily fell into his arms for another languid number. I felt safe in this intimacy with people around us.

I felt his face move along mine and he whispered, 'I love you, Vilma . . .'

I wanted the music to last forever just for this moment. This was how life should be, a dream, a dance, a scent . . .

'Vilma, I know you feel something for me . . .'

'Something, I don't know . . .' I had no need for words . . . 'Sometimes I feel confused.'

'You are always running away from me.'

'I don't know . . .' I repeated. 'When I feel confusion I want to disappear.'

The spell had ended. The music was over. I broke gently away from Roberto. He grabbed my hand and kissed it.

I turned to move off the floor to be greeted by the fiery

gaze of Elena. Fortunately she said nothing to me. Ruggero behind her was smirking.

I had another drink, then asked Ruggero to take me home. I felt melancholy for Roberto, not knowing what was for the best.

'Oh, do let's stay,' said Ruggero. I was amazed that this famed tycoon, who had impressed me with his business acumen, could now be so childish. 'It's too early to go home,' he whined, 'let's not waste the night away.'

So I danced with Ruggero, thinking of my father who would be expecting me to do my duty for the company. Roberto was now dancing with Elena, a sight that left me feeling uneasy.

After a while I said to Ruggero, 'Get my coat.'

Back at his home Ruggero tried to kiss me.

'Do that again and there will be no business between you and my father's company.' I was severe.

In the morning I rose early. Ruggero himself drove me to the station. Lina did not bother to say goodbye. Inwardly I knew this 'meeting' had been a success and that my father would be happy, so a good purpose had been achieved despite my sadness now.

'May I say something Vilma,' said Ruggero. 'I have never come across a woman as unusual as you. You fascinate me.'

'I'm sure many women have heard these words, Ruggero.'

'Not at all . . .'

'I am not unusual or different from any other woman, except that I know what I want – or don't want – or maybe I'm just honest about the fact that I don't know what I want!'

Ruggero accelerated the car unnecessarily. But I said nothing. He must learn that I could not be intimidated.

At the station he wished me a safe journey and shook my hand business-like. He looked forward to doing business with a company as esteemed as Bertolini's, he said.

Then to my astonishment, as I waited on the platform, I spotted Roberto running towards me—

'I had to see you off,' he said, breathing hard. 'Ruggero told me you'd be leaving about now.'

'You amaze me,' I laughed.

'We should keep in touch, at least. I know you have feelings for me, I shall never forget last night.'

Nor would I. But I could hardly tell him that it was the music (and perhaps his scent) which made me sentimental. Now, on this station platform, was another day, another mood, and last night already belonged to another time.

The train pulled in. Roberto embraced me, I allowed him to kiss me tenderly on the lips.

'I will call you Vilma,' he murmured.

He stood on that spot as the train pulled out.

I got back home around lunchtime and hailed a taxi. My father was relieved – Collini had already phoned him full of enthusiasm, and compliments for me. I said I was satisfied with all the figures provided.

'Now that I've been so good, papa, do you mind if I take the rest of the day off?'

'I don't mind,' he said exultantly. 'Just give me the figures and you can do what you like!'

We agreed I'd come round for dinner later. So I went shopping and in the afternoon had a rare siesta.

At around five I awoke. I carelessly jumped out of bed and in doing so knocked down one of Valentino's portraits on the bedside table.

I picked up the frame and gazed at his face . . .

'Hello handsome,' I whispered and kissed the glass. 'Please forgive me.'

My father was waiting at the door when I arrived for dinner.

'How on earth did you know I was coming at this moment, papa?' I said as I stepped out of my car.

'I didn't,' he said, 'I just happened to to look out the door and here you are.'

He kissed me on the cheek.

'Now, I could be wrong about Collini's,' I said as we walked into the house.

'No way, Vilma. You have always had a brain for business and the soundest judgement. I use you, you know. Did you realise?'

'Of course, papa! I allow you to use me.'

Mamma sat in the living room. She lit a cigarette. 'Hello *cara*, so how did you find the big man?'

She meant Ruggero − 'He's very clever, but a bit of a lad − and as for his dreary wife . . .'

Mamma laughed and gave me a hug.

Over supper we talked much about Collini and his business practices. There were many stories of his adventures, not all of them flattering.

'Do you have to make so much noise chewing on that chicken leg?' mamma said to my father at one point.

'Ah, you never eat,' he replied picking meat off the bone. 'You just smoke all day. If they opened you up they'd just find a smoked kipper from years back.'

My mother raised her eyebrows at me.

'Now Vilma, I was thinking,' papa said. 'I was thinking you need a new car.'

'Yes, it's a bit much that the manager has a better one than mine.'

'So I shall buy you one – what do you want?'

'I can't accept a car just like that.'

'Yes you can – the company will buy the car – as my business associate you must look right – your car should look as expensive as all those clothes you wear.'

'Vilma,' my mother said softly, 'stay tonight . . .'

'I can't. I have to get back to the flat.'

Back at the flat I sensed an oddness in the air that reminded me of the other night when I returned to find the lights on. I decided this was the price of living alone – the imagination playing up in an empty place.

In the early hours I awoke gently to a dreamt whispering in my ear. Then I realised I wasn't dreaming but conscious. For a moment I thought it might be a sound in the street outside . . . but, no, it was close to me, human speech. I could not distinguish the words.

I switched on the light. Nothing. Perhaps it was next door, arguing again. Yet I knew I'd heard a voice in my bedroom. After a while of straining for new sounds, I switched off the light and fell asleep.

More curious disturbances of this sort followed on subsequent nights, nothing to frighten me out of my wits, just troubling inexplicable incidents. Some nights I might feel strangely restless in bed tossing and turning with unease. My sleep began to suffer. Soon I was arriving at the office more tired than when I left it. Was I ill? I needed to talk to someone about it. I didn't want to trouble my grandfather.

So I called my best friend Lisa.

She knew just about everything about me . . . or so she thought. I had never discussed my obsession with Valentino with her. She came the day after I phoned her.

'Oh, your new flat – you've finally flown the coop,' she said, 'but you do look tired. Have you a lover?'

'As if!' I said.

'Why not? You're free now . . .'

'I didn't leave home to find a lover,' I said, wishing I hadn't.

'The same old Vilma. So what's wrong?'

Where to start. I didn't really know what to say . . .

'Does this flat feel right to you, Lisa?'

She furrowed her brow mystified by my question. 'It's a lovely flat, Vilma. Why, have you rats?'

'I can't sleep here. I hear things – they wake me up.'

'What things? Maybe you're nervous being alone. First time, remember.'

'But I hear things—'

Lisa grew serious now, realising I wasn't kidding. Perhaps she was thinking I was a loony. Certainly I was a puzzle, not least to myself.

'Now what exactly is going on here, Vilma?' she said in her no-nonsense voice which I loved her for.

'I don't know where to begin—'

'So there is a beginning. I'm interested.'

'You have to promise not to talk about this with anyone else. I trust you Lisa.'

'Have I ever let you down? Come on, talk to me.'

I confined my story to the strange happenings in the flat. When I was done she said, 'I don't know much about this sort of thing, I don't know what to think. I'm inclined to think it's your imagination . . . I mean, you do work very hard, Vilma. You look exhausted, perhaps you need a break.'

But she knew that's not what I wanted to hear. 'I just don't think you understand,' I repeated over and over again.

'Now don't try that old trick. What is there to under-stand? So you hear noises and whisperings. What do you want me to say? That you're haunted? I have an idea, why don't I stay here for a few nights with you. Then we'll see what happens.'

'You'd do that? You're not afraid?'

'Afraid of what? You've said nothing to be afraid of. Say,' she added, gazing at the walls, 'what's with all these Valentino pictures on the walls – I've just noticed.'

'I'm a film buff – you know that.'

'Just Valentino films?'

It was at this moment that I decided she may as well know the whole story. 'There is something else I have not told you . . .' Her eyes widened perceptibly. I had never seen so happy!

So I confided my Valentino obsession. All these years we had known each other and I hadn't told her.

'I think this obsession has stopped me from loving any man.'

She held my hand – 'You mean . . . you're fixated on a dead actor . . . ?'

'You can see all the pictures. Look in my bedroom, pictures of him everywhere . . .'

'I find it hard to believe . . . but you're so cool, Vilma, how could you hide this . . .'

'I used to hide the pictures . . .'

'It's so unlikely, after all these years you tell me now . . . but it makes sense. You never went out with anybody. You turned down every boy.'

'Now I wonder if Valentino haunts this flat. I wonder if he is trying to tell me something.'

Lisa hugged me. 'Now come along, what nonsense is that. But let's be rational. Let's suppose the great screen lover is haunting your flat – what have you to fear?

201

You mustn't tell anyone else Vilma. They'll think you mad.'

I felt relief I'd told her at last. At least she had not laughed. I poured wine.

As we sipped Lisa played psychologist. 'So tell me,' she said, 'what is it about Rudolph Valentino, bearing in mind he's dead and buried?'

'That's not something I can explain, Lisa, it has just happened to me.'

She rose from the sofa and peered closely at a Valentino photograph. 'Mmm, yes, he was a very good looking man – I wouldn't have minded him.'

'There's more to him than looks,' I reprimanded her.

'It's all in the eye of the beholder,' she said. 'Shouldn't you throw his pictures away to break the spell?'

'I don't want the spell broken.'

Lisa decided to stay with me the week. There were no more noises or whisperings and I did sleep better, and felt improved in myself.

But any idea that Valentino – in whatever shape or form – had been exorcised was soon dashed. One day at the office Lisa phoned inviting me to a party. I wasn't keen but on second thoughts allowed myself to be persuaded, if only in gratitude for her support.

It was a birthday party for one of the sons of large, rich family. I knew them vaguely.

I wore yet another one of my flimsy red dresses (which my father so disapproved of) while Lisa wrapped herself in a tight white one-piece. It was so tight that she could only take little steps, like a geisha girl.

It was a warm evening. Skylarks dotted the sky – thankfully the party was in the garden so there was air and space. Already stars shone bright thanks to a moonless sky.

At the back of the garden a stage had been erected for the band, with a dance floor in the foreground improvised from polished wood panels. This was a money-party – everyone wore money of a sort – expensive clothes and jewellery, perfect teeth and shiny hair: everything was glamorous and young and enchanting.

It took only two glasses of champagne to get me in the party mood. One moment Lisa was with me, next she had disappeared, so that I was reduced to wandering about like the party-ghost since I hardly recognised anyone.

I had just slipped through a small crowd when I felt a hand on my shoulder. I turned around. At first all I could see were long male legs. I looked up at certainly the tallest man at the party. He was good-looking, about thirty.

In a deep, slow voice he said without introduction, 'Signorina, may I have the next dance?'

To my surprise I replied, 'Sure.' And put my glass down.

Within moments his arms had wrapped about my waist like a boa snake as the band started up an Argentine tango – a perfect cue for me.

Whoever he was, I thought, he could dance. For a man so huge he moved with amazing lightness, turning his body without flamboyance, holding and catching me perfectly. As we found our rhythm I felt I was in *The Four Horsemen of the Apocalypse* where Valentino dances the tango in a smoky dive, so that when I looked again at this nameless man – someone who meant nothing to me – I was able to imagine Valentino in his face, and with that image in my mind, I turned and spun and posed without inhibition.

Yet I was embarrassed when at the end of the dance other guests applauded us.

'Did you train to dance?' he asked afterwards.

203

'Not really,' I said mopping my face with a napkin.

'I was sure you were a professional dancer – you're the best dancer I've ever been with.'

At last he told me his name, Luca. I said I had to find my friend – Lisa. He shrugged sadly. He thought he'd found a dance partner for the evening.

In any case, knowing he was 'Luca' spoiled my Valentino fantasy of him. I was troubled that even here I couldn't get the Great Lover out of my head.

As I hunted for Lisa I picked up a fresh glass of champagne from one of the waiter's silver trays held at shoulder level. I soon spotted her – same old Lisa, kissing a man in some far corner.

'Lisa!' I called out.

I assumed the man couldn't have meant much to her because the moment she heard me she leapt from him without ceremony – 'Vilma! Where have you been?' as if her disappearance were my fault.

'What about you?'

'Isn't he dishy?' she said looking her at her crest-fallen kisser.

'They're all dishy, Lisa. He's just for this evening, I can tell.'

'Oh! What do you know! You're wrong. What have you been up to?'

'I danced with Valentino.'

She gave me a pitying look. Dear Lisa. Not a looker. Never without a man. Never with the right man . . .

We left the party at two in the morning – together.

Thank God it was Sunday. I had a thundering hangover, not helped by the phone which squealed at me.

'Mamma. What time is it?'

'At last I get you. What happened to you? You sound drunk.'

204

'I was last night.'

'Good. At last you're being a teenager in your late twenties and taking after me! Where did you get drunk?'

'Oh, I went with Lisa to someone's birthday party . . .'

'Whose?'

'The De Vito's.'

'Oh yes,' she said in one of her sniffy voices. 'Your father and I have little to do with that lot.'

'Why?'

'Total vulgarity. All money, no class. I bet they booked the biggest band . . .'

'Why, were you there, too, mamma? Incognito?'

She laughed briefly. 'But I called you to ask you to lunch. Do you want to come over?'

I hesitated . . . we compromised. I'd visit later at five.

'So how did you really find Collini?' papa asked me later that day.

I was complimentary about the rogue. I didn't mention the attempted kisses.

'I have gone through the business proposal,' said my father, 'but before I sign it I want you to make another visit. Certainly he is very clever, he knows the market inside out.'

'As you do, papa.'

'Yes – and you!'

Mamma added, 'So much cleverness!' And we all laughed.

'Now look,' said my father, 'I'm going to disappear to the office and go through this proposal one more time, so keep your mother company.'

In the sitting-room mamma poured wine, threw off her shoes (which she often did when papa left the house) and sprawled her long legs over the chair rests.

'So what is this Collini really like?' she asked, echoing my father's query.

I giggled. 'Do you really want to know?'

'Gossip is the best way to find out about a person's true nature,' she said. 'Forget about business proposals or the twaddle spoken over lunch tables. It's what people get up to in bed that matters!'

My mother never failed to amaze me.

'All right, but you mustn't repeat anything to papa.'

She lit a fresh cigarette in eager anticipation – 'Your papa? Why would I tell him anything? It's not my style to let him know too much.'

I coughed as a draught carried a cloud of smoke over me – 'Oh mamma, I do wish you'd give up that dirty habit.'

'Stop whining! Tell me the gossip. I will never give up smoking. When I die I shall insist a cigarette is stuck between my lips. That'll give you all a shock if I lie in an open casket.'

I shook my head in mock despair. So I told her all about Collini and his ghastly wife. 'He even tried his luck with me,' I finished.

Mamma smiled, and blew up a mushroom cloud of nicotine. 'Tell me more about his wife. Lina? What does she get up to?'

'She is resigned to his infidelities I imagine, and like most Italian women closes her eyes.'

'The poor little mite,' said mamma. 'She should take a lover and stop feeling sorry for herself. I guess I must be one of the lucky women. Your father's always been good to me and never been unfaithful. We still love each other after all these years.'

She coughed, then changed the subject. 'Now your grandpa. He's not well – he wants to see you.'

This news, thrown in in her usually casual way, shocked me.

'What's wrong with him?'

'Could be just old age.'

'Should you not see him?'

Mamma was irritated. 'Oh I will, just so long as I don't find him in bed with one his tarts.'

Her words upset me, revealing more anger at her father than I had imagined. I suddenly felt restless, a desire to go.

'You go then,' mamma said. 'After last night you must be tired. Don't worry about your father.

Back at the flat Lisa phoned.

'Vilma, I've been trying to get hold of you.'

'I was at my parents'. What's up?'

'Have you got someone staying with you that you haven't told me about?'

Puzzled, I said no.

'I tried to call you once before,' she continued. 'So you were out?'

'I told you so.'

'Well when I called earlier someone picked up your phone. And when I said hello it went click.'

'Perhaps you called a wrong number, Lisa. It's easily done.'

'I don't think so. I'm very careful when I dial. In any case I phoned once more after that and the same thing happened again. Perhaps it was a burglar – best to check the place out.'

I felt chilled at the thought of a stranger in the flat. 'No, there's no sign of a break-in.'

'Look around now while I'm on the line. If you scream I'll phone the police.'

This I did. I opened cupboards, wardrobes, peered into corners and under the bed.

'It's just me here, Lisa.'

That night, after her call, I was awoken by yet another noise. I'd thought the disturbances had ended with Lisa's stay.

I spun out of bed and searched the flat once again. It was a small apartment, just the bedroom, kitchen and sitting-room.

I returned to my bedroom feeling relieved. I looked up at a Valentino portrait and said, 'You're supposed to look after me, my lover, and not frighten me.'

I knew the absurdity of this, and laughed to myself. I couldn't be entirely deranged if I was able to laugh at myself.

An immense tiredness came over me and before I knew it I was out and woke up at nine. I'd be late for work, I angrily reminded myself.

I needn't have worried. Papa had been held up, I was told, so I was running the place. Later in the morning Lisa phoned to see how I was.

'I was wrong about you, ' she said. 'I'm sure there's something going on in that flat of yours . . .'

'Don't say that Lisa. You'll worry me.'

She wanted us to meet but I put her off because of work and my grandfather.

Passed mid-afternoon my father eventually turned up at the office . . . and headed for the scotch. It was a pick-me-up, a tonic, not a drug for him, or so he said: he poured a second glass before he spoke.

'So, papa, are we still joining up with Collini?'

'Well, I've analysed his report carefully − yes, we can do business, except there are one or two points to clarify.

I have decided to meet up with him myself in the next few days . . . I'll leave the place to you to run. Can you manage that?'

He knew full well I could, but liked to keep me on my toes.

Later that day, at about seven, Roberto called at my flat. I was very surprised, and pleased in a way.

'I came on impulse,' he said.

'You should have called first . . . I might be planning to go out.'

'I took that risk – are you going out?'

'I've not decided yet,' I said coquettishly.

'So can I come in?'

'For supper?'

Naturally I let him in, though I wished I'd had time to take down some of the Valentino pictures and icons.

The door shut he came close and stroked my hair, trying to resume the intimacy at The Club . . .

He said, 'I have a better idea. We'll go out for a meal. Why should you cook for two?'

It was tempting, but I felt tired, and I was nervous of his intensity. Going out would put him in control. I offered to cook him something instead.

He followed me into the kitchen.

'So, do you think of me now that I'm not working with you?' he asked. He put his hand on my shoulder and whispered, 'I miss you terribly. I had to come.'

His touch made me tremble, I felt weak again as I had the other night when we danced.

He took hold of me and kissed me passionately. I wanted to be loved because he was here.

Over supper we gazed at each other, saying little for

some time. I was full of warmth, relishing the idea of his attention . . .

'May I stay the night?' he asked.

The question focused my mind in mild panic. I was tempted, but we hadn't known each other very long. I thought of a hundred different complications if he stayed. Then on a whim I said to myself: why not?

It was time to spend the night with a man.

Certainly the ground did not move for me. I felt no grand passion, only some relief that I would have something very surprising to tell Lisa who I think had already written me off as either a nun or a lunatic. I reasoned to myself that I couldn't expect too much from my first time.

Before I led Roberto into the bedroom I had managed to remove some of the Valentino pictures. I couldn't have done anything knowing my screen lover was a witness.

Roberto left my bed as I still slept. On the kitchen table was a brief note:

'Thank you for a wonderful night. I love you, Roberto.'

My grandfather was surprised to see me. He was getting used to my long absences.

'You need surprising,' I said. 'Mamma tells me you've been unwell.'

'I'm not too bad given I'm an old wreck. I feel better for seeing you.'

Grandpa looked good, I was getting used to his peppery-grey beard now.

He added, 'I'm certainly not going to waste our time discussing the creaky workings of my body. I can't stand people who go on and on about their health.'

I gave him a kiss. 'OK, I said, let's talk about me, then.'

'Oh yes . . . you have something new to tell me, haven't you?'

'How can you be so sure?' I flirted.

'Oh, I know all about you women – I'm sure your mother will agree with me on that! You wouldn't have come if you didn't have any news.'

In fact I didn't feel ready to tell him about Roberto, especially after what I had last said about him. All I wanted to talk about was Valentino.

'Valentino?' he said. 'Then in that case we must open a bottle in his honour. But I know you have something to tell me. Your eyes are telling me but your brain's in the way!'

'You a mind-reader suddenly?' I said as he poured the red wine.

I relented a little after a glass. I told him I had seen Roberto, but didn't go into all the details. Instead I told him about the disturbances at the flat, and how Lisa had stayed with me for a week.

'Sounds like ghosts to me,' he said.

'How can you say that, grandpa? I'll never sleep. Since when have you believed in ghosts?'

'Since forever. Of course there are ghosts and whatnot. It makes perfect sense. You should see a clairvoyant medium.'

It was news to me that grandpa knew anything about the after-world – we had never discussed spirits, or life after death, though he frequently mocked the Church and its teachings. 'Why would God choose these men of the cloth to do His business?' he might say. 'These narrow-minded virgins who look down every woman's bosom!'

Papa was appalled by these words; mamma simply laughed – she'd heard it all before, and shared her father's scepticism.

My grandfather refilled my glass. 'Now, are you still attached to the screen lover?'

'Oh grandpa! Yes, I even felt I danced with him the other night ... well, I imagined it with someone at a party.'

He gave a great sigh – his first real sign of concern for me and my love of Valentino.

'I blame myself for this fantasy,' he said. 'I should never have taken you to that Valentino picture all those years ago ...'

'Don't be silly – how could anyone have known ... I mean, Valentino gives me so much pleasure, I think he has saved me from many pointless relationships.'

'A whole life can be taken up with pointless relationships, my darling. It's called experience.'

Yes, he was right. But I was right, too. It's so easy to generalise about life and forget each individual's need.

'Grandpa,' I said. 'Valentino was a sensitive man, he had a gentle nature, these are the qualities I love. His life with women was a total disappointment, yet there is he is – the screen lover!' I laughed.

'He could have lived a long life had he not neglected himself,' he said. 'He wanted to die, I think. Part of him had had enough. Never confuse fantasy with reality or the two will collide, Vilma.'

'I know that!' I said sharply. The wine had taken effect. 'But look at his life. He was rich, famous, women worshipped him. How he struggled to achieve – nearly starving for his dreams. Then when he had everything he realised none of it really mattered. If only I had been alive when he was on this planet – I would have met him, loved him, cared for him like no other ...'

'*Mia cara*, my sweet Vilma, try to think about what Valentino means to you. He is just a lovely dream. And when you wake up you will realise that you must get on with your own life.'

'I know that, grandpa, but what a lovely dream. I know I will meet no Valentino. But why shouldn't a man not be gentle and sensitive? Think of the odds against a man being those things.'

Oh, the wine had made me say too much. I kissed my grandfather again . . . 'I love talking with you – you have never reproached me before about Valentino . . .'

'It's not reproach, Vilma, it's concern. You will never be happy with phantoms.'

Shortly after I got back to the flat there was a knock at the door. It was one of the neighbours. Somehow Roberto had got hold of her number and called to leave a message for me. I wished he hadn't done this. I hated neighbours knowing my busisness.

'He wants you to phone him as soon as you get in,' said Evelina, winking at me. 'Must be love if he goes to the trouble of getting my number.'

'Thank you for the trouble,' I said.

I didn't phone him till the morning at the office. When I did he said: 'Where were you?'

I exaggerated the time I had spent at my grandfather's.

'I just wanted to talk to you and hear the sound of your voice – it's like music to me.'

I wanted to giggle. He sounded quite the poet . . .

'*Mio amore*, if only you knew how much I want to hold you again,' he said, 'how much I enjoyed our night together . . . can we see each other this week? I know you won't say no because you love me.'

But I didn't love him, or at least not at that minute. Nor was our night together a passionate moment for both of us, though maybe for him. He was projecting his own feelings onto me . . . but I didn't want to hurt him.

'When can I see you again? Sometime this week? – you have not given me an answer.'

I was uncertain what was for the best . . . the easiest thing to do would be to see him but . . . 'No, Roberto. I can't make this week. My father is away on business and I have to run the company. It means working late nights. Don't be too disappointed. I shall let you know when we can see each other.'

'I hope this isn't an excuse to stop me coming.'

'Don't be silly Roberto. I don't make excuses, you have to trust me.'

Poor Roberto, I thought. I didn't want to lie to him but he persisted and in persisting left me no room to move. So I made the room.

That afternoon Lisa phoned asking me if I could see her that evening for a chat. Even she I put off. I'd see her tomorrow night.

She finished, tantalisingly, 'I have something to tell you but it'd take too long to explain on the phone.' I still resisted temptation to see her immediately.

Back home I arrived exhausted, too tired even to cook. I collapsed into the sofa and fell asleep. You'd think a tired mind would have a rest from dreams, but no; it worked overtime with hundreds of different images and stories.

One dream stuck in my memory, of Valentino. He came to me adorned in his *Sheik* Arabic clothes and smiled at me. Every feeling I had for him intensified in this illusion, I could feel his charisma as a magnetic force pulling me towards him. I still saw him as I came round from sleep, leaving me happy and contented.

I got up and went into the kitchen, yet I still felt his presence. It was as if he had leapt from the dream into

real-life; or was it something else, this presence, something
real to account for the disturbances?

I could scarcely believe what was happening to me. I was
once, despite my obsession, a generally down-to-earth person. Now I was wondering irrationally whether Valentino
was here in my own home.

'Good morning.'

It was my grandfather on the phone.

'I'm glad I caught you because I have some good
news, Vilma.'

'Oh, tell . . .'

'I have found you a medium.'

'Oh, grandpa . . .'

'No, you should see her as we discussed. She's an
acquaintance of mine. Her name is Rosa and I'm going
to give you her address – she's just outside town, lives in
a charming little cottage by the river. I promise you she
won't disappoint you, she's really very good.'

'You have seen her?'

'Yes, why not? Even at 75 I have a future, you know!'

'Should I see her . . . ?'

'Valentino frequently consulted mediums.'

This piece of information persuaded me.

'I'll go then. Bless you, grandpa. OK, I'll see this Rosa,
but only when papa returns.'

'What's he up to?'

'It's secret but he's planning a partnership with another
company.'

'My lips are sealed. I suppose we shall see your father
sitting on a great mountain of chocolate. That should keep
him happy.'

In the evening I visited Lisa as promised. She had a

spacious living-room – and a spare bedroom which was often occupied, with her latest boyfriend or couples. She had a phonebook of friends.

I was hit by a wonderful aroma of cooking as I entered the flat.

'I've a beef casserole on the boil,' she said. 'You need feeding!'

'I can't remember the last time I cooked anything decent.'

'On your money you could hire a cook.'

That seemed a good idea until she started giggling.

She ladled the casserole with small potatoes onto a bed of cold salad – all to be washed down by a bottle of wine, or three. I had a suspicion that a good half bottle was already seething with the beef, judging by the intoxicating smells rising on the steam.

We sat and ate and it was like old times again. At some point I asked her what she had to tell me.

'I was going to wait till after our meal, but since you ask . . . it's to do with my boyfriend Mario.'

'Who's he? I can't keep up.'

'Oh really, Vilma. He was the one you saw me kissing at the De Vito's party.'

'I thought he was just a party kiss.'

'He's still with his girlfriend. They've been going out a long time. Obviously that's no good, he has to decide what he wants.'

'What an awful situation,' I said, thinking this was typical Lisa. 'You must be careful he doesn't use you.'

Lisa was well into the wine now. 'But he loves me.'

'Don't you think it's a bit unfair? His girlfriend won't be too pleased when she knows you're on the scene.'

Lisa finished her plate with a spoon. 'That's too bad,' she

said coldly. 'That's life. What's the point of him sticking with someone he doesn't love.'

'You don't know that for sure, Lisa.'

She gathered up our plates in a rush, evidently annoyed with me – 'Go on, Vilma, open that bottle you brought. We may as well have that as well.'

She returned from the sink with something else on her mind.

'You remember that guy you danced the tango with at the De Vito's?'

'But you didn't see us . . .'

'No, but I have spies, and everyone's been talking about your risqué tango! You dark horse Vilma.'

'Luca'

'That's him, Luca,' she slurred.

'Long legs – I thought they might get caught in my shoulder strap at one point in the dance.'

Lisa laughed loudly. 'Yes, he has legs like a giraffe – I know who he is. But look, he's not just got long legs. He's got a heart. He's been asking after you. You don't do badly for someone who always says no! So do you want to see him?'

'Not really.'

'Oh Vilma . . .'

'No wait. I don't want to see him because I'm seeing someone already.'

Lisa looked outraged. 'What? Who? You never told me. You tell me nothing.'

'Roberto. I mentioned him to you before.'

'You said you weren't interested.'

'I'm fond of him for the moment. I can't tell you how serious it is.'

We went into the kitchen to make coffee. As she ground the beans I said, 'Lisa, don't you feel guilty about Mario's girlfriend?'

She stopped grinding. 'Vilma, don't be so naive about life. Life is for the living – take it when it's offered and don't worry what others think.'

'I'm sorry, it's none of my business to preach at you. I don't know what I would do in your situation . . .'

Lisa looked at me with a new sweet expression. 'I know I'm not a very nice person, I can be very selfish. And if I love someone I'll fight, God forgive me.'

As she spoke my mind turned to Valentino. What would I not do to have him if he were in my life now, in the body. In an instant I understood Lisa and sympathised. She looked understandably surprised when I said, 'I wish you well with Mario. I hope you find happiness with him.'

Now she became pensive as we sipped our coffee. Perhaps the reality of what she was up against had hit her. She was not hard, despite her claim. But I knew she was always cursed in her choice of men, and always ended up hurt.

'What are you thinking, Lisa?'

'Nothing. I'm just tired.'

The next day I could resist it no more and phoned Rosa, the medium. No answer. I tried again and again, no luck. Later in the morning I phoned on impulse.

'*Pronto*. Yes? Who is it? What do you want?'

It was a thick, deep voice, tarred with nicotine by the sound of it.

'Is this Rosa?'

'I am she. What can I do for you?'

'I would like to make an appointment to see you.'

Suddenly the phone erupted with a ghastly coughing sound, as if someone's lungs were being torn out of them. After a breather, and without apology, she said, 'And is this by recommendation?'

'Yes. Someone you know well spoke highly of you.'

With that she became friendlier and we agreed to meet next Wednesday — I would have to take a day off work.

Back at the office my father had returned — extremely pleased with himself.

'I take it you had a happy time with Collini,' I said.

He was flushed, excited. 'It went so much better than I expected. He's a smart fellow. And he was greatly impressed with you, Vilma. He thinks you're a clever one.'

'I'm flattered. Just so long as he just has business on his mind.'

Papa looked oddly at me. 'What are you saying, Vilma? Did he make a pass at you?'

'I think I flattered his ego, a little . . .'

'You mean he tried it on with you — and he's married!'

'He tried his luck, papa, but I showed I can look after myself.'

'Now you're talking! I'm even more proud of you. I suppose I should have expected this would happen. Just how many attractive young women are in a business at your level? I must say Collini struck me as a man who's been around a bit — not a bad thing in a businessman.'

'He may have just been testing me . . .'

'Never mix business with pleasure, that's what I say.'

We both laughed as we embraced.

'Come over to dinner tonight, Vilma — tell me what you think of your mother.'

'Why, what's wrong?'

'Her smoking, she's always coughing. And now she has problems with her chest.'

'She was coughing a lot last time I saw her.'

'I doubt if she'll ever pack it in. You know she was smoking at 18?'

He reminded me to go to the showroom to select a new car 'so that Collini can see what we're made of'. I was relieved I hadn't had to ask for it, that it was offered. It made all the difference.

'Have you been thinking of me Vilma?'

It was Roberto on the phone.

'Of course.'

'Let's meet next week.'

'Sorry, Roberto, next week is out of the question. Something's come up – I'll let you know when I'm free.'

There was silence on the line. After a few moments I said, 'Hello, are you still there?'

At last he said, 'I don't know what to make of you, Vilma. I don't know where I stand with you. We never get anywhere. Why not be honest and tell me if there's any point in me calling you.'

Once again I wasn't sure what to say. I didn't want to stop seeing him, yet I always found an excuse for avoiding him.

After a second's hesitation I said. 'Let's meet the weekend after next. We can decide which day later.'

'Is that the soonest you can see me?'

'I can't postpone things.'

'OK. But we must talk honestly with each other.'

I groaned inwardly as I replaced the receiver.

I drove my new car to my parents' home the next day. Recklessly I had chosen the most expensive model and dreaded papa's reaction – I even had the bill for him in my bag.

I needn't have worried. He was over-joyed by my taste and style, knowing this newly acquired status symbol would help whittle down the company tax bill.

'Collini will be chasing you in his Rolls when he sees this,' shouted papa, passing his hand over the car's silver body as if it were a new pet. 'I wouldn't mind driving this myself!'

Mamma came out. 'Oh, a new toy, how wonderful. Make sure you drive this past the De Vito's. By next week they'll have bought the same model, mark my words.'

Despite my father's worries she looked pretty good to me. I grew annoyed when she lit up a cigarette.

'I know your father's been talking to you, Vilma. Don't waste your time. I shall smoke till I drop.'

'Fine, until you choke to death.'

'Charming! What a world we live in that a daughter can talk to her mother in this way. Still, with your big new sporty car I suppose I'll have to be grateful you deign to talk to me at all.'

She spun on her heel and marched back into the house as papa threw up his eyes.

We followed her and soon we were seated together in the verandah as papa left us to make phone calls.

'So any news for me, daughter dear?' And then she did an odd thing. She lit two cigarettes at once, put one in each hand, and proceeded to puff on them in turns, filling the room with smoke.

'Oh mamma! And you call me infantile!'

I opened the window, and she extinguished one of the cigarettes, laughing. 'That's to teach you a lesson, Vilma. Do not concern yourself with my personal habits. For every complaint about my cigarettes I will smoke an extra one each day. You and your father have been warned. Now give me some gossip. I'm running out.'

How I wished mamma could be different. If only she did charity work or something she'd be less interested in petty goings-on.

'I've nothing to report. No one is sleeping with anyone and no one is about to die. Everyone is behaving themselves. The newspapers could go out of business if people continue to behave themselves in this way.'

Mamma pursed her lips in disapproval. 'What a spoilsport you are – like your father. He wouldn't know a scandal if he tripped over it in the garden. Have you seen your grandfather?'

'Yes.' I told her he didn't strike me as unwell at all.

'I made that up just to get you there.'

'Oh mamma!'

'Any of his lady friends there?'

'No,' I said sharply. 'Why do you always run him down? You should show him more respect.'

'Oh really,' she said, cross. 'How can I respect him after the way he treated my mother? I will never forget it. I know you're very fond of the old man. But then he tells you what you want to hear.'

This, I guessed, was a hint at my Valentino obsession. Now I was annoyed. 'I don't know what you mean by that, mamma. Grandpa is not like that.'

At that moment my father re-entered the room, interrupting us.

'I've just been talking to Collini. We are to hold a party to celebrate our partnership.'

'At last!' said mamma. 'Something I can look forward to.'

'The party will be at the Collini's – at the end of the month, two weeks today to be precise.'

'That's a new wardrobe for me then,' mamma said. 'At last I shall meet this Collini and his wife—'

'To create mischief,' I said lightly. 'You should be careful – he might try to seduce you.'

'At my age?'

'You're well preserved.'

'Oh thank you. You make me sound like something at the butchers.'

As we laughed and planned, I heard a car draw up on the drive. I rushed to the window – it was Lisa, looking miserable.

'She's tracked you down.' said mamma. 'More men problems, I suppose. Tell me later, Vilma.'

I met Lisa at the door and gave her a hug.

'Your neighbour said you'd be here,' she said.

'You've a new car – like me,' I said. 'You never said you were getting a new car.'

'It not mine – I had to borrow it. Mine's broken down. But look at yours. God, it must have cost a fortune.'

'We'll drive to my flat in it.'

She brightened a little. 'I need wine,' she said as I turned the ignition key.

'That bad?'

'Worse.'

'Why do I think this is to do with Mario?'

'Because you're psychic? You're right. I've been such a fool. His girlfriend went berserk when she heard about me. She even took an overdose – she's all right, but Mario was shocked, he's decided to stay with her. Now he's told me we shouldn't see each other again.'

At the flat I threw my keys onto the table and opened a bottle of white wine.

'I am truly sorry, Lisa, but there'll be someone else. Try to forget about him.'

'I can't imagine it.' She took her first sip. 'I don't believe anyone can make me happy.'

'What would you have done in Mario's place?'

'I know I would have fought a lot harder if I loved someone. I wouldn't have given up because someone threatens suicide.'

I pulled paper tissues from the box as she began to weep. 'Come on now, look, I have an idea. Stay here tonight, and in the morning you may not feel so bad. Also, show Mario you're stronger than he is – you won't be allowed to contact him here!'

She wiped her tears – 'You're a true friend, Vilma. I'll stay.'

She was still sound asleep as I made coffee the next morning. Eventually she rose, bleary-eyed.

'It took me ages to get off,' she yawned.

'You've still time for breakfast – how do you feel?'

I could tell she felt as rough as she looked. Then I had a mad idea.

'Friday's my day off,' I said, 'Why don't we go for a cycle ride in the country – the way we used to. You need fresh air. It'll get you out of yourself. I need to get out, too.'

She sighed – 'I'll get back to you on that.'

Later she phoned me at work to say she could get Friday off.

Our hair played on the warm breeze as we sped down hills on hired bicycles. We screamed and laughed, pretending to be free again, free of work, duty, men. We travelled past farmlands tall with wheat, along arcades of overhanging trees, and wobbled around ruts in the lanes. Childhood returned so easily amid the timeless wild – or what seemed wild.

I rediscovered muscles I'd forgotten about as I tried to ignore the growing ache in my legs. I promised to myself that I would do this more often – a resolution I knew I wouldn't keep.

Lisa's occasional silences told me of her pain and disappointment. She wore decorous trousers, while I'd opted unwisely for a fly-way skirt which billowed far above my knees as we rode through a village. Hens scattered every which way as a cock crowed in a nearby barn. Windows were battened against the sun, a narrow stream alongside the road added a constant note.

'Signorina!'

We both turned

'*Mi piace le sue mutante bianche*,' – I like your white knickers.

A young man sitting on an ancient stone wall waved and laughed at us, but his comment was clearly directed at me.

So I cried back, '*Mettati la corda al collo stupido*,' – Hang yourself, stupid.

'Ignore him, Vilma,' said Lisa. 'He's just a village oik. It's not like you to get worked up over such a silly thing.'

'He was rude,' I said. 'Why shouldn't we be able to cycle freely without abuse.'

As we rode from the village two young men followed us on bikes.

'They have something in mind,' I said to Lisa.

'They're just students,' she replied.

But I wasn't convinced – though like travelling students, they had huge bags on their backs.

At a river we stopped to rest – as did our two new admirers who placed their bags on the ground. We rested our bikes against the tree and settled on the green bank.

'Signorina, I hope you don't mind, may we sit near you?'

said one of the lads as the other propped their bikes against another tree.

'My name is Giorgio and my friend's Ernesto – we could do with some company, especially ladies as beautiful as you.'

He was a handsome youth, no more than 18 I guessed, with very dark features. His friend was fairer skinned and taller.

Lisa threw me a glance, and said playfully to him, 'It's a free country but there's plenty of space for you to rest elsewhere. The air gets stuffy if you sit too close together, like a bunch of bananas.'

To my amazement I felt an arm about my waist. It was Ernesto (not so earnest!) who had somehow slipped behind us, and was now sitting right up against me. He moved forward to kiss me. At the same time, Giorgio moved in on Lisa. She jumped up and ran – with him in pursuit.

A great rage gave me strength. I threw my arm blindly behind me, my hand catching Ernesto flat on the ear. He roared with pain and rolled away from me. I shot up and ran to Lisa's aid who had been brought to the ground by Giorgio. I kicked him in the behind with a tremendous swing. It was such a powerful strike that he bowled over on his side. Lisa got to her feet and with perfect aim kicked him between the legs. He howled with pain and gripped his crotch with both hands.

We screamed and laughed as we ran to our bikes, leaving the two wimps whining like beaten dogs.

We rode hard for a good mile, fearing that they might come after us. But I knew they wouldn't dare.

At another village we stopped to rest.

'We should have killed those rapists,' said Lisa.

'Then we could have thrown them in the river as a service to all women,' I replied.

We noticed a public house and soon we were seated outside with wine, bread and cheese. Somehow the incident with the two lads had lightened Lisa's mood – perhaps that kick she gave Giorgio had also been intended for Mario.

Afterwards we resumed our travels and later stopped at yet another tiny village.

We entered its church. A vague but familiar incense lingered in the cool air. I suddenly thought of the medium Rosa for a moment, wondering what the priest here would think of me visiting such a woman. Candle flame danced before a picture of the Madonna and child. It felt like a blessing to have found this simple sanctuary.

Lisa knelt down to pray in the pews. I hoped she was not wasting her time beseeching Jesus to send her Mario. I didn't ask about her prayers as we rode back, happy, energised, exhausted.

After a refreshing shower back at my flat I sipped wine and played gentle music. To my annoyance the phone rang as I towelled my hair.

'Pronto.'

'Guess who?'

'Who's this?'

'Dum-de-dum!'

'Who is it?'

'Hee hee hee.'

'Whoever this is, have you nothing better to do.' I hung-up. A moment later the phone rang again. I was about to launch into a tirade when the caller said, 'It's Ruggero – you didn't recognise my voice. Not a good start now that we're partners.'

'Oh Ruggero.' Had I said anything offensive? – I quickly racked my mind.

'I was having a shower.'

'Oh – should I come round and dry you?'

'That won't be necessary Ruggero – but I am pleased Collini's and Bertolini's are in business.'

'*Mia cara*, Vilma, I would like to see you, but not to discuss business. Mostly for pleasure. You are the most intriguing woman I have ever met.'

Casanova has such self-belief, I thought to myself. Time to act swiftly I decided.

I said sternly, 'Signor Collini, It is strictly business between us. But if you persist in making calls of this sort I shall have no choice but to tell my father.'

'No need for that,' he said quickly. 'We don't want to do anything that spoils our business association.'

'I'm glad we are in agreement on that.'

As I replaced the phone I remembered fleetingly that I had not confirmed a day to see Roberto.

My appointment with the clairvoyant Rosa soon arrived. I thought twice about going but then curiosity got the better of me.

She lived in an old farm cottage outside the town. For a moment I wondered whether this was the right place. Then I heard a hacking cough from within – reminding me of her seizure on the phone. Chickens clucked in a back garden.

House and door could have done with a lick of paint, yet the best preserved part of it was the door knocker, a gold lion's head, which gleamed in the bright light – I actually used it as a mirror to check my hair before I took hold of it.

After some delay, the door opened. I was surprised. I had half expected an old woman. Rosa was only in her mid-forties, I guessed.

'Come in Signorina.'

'Do call me Vilma.'

She led me to a small sitting-room at the back of the cottage full of surprisingly orthodox religious icons – crosses, triptyches, paintings and healing objects, such as a phial of water from Lourdes. Everything gleamed like the knocker outside and smelt of polish mixed with a curious incense I failed to identify.

She indicated where I should sit. 'Have you had a consultation before, Vilma?'

'No, this is my first time.'

'Very well. Now I can only tell you what I get so it's pointless asking me questions about what I give you. The spirit will only give you so much information. You must make all your own decisions in life. Now, do you have an object I can hold? This will help me establish a link with the other side.'

My grandfather had told to bring something I wear often. I took off my watch and placed it in her hand. She closed her eyes and stroked the watch with her fingers, gently toying with it. I suddenly felt a little apprehensive, unsure of what to do.

'Yes,' she said to herself, her eyes still shut, 'you are in some sort of business, aren't you?'

'Yes,' I replied gently.

'I feel a wealthy and powerful man, yes, it's a warning from your spirit friends. Be careful of this man.'

I thought of Ruggero immediately.

. . . 'There is some business connection with him . . . you are not happy in your life, are you. It's as if some past influence holds you, a man, and he is here now, standing behind you . . . is he a boyfriend or husband who passed over, dear?'

I shivered. 'No, I'm not sure who you mean.'

. . . 'Mmm, a young man. he passed over young, he

229

knows you certainly, they come to me at the age they died. He tells me you must live your life and if you get on with it you'll make him very happy . . . strange, I see film cameras around him, did he work in a cinema, dear?'

I breathed deeply hardly able to control myself or speak.

'I need to hear your voice to keep the contact. Do you know this man?'

'I'm not sure who he is,' I said.

'Pity, because he knows all about you. I can't see his face, I just know he's here, he's very close. Don't you ever feel him in your home? Have you not seen him?'

It was too fantastic to think that Valentino had appeared before this medium to talk to me. I didn't know what to think. I prayed that my grandfather had not told her anything.

She went onto say many other things of a very private nature, things which proved to me that there was something in this clairvoyance.

She finished by saying, 'Ah, your spirit man, he is sad you do not acknowledge him. But he says your life will change in a most unexpected way, quite soon. But will you let go of the past? Only you can decide.'

Rosa opened her eyes. 'Ooooh, that was a powerful presence, he didn't want to go,' she said.

'I'm astonished by what you've told me.'

'All from the spirit, my dear. I'm just the vehicle.' She handed back the watch.

'May I ask you something? It's why I came.'

'You can ask.'

'There have been strange disturbances in my flat. Noises, whisperings. At one point I couldn't sleep.'

'Nothing to worry about. It's your spirit friend. It's his way of saying "wake up!"'

'How can you be so sure?'

'I know these things. When a spirit comes that close as this one did today, they're bound to make themselves known to you sooner or later. Just acknowledge him next time and he will go away.'

'Can you hear these spirits?'

'Oh yes, chatterboxes all of them. Of course, it helps if sitters acknowledge the spirit! Still, you must have your reasons . . .'

'I wasn't sure, Rosa.'

'Oh I think you were, Vilma. And before he left he revealed himself to me . . .'

'Who?'

'But I promised not to name him!'

'You should have said yes when Rosa asked if you recognised the spirit entity,' my grandfather said on the phone.

'Oh grandpa, it's too ridiculous. Why would Valentino come to a simple seance for me?'

'Why not? He was only a man, after all. Not some god. And what he said to you makes perfect sense. Do you feel better for having seen Rosa?

'Yes, definitely, It's opened my mind. I feel so much better. Thank you grandpa.'

'Don't mention it.'

The moment I put down the phone Lisa called to talk about our country adventure again.

'And have you heard from Mario?' I asked.

'Yes, much to my surprise.'

'Yes . . . ?'

'You won't believe it but he said he wasn't happy with his girlfriend and that he missed me.'

'So you'll take him back?'

For a change she was struck by commonsense. She said,

'He needs to sort himself out. If he wants me he must free himself of her so that we can start again.'

'Stick to that, Lisa.'

The weekend of Roberto's visit was upon me. On the Friday he'd asked if he could come round at six next morning for a cuddle and breakfast in bed. Naturally I said no to that so he came later and we drove out into the country.

At a layby he stopped the car and rested his chin on the wheel.

'Can you guess why we've stopped here?' he said.

'You want to attack me?' I joked.

But he didn't laugh. 'We have to talk. We have to decide where we go from here.'

'I don't know. I know I like you very much but I need time to think this over.'

Nothing I said pleased him. He wanted me to love him. After a long pause he said, 'I'll be straight with you. I have tried to get you out of my mind many times but I just can't. I'm so miserable – you need to tell me what the problem is, why you can't decide one way or the other about me.'

It could simply be that I didn't love him. But there was also the question of my Valentino obsession. Perhaps it was that which prevented me from loving Roberto.

'There is something you need to know about me,' I said finally. 'This is hard to say, and you must not laugh, because there is no easy way to say it . . .'

Roberto's face had lightened with curiosity. For a moment he didn't have to feel sorry for himself.

'From a very early age I have had an obsession with Valentino. So now you know.'

'Valentino? Do I know Valentino?'

'Rudolph Valentino.'

232

'What, the actor?'

'Yes.'

'But . . . what do you mean "obsession"?'

'I'm obsessed with him. He is the man I love.'

Roberto screwed his face in disbelief. Perhaps he had prepared himself for all sorts of explanations, but not this one.

'At your age . . . but this is a schoolgirl crush . . .'

'It started that way and has never left me.'

'Have you seen a doctor?'

I was indignant. 'I'm not ill!'

'No, no . . .' He put his arm around me. 'But he's dead, isn't he? Long dead. How can he . . . ?'

'I've given you the reason why I can't love you Roberto. Few can understand me . . .'

He held me tighter. '*Mio amore*, I expected something a lot worse than that . . . I mean, you're not the first to be in awe of someone out of reach, I can understand that, but you can't allow this to ruin your life . . .'

'I'm only just starting to talk about it . . .'

'I will help you overcome this.'

I was tempted to tell him about my visit to Rosa but decided he'd suffered enough for one day.

We drove back to my flat and I cooked supper. I had thought to slip away to the bedroom and remove the Valentino picture from the bedside table, but the impulse to do that left me. That pleased me.

We drank too much wine and held each other on the sofa, talking about everything and nothing and at one point we dozed off. I stirred when I felt my hair being stroked . . . 'Oh, Roberto, that's nice . . .' I opened my eyes to find him still asleep.

I slipped out of his arms to have a shower. As I turned the tap off I heard Roberto calling me. I made a toga around my body with a huge white towel and returned to him. He'd helped himself to the scotch, usually kept for digestive or emotional emergencies. He was shaking and troubled.

'What's wrong, Roberto?'

He gulped his drink. 'Something very odd has just happened.'

'What?' I sat next to him. He was cold to my touch.

'I went into your bedroom. Maybe it was the wine, but I looked up at one of your Valentino pictures and jokingly said to it "let Vilma go". At that moment I swear I felt a hand grab mine, it was so real. I was so shocked that I kicked out at your bedside table in panic and his picture fell to the floor. Then I ran out. I don't think I can go in there again, Vilma. Your flat is haunted by something.'

I was astonished and relieved all at once. So I hadn't imagined the disturbances. But Roberto was deeply affected and upset.

'Come, Roberto. You're still alive. Odd things have happened to me but I'm still in one piece. Whatever it is, it's harmless.'

He looked at me almost accusingly. 'How can you be so calm? How can you take this so casually? I don't understand you Vilma?'

'Now don't be like a child and come with me to the bedroom. I'll show you there's nothing to fear.'

It took some persuasion. In bed Robert still trembled and was quiet. I felt his fear and tried to fight my own disappointment in him. He didn't even try to make love to me that night.

Sunday morning he announced that he wanted to leave. I wasn't surprised. He made some excuse about having to attend to some business at his new company. Then he added:

'I want to see you again, Vilma, but not in this flat. I want you to move out.'

'Really. I shan't be moving out Roberto—'

'I know what happened to me last night and I'm not going to try to forget it. Are you involved in witchcraft? Even this Valentino obsession of yours seems sinister to me now.'

I raised my eyebrows in mockery . . . 'And to think I thought you a sophisticated worldly man, Roberto. Next you'll be accusing me of casting spells!'

'You certainly cast a spell on me.'

Mischievously I turned to a picture of Valentino on the wall and said, 'Well done my love. You have saved me.'

Roberto got up to leave. 'Now you're mocking me! Despite this I still love you Vilma. I just wish you would be . . . normal.'

I opened the door for him. I felt cool, detached. 'Goodbye Roberto. I'm sorry I'm not normal enough for you. I shall not be selling the flat. And I shall not remove Valentino from my life. So that's it.'

It was over between us.

His very fragile love had evaporated in fear.

I phoned Lisa to tell her all about Roberto.

'You a witch!' she laughed

'Hubble and bubble, toil and trouble . . .'

'Tonight we shall catch a toad . . .'

'And an old woman's wart . . .'

'And abduct a kitty cat . . .'

'Then fly on our broomsticks.'

'Well, I think Valentino has done you a favour, Vilma. Roberto's obviously not for you.'

'He took the news of Valentino rather well, it was the experience in the bedroom that got to him.'

'He was just humouring you over Valentino. Maybe privately he thought you were a bit nutty but could cure you.'

'Oh thank you, Lisa. Now I'm nuts.'

'You know what I mean. But what about his experience? Was it a ghost? There is something going on in that flat of yours.'

I told her of my visit to Rosa.

'Well, Vilma, it's as well I know you. I don't know what to think. Maybe I should see this medium myself. So do you want to see Roberto again?'

'No. What's the point? In any case he's gutless and weak-minded.'

'You're so harsh, Vilma. Not many men could cope with the ghost of Valentino!'

'No, but maybe this ghost has my best interests at heart.'

'Oh, Vilma!'

'Do I have to attend the Collini party?' I asked my father.

He looked at me surprised. 'It's not fatal if you don't but it would be impolite not to. This party is symbolically important – there will be potential buyers there, it'll be good for you, Vilma. You can deal with Collini.'

I decided not to tell him about Collini's recent call to me – the last thing I wanted to do was imperil our new association.

A new awareness took hold of me at this moment, that one day I might not be working with my father. I might move on, I might marry . . . something so simple and obvious had not occurred to me as a reality before now. It left me feeling vulnerable and slightly sad . . . about the inevitable.

I left my father in the kitchen and joined my mother in her bedroom. Dozens of frocks were hanging from all parts of the room, even from the curtain rail.

'Oh Mamma . . .'

'I can't go to the Collini's dressed in anything. I'm putting up my dresses to see if they still look right. I'm imagining I'm at the party and these dresses are my guests. And I'm deciding what I think of each guest. That ghastly flowery guest can leave . . .' She grabbed the dress and put it back in the wardrobe. 'Look at that awful glitter job.' That joined the flowery job. 'Do you think I should buy a new cocktail dress?'

'With all these dresses to choose from. Come on, mamma.'

'What are you wearing?'

'I haven't thought about it.'

For the party we hired a limousine and were driven all the way to Milan, arriving about midday.

'A beautiful house,' mamma said as the Collini residence came into view. 'Ours should be that big.'

'Listen to her,' said papa.

Young men in white and gilt edged livery met us at the gates and parked the car as we were led to Signora Collini and Ruggero who stood together at the front door to greet guests.

'Ah beautiful Vilma,' he said before kissing me on both cheeks . . . 'and this is your equally beautiful mother?'

'Signor Collini. Call me Rosaria,' she said, holding out her hand to be kissed in the old-fashioned way.

Ruggero's wife Lina gave us all a wintry smile before uttering, 'The servants will take you to your rooms. I hope you like them.'

Ruggero placed his hand gently behind my back as he

escorted me into the house. 'I am looking forward to dancing with you again, Vilma.'

'Yes, I said, but mind you remember you'll be dancing with one of your business partners.'

He pulled a face and fell quiet.

My parents' bedroom was done out in eccentric English Regency while I was given what looked like an oversized creche, complete with spooky dolls standing guard on every surface.

Later I joined Ruggero in the conservatory downstairs.

'This is my favourite room,' he said as he handed me a cool spritzer.

'Thanks. Have you seen my parents? I've lost them.'

'They're with my wife. She's giving them the tour of the house and gardens – your mother insisted on it.'

I looked at him squarely, 'You will have to behave yourself, Ruggero. No hanky-panky.'

He laughed long at that, revealing a well-preserved set of white teeth set off by his dark complexion.

'Expensive choppers, I see.'

He laughed afresh – 'Stop it. Everything you say amuses me – even when you cruelly reject me. Are women today so frank?'

'Women have learned to keep men on their toes . . .'

'I'll show you, Vilma, I'm not as bad as you think. I'm no worse than the next man, I have my faults . . . Now let's change the subject. I'll show you the garden.'

We wandered out onto the terrace and walked towards the orchard. Manicured lawns unrolled into the distance. I stopped at a young tree and shook it for no reason at all. A single apple fell, bouncing off Ruggero's head.

'Now you assault me. What am I to do with you?'

Back in the house, servants were carrying bouquets

upstairs and making beautiful flower arrangements in various rooms. More people had collected in groups here and there, and Ruggero made introductions, often to people I knew already.

As I crossed the drawing room for water I noticed I was being observed by a man. He was not especially handsome but something in his countenance interested me, he was heavily built but not overweight, and dressed already in an evening suit even though it was still afternoon. His most attractive feature were his deep brown eyes which held mine a little longer than strangers usually allow.

'Ah,' said Ruggero, almost pouncing on me, 'I see you have a new admirer . . .'

'Riccardo,' he said to the stranger, 'come and meet Vilma.'

He seemed momentarily embarrassed by Ruggero's lack of tact but stepped forward, still gazing at me with a tentative smile.

'Vilma, meet Riccardo Righieri. Riccardo meet Vilma Bertolini, who is now my business partner.'

We shook hands. 'Hello,' he said.

'You're staring at me,' I said lightly.

Ruggero thankfully was distracted by new people waving at him across the room.

'I was wondering,' he started, 'if you're alone.'

'Why, are you?'

'Yes, yes . . .'

'I'm with my parents actually . . .'

'Oh, I see . . .'

I was instantly attracted to him, amused by his gentle hesitancy. But something in his gaze hinted at a bold nature. I decided to be bold as well to see what would happen.

'So, you're alone – a handsome man on his own. You should watch yourself.'

He smiled broadly. 'I'm a widower, of two years. I've got used to being alone . . .'

'I'm sorry . . .'

'No, it happened . . . and you, why should a beautiful young woman be on her own?'

I suppose I'd asked for that. We exchanged smiles, uncertain as to what to say next . . .

'You couldn't have been alone for two years,' I said.

He replied he'd had casual girlfriends, nothing special. He hadn't looked for a serious relationship.

'And how do you know Ruggero?' I asked.

'Business. He's a rogue, but a trustworthy rogue, if there's such a thing.'

Yes, that was correct, a trustworthy rogue.

'I hope we can talk more,' he added.

Over his shoulder I caught my parents observing us, my mother giving me a wink.

The room was now quite full, many of the guests here only for drinks, not planning to attend the dinner. Another man came over to Riccardo and held him in conversation as my attention drifted here and there. At one point I spotted a familiar pair of very long legs – Luca's legs, the man I'd danced with at the De Vito's. Before I could make an escape he saw me—

'Signorina! How good to see you again,' he said in a great rush, almost stepping over people like a great ostrich. We must do the tango again—'

'Oh Luca,' I cried, giving him my most false smile, 'we'll have to see. Perhaps they don't play tango music here.'

'A friend of yours?' said Riccardo, free again.

'A dancing partner – we tangoed once and he's never got over it.'

'Do you usually have this effect on men?'

240

'Of course!'

A servant announced that dinner would be served within the hour, giving time to dinner guests to go to their rooms and change.

'You're dressed already,' I said to Riccardo.

'I shall wait for you down here,' he smiled.

I walked rapidly to the staircase where I found my mother blowing cigarette smoke in Lina Collini's face.

'*Mia cara,*' mamma said turning to me as I passed. 'Who's that attractive man you've been monopolising?'

'His name is Riccardo, mamma.'

'A very good man,' said Lina, almost as if I were not worthy of him.

'He's a widower I understand,' I said.

'Yes, though his marriage wasn't entirely happy.'

Unpleasantly, this news satisfied me. As I dressed, my thoughts were totally preoccupied with Riccardo. I was appalled with myself because I knew I had fallen for him.

My parents and I descended the stairs in a queue of ruche, brocade, feathers and bowties. I wore a strapless green silk dress leaving my shoulders bare while my mother, for a change, was dressed chicly and simply in a full-length silk white sheath. She looked beautiful and young.

All the guests congregated in the drawing room for aperitifs. The word was out that the Collinis were about to give us a surprise.

'What is this surprise, Luca?' I asked as he squeezed by me.

'The Collinis – anything's possible. Crazy.'

Moments later some in the crowd began to clap while others laughed. I gazed up at the top of the staircase, on which everyone else was focused, and there stood a proud

Caesar and Cleopatra in all their glory, Ruggero and his dreadful wife in fancy dress.

He was swaddled in a toga edged with the emperor's purple. A laurel-leaf crown decorated his head and a sword hung from his waist. He even wore a bald wig with a few ironed curls at the back and the sides of the head. At one point he turned around to reveal a variety of daggers sticking out of his back.

Lina's Cleopatra had adorned a black wig, with its curious half-mast even fringe, upon which sat a crown topped with a cobra's head at the front. Her eyes were heavily kohled into great black almonds while a short metal dress fell from her girdle. How my mother laughed.

The historical pair walked slowly down the stairs, with Cleopatra waving her sphinx-head sceptre at us, as everyone cheered and applauded.

'Why appear in fancy dress?' asked my mother to no one in particular.

'They do it at all their parties,' said Luca. 'Each time they appear as a different couple from history. One year it was Hitler and Eva Braun.'

'What have you got involved with?' my mother said to papa. He shrugged his shoulders and finished his drink.

When the party had calmed down we filed through to the dining room.

The table, with fabulous bouquets staggered along its length, was laid for eighty, with Caesar and Cleo at either end. I was seated to Ceasar's left, my father to his right with mother to Cleopatra's left.

Caesar stood with champagne in one hand – 'Ladies and gentlemen, friends, countrymen, Romans, raise your glasses please – quiet if you please! – to a new marriage – the marriage of Orlando Bertolini and Ruggero Collini, the only time you'll ever hear of two men marrying!'

The table erupted in laughter as heads shook at Ruggero's devilment . . .

'Seriously, ladies and gentleman, a toast to the partnership between Collini's and Bertolini's, both makers of the finest chocolate in all Europe!'

Everyone raised their glasses and sipped . . .

'And,' he added, 'a special toast to Vilma Bertolini – Orlando's gifted daughter whose favourite word is "business".'

I laughed along with that but was irritated by his little dig.

I had to endure 'digs' of another sort during the course of the dinner. Ruggero so positioned himself that his sword (incongruous with the toga) constantly chafed against my leg.

'Ruggero,' I whispered, 'stop it.'

'What?'

'Remove your sword – you know why.'

'But I can't, *mia cara*. Do you know what I'd like to do to you now? Put you over my knee and spank you.'

'You're the one who needs spanking, Ruggero,' I said nibbling prusciutto.

'I'd like to undress you and love you to death.'

I giggled at his banalities. 'More likely you'd drop dead afterwards, Ruggero.' Thank God my father couldn't hear all this.

After the dessert Julius Caesar stood up and gave a boring speech on how he had founded his Chocolate Empire and how children must be encouraged to eat chocolate. My father had often told me that this was the wrong approach – targeting children. We should aim at all ages with the 'happiness food' (which is what he called chocolate) – my father glanced at me and raised his eyebrows in disapproval at our host.

With relief all around, music signalled the next stage in the party. A brief attempt by Ruggero to dance the tango with me came to an abrupt end when he tripped over his toga to reveal his white underpants. He covered his embarrassment with laughter, giving me a good excuse to try a getaway. But he grabbed hold of me – 'Don't leave me Vilma. You are the sexiest thing here and you excite me.'

I pulled his hand off me (whereas I would have hit him in other circumstances) and shouted above the music, 'I don't think Julius Caesar wore white underpants, Ruggero.'

'Oh, don't mock me . . .'

'Caesar's gear is not right for the tango.'

'Dance with me – there's a waltz next.'

I slipped away to my mother who was talking with Lina Collini.

'Vilma,' Lina said, 'What a gifted dancer you are. It takes great skill to trip up Caesar.'

'He did it all by himself.'

'You should be proud, Lina, that Ruggero was wearing clean underwear,' shouted my mother.

Lina must have been tipsy because she replied, 'He changes his pants twice a day – for good reason!'

Mamma and I exchanged glances . . .

'Vilma . . .'

I turned around. It was Riccardo. 'May I have this dance?'

I didn't have to think twice and in an instant he had wrapped one arm around my waist and swept me into the dance. He was a perfect mover, sensual and light, not ruining the moment with talk – unlike Roberto who would have smothered me with compliments and demands by now.

As he held and let me go to the rhythm, I sensed his

own independence and strength, a kind of detachment I found enticing . . .

'I think I need a drink,' I cried.

'Champagne.'

'If there's any left.'

'I'm sure Ruggero has a natural well of champagne in his gardens.'

He returned with a bottle and two glasses. We strolled out into the gardens and sat under a tree. For ages we did not talk, just stared up at the sky, sipped our drinks, listened to each other catch our breath. I had never felt happier.

In the darkness his hand gently turned me to him and I felt his soft lips on mine, first tender, then passionate, pressing against me as if he had a lifetime's worth of kisses to give me. I sensed no resistance in me, no reason to stop.

'I won't apologise,' he murmured in my ear.

'For what?'

'For this.'

'Then I should apologise.'

'For what?'

'For lying under a tree with you.'

He kissed my neck – 'More champagne?'

'I don't think I can drink anymore.'

'I'll get another bottle . . .'

And he was off.

My head was spinning. I could hear couples running and giggling around trees nearby, and the odd groan. I had visions of a Roman orgy in Ruggero's orchard.

I got up imagining Riccardo had been away for hours. 'Where's my Riccardo?' I was muttering to myself. The house lights were my beacon back to civilisation.

I barely had got into the house and I felt myself grabbed by some strange creature (an octopus?) which deposited on the dance floor. My body must have a mind of its own because it moved to the music without any help from me. At some point I recognised the octopus as long-legged Luca – he seemed to have so many legs now, whirling all over the place, all eight of them coiling and uncoiling about me, the dancing octopus – how did he grow so many legs?

'Get away from me!' I suddenly screamed drunkenly, alarmed at the sight of hallucinated legs. 'How dare you!'

'It's only me – you've had too much to drink.'

I held my head. Drunk or not I was grabbed again as the tango started up. Luca had reclaimed me. To my astonishment I threw up my skirt and shook my body with total abandon, like some crazed gypsy around a camp fire. Luca held me by the waist and swung me into the air, I seemed to soar towards the stars, before falling within inches of the floor. I had no idea, in my head, what I was doing; I was only aware of sensations, music, extremes . . . and legs!

When the music stopped the crowd which now encircled us broke out in rapturous applause. I had little sense of what had happened, but I registered the astonished expressions on people's faces – people who perhaps only knew me as a straitlaced daddy's girl who worked all hours.

The octopus tried once more to draw me into another dance. This time I said no emphatically. Sobriety was beginning to break through. I remembered with a sudden jolt what this party was really for.

Ruggero came up to me, his laurel-leaf crown resting off one ear, 'Vilma, you were fantastic! I will pay you twenty million lire to dance for me privately like Salome. You erotic devil.'

'I don't do private shows,' I said sweetly.

Luca took Ruggero's place . . . 'I do apologise Signorina for grabbing you like that.'

'I forgive you. Where's the rest of your legs?' He only had two now.

A strong pair of hands grabbed my arm and pulled me towards the garden. I daren't look to see who it was. Of course I knew it was Riccardo.

He had already lain a blanket under our tree. He was angry with me . . .

'I went to get another bottle of champagne and then you disappeared to make an exhibition of yourself with that cretin Luca.'

'I did not make an exhibition of myself, I just enjoyed myself.'

'You danced brilliantly . . .'

'Thank you.'

'People won't think of you the same way after that performance.'

'What do you mean by that?'

'You will appear easy from now on.'

'Easy?' I repeated furiously. 'I didn't realise you were some sad little small-minded peasant. Go to hell! Come back to me when you've lived a bit and expanded your mind, you dried up priest.'

I ran back into the house almost screaming with disappointment. Fury had sobered me up. I was back in control.

The party was quieter now, subdued. I sat on the conservatory step watching couples melt into each other as a lonesome trombone made them liquid – at least that was the impression. Had drink made Riccardo speak so foolishly? I couldn't believe I had misjudged someone so badly.

Ruggero sat beside me. '*Mia cara*, what are you doing here alone?'

'Recovering my reputation,' I said drily.

'You are the star of the party. Have you enjoyed it?'

'I was till you sat next to me.'

At last he was offended. 'Why are you so unpleasant to me?' I said nothing. 'And where is that lover boy Riccardo?'

'You'll find him buried under one of your apple trees, Ruggero. You should have a good crop next year. He'll make a good compost.'

'You'll find me a better lover, you know.'

'I'm just a challenge to you, Ruggero,' I said. 'Business before pleasure, Ruggero. There are plenty of women you can pay for what you're looking for.'

Ruggero silently walked away – I knew I had taken my anger out on him. But he had it coming.

I walked back into the warmth of the house. My parents were seated together in the drawing room.

'What is this?' my mother said, 'why aren't you outside making a fool of yourself like any decent woman at your age?'

'And who taught you to dance like that?' asked papa. 'Everyone asked me afterwards. I've met two new potential customers because of you Vilma.'

My mother said, 'I thought you were with that Riccardo. Run off already?'

'He couldn't cope with my dancing. He thinks I'm a woman of the night now.'

My mother laughed. 'He's been watching too much opera.'

'Don't worry, Vilma,' added papa, 'he'll be back after you, if I'm a judge of these things. He's just a bit jealous like I was when your mother danced.'

'I never knew that,' I said.

'Oh, yes,' said mamma, 'he'd get furious with me.'

'I dreaded parties,' he said, 'I dreaded your mother parading herself on the dance floor. Fortunately she took no

248

notice of me. The tango takes great skill. Your Valentino was the greatest dancer I've ever seen – yes, I don't mind saying it. Your mother was brilliant, even if all the men only watched her to catch a glimpse of her knickers.'

We laughed and I sat between them, proud of and amazed by my parents.

'But you both never told me these things. Why wait now?'

Mother lit a cigarette. 'This is all history, ancient history, like Lina's costume. I'd completely forgotten.'

'You had not, mamma. You just hate nostalgia. I know you.'

She smiled, 'Maybe there's something in that. But enough of all that. What about Riccardo? That was your other surprise tonight. I think he has the intelligence to say sorry. And what about Roberto?'

'That's all over. Roberto's not what he seems.'

'No one is darling.'

Papa left us to talk with Ruggero.

'I've a lot to tell you about Roberto but I didn't want papa to know.'

'That's all right. We'll talk another time.'

I wandered back into the garden. A couple danced silently on the lawn. Drunks slept or brooded against the trees. I felt sorry for the gardener. He'd have a lot of clearing up to do in the morning.

I made my way in. It was time to call it a night. I had barely mounted the stairs and I felt a now familiar hand on my shoulders. Not Ruggero's grip, nor Luca's.

'Riccardo! You frightened me.'

He looked intense and tired.

'I didn't mean to scare you. I want to apologise for the silly things I said. What I didn't say was how much

I enjoyed your dance — I just got upset when I saw the way Ruggero looked at you.'

I smiled, 'Well, you've changed your tune. Ruggero looks at all women that way. We're in business remember — I know how to deal with him . . .'

'I must see you tomorrow.'

'You're sure? I'll give you a call.'

He took out his wallet and gave me his card.

I rose late and happy next morning. To my surprise I had no hangover.

The garden was indeed a mess as I surveyed it from my bedroom window. A hot sun blazed down on two gardeners raking rubbish up on the lawns — and a guest still lay against a tree, unmolested.

I passed a finger over the embossed lettering on Riccardo's business card. Should I call before I shower? Or after breakfast? Or perhaps lunchtime? I picked up the phone that instant.

His first words were, 'Have you forgiven me?'

'Would I have phoned otherwise?'

'I worried whether you'd call.'

'So are you going to take me out?'

His flash white car — matching my white dress — turned into the Collini's early in the afternoon.

'You look beautiful,' he said.

'Ah, flattery . . .'

We drove for miles into the country. I didn't care where we were headed. Eventually we stopped at a lake and rested at its edge on a white blanket under the shade of trees.

Last night's party had caught up with me. I lay with a heavy head, throbbing a little to the cries of waterfowl nearby. A welcome breeze fought my body heat.

We talked little, happy in each other's company. Never

before had I felt this – this sense of at-one-ment with a man.

He moved towards me and kissed me passionately on the lips . . . 'I don't know what's happened to me,' he whispered. 'I just want to be with you.' He caressed my hair. 'It's a pity you have to go back tomorrow.'

'You sound as if we won't see each other again,' I sighed. 'I love being with you.'

'Do you?'

'Mmm – with that car of yours, it wouldn't take you long to visit me.'

'I know I'll see you, but not everyday as I'd like.'

'Wouldn't that be a good test? Will you feel like this about me when I'm not around?'

He gently pinched my cheek. 'You needn't have any doubts. I have never felt like this before, believe me. I know what I want.'

Time would tell, I thought to myself.

The next morning we loaded the limousine. My father was in heavy conversation with Ruggero, planning the next stage of our association. Riccardo had said he would come to wave me off but had yet to arrive. Had he changed his mind? I wondered.

The car had already crept forward on the drive when I spotted Riccardo's car race up. I ordered the driver to stop, ignoring my parents, and jumped out to embrace him. As much as the pleasure of seeing him was the relief that he kept his word. He kissed me many times oblivious of my parents in the limo who must have giggled in amazement at the spectacle.

'Who are the red roses for? I asked.

He took them from the back seat of his convertible and handed them to me. 'Who else?' he smiled. 'I'll come and see you in the next few days – but I'll call you first, I got your number from Ruggero.'

So Ruggero had served a useful purpose at last.

As I made my way back to the limo I waved at the Collinis standing at the front door. Ruggero did not look entirely ecstatic, but Lina gave me such a dazzling smile as if we were old friends. I think she had approved of our goodbye.

'Well,' said papa in the car, 'I never thought I'd see the day my daughter actually finds a boyfriend.'

'Oh, Orlando,' said mamma. 'What a thing to say. I thought Riccardo was very romantic – what a lovely scent those roses have. Can I have them?'

'Mamma! You can have three stems.'

'See how she treats me Orlando.'

'Kids today . . .' laughed papa.

'Yet I thought Ruggero was your suitor last night,' said mamma, making mischief.

'He tried his luck. I just teassed him. He's a big flirt.'

Papa looked concerned. 'You must remember, Vilma, that we are in business with him.'

'I shall never take him seriously again after that ludicrous Caesar outfit,' said mamma. 'Lina was obviously bullied into becoming Cleopatra.'

My father said, 'They maybe slightly eccentric but they are no fools.'

Our mood changed when the car was held up by a terrible car crash ahead. Twisted metal and burst tyres lay across the road, and ambulance flash light filled our limousine.

'How terrible. To think death is that close,' said mamma.

I was dropped off at the flat.

The first thing I did was to shower and relish my own

company again. What I used to call freedom was simply my right to be alone at times. Yet there was a price to be paid for this freedom. I only had two eggs in the fridge. At my parents I would have feasted.

I wandered into my bedroom as I towelled myself off and gazed up at a Valentino portrait.

'I've missed you,' I said to it. 'In my heart you'll always be my first love.'

The phone rang. It was Riccardo. I had half expected him to call.

'*Mia cara,*' he said, 'I'm missing you already. I will always be straight with you. There'll be no secrets between us.'

'Secrets? Do you have any Riccardo?'

'I don't like secrets, er, so you have a right to know something. I have been seeing a girl for the last few months. It's not serious.'

I was not entirely surprised. It would be too much to expect that a man live like a priest – or a woman for that matter.

'You must tell her immediately,' I said gently. 'But why wasn't she with you at the Collini's?'

'Like I said she's not important.'

'We can't see each other until you have told her.'

'I can't just drop this bombshell,' he said quickly. 'I'll have to be gentle with her. The important thing is that she's not between us.'

'No, Riccardo. You must finish with her first.' I hung-up.

How quickly happiness turned to uncertainty. We did not communicate in the next few days. A week passed and still I heard nothing. I began to wonder whether I had misjudged him again. Nearly two weeks later I had a phone call from a young woman.

'Signorina Bertolini?'

'Yes.'

'You don't know me but I know Riccardo. He's told me all about you, and let me give you some advice. Forget him. He is not worth thinking about.'

'Who are you?'

'I'm Marianna. I've been going out with him for four months. He's just got carried away with his feelings for you – we are planning to marry soon.'

I could hardly speak. I swallowed and controlled my breathing.

'Thank you for telling me. But I won't believe it till I hear it from Riccardo himself.'

'I wouldn't get your hopes up. He hasn't the courage to tell you. He's a weak man, but because I love him I forgive him.'

A weak man? Nothing in my experience suggested weakness in him. Yet he hadn't called me – could this Marianne be right?

'I shall talk to Riccardo,' I said.

The girl laughed. 'He's mine!'

I replaced the receiver. A familiar doubt passed over me. I couldn't cry. I relived our few moments together. If I was wrong about him, then I could never trust my judgement again. I knew nothing.

'What do you think?' I asked the picture of Valentino. 'What will happen next, do you think?' No answer. The dead don't talk.

Work was the best remedy and work I did the next day. I decided not to call Riccardo – it was important he call me if he had anything to say. Ruggero's new contracts had revitalised the company. We would soon need to take on new staff. In the afternoon Roberto called.

'Surprised, Vilma?'

'Yes. What can I do for you?'

'Only that you see me. I behaved stupidly the other day. Will you forgive me? I want to explain how I felt in your flat so you understand me better.'

'No, Roberto. It's pointless. The ghost in my flat is still there and I'm not moving out. And I shall continue casting spells. Now I'm very busy with no time to waste.' And I hung up.

I could have been pleasant but I had no patience with him. Why waste time? Another episode ended.

Back at the flat a neighbour called in to tell me a 'gentleman' had left a message for me as I was out.

'Oh, yes,' I said, thinking it Roberto. 'Did he look pale by any chance?'

'I didn't notice but he's left his phone number. You are a popular girl, aren't you?'

She handed me a scrap of paper with scrawled numerals on it. I recognised the number as Riccardo's. I began to tremble a little. My first instinct was to call. Then I thought better of it. He could call again, or phone my office. I decided to give him a taste of his own neglect and make him wait.

The next day I went to my grandfather's. I knew he wanted to talk more about my consultation with Rosa.

'Is he all right?' I asked the housekeeper, Clara.

'He's better now.'

'What do you mean?'

'He's been complaining of feeling unwell.'

He must have made a remarkable recovery because just outside his living-room door I could hear him giggling.

'Has he company?' I asked Clara.

'Yes. Two nice ladies came to visit him when they heard he was unwell. He's greatly cheered up.'

I decided to gatecrash his little party.

He jumped up like a frightened rabbit – '*Cara*, how wonderful to see you.' He rushed over to embrace me.

'I didn't realise you had company,' I said throwing a glance at his two guests. I'll come back another time.'

'I won't hear of it,' he insisted. 'My friends were just leaving, weren't you dears.'

They made a great fuss of him with goodbyes, confirming all my mother's words about him. But I couldn't be harsh.

Alone together I said, 'You certainly like the ladies, grandpa.'

'You sound like your mother.'

'Just joking.'

'It's not like you to make observations like that. Now, what do you want to drink?'

We sat on the sofa with wine. 'You know, Vilma, I have always found women more intelligent than men. That's why I prefer their company – women's, I mean. Men are only good for business. Your mother always got it wrong about me. She always assumed I was up to no good. Her mother was the same, so I am the bad boy of the family.'

'But I love you, as does mamma.'

'And I love you both, too.'

I said more about Rosa's psychic reading – he had no doubt that the 'young man' who communicated through her was Valentino.

'Remember his words – live your own life. You are still young with a long life in front of you. It doesn't matter if I die tomorrow, I'm an old man. I'm sure your mother will be happy when I'm gone.'

'Oh no, grandpa, you're wrong. I think she would be the most upset. And I love you and pray you live another twenty years.'

'God, no, not another twenty years!'

'Shouldn't you try to make peace with mamma?'

'No, there's no point. It's all to do with the emotions. She feels wronged. If I say anything to her she thinks I'm trying to salve my conscience.'

I told him about Riccardo. He got the full story to date, about his girlfriend and how he must drop her.

'You don't waste time do you, Vilma. First Roberto, now this Riccardo. You know the answer. If he loves you he'll know what to do. You're right not to phone him – make him want you. And you're right to insist he tells his girlfriend. It would be more hurtful to deceive her, though she sounds a nasty piece of work to me. I hope he sees sense. But are you sure he loves you?'

The question made me weep.

'Oh, my child, you must be in love!'

'Yes, I am. I wish I weren't.'

He cuddled me. 'It's good to cry. I've never seen you cry over a man before.'

At the flat I was torn over whether to phone Riccardo. It was like a war of nerves. I was about to dial him, but my fingers found their way to Lisa's number instead. She wasn't in.

I was already in bed when the phone rang.

'*Pronto, pronto . . .*'

Just silence. Then just as I was about to put down the phone Riccardo spoke.

'Are you there, Vilma?'

I had an impulse to put the phone down in panic.

'Yes, hello.'

'Are you talking to me?'

'Well, I'm here now.'

'We must talk to put things right. Can I come this weekend?'

257

'After all this time? And no word from you. What was I to think? What about your girlfriend? Are you still seeing her?'

'Of course not.'

I decided not to tell him of her phone call at this moment.

'I will book a hotel nearby and then I will come and see you and we can talk about everything.'

Excitment overwhelmed me as I replaced the receiver. I planned to ask him to stay with me though he could book his hotel if he wished.

I wanted him in my bed. How would he cope with my 'Valentino ghost'?

He phoned again Friday to say he'd be over later that evening, around eight. I was delirious with fear and happiness. Much as I wanted him, I knew one wrong word could end it. Our relationship seemed to hang on a fine thread. I was not prepared to go forward at any price.

I bought a new tablecloth and candles. I prepared a feast. At a few minutes past eight the doorbell rang. For all my plans to be cool, I rushed to the door like a child, full of near-hysterical emotions.

Riccardo stood there with a bunch of red roses in his hands. I'd almost forgotten the intensity of his gaze. We smiled, I took the flowers, his eyes would not leave me. We must have stood like this for sometime.

He broke the silence at long last. 'I can't believe I'm here at last. Or am I dreaming?'

'If you are, so am I,' I said. 'Champagne. It's cooled.'

We sat close. 'You know your girlfriend called, Marianna.'

'My ex-girlfriend,' he corrected. 'She told me. She claimed you said you never wanted to see me again.'

'She said something similar to me.'

'We never discussed marriage. It was a fling, that's all. She reacted very badly when I told her about you and flew into a violent rage. I shouldn't have told her your name.'

'That'll teach you to have flings!'

'No more flings for me. I've found you. I shall be the last man in your life.'

'Really. Then I'll be your last woman.'

We sat at the table to eat.

'We must start again,' I said. We began to kiss – the scream of the coffee percolator threw us apart, and we laughed.

We talked about our lives. And when it was late and we were both tired he said he'd return to his hotel – 'not that I want to leave you.'

'You don't have to, Riccardo. I have a bedroom which can be shared.'

To his credit he looked truly astonished. 'Are you sure? Is that what you want?'

'I always know what I want. That's why I waited for you. Forget about your hotel.'

In the bedroom he was drawn to my Valentino pictures. 'So, who is this handsome fellow? An old boyfriend?'

'In a way,' I said, 'except he's dead. Don't you recognise him? Rudolph Valentino?'

'I knew that! Why so many pictures? Do you run his fan club? You've even his photograph on your bedside table.'

'It's a long story,' Riccardo. 'I'll tell you sometime.'

'I could be jealous of him,' he joked, as he pulled off his jumper. 'But I won't fight a duel with a ghost.'

I threw off my slippers and lay on the bed. 'Do you believe in ghosts Riccardo?'

'Oh, yes.'

'And have you felt Valentino's hands shake yours since you arrived?' I giggled.

'Not yet!'

'You think I'm joking, but a friend of mine swears he felt an invisible hand shake his in this flat. He ran out shrieking. He went home and has never been back since.'

Riccardo laughed. 'What a story. Was he kidding? Maybe he wanted your sympathy. Well, Valentino has not shaken my hands so he must like me,' he added tapping a portrait.

'And what would you do if he did?' I asked.

'I'd shake his hand back. I'm a gentleman. I don't think he will bother us tonight. In fact I would like him to be our witness. Because tonight I am going to make love to you.'

He gently pulled off my dressing gown and we got into bed. As he kissed me tenderly about my neck he whispered, 'I think Valentino would love to be in my place right now.'

I was in the kitchen making us coffee when I heard a commotion from the bedroom. I rushed in to find Riccardo flat on his back on the floor with blankets thrown all over the place.

'Riccardo, what happened?'

'I was attacked!'

Then he laughed loudly. And jumped onto the bed.

'What . . . ?'

'I didn't know what hit me.'

'Oh, you're a joker are you.

'Valentino attacked me – his ghost.'

I threw a cushion at Riccardo. 'Don't mock the ghosts or they'll haunt you.'

'Oooooooooh!' he cried, throwing the cushion back at me.

'What I told you last night – it did happen. I have another

friend who thinks this flat is haunted. You've been warned. I've your breakfast ready.'

I had hardly turned and two strong arms enciled me and lifted me off the ground. Riccardo swung me about the room like a toy.

'Put me down, you devil!'

'But I am a devil.' He threw off my dressing gown and made love to me again with such passion that I was left breathless.

We lay a long time on the bed before I made another attempt at breakfast.

'I'll have you for breakfast,' said Riccardo, 'between two slices of toast.'

'Very amusing,' I said, putting on my dressing gown.

'I will amuse you in many ways,' and he winked at me.

The weekend passed wonderfully. He was true to his word, funny, entertaining, a complete contrast to anyone I had known before. His mind fizzed fearlessly with new adventures.

I went straight from my office to Lisa's on the Monday after she'd invited me to supper during the day.

'I tried to call you last week,' I said. 'You were out'.

Lisa was spooning boiled eggs from the steaming pot.

'I was out with Mario,' she confessed, 'and he's still seeing that other woman. He keeps saying I must be patient while he sorts himself out.'

'You shouldn't put up with it, being treated second best.'

'I know, I'm silly, but he won't do anything and I love him.'

'You must be more firm with him.'

'I know all this,' she said, tapping the eggs before peeling off their shells.

Eventually I told her of the Collini party and Riccardo. 'He's just spent the weekend with me.'

'Vilma! What has happened to you? Is this the Vilma I once knew? What tricks did you get up to?'

'It was wonderful.'

'And you're sure of him?'

I dressed the salad with virgin olive oil.

'I just know I feel very happy with him.'

'And your Valentino thing – do you think that will fade away now?'

'Perhaps . . . but Valentino is another matter, he is part of my dream. Were he alive we'd have met—'

'Oh Vilma, how can you say that?'

'Valentino is more than a dream. I think this so-called obsession of mine prepared me for Riccardo. I won't settle for less. But in different circumstances, Valentino could have ruined my whole life.'

'OK, the salad's ready.'

Over the meal she said, 'The problem with your Valentino dream is that it has nothing to do with real-life. It's simply fantasy. It's nothing like reality. Look at me and Mario. That's the reality of romance. And what is romance? Between Mario and me, it's more to do with sex than anything else.'

She paused in thought . . . 'I think you're far more spiritual than me, Vilma. You think and feel differently from me.'

'Sex isn't love.'

'But look at you and Roberto. Only a short while ago he made you happy. Now it's Riccardo . . .'

'I knew from the start Riccardo is the one for me. I was always finding excuses to avoid Roberto. You know that. If Riccardo asked me to marry him tomorrow I'd say yes. I could never have said that of Roberto. But you may as well know, I had to put my foot down with Riccardo. He had a girlfriend. I insisted he dump her – or else that was it between us.'

'Like me and Mario.'

'He put up a bit of a struggle because men are hopeless at emotional confrontation. In the end he got rid of her.'

'That's a lesson! You are heartless, Vilma.'

'Not at all. It would be heartless to deny what Riccardo and I feel for each other. He couldn't carry on seeing this girl out of pity. It's the same with Mario. You have to face it. He's seeing one of you out of pity. So he must be forced to choose to end the nonsense.'

'Ruggero!'

Our new business partner stood in the doorway to my office.

'Are you too busy to see me? I have something to discuss,' he said.

'Not at all.' I was professionally charming. 'Would you like a drink?'

He took a seat as I poured a little scotch.

'What a delightful office you have, Vilma. Quite spacious. Have you sacked anyone today?'

'We try not to sack anyone, Ruggero. Sacking someone is always an admission of failure by the employer – and we never fail.' I handed him his drink.

'You're formidable, I'll say that. Now this project I have in mind—'

'Should we not call my father in?'

'Er, no. I don't do business that way. I like to discuss things one-to-one. That way I get to know what the individual is thinking as opposed to what people say in each other's company.'

'I can assure you my father and I are of one mind.'

'Of that I am certain. But this is my way.'

'Well, we all have our . . . little ways.'

I gazed at him on alert. He was clever, but not that clever. Perhaps this was his way of trying to discover whether my father and I had our professional differences.

For over two hours we talked over his ideas on expansion. I was impressed, he was canny and shrewd.

'I think this calls for a celebration, Vilma.'

'Why, because we agree?'

'Don't you think that's cause for celebration? By the way, your father has invited me to spend the evening with him and your mother. I'm sure you will be joining us.'

'Naturally,' I said, inwardly annoyed that my father had not consulted me first.

Ruggero took my hand and planted foolish little kisses in a manner that sugested he would have liked to go further.

'I so much admire you, Vilma. As does Riccardo. You've got a good one there. I've known him a long time and he's a man of true worth.'

'I agree,' I said smoothly, withdrawing my hand. 'I am glad we also agree about my choice of man.'

'I'm not all that bad. I know good when I see it. I am not a good example myself, granted, I have many faults. I couldn't possibly be faithful to any woman – you see, I admit it. I don't pretend to be a good husband. My poor, long-suffering wife! But she's accepted me as I am. I certainly don't deserve her.'

I laughed. 'Well, at least you're honest. Or do you think that this honesty excuses you?'

Now he laughed. 'Only you could come up with that one.'

'Personally, I would never tolerate your behaviour as your wife, Ruggero. Thank God you are not my problem.'

'You expect total loyalty in your men, don't you? I can't blame you. Riccardo will give you total loyalty, like a doggy.'

I laughed again. 'You are a classic rascal.'

'But it is so hard to resist you. Nonetheless I will make an extra effort not to annoy you.'

'I think I've heard that before, Ruggero.'

He sighed, 'Well, it's time I left you. I've many things to do.' He managed to sound as if I'd held him up. 'I'll see you later, Vilma.'

Later my father apologised for not alerting me to the evening do with Ruggero. 'It'd be nice if you came.'

I returned early to my flat to shower and find something to wear for the evening. I was on the point of leaving when the phone rang. It was my grandfather's housekeeper.

'I thought I should let you know he's been taken ill,' Clara said.

I felt sick with worry. 'What's wrong with him?'

'I don't know. The doctor is with him now. I phoned your mother and she is on her way.'

I popped into see my father en route just to show my face. I prayed to God to give grandpa – my best friend – extra life.

'I'm sure he'll be all right,' was the first thing papa said to me.

'Don't worry about me,' said Ruggero, already there. 'We can celebrate another time if you wish to see your grandfather.'

My mother was already at grandpa's bedside when I arrived. He was asleep. She got up with a finger at her lips and mouthed to me not to make a noise. She shut the door soundlessly behind her.

'Let's have some coffee in the kitchen,' she whispered.

We joined the doctor and the housekeeper.

'He must take it easy,' said the doctor. 'His heart is not as strong as it was.'

'I'll stay the night,' I said.

My mother looked at me with relief. 'Oh do.' She wiped the tears that had run down her face. 'Don't think I've been too hard on him . . . I do love him despite everything. I want to talk to him.'

Grandpa didn't rouse that night. In the morning I went to the office having changed clothes at the flat. To my surprise Ruggero was there, having stayed the night at my parents'.

After I told him about my grandfather he said inappropriately, 'I'm planning another party – I'll be in touch.'

It was a morning of tiresome distractions all building up around my anxiety. With perfect timing Roberto called demanding we meet to talk about 'us'.

I shouted down the phone, 'How dare you call after your disgusting conduct. There is no "us". There is nothing between us, nothing! Do not call again.' I slammed the phone down.

A terrible fury gained force in me as the day progressed. Even my father kept out of my way. I prayed Riccardo would not phone in case I blasted at him too. I got back to the flat with stormy and uncertain thoughts.

It was while I clattered about the kitchen that I thought I heard my name called from the bedroom. For a moment I wondered how Riccardo had let himself in. But that wasn't Riccardo's voice. Was it a burglar playing games? Nervously I crept out of the kitchen listening for a new sound. As I entered the bedroom I was stopped by a rapping sound on the wall within. I saw nothing and for the first time felt afraid.

I jumped at the phone's first ring.

'Are you all right?' asked Riccardo.

'Yes, I think so . . .'

'You sound strange.'

'I'm fine – my grandfather is ill.'

'I'm very sorry . . .'

But as we spoke I heard more noise in the bedroom: the knocking was louder, seemingly more urgent.

'Have you builders in Vilma?'

'No,' I stumbled, 'I think it maybe the neighbours. Can I call you back . . . ?'

'I only phoned to see if you're around this weekend. I'm desperate to see you.'

'*Cara*, I am sorry I have to go. This weekend should be fine but we'll talk again. I think there's somebody at the door.'

I put down the phone quickly and marched into the bedroom, determined to confront whatever. I was struck by a new iciness in the air, a weird coldness despite the heat outside. Then with a start I saw that a framed Valentino portrait had been turned against the wall. This morning it faced me. A greater chill rushed through me.

'What's this?' I said to all the other Valentino pictures. 'What's wrong? Is this to do with my grandfather . . . ?'

I phoned him and spoke to Clara.

'Don't worry,' she said. 'He's a lot better but the doctor says he should stay in bed a while longer.'

'Is my mother there?'

'No, but she'll be back soon.'

I was mystified by the curious activity in my bedroom. I thought of Roberto, how he must have felt when an unseen hand gripped his. Perhaps I had been too harsh towards him.

Riccardo called again. 'I just want to know why you hurried off last time I phoned. Is there a problem?'

'No, somebody was at the front door.'

'Who was it?'

'No one in particular. They had the wrong address. I should've called you back. I want to see you Riccardo. I miss you . . .'

'I miss you, too. This weekend then? Goodnight . . .' He made kissing noises.

As soon as I had replaced the receiver a single loud noise from my bedroom stunned me. A moment later the doorbell rang, two sounds almost but not quite simultaneous. I felt relief of company. I opened it . . . it was Ruggero.

I nearly fainted on the spot. How much more could I be expected to tolerate?

'Ruggero! What are you doing here?'

He wore an inane smile . . . 'Sorry to intrude but my car's broken down. It's at the garage but it won't be ready till the morning.'

'You had better come in then. I was about to make some supper.'

'Thank you, that's very kind. I've eaten already but I wouldn't say no to a scotch.'

I didn't believe his story about the car for one moment but was happy to have someone in the place after all the disturbance. I was curious to see if the rappings continued with Ruggero here.

As he nestled down into the sofa with a huge tumbler he asked casually, 'Can you put me up tonight? I've nowhere else to stay.'

'Certainly not, Ruggero. You have plenty of time to book into a hotel.'

'Oh, I hate hotels,' he said childishly, 'all that booking-in rubbish, and I deplore sleeping in hotel beds. You don't know who else has slept in them. I can sleep on this sofa.

It feels lovely and comfortable. I won't be any bother –
here, can I have another scotch?'

I took the proffered glass and refilled it almost to the
rim in the hope of knocking him out.

'As you wish, Ruggero. But you had better behave
yourself.'

I drifted off to the bathroom to refresh myself for the
night and put on my white dressing gown.

As I made my way to the bedroom he said, 'Don't tell
me you're going to bed already. It's not ten yet.'

'When I go to bed is for me to worry about. Actually,
I was about to pour myself a glass of wine. I find it's more
effective than hot chocolate.'

'As a senior executive of a chocolate manufacturing
company you shouldn't say that,' he teased.

'Well, Ruggero, you're welcome to hot chocolate
instead of all that whisky you're guzzling.' He had refilled
the glass again in my absence.

I sat with my wine . . . 'I hope you don't think I'm in
the least fooled about your car.'

'What do you mean?' he responded, full of humorous
offence. 'I can take you to the garage in the morning.
Do you think I'd make up a story just to spend the night
with you?'

'Yes, I do.'

'Well it worked didn't it. But my car has broken down.'

'You will leave first thing in the morning.'

'Thank you Vilma for your characteristic hospitality. It
is a novelty for me to be treated like a dog.'

'Dogs have quite a good life,' I said, getting up. 'But
can expect a kicking if they misbehave.'

'Woof woof!'

I went to find him a pillow and blanket.

*   *   *

In the early hours I was brought round by the creek of my door handle being turned from the outside. The ghost of Ruggero, I surmised. I had locked the door so I went to asleep again and dreamt of dogs.

By the time I had risen Ruggero had disppeared, leaving a note on the kitchen table. 'Thank you for letting me stay the night,' it read. 'The chair wasn't as comfortable as I first thought. I think your bed would have been better for my back. We could have had a wonderful time together. Yours faithfully, Dr Ruggero.'

I was about to tear it up, but on second thoughts decided to keep it safe. Such a note might be useful in the future for some as-yet unspecified purpose.

As I dressed I toyed with the idea that the odd noises might have been a warning against Ruggero. All was silent now. I was torn between such an idea and dismissing it as fantasy.

But I gave Valentino the benefit of the doubt and looked up one of his photographs and said, 'Thank you.'

'So your grandfather is on the mend,' said papa rushing into my office with papers in both hands.

'Yes, it's a great relief – we need to talk about Ruggero.'

'Oh, is it important?'

'Could be.'

He sat down at my desk. 'What's he done now?'

'It's not so much what he's done as what he would like to do. I'm not certain I can tolerate him much longer – it's important I tell you this because I don't want it to destroy our business relationship with him if we can help it.'

Papa appeared shocked. 'What do you mean?'

'I feel Ruggero is harassing me. His behaviour is intolerable.' I told him about last night, how I'd allowed Ruggero to stay because of his car breaking down, and everything else.

'You let him stay in your flat?' papa said incredulously. 'That was very stupid.'

'I didn't want to offend him. But I think things are getting to the stage where I may feel forced to leave the company.'

'Leave the company!' shouted papa appalled.

Hearing him say this had a sudden effect on me. Yes, this was the moment to leave Bertolini's. It was time to make my own life in every respect.

. . . 'In fact papa, I am leaving. I'm handing in my notice.'

I couldn't believe I had said this. I hadn't planned to say this at all. But it felt right. This was the moment to go.

'Go? You can't go. This is as much your company as mine.'

'I have decided papa.'

'But . . . I will talk to Ruggero. I shall make him apologise and if he doesn't then I will break up our partnership.'

'That won't be necessary. This is not really about Ruggero, though he needs to be watched. I want to change my life. I will stay another month and then that's it.'

My father blustered and spluttered but he could see my mind was made up . . . 'Where will you go?'

'Don't know. I shall have a long break first. I've been working ever since I left school. It's time I took stock.'

'You shouldn't be so attractive! Then this episode with Ruggero wouldn't have happened.'

'You would prefer a witch for a daughter would you?

271

Ruggero can take responsibility for his own actions – and choke on his chocolates.'

Later in the day my mother phoned the office. 'Is it true you're leaving the company?'

'Very true. I suppose papa told you everything.'

'Yes. Don't you think you could have handled Ruggero in a more . . . mature way, Vilma?'

'I am leaving for me, not because of Ruggero. In any case why should I have to handle him at all? What you should be saying is, "Why should such a man, in his position, behave so ridiculously?"'

Riccardo laughed when I told him about Ruggero.

'He is such a clot. You shouldn't be concerned about him,' he said. 'Are you sure you want to leave your family company?'

'I have never felt more certain.'

He hugged me. 'It's always amused me how Ruggero runs his business. I think he set it up so he could chase women.'

'It's not a laughing matter,' Riccardo. 'He's pathetic, but people make excuses for him because secretly they think that's how men should behave.'

'Come, on let's go out for supper. I've booked already.'

Later that evening we went to a new and elegant restaurant. A huge red candle burnt bright at our table.

'You look especially beautiful in that black dress,' Riccardo said.

We drank champagne. Over dessert he brought out a small black box from his jacket pocket and handed it to me.

'What is this?'

I opened it. A gleaming gold ring crowned with tiny diamonds sparkled at me.

'Put it on,' said Riccardo. 'Will you marry me?'

I had no doubts.

'Yes, yes!'

When I told papa of our engagement his attitude to my leaving the company changed in an instant.

'Ah, now I understand. You want to be a wife and mother.'

'I can still be a wife and mother and work, papa. I'm leaving to prove I can make it on my own.'

'Of course, you are,' he said completely unconvinced. 'Incidentally, I had a word with Ruggero and gave him a reprimand. But now I see you would have left the company anyway.'

There was someone else I wanted to talk to about my new life to come.

In my bedroom I addressed Valentino's portrait:

'So, my handsome lover. I am to marry soon. But that doesn't mean I'm saying goodbye to you. The candle remains lit for you. I hope we meet in another life, without your fame and glory, where you can carry me under a desert sun and our love will be forever.'

Epilogue

Now I am old but still married to Riccardo. Sometimes he jokes I wouldn't have married him had he not allowed Valentino to stay in my life.

'So I had to take my vows with both of you.'

Then he laughs as he has always done.

Arrivederci Valentino

The Mystery of Carmen

Chapter One

Where am I?

I've been driving through the countryside for quite a while not thinking where I'm headed. But then it doesn't seem to matter just so long as I stay on the road and keep my mind empty of troublesome thoughts.

It's very warm now, so much more balmy than earlier this morning when I'd set off for nowhere in particular. Now I'm parched. Then I spot a figure in the distance walking along the brown roadside scrub.

Closer to, I see he's an elderly man carrying a pitchfork on his shoulder, most likely making his way to a field. I stop the car. As he passes I say, 'Excuse me, excuse me!'

He turns and smiles, revealing fragments of brown teeth, his face corrugated by a lifetime of work in the sun.

'Yes, whaddya want?' he says, not unfriendly.

'Is there a cafe or inn roundabouts? I need a drink.'

He giggles and points ahead – 'Just up the road beyond the hill there, about four kilometres, the village, you can't miss it. Plenty to drink there.'

He waves me off and in a matter of minutes I'm greeted by the road sign for this oddly named village: Casarsa Della Delizia. The usual terracotta roofs, the rural Italian sleepiness punctuated by the occasional sounds of poultry.

A pleasant place, a place that feels like home.

I park the car and stroll up Via Valvasone. Just passed the piazza I spot an *osteria* and dart in. Not many people given the time of day but the few there are talking loudly.

I buy a drink and as I make my way to a table I overhear a man say above the hubbub, 'It's strange no one's bought that cottage.'

Another man replies, 'It's a sad house . . .'

The first man pulls a scornful face – 'That's a lot of nonsense . . .'

I smile to myself at these rustics. I drink up quickly and make my way back to the car, attracting a few desultory looks. But on a strong impulse I change direction and head towards the end of Via Valvasone. Even now I cannot explain such a pull.

At the end of the road are two cottages, one of which has a For Sale sign. It's evidently empty or at least neglected, but like the other has net curtains – an odd thing in these parts. Despite them it's not hard to see in – I wonder if this is the cottage the locals were talking about.

A sense of familiarity overwhelms me as I take in the detail of the place, though I'm a stranger. I feel curiosity, as if catching up with an old friend. I know I shall have to return, with keys next time.

I cup my hands against the window to see within a final time, and for a moment I think I see movement. A rat? Something. Perhaps a trick of light. There's nothing now, just interior gloom and the spectral shapes of furniture.

I can stay here. I want to. But Lucia, my wife, will be wondering where I am. The thought depresses me a little.

It's just before lunchtime when I get home. As I make it

into the drive I spot Lucia's anxious face framed by the window. My 15-year-old daughter Elisabeth stands in the front doorway.

'Papa, where have you been?' she screeches. 'Mamma's been frantic with worry.'

'I'm sorry, *cara*,' I say gently, closing the car door behind me. 'I got a bit lost.'

The redness of Lucia's eyes tells me she's been crying. 'Where have you been Marco?'

'I felt like going somewhere this morning,' I say sharply. 'It's not like I've committed a crime!'

Hurt by my sharp tone she turns towards the kitchen – 'Your lunch is ready.'

Let me explain. I am a romantic novelist – a strange job for a man you may think. In fact I have been writing for several years now. I've had books published under a pseudonym – I won't say who I am. But, to be honest, I don't feel I've really made it. Sometimes I think this is because I'm not sure what love is myself – and I say this as a married man, and a romantic writer.

What do I really feel for my wife Lucia? Our marriage is reasonably happy, yet there's always this sense of something missing. The deadening effect of familiarity perhaps. And what's missing? A sense of passionate commitment? A rush of mad abandon? Does my trade make me unrealistic about expectations of love? I write about love yet find it impossible to know.

Lately I have begun to think of writing another book which must somehow be true (to me) and work on a deeper level of feeling. It must feel actual, lived. Not sentimental daydreams which most romances are. For another reason I cannot explain, irrationally, I am confident that this time I will make it.

Maybe the answer is I have to get away from here – away from Lucia – for a while.

To be completely alone—

'Marco,' Lucia says, 'are you coming for your lunch? 'At least you should have told me you were going out this morning.'

At the kitchen door I observe my wife standing so intently before the cooker, as if in prayer. She's a good cook, a good wife, and above all she is such a good mother to our daughter.

My eyes fall on Lucia's tiny figure, and I am absorbed by her sharp, neat movements. The soft wave in her brown hair, the honesty in her dark brown eyes: she fascinates me at this moment as she works through her rituals to keep a family together.

I'm so very fond of her but I can't expect her to inspire me. I suppose you're thinking I'm a typical male, that I expect too much, but this is what I feel, rightly or wrongly.

Lucia turns to me and asks matter-of-factly whether I would like bacon with my pasta. I nod.

'Sit down then,' she says playfully, in a new mood.

But a sudden idea hits me. 'Hey,' I say, 'it's a beautiful day, we shouldn't be cooped up here. Let's go for a picnic. Now. Come on!'

'But you've just been out and I've just cooked—'

'It's such a lovely Italian summer's day, warm and dry and sweet-smelling, and a pity to waste indoors.'

'Not now Marco . . .'

'Where's your spirit of adventure—?'

She looks at me as if to say, 'How out of character'; but says instead, much to my surprise after a pause, 'OK, that'll be very nice.'

'It's simple. Look, wrap this food in foil, get some fruit and cheese and a bottle of wine . . .'

'That's settled then,' she says.

I know that I can be very selfish, so wrapped up in myself. Rarely do I ask Lucia what she really wants. Rarely does she tell me. I can't recall once our ever sitting down for a good talk about life together.

I want to think that this is going to be a lovely day. I shall try to come out of my thoughts. I hear my daughter's tread on the staircase. Then she appears in the kitchen, looking brighter than minutes ago.

'We're going out for a picnic,' Lucia says. 'One of your father's sudden ideas.'

'A picnic?' she says, slightly amazed.

'Come with us,' I say.

'Sorry,' she says not unexpectedly. 'I've already made other plans to see a friend.'

I say, 'Very well. But don't forget to be back by five.'

Lucia starts with the food-wrapping and I go upstairs for a shower.

Half-an-hour later Lucia appears ready at the front doorway with the packed picnic basket. She does look happy . . . and I feel a twinge of guilt because our trip out is really just an excuse for me to return to Casarsa.

'Let's make a move, ' I say. 'We want to make the most of the day.'

We drive off. And in the rear-view mirror I glance at our little house, almost as if for the last time. Home is nothing special, not at all grand, a typical, modest terracottaed *casa* on the outskirts of Venice, with its small garden now blushed with the first roses of late spring.

Out in the country I am again possessed by an almost overwhelming sense of freedom. Everything is as it should be . . . sky and grassland vivid with life, and trees blooming into bushy sentinels. It's a perfect last day of May: and it is not too hot, not just yet.

'"Casarsa Della Delizia", that's an odd name,' says Lucia as we pass the village sign. 'Why have we come here, Marco?'

'Just curiosity – it'll whet our appetite.'

We head up Via Valvasone as I did hours earlier towards the cottage with the sale sign. I never imagined I'd come back so soon.

I want to meet its owner. I know already this is the place for me – for work.

I park the car and get out. 'Stay here for a moment,' I say to Lucia. 'I just want to look at something. We can eat soon.' I don't wait for her response.

Before, I hadn't noticed the ancient iron spring pump in the cottage's back garden, fed I guess by the waters from the Dolomite Mountains that stand some thirty to forty kilometres north. That far away yet they dominate the skyline. I see their snowy peaks and scalloped greys . . . to gaze at them all day would be paradise.

I cup my hands over a window again, to spy within, but the sun's angle on the net curtains fazes me now. I wonder why the owner didn't prefer wooden shutters – known as *persiane*?

'Marco!' Lucia has popped her head out of the car window, clearly irritated by what she sees as time-wasting. 'What are you doing? Come back before the food goes off!'

I can't very well tell her what I'm thinking; not this minute anyway, as time mustn't be wasted. But I'll explain things later. We must talk.

Ignoring Lucia (what must she think?) I stride next door and knock at the door.

After the third rap on the old knotted wood, the door opens and a large woman in a body-length, stained apron looms in the threshold, gazing at me as if I were mad. With the defensive, unfriendly manner of a peasant she asks me what I want.

'I am interested in the house next door,' I say. 'Who owns it – can you tell me?'

'Well,' she says pompously in the fast-talking Friuli dialect, 'if you want to buy the property you must go see Signora Martina.' Then she adds unnecessarily, 'She is a very old lady and she cannot look after herself anymore. She lives with her daughter.'

I find it hard to follow all she says. It's a long time since I last heard Friulano, not since the War when I was stationed about forty kilometres away from here (though I'd never heard of Casarsa), and it takes a moment for me to tune-in to the rapid rhythms of the old language.

'So where does this Signora Martina live?'

'Turn back up Via Valvasone,' she says, stepping out to wave a fleshy arm to give directions. 'And go to the end of it. Turn right down Via Pordenone and go to number eleven. That's where she lives.'

'*Grazie, Signora,*' I say.

Back in the car Lucia asks me what the hell's going on and why I am so interested in the house.

'I will tell you all about it later,' I say cryptically. 'And now I have to see an old lady about the property and I will see what she has to say.'

'You can't be seriously thinking of buying the place,' Lucia says crossly.

'I am not buying it,' I say sharply. 'That's not what I have in mind.'

'So what do you have you in mind, then? I thought we were going to have a picnic!'

'I can't talk now!'

At the end of the road I turn into Via Pordenone and stop at number eleven. As I step out of the car, I hear hymn singers in full voice in the local church.

'Stay here Lucia in the car while I see someone.'

'What – !'

I have barely stopped knocking on the door before an attractive woman answers. She must be in her forties.

'*Buongiorno,*' I say. 'Are you Signora Martina?'

'No, Signora Chiavelli. Is it my mother you wish to speak to?'

'I would like to talk about the property around the corner.'

'I'll talk with my mother first,' she says. 'You don't mind waiting here first?'

A couple of long minutes later she returns and invites me in. 'You are Signor—'

'De Silva,' I finish. 'I am sorry I did not give my name at the door.'

'That's all right,' she says.

She guides me towards the kitchen where I see a huge old woman seated by the window, peering through brilliant white net curtains at the outside world. More net curtains! Everything I see in the house is very clean and very simple. I am struck by the many wood crucifixes and images of the Virgin on the walls and shelves, along with several framed family photographs: a gallery of icons and memories.

The daughter enters first – 'Mamma, our visitor's name is Signor de Silva.'

The old lady turns to face me and seems to brighten for a moment, as if she knows me. For an instant I think she's almost about to embrace me, but then she collects herself and allows her face to fall into a stern, alert countenance. She invites me to come in and take the seat opposite hers.

'Young man,' she says, 'I understand that you are interested in buying my house. Am I right?'

'Not to buy,' I say. 'But I'd like to rent it for a while – is it up for rent?'

'Well,' she says, clearly taken aback, 'you should have seen the agent.' Then a new mood sweeps over her – 'But, on the other hand, I may let out the place since I do not seem able to sell it at the moment. It has been on the market some time now.'

She pauses, as if taking time to persuade herself. Then: 'For how long would you want to rent my house?'

'Three months, Signora Martina. You see, I am a writer and it is very important I have your house. It is the perfect place for me to write my next book.'

'May I ask you what your book is about?'

'Sorry, Signora Martina. I can only tell you it is about love.'

'How lovely. I wish I were young again.' She smiles at me for the first time, with warmth and an unlikely twinkle in her eye.

Then abruptly her face registers yet another new mood.

'Look, Signor de Silva,' she says. 'I will let you have my house for three months. And tomorrow morning my daughter will take you to the agent and there you will agree a rental and he will give you the key to the house.'

'I will pay you in advance,' I offer.

'Talk to the agent,' she says quickly. 'Well, Signor de Silva, I say *buongiorno* to you and I am sorry if I cannot come with you tomorrow. But my daughter will see to everything.'

I say goodbye and agree a time to meet the daughter. It's all been so easy, I am amazed.

In the car Lucia waits patiently and says nothing as we drive off. Now the church decants its worshippers and the

285

street is alive with chattering people in their Sunday best. Old women in black garb cluster together, bobbing their heads as they chatter like tiny finches.

Lucia has clearly decided I must volunteer an explanation for my odd behaviour. We have a war of silence. I drive out of Via Valvasone and down a country lane and soon I am drawn to a beautiful, large acacia tree.

'Let's picnic here – how about it Lucia?'

'Lovely,' she says simply, neutrally.

We park by the curbside and I hoist out the basket. Lucia opens a blanket under the tree. As she arranges the food I think how wonderful it is here, how tranquil.

'A glass of wine?' suggests Lucia. 'Do you want a cheese or ham roll? Salad?'

'I'll have one of each with a bit of salad.'

It is typical of Lucia to focus all her attention on arranging the food, and engaging in small talk, when she is upset. Only when we are half way through our meal *al fresco* and a little more relaxed because of the wine (she knows I am less likely to grow angry and walk away when I've had a glass or two) does she say what's on her mind.

'Tell me,' she says, 'what is it about that cottage? Was this picnic an excuse to see it?'

'Not at all,' I lie, astonished. 'I've never been to Casarsa before today.'

I pull out a slippery slice of cucumber from a ham roll and throw it to a hopeful starling nearby. Then I add, 'But when I saw that cottage I realised it was the perfect place to work in for a while.'

I tell her I don't plan to buy the house but that I've already arranged to rent the place – 'After all, you should have grown used to my comings and goings by now. You know I am planning another book but this time I feel I want to be completely alone to concentrate.'

'Alone? Why? What will you write about?'

'Another love story but this time I'm doing something different . . . I know it will be unusual.'

'Can't you tell me a bit about it?' she asks sharply.

It dawns on me that this is the first time I have excluded her from my life. Once I shared all my plans with her. Now I seem secretive, furtive.

'I can't talk about it,' I say firmly. 'In fact I shall not let you see it until it is completed.' Then somewhat cruelly I add, 'Try to understand a bit more about my work and why I want to be on my own.'

Lucia throws me a hard look. 'But you have written so many books and this is the first time you've ever wanted to spend time alone.'

'This book is going to be very different and it will be different because I am alone and it will be the best I have ever done.'

Lucia gives up and sinks into her thoughts. I lie back in the grass. The wine has gone to my head and I lose myself for a while in another world.

A hundred half-thoughts pass. Will I be able to afford the rent? Will I complete the novel in time? But what novel? I have no story, no ideas, only a feeling. What's happening to me? . . .

Suddenly I'm stirred by an angry voice – 'Get off my land!' – as if from far away. I think I am dreaming. I look up. Lucia has also been dozing judging by her alarm.

By a fence about fifty metres away I see the source of the disturbance, a thin scruffy man, probably one of the village folk judging by his raggedy clothes. He is pointing his large pitchfork at us in a threatening way.

'You're on my land. Clear off!' His face is red with fury. He looks like a bull ready to charge.

'Calm down man,' I say. 'We didn't know this was your land.'

'And take all your rubbish away as well and don't let me catch you here again!'

'Don't worry,' I say. 'There won't be another time. Not here anyway.'

And with that I draw up the four ends of the blanket to make an impromptu sack. The plates and cutlery crash and tinkle inside as I carry it to the car.

'Come Lucia,' I say. 'This oik means what he says.' She almost leaps into the car and we drive off.

In the rear-view mirror I watch the yokel with his fork and his brown cotton trousers, probably still shouting at us, as untouched by time as his great grandfather once was.

We pass back up the narrow country lane and head towards Via Valvasone.

'Well,' says lucia, 'are you still planning to come and stay here after *that*?'

'Sure, I'll come back. It'll take more than a bumpkin to scare me off. It will only be for three months.'

'I shall miss you Marco but I will try to understand.'

Touched by her words I say something I had not planned. 'We can see each other on Sundays. And then we can travel around the countryside. If you like. I'll explain to Elisabeth why I have to do this, and I hope you'll support me – I want you both to visit me. I'll get lonely.'

Lucia says nothing, but nods. I'm certain she's not sure what to say.

Chapter Two

Monday morning I call at Signora Martina's house in Casarsa. The first thing her daughter says to me is that her name is Caterina but I can call her Kate.

Signora Martina is sitting in the kitchen by the window as if she hasn't moved since yesterday. She apologises again for being unable to come to the estate agent's.

'My legs would give way, I know it.'

She's certainly a heavy woman and with height to match. I notice two walking sticks propped by her side.

'Not to worry,' I say. 'I will come and visit you when I move in.'

'Before you go would you like a glass of wine?'

'Not right now, Signora. Best if I have a clear head for your agent!'

She smiles.

Kate leads me away. Out in the hot sun I see a farmer – dressed like the oik who abused Lucia and me in the fields yesterday – lumbering by.

'The farmers work very hard at this time of year,' says Kate, noticing my interest. 'After lunch they have their siesta till four or five and then they return to the fields. They rise very early in the morning to avoid the heat and they work till it's dark. That has been the way since time begun.'

'Were you once married to a farmer?' I ask, partly in jest.

'Oh no!' she laughs. 'He was an estate agent – he died four years ago.'

'I'm very sorry; I didn't mean to pry . . .'

'Not at all. I still miss him.'

As we stroll down Via Pordenone I ask Kate about the house I want to rent – about its past.

'Why do you ask? What do you want to know particularly?'

'I'm not sure. It's odd how I was attracted to the house the moment I saw it and I can't explain why. I'd be fascinated by its history – a house can have a character all of its own . . .'

'Well, there's no tragedy attached to the place,' she says, perhaps as a precaution. 'But my mother has many memories in that house, and she never talks about them.'

At the estate agency I am greeted by a man in his late thirties, and I notice that he throws Kate the type of glance I have seen many times before, a glance of conspiracy or . . . of familiarity.

Perhaps they are having an affair. Then I wonder whether her late husband worked here.

But no more time to wonder for the moment. He's not too pleased that I only want to rent the house. Less commission for him, I suppose, and less chance of selling the place with a tenant in it. We agree a weekly sum for three months, I sign a simple contract and he hands me the keys. Again, it all seems so . . . easy, as if this should be happening.

Back in the street Kate says, 'There's one thing I want to say about the house before you go.'

Instant curiosity. There is a secret after all.

'There are two bedrooms,' she continues. 'My mother

would prefer you to sleep in the east bedroom if you don't mind. The linen's kept is in a cupboard to the left of it – you'll see anyway when I show you around in a minute.'

So much for secrets!

I arrive home about two in the afternoon. 'At last you are back,' says Lucia. 'I was just beginning to wonder . . .'

'Sorry,' I say. 'I tried to get home in good time.'

'Lunch is ready – was an hour ago.'

'Give me a minute to wash my hands,' I say as I head for the stairs.

When we're seated, and Lucia has me in her grasp again, she asks me if everything is settled with the cottage.

'Yes, I have the key,' I say, fishing it out of my pocket. Unnecessarily. 'And I have decided to move in tomorrow. I shall leave about ten in the morning.'

Lucia puts down her knife and fork. 'So soon?'

'Remember Lucia, I am only there for three months to get this book done and I want to start immediately. Please, don't look so worried.'

'I am not worrying,' she says, taking up her knife and fork again. I can see she has no appetite. 'I just cannot get used to the thought of you being away. But don't worry. I will find plenty to do. I will visit some friends more often. I have neglected them in the last few years. Perhaps you being away will be good for both of us.'

Can she mean that?

'Come see me next Sunday.'

'I will. You'll need food in your new house – after lunch I want to get some groceries for you.'

'No need for that. I will have plenty of time to do all that in Casarsa.'

Though part of me feels guilty about leaving her, I know she will only try to develop a routine of bringing me food – and then we'll back to square one with her in the kitchen.

Elisabeth joins us. She's happy, smiling. We've told her of my 'project'. I suppose she thinks she will be a bit freer for three months. If only Lucia felt the same.

'When do you leave? Mother will miss you.'

'I know, but I'm sure you can look after her.'

'Of course,' she says lightly, thinking only of herself.

'Visit me sometimes,' I say. 'And bring a friend if you wish.'

That night Lucia and I just lie in bed in the dark, and I know she wants me to make love to her. Neither body nor spirit is willing. It's as if I have met someone else and Lucia is a stranger. I cannot respond to her.

This is a new, terrible experience for both of us.

Poor Lucia. I just wrap an arm around her shoulders, and in the flash of sleep it is suddenly morning.

'Sorry about last night,' I say to Lucia as we dress.

She turns from the mirror and asks me something she has only asked once before.

'Do you love me Marco?'

Without thinking I say, 'You know I do.' But I think, 'Do I?'

I only know that I am more aware of myself. Perhaps this little separation will give me time to think, not just to write this book – this book that I still know nothing about.

'I am going now Lucia.'

She throws her arms around my neck and kisses me tenderly in a silent display of affection. For the first time I am aware of her complexity – or am I just projecting my own confusion on her? She is a woman who buries her feelings, and does not say truly what is in her mind.

292

She forces me to analyse her, when now I need time to examine myself.

In the car I feel free, like the first time I left my parents. What an awful, wonderful, feeling.

I don't see many workers toiling in the fields. The day – the season – is hotting up, and the sense of adventure overtakes me.

On my arrival in Casarsa I decide on impulse to enter the church. The huge iron door I suppose is always open. Though virtuously chalk-white on the outside, with its simple threat to sinners of judgement and damnation, the church within is all soft, sensuous, rainbows; the stained-glass window saints hinting at a gentler God.

I kneel, and though I am not one for prayer, I speak to Him. I pray for Lucia and Elisabeth. And for myself. But really I am wishing.

Down Via Valvasone people in the streets stare at me as if I were from Mars. Strangers are treated with suspicion. I can imagine little happens in these secluded places where life is dictated by the seasons and by the sun.

Why are they so curious?

When I open the door to the cottage I am impressed again by the ancient forge in the old kitchen. No door bars your way to the living room which looks out onto the garden and its pump. Since yesterday, when Kate showed me around, someone has dipped into the beeswax because the air is fresh with polish, and the dark old wood of the furniture gleams its welcome.

Kate had asked me to sleep in the east bedroom. Naturally I try the door to the west. Naturally it is locked. What better way to arouse my curiosity?

I go downstairs and decide to do some shopping first. I'll unpack when I return.

Before I make it to the door there's a knock. I peer through the kitchen window and see a large woman standing out there. It's the next door neighbour I talked to when I first discovered the house.

It's best if I answer, I can't very well ignore her.

She says to me in the high voice of these parts, in her Friulian dialect, '*Buongiorno*! Would you like to eat? I hear you're on your own!'

'Thank you,' I say, astonished at her generosity. 'but I'm on my way to do some shopping.'

'I hope you don't mind me barging in like this. I saw you moving in and I wondered if you needed anything. You have only to ask.'

How friendly she has become. Not too friendly I hope.

'I think you are very kind,' I say.

'My name is Vilma.'

'OK, I'll remember that.'

I won't encourage her by volunteering my Christian name just in case she bangs on my door every five minutes. In any case, she probably knows all that she needs to know about me already.

When she's out of sight I make a dash for the town square. The one general store seems to cater for most of Casarsa's needs. As I study the shelves I confront the reality of looking after myself – will I need salt for the gnocchi? How long does it take to boil spaghetti? This will be a challenge after Lucia's cosseting.

I settle for a couple of ham rolls for lunch.

Early in the afternoon I'm still not in the mood to write so I decide to investigate Casarsa further. In particular, I feel I want to walk down the country lane off Via Valvasone that takes you to the fields – where Lucia and I were chased off by that irate farmer.

Nobody is about because siesta time approaches; so I leap over a fence and into a field.

I hold my face up to the sun to feel the dry, comforting heat. No wonder the labourers sleep at this time of day. I am drawn to a bridge and I decide to sit here for a while, on its modest prow, above a narrow stream that's slithered its snake-like way from the mountains.

How beautiful it is here. And how peaceful, as the silvery lapping of the water below makes me sleepy.

I lie down, lost in my thoughts, aware of birdsong. Suddenly I am disturbed by a curious sound. It is hard to describe. It is like a rattling of something, a rattling from somewhere beyond the surrounding trees and bushes. The sound is hard and deliberate, not of nature.

I get up to see what could be making such a noise. But there's nothing to account for it. No mischievous kids or lunatic farmers. How odd. Still, the area is new to me; perhaps I am just no longer used to my own company, and the mind is playing tricks. What does it matter?

Back at the house I get out my typewriter. I decide I will do all my work in the living room. It's the best place because it looks out on the garden which I can gaze on when I am searching for inspiration.

The silence of the house. The absence of routine. No Lucia.

Early evening I decide to go to the *osteria* Sabatini – the local bar off Via Valvasone. The truth is I've not accomplished much today. I stared at the typewriter, then out at the garden water pump, and finally at the distant Dolomites. I didn't think a single thought.

At the Sabatini there are just four farmers at a table playing cards and sipping liqueurs.

The padrone – who has the characteristic leathery skin

of these parts and wears brown braces – wishes me a good evening and asks me what I would like to drink.

'A scotch with ginger ale, thank you.'

He asks me if I am just passing through or new to these parts. Then he adds before I can reply, 'Are you the writer?'

'I am a writer,' I say. 'Word has got round pretty quickly.'

'Well, Signore, this is a small town. Everybody knows everybody's business.'

'That's cosy,' I say, 'but I can live with that. In fact I like Casarsa very much already.'

'I'm pleased to hear it! You're staying at old Martina's place, aren't you?'

'Renting it.'

'The old girl's been trying to get rid of the place for ages. Can't give it away!'

'Surprising. It's a desirable property.'

He smirks, oddly I imagine, before he attends to someone else.

I drink up quickly because I feel ready for an early night. I am so very tired.

I'm out as soon as I hit the pillow, but at around three in the morning a noise awakens me – that strange rattling noise again, similar to the sound I heard out in the country only hours ago. It's so loud the whole house seems to vibrate.

Wood or steel – I can't identify the sound or fix in my mind what it is like. I think of the sound that sometimes warns of an earthquake – but surely the neighbours would be in hysterics in the streets by now.

I get up and go downstairs. I even prowl about the garden. But I see nothing which explains this disturbance. Now I do feel a little unnerved.

Perhaps a local is trying to scare me off.

Soon afterwards I return to bed and manage to doze off. In the morning my first thought is of the night event, but I decide to try to forget about it. Soon I will be used to the sights and sounds of Cararsa – and not exaggerate the little things I probably wouldn't even notice if Lucia were here.

The days rush by quickly. Sunday morning Lucia arrives by rail. I think she preferred this to my picking her up in order to discourage Elisabeth joining us (who gets madly bored 'hanging about' at stations). So Lucia has me to herself.

I go to meet her. I tell her she looks so pretty in her blue dress, her dark hair freshly done.

To my surprise the first thing she asks me is not whether I've eaten well but how I am getting on with the novel. Slowly, I lie.

'And what about you, dear?' I ask. 'How do you spend your days – all alone?'

'I keep busy,' she says. 'I visit friends, and so on.'

I tell her that I have booked a place for lunch in the village – 'I am sure you will like it.'

'You didn't have to do that,' she says, put out. 'I could have done the cooking myself and it would have been much nicer – just me and you in your little house without going to a restaurant!'

I feel very annoyed with Lucia about this.

'Don't you ever want to get away from the cooker once in a while?' I say snappily, as we stand on the steps outside the station.

'Well, I am sorry you feel that. I was only thinking that the afternoon goes very quickly, and we haven't got much time together . . .'

'We will have enough time,' I say gently. 'We don't have to spend all afternoon in the restaurant.'

After lunch we return to the house in a much better mood – 'We've still got hours to go', I say, teasing her a bit. The wine has loosened us up, so I add grinning, 'Would you like to have a little siesta with me? I want to make up for lost time.'

And then, without thinking, I grab hold of her and kiss her fully on the mouth. She responds with such passion that I can't remember the last time it was like this – not even on our honeymoon.

I carry her upstairs and we lie on the bed and kiss feverishly – as if we are about to part forever.

Afterwards, lying there together, Lucia asks me again if I love her.

'Have you any doubts?' I reply.

'I just want you to say you do.'

Instead, I put my arm around her to show that I do care about her. And we sleep.

When we wake it is nearly time for Lucia to return home. 'Don't worry,' I say to her. 'It will only take a few minutes to run you to the station.'

On the platform waiting for the train she turns to me and says she loves me very much – 'I want you to know how I feel about you.'

I stand there looking at her wondering: do I really love this woman? I just cannot bring myself to say I love her. I only feel deep sadness, loss.

The train arrives and I kiss her goodbye and I ask her to give lots of kisses to Elisabeth from me. On the way back to the house I wonder whether we should see each other again in the next three months. I need time to sort myself out.

As I draw up to the house I see Vilma sitting on her

doorstep, drinking up the last remnants of sunlight as they do here. She waves to me – no doubt she will be telling the village tomorrow about my 'mystery woman' as she shops down Via Valvasone.

Back in the house I sense once more that feeling of freedom without Lucia around. I cannot ignore this sensation, no matter how wicked it is. I need to know why I feel this way.

Monday. I feel curiously excited, a sense that something dramatic is about to happen – but about what I do not know. In the morning I do some work on my novel. And later, as usual, I decide to go for a little walk out in the countryside.

I have an established route: down the narrow country lane and into the field which takes me to the bridge – always deserted.

Today I walk beyond the bridge. I am fascinated by everything around me, by the mysteries of the countryside. I gaze up at the twittering skylarks, a sound of summer I have started to take for granted. It's a sound, which after a while, like the lapping of the stream, sends me into a trance; a kind of waking sleep where I feel I no longer have control . . . I lie down . . . my eyes are heavy . . . do I sleep now?

I am fascinated by the loops and turns of the skylarks, and just as one seems to swoop to the ground, my attention is caught by the sight of a distant human figure in red who appears from nowhere.

In my dream, it is a woman, and by her purposeful movements I see that she is heading towards me. As she approaches I see that she is very young, slender, dark haired and with very dark looks – certainly not someone of Casarsa, and probably from the south if she's Italian.

I get to my feet. Why does she not move away from a man in a lonely place? She continues to advance and for a moment it idly passes my mind that she maybe be an apparition.

A few metres away from me and she pauses and smiles. I still don't know if she's real, but to me she's the most beautiful woman I have ever seen in my life.

I cannot take my eyes off her. And *her* eyes – as black and polished as jet beads – meet mine with an intensity that entrances me. I have this immediate and absurd fantasy that we have been waiting for each other, and there are no doubts.

For how long we stand here gazing at each other I do not know – time, as in sleep, as in death, does not exist. I dream that she is inside me. A stranger enters my life and in one moment touches something deep within me.

On impulse I break the silence: 'What is your name?' I ask.

'Carmen,' she says without hesitation.

'My name is Marco de Silva.'

I wanted to add: 'And I have been waiting for you all my life.'

'I was waiting for you, too.' she says.

Can she read my mind? I am astonished. I don't think to ask her why she has been waiting for me.

Instead I say, 'You are not wearing shoes – don't you feel uncomfortable?'

'I feel much better without them,' she says. I notice a slight Spanish inflection in her voice. Then she adds, 'I do wear shoes on special occasions.'

She raises her tiny hands to me and I take and kiss them.

'Where are you going now Carmen?'

'I am going to see a friend who lives not far away from here.'

'May I walk with you then?'

'Sure,' she says lightly, 'but only half the way.'

'Why half the way? Don't you want your friend to see me?'

'There is no need for you come any farther.'

'May I see you again, Carmen? I would like to see you.'

'You will see me again, and you know why.'

What does she mean? I am unable to ask her. Instead I ask her where she lives and when I am going to see her again.

'I live in the next village,' she says, 'in San Lorenzo. It is not far away from here. And in the next few days I will come to see you. Where do you live Marco?'

'In Casarsa. I have rented a house for three months – at the bottom of Via Valvasone.'

'Well,' she says, almost teasingly, 'I know where you live. You are the writer?'

'How did you know that?'

'Often I am in Casarsa and I hear the people talking, and you must know in these little places like this . . .

'I know,' I say, thinking of Vilma.

I ask her to tell me precisely when she will visit me.

'I will see you the day after tomorrow.'

I cannot help but cup her face in my hands and kiss her tenderly, as if she has willed me to do this.

'I'll see you soon,' I hear her say as she wanders away from me, as light as silk.

As I stir in the grass I whisper: 'My life is yours now, and you will have the power to do what you like with it.'

I am fully awake now – but was I asleep? I can't tell. Never has a dream seemed so real.

Only when I am back at the house do I remember that

Carmen said I could accompany her half way to her friend's house. And I had forgotten!

My mind is in a storm. Did I meet a real Carmen or did I just dream her? In sleep we assume we know so many things for no reason. Our meeting had the texture of a dream.

Carmen is real in one sense. She has made me more aware of what I do *not* feel for Lucia and of what has been missing in our marriage. Am I infatuated? Deluded?

Something has opened within me at long last. And nothing can be the same again.

And though I have just left Carmen I have this feeling she is still with me here in the house, and she is in me.

I never imagined anyone could affect me so. What if one day I had to tell Lucia about Carmen? About a dream woman?

Everything I wanted for my novel is all here, me and Carmen. I shall start the book again!

Chapter Three

As I pour myself some wine I hear a knock at the door. I wonder who it can be at this time.

In front of me is a thin man who seems familiar to me – at least I recall the body type.

'Sorry to bother you,' he begins, and takes off his felt hat, 'but you must remember who I am.'

And suddenly I do – he's the farmer who threatened Lucia and me the other week because we were trespassing on his land.

'Yes,' I say. 'I remember you – and what can I do for you? I hope you don't have any more complaints.'

The farmer registers the edge in my voice with a smile. Then he adds that he has come to apologise. He didn't mean to be unpleasant and asks me to forget about it, no hard feelings.

Well, perhaps he's not so bad after all. I do hope I can find time to get to know these good people of Casarsa who are so different from the cynical town-dwellers. They maybe peasants but they are not unreasonable – or maybe I am the peasant!

'So will you allow my wife and me to eat under your tree next time?' I ask, smiling.

'Anytime! No bad feelings?' – and he holds out his large, bark-like hand to shake.

'No,' I say, taking his hand, 'no bad feelings.'

He replaces his hat. 'I must return to the farm, Signor De Silva.'

So he knows my name.

At my desk I struggle with the new thoughts and feelings that Carmen has planted in me. Something new is taking shape in my heart, not yet ripened – something exciting and true.

At three in the morning I am awoken by that horrible sound again – the rattling sound which could be from hell. It can't be my imagination.

I am not dreaming it for the sound is real; it's hard and grating and I can almost feel its strength surging through the house. A storm would explain it. But outside is still.

In a place like this it's possible someone is playing a little joke on me, the newcomer. No one's going to scare me off.

Brightened by this thought I return to my bed and sleep.

Next day, to my surprise, my daughter Elisabeth visits me.

'I can't stay long, papa, but I thought I'd just come and peek at you. How's the novel coming on?'

She sounds so flippant about everything – 'Fine! Everything is going fine.' She never asks to see a manuscript. 'How is your mother?'

'She's OK but she misses you very much. Why don't you visit home and see her? We're not that far away.'

Like most children she would be running her parents' life given half the chance.

'I can't darling, I am far too busy; besides she will be here next Sunday.'

'But you've got the car – you could visit her in the week if you wanted to.' She curls a lip.

'That's impossible. You don't understand and please change the subject. Tell me about you. How's school? Still thinking of becoming a teacher?'

'Well, yes,' she replies, allowing herself to be deflected. 'But there's plenty of time yet—' Elisabeth stops, turning to face a new figure in the doorway.

'Sorry,' says Kate to me. 'I didn't realise you had visitors.'

'No, no, come in,' I say. 'Meet my daughter Elisabeth.'

'Pleased to meet you,' says Kate.

Elisabeth just smiles back. In fact the smile is more of a leer, which means mischief.

Kate continues, 'I called Marco because I was wondering if you need anything. Just let me know.'

'Thank you but everything's fine.'

'Well then I must be off – my mother asked after you by the way.'

'My regards to her – tell her I shall be visiting shortly.'

As Kate disappears down the short path Elisabeth spins round to me with a devilish look on her pretty little face.

'"Marco!"' she echoes, mockingly. 'How friendly of her. Do you fancy her dad? She's quite attractive – for a country girl!'

Sometimes I could smack her but I say, calmly, 'Not in the least, darling. Just because she's attractive doesn't mean I fancy her, as you put it.' Then I tease her – 'There are plenty of attractive women in Casarsa, many big families with beautiful daughters, but I only have eyes for you.'

'Mmmm . . .' Elisabeth bats her eyes playfully, and giggles.

How many men will fall for her? She has my dark eyes and hair, kept short and curled, but a classically framed face:

305

oval with high cheek bones and a permanent half smile on her face. Who does she take after in the family? Certainly not Lucia.

An hour later I run her to the station and soon again I'm back at the house alone. Even with Elisabeth here I was aware of Carmen around me, in my thoughts; and now that I am alone I feel her presence more intensely, which maybe just the longing that she is real and not a dream. I need to see her.

Tomorrow I pray to see her . . . dream or not.

I sleep soundly for a change, no disturbing sounds. Perhaps the local prankster has grown bored.

I wake up full of new ideas. I feel even greater confidence about my new book.

Normally I put off the dread moment of writing as long as possible. I'll potter about in the garden or read a paper. But today I feel possessed – inspired might be a better word – and I get to work as soon as I've washed and dressed.

The words pour out on the page like a deluge, as if a dam has burst within me at last, and I feel free to say all that I ever wanted to say.

So driven am I by this new venture that I forget about time. So I'm amazed when I look up at the wall clock to see it's just passed one in the afternoon.

Who or what has stolen my time?

Just as I am about to resume work after a quick lunch there is a knock at the door; or rather a gentle brushing sound.

Who now? Another curious villager?

I open the door. It is Carmen. Nothing could have prepared me for this.

She is no dream.

A living, breathing Carmen.

She looks at me as if to say, 'I love you.'

I take her hands in mine and feel the warmth of her flesh, the softness of her skin. I cannot help myself when I say, 'If only you could know how much I have missed you.'

'I have missed you too,' she responds gently.

I have the sensation that everything already has been said and that we already know each other as lovers.

Have I fallen asleep at my desk and returned to the dream where I first met her?

'But,' she continues, 'you have to understand that I have many things to do to help my aunt on the farm. I have many chores to do in the house. As much as I want to be with you I am left with little time for myself, but I want you to know that I am always thinking of you.'

'My darling,' I say. 'If only you knew how much you mean to me – just to see you makes me feel so happy.'

In the back of my mind is the thought that Carmen has not mentioned her aunt before, or her farm – yet she speaks as if I know all about her . . .

I admire her beautiful face, her dark hair and eyes, her slender figure . . .

'But I know nothing about you,' I say. 'You are Spanish?'

'My parents are Spanish,' she says simply. 'I now live with my aunt and uncle in San Lorenzo, for the time being . . . and one day you will know why I am here,' she adds oddly.

'Why you are here? That sounds mysterious.'

She does not explain. Instead she says, 'There's one thing I don't like about my aunt – she does not give me much freedom. She's very old-fashioned and always keeps a close eye on what I do and where I go.'

'Let me meet your aunt and uncle, Carmen—'

'Not just yet,' she says with certainty. 'Give me time to prepare them.'

'But I can drive you back. We can go out – I have a car. We can be together – just me and you.'

'Yes,' she responds, 'but please give me time.'

'When do I see you again?' I feel slightly desperate, as if I fear she is a dream and won't return.

'Maybe tomorrow at the same time as today,' she says.

'Well, since I can't come to you, you must come to me. Don't stay away too long. You'll make me very unhappy.'

I then take hold of her and kiss her lovingly, almost delicately. She holds me and kisses me with the same tenderness, and I know this cannot be a dream despite everything.

After a few moments she slips out from my embrace. She tells me she has to go, and asks me whether I shall forgive her.

'I'd like to force you to stay.'

She waves gently and then walks quickly away down Via Valvasone and towards the fields and San Lorenzo.

I am tempted to follow her, not to allow her out of my sight, but something restrains me within. This time I am more aware of her strangeness, and her total hold over me in our brief moment together.

There are so many things I do not know about her.

This air of mystery, the intensity of our passion. Are not dreams like this?

Back at my desk I rub my eyes as her spell weakens its hold over me. I wonder why she does not ask me anything about my life. She has not asked me whether I am married and yet when I see her I am certain she knows that I am.

Like the way she knew I was a writer when we first met.

Not that any of this matters to the love we feel for each other. Can you love a person you do not know?

The next time I see her I must tell her everything about me – just in case she does not know already. And I want to know all about her, the facts of her life.

No secrets must be between us.

I feel she is by my side even now.

I cannot imagine ever feeling this way for another woman. Certainly not for Lucia. Only once in a life can you experience such magical, complete love.

I am looking now at my typewriter. And since I do not have the will or the energy to go out for a walk, I shall try to shut out what has just happened and get back to my novel where perhaps I can make some sense of my life.

Chapter Four

During the night the terrible sound returns to haunt me, the rattling again, at its appointed time – three in the morning. The usual noise, then new, strange sounds of scratching and rubbing, which could be coming from the west bedroom, or downstairs or even outside. I don't know.

'What can it be?' I ask myself as I wearily throw back the bed covers, trembling a little now.

It can't be mischief. The regularity, the sheer cacophony, puts it beyond a joke.

I get up and look around but of course I'm unable to trace the source of the sound. When I think I've located it, it seems to shift to another place.

A game maybe, but no joke.

In my heart I knew Carmen would not turn up today. I had sensed her own uncertainty. So, disappointed, and troubled by the night activity, I decide to visit Signora Martina.

I haven't seen her since I moved in, and I'd like to ask her about the house.

Kate answers the door when I pop round later in the afternoon. She looks surprised to see me.

'That's good timing,' she says. 'I have just made some fresh coffee. Will you join us?'

'Yes,' I say, welcoming her friendliness, 'I'd like that very much.'

I see her mother is not in her customary place this time, by the window in the kitchen.

'Is your mother all right?' I whisper.

'Yes, she is fine,' says Kate, pouring coffee into cups from a percolator. 'She will be down in a few minutes.'

'Sugar?'

'Please, just one, thanks.'

'Your daughter Elisabeth is pretty.'

'Yes, yes . . .'

I hear the staircase groan, announcing Signora Martina's perilous, slow descent.

At the foot of the stairs she smiles broadly at the sight of me.

I say, 'I am glad to see that you are keeping well, Signora.'

'I must not complain,' she says resignedly. 'And how are you getting on with your novel?'

She lowers herself carefully into her favourite chair in the kitchen.

'Very well—'

'Good! And how rewarding it must be.'

Kate serves her coffee.

'May I talk to you Signora,' I ask, 'about a private matter . . . ?' I add that I haven't come just for that, of course; but to find out how she is—

'I know that,' she says, bringing the cup to her lips. 'But what do you want to ask me?'

At this point Kate diplomatically leaves us – 'I've got a lot to do,' she says without taking offence.

The Signora does a quarter turn in her chair to me – 'So, Signor de Silva . . .'

'I'm not sure what you will think about this, Signora.

But I'd be grateful if you kept this between us – this matter I want to discuss.'

'You don't have to worry about that!' she says, smiling with interest. 'I am not one of those nattering rustics in the village with a loose tongue, you know! I do know how to keep a secret.'

'Of course. I want to ask you Signora – is your house – the house I am renting, is it haunted?'

The Signora almost drops her coffee and looks at me with horror.

'Haunted? Look here, young man, I lived in that house for many years, for longer than you've been on this earth probably, and I never heard such a thing.'

Then she composes herself, rearranging her colourful shawl, for she is evidently fascinated. She wants more details.

'What actually happened?' she asks.

'Three times now in your house, at three in the morning, I have been awoken by an odd sound, a sort of drumming or rattling in the whole of the house. Despite my searches I have found nothing to explain the disturbances – certainly I have seen nothing.'

'That is really very weird,' she remarks. After a moment a thought occurs to her – 'Maybe some local lads are having a little fun with you? I know in the village there are a few lads, who after a few drinks . . .'

'I have thought about that but I am not so sure any-more.'

I then tell the Signora about the noise I heard in the Casarsa fields.

She looks thoughtfully at me. She says, 'So, then, perhaps it is not the house which is haunted . . . maybe it is you! But still, there maybe something in what you say but don't let it worry you. I know these things can be very alarming.'

She adds that if I hear these sounds again I am to tell her – 'And I will deal with it.'

'What could you do?' I ask the old lady, mystified.

'I'll tell you next time – if there is a next time. Now, why don't you stay for supper.'

'Thank you, but I have so much to do and I must go.'

'Well then,' says the old lady, half-shrugging. 'Some other time, Signor de Silva. What you have just told me – it will stay just with me.'

'I appreciate that.'

I notice a man and a woman seated in their doorway – the Casarsa way of amusing oneself before bedtime. As I pass by they look up at me boggle-eyed, silently, as if I were some kind of alien.

On my doormat is an envelope. Who can this be from? I don't recognise the hand. It can't be Lucia. Then as I open it I have a premonition it's from Carmen.

It is.

I am breathless with excitement, and astounded. This is the first piece of evidence I have that she is not a fantasy. I am certainly not asleep now.

She is real, not a dream-lover who comes to me when my mind is disturbed.

She writes: 'Forgive me my love, something here has held me up. I'll explain to you, as soon as I am able to see you. Forgive me again, my love, my life. Carmen.'

Just a little note, but it overwhelms me. I feel I want to weep.

Who delivered the letter? Carmen herself, or a friend? That I won't know till I see her.

I kiss the note and place it in my wallet.

A week rushes by and no sign of Carmen. I feel bereft,

313

sometimes desperate. I am tempted to go look for her in San Lorenzo. But any minute now Lucia arrives and I have to wait for her.

Do I tell her about Carmen? Is it too soon? What is there to tell but that I have met a girl I do not know, know nothing about, except that she lives with her aunt and uncle — someplace.

At eleven Lucia arrives, prompt.

I try to behave normally by being chatty. I talk about the village people, the shopping, the crops, anything. But I am not normally talkative, the reverse in fact. Lucia knows something is not right.

'What's wrong?' she asks finally.

'Nothing really.' I sit down.

I have never been able to live with guilt. When something has to be said I can't stop myself.

'What do you mean, Marco?' She stops unloading the food hamper she has brought. To look at it makes me feel awful, thinking of all the time and love she has put into packing it. 'Is there something I should know?'

'Yes,' I say. 'There is something you have to know.'

'I am listening.'

'Come and sit down and have a glass of wine.' I pour.

'I can't drink now.'

I gulp down my wine, throwing back my head, then fill the glass again.

I start to tell her that I have met someone else.

'Here, in Casarsa?' She says it as if such a thing were not possible. In Casarsa.

'I have to tell you this. I feel for her very . . . much.'

'Already? You've only been here three or four weeks. Or did you move here to be with her?'

'No, I have just met her.'

'But, how can you . . . ?'

314

She stays quiet for a full minute staring at me.

Then: 'So, this is it?'

'Yes.'

Lucia rises from the seat and fiddles with something in the hamper.

She is calm though I know she is devastated. She does not say she is in pain. She does not ask me how I could have done this to her. This is not Lucia's way.

'Strange,' she says. 'I always knew that one day you would find someone else. I never felt you were close to me. I know I don't always express my feelings but I love you and I've never wanted anyone else. What do you intend to do?'

I am staggered by her words, by her painful acceptance. What else did I expect? I could understand it if she screamed at me. Tried to kill me. Instead, this terrible acceptance of all that life gives to her and takes away.

'I don't know,' I say. 'Only that I want to be with her more than anything in this world. I am sorry, Lucia, but that is the way it is.'

'And what about Elisabeth? Don't you think about her?'

'Of course I do. I love her. One day she will understand.'

Lucia closes the hamper and puts on her wrap. 'There is no point in my staying. There's a train in less than an hour.'

'Are you sure you want to go now?'

'Of course I am,' she replies sharply. 'There's nothing here keeping me now and you know it.'

'I'll take you to the station then.'

On the station forecourt I say, 'Give my love to Elisabeth and tell her that I always want to see her.'

Lucia nods. Then she opens the car door.

As the train comes into the station I say: 'Forgive me.'

She looks at me: 'There is nothing to forgive. I never felt I had you.'

I watch the train move away and disappear down the track.

What have I done? What happens now?

Later in the afternoon Kate calls. She knows this is Lucia's day so I suppose she's picked her moment to meet her. She must be surprised to find me alone.

'Sorry if I am intruding, Marco, but I am here just as messenger. My mother would like to see you when you have a moment.'

'Oh, well, tell her I'll be round as soon as possible.' Kate leaves.

Maybe the old lady has something to tell me about the house, about what I have told her.

I look at the hamper on the table and think of Lucia and how I have no appetite. She is a strong woman. Strong, but emotions are the hardest thing in life to control. I feel suffocated – I need to get out into the air and breathe.

I daren't admit the hope to myself that I may bump into Carmen on my walk, so I take the narrow country lane which takes me into the country.

Then on impulse I doubleback and decide to trek to San Lorenzo – about half-an-hour away on foot. I kick stones on the way, stirring up small dust clouds. Dogs bark menacingly in the distance. You always hope they are well leashed.

If anything San Lorenzo is quieter than Casarsa, less affluent with many abandoned, dilapidated farm houses. It could be the nineteenth century if I knew no better.

In the village square a group of boys are playing marbles. No harm asking them if they know where Carmen lives. After all, everyone knows everyone.

They look at me as if I am the village idiot. One *ragazzo* – boy – says to me in crude Friuli dialect: 'There's no one round here with that name.'

'Are you sure?'

'Course,' says another, getting off his knees, hoping for some lire I suppose. 'Nobody lives here with a funny name like that.'

'Funny? There's nothing funny about the name Carmen.'

All the boys laugh and mimic my out-of-town accent.

Silly peasant boys.

I retrace my steps along Via San Lorenzo, heading back to the narrow lane that leads into Casarsa, close to where I met Carmen for the first time that magical day. I shall never forget that moment till the day I die: and even after death I will look for her.

Back home I drink more wine.

At my desk I think again of that tremendous moment when I first saw Carmen, in the hope of capturing the sense of dream and awe for my book.

I hear a soft knocking at the door but choose to ignore it, thinking it might be a breeze as the door is ajar. I hear the door open wider. I turn. There in the threshold is Carmen.

She steps in – 'Carmen!' I shout.

I take her in my arms and we hold each other for many moments. She is real, I feel her, I can smell her.

'I have been looking for you all afternoon – I went to San Lorenzo,' I say.

'Did you get my note?'

'Yes – what held you up?'

'My aunt was unwell – you must not torment yourself. I will always be near you.'

Suddenly I notice something on the table – I didn't see Carmen carry anything in. It's placed next to Lucia's food hamper.

It is a plastic folder with a reddish floral pattern tied with a thin elastic band.

'Did you put this here?' I ask Carmen, pointing at it.

'Yes. It contains my diary and I want you to read it when you have time. It is my life story and it will tell you everything you want to know about me.'

'Your life story? You are too young—'

'Please read it.'

I hold her gently this time – 'Why don't you tell me yourself. There are many things I want to tell you about me.'

She holds my gaze, then says: 'I know that you are married. Your wife is called Lucia and you have a young daughter.' Then she adds: 'Is this what you wanted to tell me?'

'How do you know all this? Need I ask!'

'My darling, there is nothing you can hide from Casarsa. I know many people here, and when I pass this way I discover many things about everybody. I want you to read my diary and use it for your novel.'

'But my book is already about you – it will be my best book.'

'May I see it?'

'When it is finished, and then you will be the first to read it. Are you upset about me being married?'

'I am not upset, it isn't very important to me. The most important thing is that we are together as one. We will always be together and no one can separate us.' She pauses, then adds, 'How would you feel if I asked to stay with you tonight?'

I can hardly believe my ears or describe how dreadfully excited I feel. I hold her tight as if she is about to disappear again and kiss her passionately and tell her how much I love her.

'What will your aunt say about you staying out all night?'

'I don't worry about tomorrow,' she says gently. 'Tonight is our first night together and nothing else matters.'

'Are you sure?' Then I say how much I want her, with all my heart, soul and all my being. 'You are mine already in the eyes of God. Since I have known you Carmen I feel more closer to God.'

I want to celebrate our first night! I pour wine into glasses, I lay out the tablecloth and arrange the food Lucia brought for our lunch. I am too happy to worry about anyone else. There is no guilt, only a sense of rapturous abandon, total joy.

We hardly touch the food. I can see so much love in Carmen's eyes that I take hold of her and carry her upstairs.

I drift in and out of sleep for about an hour. When I stir Carmen is not in bed. I look at the clock – it's five in the morning. She must be downstairs so I call her. She's not in the house.

All I can hear is the cock crowing in Vilma's garden, a depressing reveille.

In the kitchen I find a note placed on Carmen's diary folder. It reads: 'Forgive me my love but I had to get back to San Lorenzo before my aunt wakes. I'll see you soon. Always, Carmen.'

Why does Carmen do this – why did she wait for me to sleep before slipping out? She said she did not care about tomorrow. Her aunt must be a horror.

I can't stand this separation. I must work out a plan for us to be together. There is much to sort out with Lucia, and none of this is going to be easy.

I place my hand on Carmen's diary but I don't feel ready yet to read it.

Chapter Five

Later in the morning I think of Signora Martina's request to see me. Though tired and irritable I'll go see her. Perhaps she can resolve at least one of the mysteries in my life.

There she is, back in her usual chair near the window of her kitchen.

'I was expecting you,' she says.

'*Buongiorno.*'

'Sit there then.' She points to the seat opposite hers as before.

'Kate said you wanted to see me.'

'I think that I maybe able to put your mind at rest—'

'About the house?'

'Yes. I have some information which – as I was saying – may put your mind at rest. As I suspected, I have discovered that there is indeed a small group of lads in the village. And after a few drinks they become a nuisance and play practical jokes – this is the nearest to crime in these parts, you know Signor de Silva. Anyone new around here, and they tease them for a while. Take my word for it. They soon grow bored of their sport. And then they look elsewhere to lark about.'

She is simply repeating what I first suspected.

'And what about the noise in the country, on the bridge?' I ask.

320

The old lady rolls her eyes towards the window for a moment. 'Well, that was probably an act of nature – "His wonders to behold",' she adds, dipping into the Bible for an answer.

'Sorry Signora Martina, I don't think so. But I am grateful to you for going to the trouble of trying to solve this mystery. Now I'd rather forget all about it. Just one question. How do these village lads ever get any sleep if they stay up till three in the morning?'

She gives me a half smile, as if I know nothing of the world . . . 'Well, of course they let off steam on Saturday nights after a week's work. Even I was young once, you know. All night they play, because they know the next day is Sunday and they can lie in.'

'So there's the problem, Signora Martina. These strange sounds have all happened at the beginning of the week, never on a Saturday. So I think we can rule out the *ragazzi*.'

The old lady visibly collapses into her seat, whereas a moment ago she had sat upright in her seat.

'Well, you have got me there!' she says with exhaustion. 'Whatever is the cause of these "hauntings" must come to light one of these days.'

'Perhaps,' I say rising to leave. 'But I am not worrying about it anymore, and it's best forgotten.'

To my amazement she struggles to her feet before she grabs at her stick.

'Signor de Silva, before you go, I should like to show you a photograph of my nephew. I meant to show it to you last time you were here. He is – was – so like you. The resemblance is quite remarkable. Will you excuse me then? I will have to go upstairs to my bedroom to get the photo – it's on my dressing table.'

I groan to myself at the prospect of poring over her

321

family album. Her huge body passes by – it's extraordinary that she can walk at all, her stick thudding on the hard floor every other step.

Like most of the older women in the village she only wears black. An ankle-length black dress, a black scarf. In my bad mood I ask myself: do these good Catholic ladies in black actually wear drawers? And, if so, are they black, too?

Perhaps one day I shall find out.

My lewd thoughts are broken by Kate who enters the kitchen carrying a bottle of wine and three glasses on a tray.

'Oh, where's mother?'

'Upstairs, to get a photo of her nephew she wants to show me.'

'Ah,' she says slowly, lowering her eyes – clearly mother and daughter have discussed this picture. Then: 'She's so independent! She could have asked me to get it – would you care for a glass of wine? It's a local wine, very good for the digestion.'

'Thank you, I will.'

We hear the thud of the old lady's stick on the staircase. Kate and I take hold of her on the bottom stair.

'You should have asked me, mamma—'

'Don't fuss over me!' explodes the old woman. I imagine she is about to hit Kate with her stick. 'I'm not an invalid yet! I managed perfectly.'

When she has rearranged herself in her chair she hands me the photo. It's quite old, with white creases . . .

'Don't you think he is just like you?' inquires Signora Martina. 'A remarkable likeness?'

Indeed it is. A chill passes through me at the similarity. The same expression in the eyes, shape of nose – everything. It is as if I am looking at a photograph of myself, or a twin.

'What happened to him?' I ask.

'I am afraid he is no longer with us,' replies the old lady. 'He died many years ago, and so very young, and I wish not to talk about how he died . . . one day perhaps . . . I'll tell you all about him. I was so very fond of him . . .'

Her voice trails off. Then she says wistfully: 'I have missed him for such a long time. It was a tragedy. I think of him every day.'

I finish my drink. This is tantalising – to know of a secret but not to be told it.

'I am sorry about your nephew, Signora Martina – I shall have to be going now, but I will see you again soon.'

'I want to say something before you go,' says the Signora, excitedly. 'When I saw you the very first time I thought, for one brief moment, that my nephew had come back to me. And I think that is why I allowed you to rent my house – because you look so like him. It's not my practice to rent my property out to anybody!'

'Perhaps your nephew was looking down on me the day I passed your house. I can always thank him.'

She and Kate are not sure how to react to my joke – have I been facetious?

'And now I must go.'

Kate sees me to the door as the old lady cries out that I should return for supper one evening.

As I stroll back home I marvel at how I had gone to *la casa* Martina in the hope of solving a mystery but instead am saddled with more: the fate of the nephew and the old lady's reluctance to discuss him. Also I forgot to ask her his name.

Another thing to wonder about when I cannot sleep.

I have hardly closed the door when Vilma calls with a parcel – 'From your daughter!'

'Why didn't she wait for me? I am very disappointed.'

'She told me she didn't have much time – she waited an hour! But she did say she'd be back next week.'

'Thank you, Vilma. You are very kind.'

But why the hell didn't Vilma let me know Elisabeth was in town? She knew where to find me: she follows my comings and goings like a society gossip – I am almost in the mood to say these things to my neighbour; but best not.

I close the door and open the parcel. As I thought, it is my clean laundry from Lucia, with a short note attached to the tissue paper in which my clothes are wrapped.

The note reads: 'Dear Marco, in spite of what has happened between us, I am still willing to do your laundry for you.'

I shake my head in disbelief. I almost want to laugh at the absurdity. She is trying to make me feel guilty by doing little things for me – and after all that I said to her!

Or is it possible that she still loves me and by doing things for me she hopes to remain near to me?

Flames of guilt sear through my gut. I will have to see Lucia and discuss a formal separation. The Church won't let us divorce, but we can separate. I cannot bear all this. That will be the best thing to do. And sort out the finances.

It's all going to be so unpleasant for both of us but it has to be done.

Yet another caller at my door. I came to Casarsa for peace yet I have had anything but.

I surrender my lunch and wearily open up my house. To my surprise – though I should expect to be surprised these days – it is an elderly man in what looks like a black frock. A man of the church, he also wears a large, wide-brimmed black hat and sinister steel-rimmed spectacles.

I am in no mood for a sermon. I say: 'I think you have come to the wrong house, padre.'

'Good afternoon,' he says, ignoring my impudence. 'I am the parish priest of Casarsa, Don Giovanni. As you are new to the village I thought I should pay you a visit. Is this convenient? I can come back.'

'I don't mind you visiting me so long as it is not to give me the last rites.'

His thin mouth – as wide as a frog's – stretches outward almost to his ears in a wintry smile. Perhaps he has a sense of humour.

'I had wanted to visit you before now,' he says, 'but I have been very busy.'

'Please, come in, reverend.'

He glances at the bottle of wine on a table, and on cue I offer him a glass.

'Thank you, I will,' he says. 'Oh, I see you have not finished your lunch.'

'I am running a little late today. But not to worry – I shall carry on eating if you don't mind. Would you care to join me?'

'Thank you, I have already eaten.'

No sooner than I've picked up my fork I see he has finished his glass of wine, and he blesses me as I pour him a second.

'Tell me, Signor de Silva, are you a religious man?'

I decide to give up buttering my roll.

'I don't disbelieve.'

'You are married?'

'Yes. And I have a daughter.'

'A pity they are not with you,' he says, shaking his head gently as if at the shame of it. 'Family has responsibilities.'

What does he mean? Is he hinting he knows of Carmen?

'The temptations of being a single man . . .'

'My work is my only temptation, padre.'

'You are a writer, I understand. A writer of, er, modern love.'

'I write romantic novels.'

'Yes, I don't think I have seen you in the church just yet.'

How could he possibly know that with his flock of three thousand to watch over? He must keep a register of who attends and who not, like at school. Still, he has the air of a natural-born listener and I can imagine that smile of his in the confessional box.

I say, 'The problem is that I am very busy . . .'

I attempt to explain my day, my problems. His mouth widens yet further in understanding – which is to say, I don't think he is listening at all – and before I know it I am pouring him his fourth, or fifth, glass of wine.

'Bless you, my son.'

I wonder whether I should open another bottle. Like a magician he empties his glass in a trice. Presto!

'Now I must be on my way, for there are others to visit.'

Don Giovanni rises unsteadily to his feet. 'Thank you for the wine, and try to call at the church sometime. Remember, God is always near.'

'Surely,' I say. 'I don't disbelieve.'

What a day. I look at my lunch, almost untouched: I don't feel like eating now. I open another bottle of wine and wish that Carmen were here. I miss her so.

I still wonder about her aunt. I dread to think that Carmen fell foul of her. The urge to return to San Lorenzo pulls at me – but then I turn to her diary on the sideboard which I promised to read.

I pick it up as if it were a delicate ornament, slip off its elastic tie and open its cover. Her hand is strikingly mature for one so young: firm, small, upright strokes. This is not the writing of an immature girl.

On the first page she tells the world that she is Carmen Fernandez and Spanish. I read on:

> *I had always loved to go to Italy for holidays. There I felt at home. I was planning to go again soon for three weeks.*
>
> *I worked in a lawyers' office as a secretary and the money was not bad. It earned me enough to play with. I would never ask my parents for money because I needed to be independent of them.*
>
> *They had done enough for me and I was grateful for the freedom they had given me. There are not many girls of my age who would be allowed to go abroad unchaperoned.*
>
> *When I did not work I attended flamenco dance classes — perhaps once I would have taken it up professionally and become the gypsy my parents always said I should have been. Everyone said I should have become a professional dancer.*

It is a cliché that you can never know another person. But it is still bewildering to observe another side of a loved-one: to learn of something which alters your original view. Carmen, a dancer! Already, a new Carmen is taking shape in my mind, and I need to know her.

I turn to another page:

> *I will never forget that July in Rome.*
>
> *It was so hot. I stayed with my aunt in San Lorenzo for a few days and then travelled to Rome. I wanted to see as much of Italy as possible.*
>
> *Also, I did not know when I would ever be able to return again.*

Then I headed back north towards Treviso but on a whim decided to return to Rome. I love the city though it terrifies me in some ways. I could never enter the Colosseum. I had read too much about it, and I think it must have played on my mind to think of all the people who once died there – for entertainment.

At night I wondered if I was once a Christian consumed by one of Nero's lions. Nothing could induce me into what is now just rubble surrounded by roads and traffic.

One morning I decided to shop near the Piazza di Spagna – I love just sitting on the steps and watching tourists. I was drawn to a pair of dainty shoes in a window display. As I wondered if I had enough money I couldn't help noticing a man standing behind me and looking at my reflection.

He said something silly in Italian – bellissima, I think – so I turned around to face him. I was immediately struck by his dark eyes, by the intensity of his gaze.

So many Italian men have tried this ploy with my – as if I were the only woman in the world. But he was different – there was kindness in his eyes, not that hard cynicism.

I was immediately attracted to him. I asked him in Italian what he had just said. Oh God! He said that he thought I was the most beautiful woman in the world.

Only an Italian could get away with that. I just smiled. Then he asked me if I would join him for an aperitif in a nearby bar on the Via Condotti. I said I needed something a lot cooler. He said, 'Let me introduce myself: I am Marcus Fiore.'

I told him I was Carmen Fernandez. He thought that was a lovely name – and repeated it over and over as if not to forget it – then took my hand. It was such a natural thing to do that I could not object.

We walked to a cafe on the Via Borgognona and sat

outside under an umbrella. As he sipped a liqueur and I an orange juice, he asked me what I was doing alone in the big city. I told him and then he said, 'Well then, it just so happens that I am also on holiday – would you like us to spend sometime together?'

I felt torn. I couldn't simply follow my first impressions like a silly girl, but I didn't want to refuse him as I might not see him again. So, really, I found it very easy to say that I would like that very much.

I told him I wanted him to show me as much as possible – now he was my tour guide.

'Of Rome or of Italy?' he asked with a grin. Yes, that was a good question. Then he said that I talked as if I would never return to Italy again – so greedy was I to see everything. In a way that was true as I did not think I could afford to return for a while.

Then I thought: Why do I trust this man who I have only just met? For some reason I did, and I knew I would be safe wherever he took me – anywhere. What he wanted to show me I would be happy to see.

'Carmen,' he said, 'it's a ten minute walk to my automobile.'

I was very impressed by that, and amazed when I saw it. It must have cost the earth. I thought then he must have lots of money and certainly he always spent it freely wherever we went as if there were no tomorrow.

We got into his automobile and drove off.

I put away the diary for now. Strange she uses an old expression like 'automobile' instead of car. I shall read more later. I am surprised that Carmen has put her thoughts on paper because she is so elusive. I imagine her as a butterfly, not wishing to be pinned down.

But I can see already how her diary could be used as a

basis for my novel. I have noted passages which I could quote . . .

I feel like getting out for a walk in the country. You never know, I may wander to San Lorenzo again for any sign of Carmen . . .

From my now familiar country lane I see four farm workers with their pitchforks toiling in the late afternoon sun, and others perched on their carts until the night takes them to their beds – after the bars.

But these good people do work hard. Not like me, who works when the mood takes me and has time and energy for walks. The women I think work harder than the men. They work the fields and then run the home.

Who would want to be a woman?

I wake as from a sleep-walk and find myself half-way to San Lorenzo. I spot a middle-aged woman dressed in black emerge from a narrow side road, almost as if she has been lying in wait for me.

She walks towards me. Then to my astonishment she stops in front of me and says: 'Are you Signor de Silva?'

'But, yes—'

'I have here a letter for you and it's from Carmen.'

My heart pumps hard just at the sound of her name. From a fold in her dress the woman hands me an envelope. And then she walks away – back down the side road.

I cry out, 'Wait a moment, who are you?'

But she does not answer, scurrying into the wheat fields, where she disappears.

I open the envelope. Carmen writes: 'Don't worry about me my love. Everything is all right with my aunt but I have to go to Spain because my mother is unwell.'

Something collapses within me, as if I have been told of her death.

'I hope,' the letter continues, 'that I will see you soon. You are my life. Carmen.'

Once again I sense her presence. But that woman in black, where did she go? I scan the fields; there's no sign of her. Could she have been the aunt? And what a coincidence that we should meet on the road like this – it is too bizarre. How did she know who I was? – I think she knew, though she asked my name. As everything else to do with Carmen nothing makes sense.

Her diary will keep her close to me. Her absence will force me to read it all. The air of mystery is as intoxicating as love itself – I hope the two have not fused in my heart. That without the mystery I cannot love Carmen.

Nevertheless I walk all the way to San Lorenzo in pathetic hope of spotting her. Maybe she has changed her plans . . .

By the time I return home I have convinced myself that we have no future together. I think of her diary again. Somewhere in its pages lies an answer to all this confusion – that's the only thing that makes sense.

One mess I can try to sort out in is my marriage. I must see Lucia tomorrow. I still feel angry that I missed Elisabeth last time she was here.

After a light supper I work on my novel for an hour or so and then think it would be nice to visit the Sabatini for a couple of drinks.

In the bar are a few of the usual farmers playing cards and arguing. Two are playing the traditional *morra*, a game of fingers and numbers which can lead to fights. There is something primitive – or perhaps timeless – about the village but the atmosphere is so relaxed, despite the bickering.

As I sip whisky a rough-neck farmer in a grubby,

collarless shirt looks up at me and invites me to join their game with the wave of a huge, rock-like hand. Everyone knows me now.

'Can't stop,' I say. 'I have something else I must do.'

'Another time then Signor de Silva,' he says.

'Sure.'

On my way home I notice groups of girls flirting with boys – 'Bello! Bello!' – and wonder what Don Giovanni will make of all this licentiousness under his very nose. I had been very tempted to ask him why he wore the heavy hat and cloak in hot weather. Perhaps he wasn't very well.

I am drawn back to the diary. To discover more of Carmen.

First I pour myself wine – I am much more a wine drinker – to wash away the taste of the scotch. Then, feeling nervous for some reason, I open the diary:

Marcus drove me to so many places and at all times he was a gentleman. He was charming and considerate; in fact he was too perfect and at times he left me wondering how long it would all last.

After our first week together he asked me to marry him. It was very sudden but natural. Though I barely knew him at all, I had to say yes because I loved him.

I said yes but told him I wanted to wait a little while longer. I also said that once the holiday is over I would want to go back to Spain to tell my parents about us.

He understood. He said that after the holiday he would have to return to his business for a while – 'Then I will join you.' He said that he had to settle a business matter – he didn't say what – and then he would come for me in Spain and arrange our marriage.

'We can marry where you wish to,' he said, 'but I shall have to get permission from the authorities if we have the

wedding in your country, Carmen. Or else we can marry in Italy.'

He then said, not for the first time, that he had to make an important phone call and left my hotel to make it from a public booth.

He could have easily made it from the hotel.

When I asked him why he did this, just after we had agreed to marry, he said there was no particular reason except that he didn't want anyone in the hotel listening in on important business calls.

I found that a bit strange but I forgot about it and didn't think it was very important. But I suppose I did not want to spoil the little precious time we had left. We just wanted to enjoy each other.

We spent my last night in Rome, and we booked one room instead of two. I could never have imagined such passion.

Reading that and I need another glass of wine. How terrible to read of Carmen's feelings for another man! Yet she wanted me to read this and I know she loves me. As I replay in my mind what I have just read, I feel – it must be the wine – a gentle touch on my hair, like a hand stroking me.

I throw my hand up over my head as if to shoo away a fly but nothing is there. Yes, it probably was the wine playing its tricks on me. I go upstairs to bed.

At about five in the morning I am awoken by the sound of movement downstairs. But the noise is soon drowned out by the cries of Vilma's rooster and other fowl next door. What a time they have clearing their throats for the dawn chorus.

Then to add to the cacophony I hear the rumble of farmers' carts along Via Valvasone. I just lie there listening to all this, a nightmare symphony, and wonder what the first sound downstairs could have been.

Then I drop off until seven-thirty. While I dress I resolve that I must sort everything out with Lucia. I'll drive home the country way so that I can at least enjoy the scenery.

Just as I pick up my car keys from a sidetable Vilma knocks at the door, carrying a bowl of eggs, newly-laid judging by the feathers and dirt still stuck to them.

'These are for you, Signor de Silva.'

'Thank you, Vilma, how very kind of you – do I owe you anything?'

'Certainly not!' she says, rather affronted. 'This is a present!'

I can't help thinking that I deserve the eggs after the row her cock and chickens made this morning.

I've got the door key to my own home, of course, but I ring the doorbell all the same. No answer, so I let myself in and call out. Again no answer. I make myself a coffee.

More than an hour later Lucia turns up. When she sees me standing in the hallway she seems stunned.

'Sorry. I didn't mean to frighten you,' I say.

'You haven't,' she says quickly. 'It's just I am very surprised to see you. I'm running late – I was out with a friend and we started talking and I forgot the time.'

'You don't have to apologise to me Lucia. Your time is your own now, and you don't have to answer to anybody.'

As I say this I realise, harshly, that she is not really my wife and she has never been. To me she is like a friend of long standing. A very good friend. How strange and cruel life is. How I have changed in such a short time.

And all because of Carmen.

334

'Would you like me to cook you some lunch?' asks Lucia.

'Shall we go out instead?'

'I can soon fix us something – there's no need to go out.'

'Very well, Lucia. As you wish.'

As she begins her ritual in the kitchen I say: 'Do you know why I am here today Lucia?'

'I have an idea.'

'We need to talk about us and what we are going to do.'

'Certainly. We can talk.'

I watch her fill rolls with ham and tomatoes and take out a bottle of wine.

She says, 'Come and have something to eat then. Have a glass of wine.'

'Perhaps I'm not very hungry—'

'You must eat something!'

To please her I nibble a roll but drink too much wine.

'So you realise we must talk,' I start after an awkward silence. 'We must settle things between us – about the separation and the money. There are so many things which must be discussed.'

'Are you sure Marco that you want all this. Why don't you wait?'

She pours herself more wine and does not touch her food.

'You don't seem to understand Lucia . . . I am not going over this again—'

She rises from the table – 'I was hoping that this wasn't serious—'

'There's no turning back. I love her so much that I would be no good to you in anycase – let's just be friends

335

and accept each other for what we are now, and for the sake of Elisabeth.'

'Very well. I will go see a lawyer and if I want to communicate with you from now on it will be through the lawyer.'

I am alarmed by her change of mood. Never before has she spoken to me like this.

'I want to say one more thing before I go Lucia. This house is yours and I will provide enough for you and Elisabeth.'

'You will hear from my lawyer. Money can be settled through the lawyer.'

'Yes, that's fine.'

Then in another odd turn Lucia asks about my novel, the last thing I'd expect to be on her mind.

'It's going very well. I feel that this time it will be a success, but I don't—'

'I am very happy to hear that Marco. I feel you will make it this time also.'

'Thanks – I must go now. I want to say hello to Elisabeth at the school. How did she take the news?'

'Not very well I'm afraid. But she will get over it.'

A little later I park the car outside Elisabeth's school gates. I can hear the cries of children, like gulls.

Beyond the iron railings, in a corner of the yard, I see a crowd of girls talking hysterically. I approach one and ask her where I can find la Signora Molina's class. She just looks at me and then points an arm towards the main entrance to the school building.

Just as I enter the corridor I spot my daughter talking to another girl. As I approach her I call her name. She turns to me with an expression of surprise.

'Papa!' she says. 'What are you doing here?'

'To see you of course.'

I ask her whether we can talk as her friend slips off, and tell her that I have just seen her mother.

'I wanted to see you as I was passing by,' I add, clumsily.

'Oh.'

'How are you getting on with your lessons?'

'Very well,' she responds tartly. 'Considering.'

'What do you mean by that Elisabeth?'

'You know, or do I have to spell it out for you?'

Before I can reply she says with great venom – 'But since you ask, you are very selfish, papa.' She throws her hair back with one hand – she often does this when she is agitated.

'Please, try not to be too hard on me,' I say, hopelessly. 'You will understand when you are a bit older. I didn't come here to argue with you Elisabeth.'

'I have to go now,' she says, clutching her satchel.

I take hold of her and say: 'Please don't let me go with bad feelings between us. I do love you my darling and remember what I say. I do hope you will visit me sometime.'

'Never!'

She shrugs from my grip and walks away rapidly without another word.

Back in my car I pray she will get over this and forgive me. I tremble a little to witness the hateful side of my beloved daughter.

How much more spirit she has than Lucia.

I return to Casarsa by the country route once again: trees and the fields offer me solace; perhaps they will heal me.

I will go to the church next Sunday and pray for my family. What a shock this will be for Don Giovanni who I am sure thinks I am a metropolitan pagan. I shall sit in the front pew where he cannot fail to see me.

Down Via Valvasone I see Kate by chance with her shopping. I stop the car to say hello and ask her to pop by tomorrow if she has a moment.

'Is there anything wrong, Marco?' she asks.

'Nothing to worry about Kate. I just want to ask a favour of you.'

At home I cannot resist another glass of wine as I think again of Elisabeth's shocking fury on her face, an expression of anguish and disappointment all at once. It is a tragedy that my love for Carmen should be the cause of so much heartache.

If only I could see Carmen right now. When will she return from Spain? I have so much to say to her. To talk about our future together. It is unimportant to me what she has done in the past.

Now is what matters.

I will return to her diary, a poor substitute for her presence. And I will read it because she asked me to. But first perhaps a little supper will improve my mood . . .

Later I open the diary once again:

The next morning after our night together I returned to Spain. Marcus said he wanted to take me to the station. But first he had to make one of his phone calls.

Yet again he insisted on making it from a public telephone box — almost as if I were the one he wanted to keep in the dark.

Why didn't he make it from the hotel? When I asked him as I did before he said that private business is always better done outside.

I then asked him what business he was in. He said quickly, 'It's to do with tobacco and I am responsible for

338

all the running of the business.' He then changed the subject with, 'And now it's time we got you to the station or you'll miss your train!'

In the car on the way to the station I felt I had to ask Marcus again what exactly was his business. 'I thought I had explained that to you . . . or do you have doubts about me?' he added with a half smile. 'You have to trust me, Carmen. You ask me so many questions — as if I were a criminal!'

I said I was sorry and that I didn't mean to pry. That whatever he did he must have so much responsibility and I asked him if it worried him.

'Not really,' he replied with such calm. 'Once you get organised the rest is easy enough to run. Are you satisfied now, Carmen?'

'I am just interested in what you do, in your life.'

'So, what else do you do in Spain, Carmen?'

I had told him about my work already, of course, but not about my flamenco dancing.

'That's wonderful, Carmen. Just like the opera! I'd love to see you dance. I'd like to see you in that mood.'

'You will see me dance,' I promised. 'I will dance just for you.'

We arrived at the station in good time — we had twenty minutes before my train was due to depart. But instead of waiting with me in our last moments Marcus said he would have to make yet another phone call — 'It won't take me more than ten minutes.'

'Why don't you make it after I've gone,' I said. 'We have a few things to talk about.'

'It won't take me long,' he said, rushing off. 'It's very important to make this call now.'

I was devastated. Twenty minutes passed and there was no sign of him. I wondered what had happened to him. I

boarded the train at the very last second — in fact it was
beginning to jostle as I shut the door — but still Marcus
failed to return.

As the train gathered speed I peered out of a window in
the hope of at least spotting him and knowing that he was
safe. But he was nowhere to be seen.

This was an awful moment. So many doubts flew into
my mind . . .

So what is that bastard up to? God, I feel sorry for
Carmen. Naive Carmen. Clearly Marcus is up to something illegal. Time will tell. I pour another glass of wine
and put away the diary for now. I feel tired and ragged:
time for an early night.

Chapter Six

The next morning a letter arrives. It's from Carmen. She answers my prayers. She says she will be back in a few days as her mother feels better now. 'I will see you on Monday,' she writes. 'With all my love, my darling. Carmen.'

I feel alive again with so much promise. I have so many things I want to say to her. Before I can relish re-reading her letter over and over again – even sniffing it for scent to make her more real to me – Kate is at the door, and I remember that I had asked her to call.

She looks very attractive today in a blue floral print dress.

'You said you wanted a favour from me Marco?'

'The favour – yes, I wanted to ask you a favour.'

'If I can be of any help . . .' she says, her face looking ten years younger with a dazzling smile.

'I wonder,' I begin cautiously, 'if you know some-body who could do my laundry or is there a laundry in these parts?'

Instantly Kate's face changes expression and I realise that this is not the sort of favour she was expecting to do me. She ages ten years.

'There's no laundry service here,' she stumbles. 'But if you like I shall be happy to do it for you, Marco. And if there is anything else I can do, you have only to ask.'

'I don't want to take advantage of you, Kate, but I would like to take up your offer – on one condition: that you accept payment.'

'Very well,' she says.

'Thank you Kate. I am very grateful. Would you like a glass of wine?'

Her face softens somewhat. 'Thank you. It's a little early, but, yes, I'd like that.'

As I pour she asks me how Lucia is.

'She is fine.'

Perhaps she wonders why Lucia no longer does my laundry . . . but I don't want to talk about her. Otherwise the whole of Casarsa would know before sunset that our marriage is over, and Don Giovanni would come calling with his holy recriminations.

Is Kate really interested in Lucia or just curious to know why she has not visited me lately? I detect in Kate's eyes more than just a formal regard for her mother's tenant. I must not lead her on in anyway: I shall have to tread carefully.

'How's your mother?'

'Very well,' she says, between sips, 'for her age. My mother can be very stubborn in her ways. She likes to be independent, but she does not realise that sometimes we all need other people.'

Is Kate simply talking about her mother?

'Tell me more about that photograph your mother showed me – who was he really?'

'Her nephew, as she said.'

'Yes – but I wanted to hear it from you. When she showed me his picture I felt there was a story behind it that she wanted to talk about.'

'Perhaps that is true, and if I knew I would tell you. Why the interest especially?'

'No particular reason. I just thought . . . just something your mother said about him that makes me think there is more to the matter than meets the eye. Or maybe I'm curious because he resembles me.'

'Yes, it is a strange likeness you have. I've always suspected my mother has many secrets. She keeps things to herself rather than talk about them.'

She places her empty glass on the table and says she must go now.

'I like talking to you, Marco.'

'The feeling's mutual.'

I wished I hadn't said that.

The moment Kate's gone thoughts of Carmen return and I grow excited, as a child does before Christmas. I know I should work on my novel but impulsively I decide to go out for some lunch – I'll try the Alla Trattoria dei Tortiglioni, not far (a five minute walk) from the railway station.

It's a fine, clean restaurant. I have got to know the owner who is pleasant to banter with. I can never tell whether her smile is genuine or the sign of some defect. It is fixed and lop-sided . . . but I mustn't be mean.

When she sees I have finished my meal she comes over to ask me if all is well.

'Very well,' I say.

'I'll fatten you yet with my food,' she laughs.

'That could be your advertising slogan!'

'Oh no! Everyone's fat round here already.'

Just as I reach for some lire to pay the bill I hear my name being called out by a woman.

I can't immediately identify the figure in the doorway because of the blinding sunlight behind, but I think I recognise the voice. Vilma!

She shouts my name again and again, waving her arms, until all the other patrons are staring at me and whispering. She could easily come into talk to me discreetly. But maybe she's never been in a restaurant before – so conducts herself as if at home with her chickens.

I rush up to her – 'What's wrong, Vilma?'

'Nothing's wrong. But your daughter is waiting for you.'

'My daughter? Where?'

'Back home!'

'I'd better be going then – how did you know I was here?' I ask as I pay the bill.

Vilma blushes, and for once she is lost for words.

I hurry back. On the way, Vilma rushes past me on her bicycle and makes a whooping sound. I glance at her and see a cloud of flesh in black: she certainly needs to lose weight. Her husband looks like a sardine by her side.

In the distance I spot my daughter lounging against my cottage front door with arms crossed. She is looking in my direction but does not stir, does not acknowledge me. I wave to her but she does not respond: she means to punish me, I'm sure.

'Elisabeth, I am so glad you are here.'

But she says nothing, she just glares at me with a cold expression. Then, strictly, she says, 'Shall we go indoors. I want to talk to you, papa.'

'Sure,' I say. 'Come in.'

The door shut she comes straight to the point: 'Are you really separating from mamma?'

'But you know the answer to that, darling.'

'I didn't think it would last when mamma first told—'

Then, with tears in her eyes, and that twisted expression I last saw at her school, she screams at me – 'How could you do this to my mother? You have really broken her heart, and I don't think I can ever forgive you!'

344

Shaken, I say, 'Listen, your mother and I are still friends, and she understands everything.'

'I don't believe that!' she shouts, bearing her teeth like a frightened cat. 'She is very upset, devastated!'

'Listen, one day you will fall in love with someone and you will know the strength of love and what people do for love – it makes us do so many things. I love your mother in a different way.'

Elisabeth stares at me with savage hatred, as if I am dirt. 'YOU MAKE ME SICK!' she shrieks. Then she runs out of the house.

I rush after her – 'Stop Elisabeth, please stay and talk—'

But it's hopeless. I fear I may have lost her for good.

Her words echo in me and tear me apart. Elisabeth is very young, I can't expect her to understand fully. I can only hope that one day she will forgive me . . .

These thoughts do not heal me. I open a bottle of wine. Soon I am drinking my second glass.

Later, I return to Carmen's diary – the only thing that seems real to me right now – and recall, with relief, that she has been deserted by Marcus at the station . . .:

I felt so shattered that I didn't even hear the conductor asking to check my ticket. I apologised, and I remember him saying, 'Are you all right, Signorina?' I must have looked pale. 'Of course I am all right,' I replied sharply.

Naturally there were other people in the carriage and sitting opposite me was a man who could not take his eyes off me.

I pretended to take no notice and closed my eyes. But it was no use. Minutes later, in front of the other passengers, I heard the words, 'How beautiful you are.'

I opened my eyes and I looked at him with contempt.

He immediately apologised for being rude then said – and

I was so embarrassed as the other passengers were giggling — 'But I must tell you, you are the most attractive woman I have seen in a long time and you must forgive me for saying so.'

I said nothing more. I just ignored him.

In the window reflection I decided he was a good-looking man in his early forties, but at that moment, after all that had happened, I was too upset to deal with something like this.

I just wanted to be left alone. There were other encounters on that journey back to Spain but there's no point describing them. I was a young woman alone.

My family lived just outside Madrid. My father came to meet me at the station and he was so happy to see me again.

The first thing he asked me was if I had enjoyed my stay in Italy.

'Wonderful,' I said.

I promised to tell him everything after I'd had a good night's sleep. He said that I looked tired and I asked him how was mamma — 'She is very well, and she has cooked you something special.'

As I write I can see our little villa in my mind's eye. The beautiful garden, my mamma loved to tend it. Often people would say I had the looks of my mamma. But my dancing, I inherited that from my father. I danced the way he used to, I was told.

From the garden gate I called out for her. In an instant she was in the doorway with her arms outstretched to embrace me. To think of it now makes me cry. She smelled of cooking, and her hands were white with flour. As usual she had prepared a wonderful meal but I was not very hungry — I was still too upset over Marcus' treatment of me at the station.

My mother must have sensed my sadness as she did not remonstrate with me.

That night I had so many broken dreams but one still remains vivid to this day. In the dream I saw Marcus lying dead on the ground covered in blood. He had been murdered, and the very thought of it had woken me in a panic. I still loved Marcus – the nightmare had left me in no doubt.

Three or four days after my return to Spain I received a letter with an Italian postmark and just knew it was from Marcus. The relief to learn he was safe! He begged me to forgive him – he said he'd had a very important business matter to deal with, which had prevented him returning to the station in time.

'I will be with you,' he wrote, 'in the next few weeks, and then we must get married. I leave it to you, Carmen, to decide which of our countries we should marry in. You will hear from me soon. I love you, Marcus.'

I soon forgot about my nightmare – I was suddenly in a dream of total pleasure. I had not told mamma and papa about Marcus. Now I must.

I close the diary with an empty feeling. We all secretly hope that the person we love has never loved before. I'm no different. I must leave the cottage for air.

I walk to San Lorenzo. It's about four in the afternoon, and very hot, being the end of June. Few people about. I think of Carmen's life and wish that Carmen had never met Marcus. I hate it that his name is like mine; a double thorn.

On my way back I bump into one of the local farmers I'm on nodding terms with. He is youngish and thickset – I have seen him in the Sabatini.

Without ceremony he asks me if I will play him and his mates at cards.

'OK.'

'Good. My name is Tony. We'll expect you tonight Signor de Silva. You staying much longer in Casarsa?'

'For the summer I hope.'

'Yes, and I hear you are writing a book.'

'That's right.'

'And what do you think of Casarsa?'

'What do I think? It is a lovely place, and I like the people, too.'

He stands close and looks at me straight – 'You may think some people in Casarsa are very rough in their ways, but inside they are very fine and they are good people.'

I'm interested he feels the need to say this to me. Perhaps Tony thinks he's been around a bit and feels above his neighbours. He has the air of a show-off, and none of the reserve of the country people. Come to think of it, I am not really in the mood to play cards tonight – but maybe I could do with company.

'I'll see you tonight, then,' I say. And walk home.

Back at the house I notice a hand-posted letter on the door mat. It's just a little note, an invitation from Signor and Signora Fabrisi to join them for supper on Sunday night at eight-thirty.

I have heard the locals speak of the Fabrisis – about their farmlands, wealth and snobbery. People may say to upstart neighbours – 'You're no Fabrisi, you know!' Or in the shops, a woman may say to another – 'Ha! That's a lot of food you're buying. Married a Fabrisi, then?'

The Fabrisis live in the smartest part of the area. Do I really want to have supper with them? They ask for an answer today.

I'll write a note of acceptance which I may or may not pop through their letterbox when I pass their house on my evening walk – depending on how the mood takes me. But I suppose a writer should mix with all sorts.

In the evening I slip my acceptance note through the Fabrisi postbox attached to the doorgate – instantly regretting my decision when it occurs to me that I have no special evening wear. It'll be too bad if the Fabrisis take offence at my casual clothes.

On my way back I call into the Sabatini, as I promised, for a game of cards and a drink. There's Tony with two friends sitting at a corner table.

He rises and beckons me to join them with a broad smile.

'Glad you could make it – Marco, isn't it? This is Piero and this is Giovanni and they're both good players,' he says pointing to each of his companions, unshaven and still in their farm clothes.

Giovanni smiles proudly and even throws out his chest when Tony describes him as the 'ace of the Sabatini.' For some reason Giovanni decides to focus his gaze on me for the evening, his face glazed with wine.

His mood changes for the worst when he loses the first and then the second game.

'Son-of-a-bitch!' he mutters at me over and over again in English. And 'Sucker!'

'Eh, Giovanni,' cries Tony, 'you're speaking English – but you've had too much to drink tonight – eh Giovanni!'

Perhaps Giovanni has drunk so much he can't remember any other English.

'Son-of-a-bitch!'

I show my winning hand in the third game.

Giovanni furiously bangs the table with his hand, shouting 'Sucker!' – and then throws his cards over the table – 'Son-of-a-bitch!'

I excuse myself and tell a rather embarrassed Tony that I must get home now as I have things to do.

'Sorry about that,' he says. 'Giovanni is not used to losing.'

'Please don't apologise. Goodnight Tony – Piero, Giovanni.' And I salute the landlord.

On my way home I think of Giovanni. I can only laugh about him, and then about life in general. Above the woody cicada nightsong, I hear happy band music from the open-air dance near the station, where I guess courting couples have gathered for the evening. Not a place for me.

Back home by ten, I hear Vilma shouting next door, presumably to her husband. He is probably drunk and she is giving him weekly hell (or is it the other way round?): as predictable as the seasons.

Yes, the older farmers get drunk every Saturday – but what else is there for them to do when the passion's all gone?

Chapter Seven

I think of Carmen. Monday and she is back. I miss her so much. I open her diary: she describes her life in Spain — she feels everything, so in touch with life . . .:

I was so relieved that Marcus was safe. But I dreaded telling mamma and papa about him.

One evening mamma was preparing dinner. I walked into the kitchen. 'Mamma,' I said. 'Can I talk to you? I have something very important to tell you — I meant to tell you as soon as I returned from Italy.'

I hear her words now. She said, 'My dear, can't you wait a little while, I want to finish here first.'

I was impatient to tell her, my secret was a heavy burden — I said I could talk while she cooked, I couldn't wait any longer.

'Tell me, what is so important?'

I told her that I had fallen in love with someone in Italy and wished to marry as soon as possible. I thought if I said it quickly mamma might accept it.

Instead she dropped her wooden spoon and put her hand to her mouth. It was as if I had announced my death.

'What are you saying Carmen?'

She certainly didn't know what to say. She gabbled

351

that it was so sudden, so premature. Finally she asked: 'Who is this man? What does he do for a living?'

Innocently I told her how good-looking Marcus was, that he ran a big tobacco business, that he was charming. 'My dear,' mamma said, 'don't you think he sounds too good to be true?'

'But we love each other, mamma!'

'It is far too soon to be thinking of marriage. You may feel a lot for this man but what do you know about him or what he really is?'

If only she knew how little . . . but I said to her: 'I am sorry mamma but we are going to get married soon and nothing will stop me.'

Then she said that I must tell papa the moment he returned from work. On second thoughts, she asked me to tell him after dinner, 'otherwise he'll have a heart attack – oh Carmen!'

I could not understand her attitude. 'But it isn't wrong to marry,' I argued. 'You should feel very happy for me, and besides you married for love and it wasn't a tragedy for you.'

Mamma bent down to pick up the spoon. 'That is true,' she said. 'I did marry for love but I had known your father for a very long time before we married and we have always been happy.'

'And it will be for me,' I said with certainty.

We heard the front door open – it was papa. Mamma shooed me out of the kitchen and filled the colander with lettuce.

A sudden thought occurs to me: how old was Carmen when all this happened? She is almost a child even now – when could she have fallen for this Marcus? Is this really a diary or a work of fiction?

I am nonplussed.

She could not have been more than twenty when she met Marcus, if that. And so naive with it. It's obvious Marcus is up to no good – or is that wishful thinking? Where is Marcus now?

Carmen's mother is very wise – but what do you say to a determined child who is in love? What would I say to Elisabeth in similar circumstances? Carmen has so much to learn, as we have all learned. But somehow I find it hard to reconcile the Carmen in the diary with the Carmen I love . . .:

Eventually, after an awkward dinner I told papa about Marcus. He did not appear shocked when I told him I wished to get married as soon as possible.

He only cautioned me that I should wait a bit longer.

'You didn't look very happy when you returned from Italy' he reminded me. I had told a white lie that I had felt very tired from the trip – 'In anycase,' I said, 'I had decided not to tell you straight away.'

Then I announced that Marcus would be coming next week and I said to papa: 'I hope you are going to be nice to him.'

Papa replied: 'We will do our best to welcome him here.'

The day before his arrival Marcus sent a telegram. He said he expected to be at my home at eight in the evening – 'Can't wait to embrace you. Love, Marcus.'

I did not show it to mamma and papa just in case they guessed at our intimacy.

To my surprise mamma seemed to grow excited at the thought of meeting him and said she would prepare the spare bedroom. 'You can't imagine how happy I feel with Marcus,' I told her as we pulled up the sheets.

My darling mamma looked up at me with some sudden sadness and I recall her saying: 'I'm sure you are happy with Marcus and we shall wait and see what happens.'

Marcus flew over from Italy. With all that cash he always had he could afford to. As soon as I saw him at the airport I became very emotional – he picked me up by the waist and swung me around. We were both so very happy. 'I was longing so much to see you Carmen,' he said.

We caught a taxi back home. Marcus asked whether I had told my parents about us, but I wasn't completely honest about their reaction. I was quietly praying that they would love him on sight as I had.

I couldn't accept that the people I loved might not love each other.

I told him that in his honour mamma was preparing something special for supper.

By now I had forgotten about the awful time at the station in Italy but Marcus wanted to say sorry again for his behaviour – why he had failed to return in time to say goodbye.

He held both my hands in his as he promised it would never happen again.

Even then I wondered if he really meant what he said. So I asked him once more what his work really was. For the first time he became irritated and turned his head away from me, looking out at the passing streets – 'I did tell you before what I really do,' he said slowly, as if I were backward. He said he was responsible for the export of tobacco to certain European countries – 'Or do you still have doubts about my work?'

Troubled by his change in mood I said, 'Let's forget it.'

He'd lightened by the time we had arrived at my home. He loved our villa – 'So this is it – very nice!' I was so keen to show him everything – mamma's beautiful garden, the neighbourhood – that we almost forgot about my parents standing at the front door waiting for us. They had not called out, but simply gazed at us.

As I introduced all three my heart sank – my mother was forcing herself to smile. My father, too. I think he felt the same. They were courteous but not warm or natural.

Over supper papa was very direct with Marcus. 'When are you thinking of marrying my daughter?'

'As soon as possible,' Marcus replied.

I smiled at him – then he added, 'That's why I am here. To meet you both and make arrangements before I return to Rome, sooner than planned I'm afraid.'

I asked Marcus why he had to return in a rush. 'An important business meeting. But I will be back here in two or maybe three weeks time – I would like to discuss our wedding plans with your father and mother—'

Papa interrupted, 'We will talk after supper.'

As I feared, Marcus and papa left the table after dessert and went into the sitting room while mamma asked me to stay with her and help her clear up and make coffee.

I suspected my parents were up to something to ruin my happiness. Later, Marcus told me papa had asked him to consider that we were marrying too soon. Marcus had replied that he loved me, and that because of his business he hadn't enough time to travel back and forth between Italy and Spain.

Marcus said he explained to papa what his work involved and that he had more than enough money to support me. Papa had asked him how well he thought he knew me? Marcus had replied, 'We know each other and understand each other – we've always known each other.' This was true. I did feel that I had always known Marcus.

In the kitchen, straining to hear the men in the next room, I could only curse the coffee percolator as its hiss drowned *their words. And mamma seemed to be making more noise than usual as she dried the dishes and cutlery.*

I was terrified Marcus might be talked out of loving me — I wanted to throw everything to the ground and rush into the sitting-room . . .

Instead the coffee grew hot and mamma at last placed the cups, saucers and coffee pots on a large silver tray. When we entered the sitting-room I looked hard at Marcus for any sign he no longer wanted to marry me. He gazed up at me and I could feel the warmth of his love — at that moment I knew for certain we would marry.

As mamma poured coffee, Marcus said he wanted to help with the expense of the wedding. Papa would not hear of it. 'That is not your responsibility,' he said firmly. 'Carmen is our only daughter and we will pay for her wedding — we shall also discuss her dowry with your family.'

Marcus turned to me and asked me if I was happy with this arrangement. I was embarrassed by his question — perhaps these things are handled differently in Italy — but he shouldn't have asked me this in front of mamma and papa — 'I agree with my parents,' I said weakly, 'with whatever they decide.'

Mamma gently gripped my arm for a second — poor mamma, I am sure she could feel all that I felt.

Then papa did an amazing thing. He took out a bottle of champagne and said, 'Shall we toast the new life of Carmen and Marcus!' When the glasses were filled — we hardly touched the coffee — my parents said 'Mucho felicidad to you both!'

From that moment the rest of the evening passed like a dream. I remember papa asking Marcus about his family and, of course, what he revealed was new to me as well.

He said his father had died when he was just a little boy. His mother had remarried someone quite well off, and was living in Florence with him. She knew of Marcus' plans but it was unlikely that mamma and papa would be meeting her before the wedding ceremony.

Papa became quite excited when Marcus said his favourite aunt lived a little way outside Venice. 'What a coincidence,' Papa said. 'I have a relative in San Lorenzo, Carmen's aunt. Maybe you've heard of the place?'

'Of course,' Marcus said, amazed. 'San Lorenzo is in the same region as my aunt's village – the Friuli region I think it is called.'

'That's right!' my father replied laughing.

Later, when my parents had gone to bed, I whispered to Marcus – who looked drawn and tired – 'Don't think I am going to share the bed with you, not here. I hope you respect that.'

Marcus smiled and held me – 'I will behave myself, Carmen. Tomorrow I'll take a room in a hotel.'

I told him mamma would be very upset if he did that.

'I will explain to your mother,' he said, kissing my forehead.

I hear the clock which tells me I am back in Casarsa. It is midnight already! Carmen's diary takes me to another world and I lose time. Everything about her obsesses me.

I feel very tired and go to bed. In half-sleep I sense again the gentle touch of a hand stroking my hair, very lightly. I come to with a start. Am I dreaming or does a ghost linger around me seeking attention?

My mind turns to the other bedroom in the cottage, the west bedroom. Perhaps I have seen one too many films but it's time I investigated it.

I swing wearily out of bed and pad gently to the door of Signora Martina's mystery bedroom. It was secure last time I tried it, but now, to my surprise, I find it unlocked:

Kate must have forgotten to turn the lock last time she was here – with my laundry. To think, I could have wandered in anytime . . .

I open the door warily. To my disappointment there are no skeletons, nothing spooky, not even some suggestive cover sheets. All to be seen is a lot of old furniture with braid edgings. Perhaps, for old time's sake, Signora Martina simply doesn't want her sacred memories disturbed . . .

As I close the door behind me, I realise why Signora Martina has been unable to sell the place. She has never really let go of it. People sense its secrets and are put off buying it.

Or maybe my imagination is working overtime. No wonder I am a writer!

After breakfast I make for the church. Odd it has two names: the SS Croce e Rosario. A new church must have been built on the site of the old. Mass is at ten-thirty, and I am determined to get there early to grab a front pew.

A front-row seat to observe Don Giovanni in action before the good people of Casarsa.

The blinding spots of sunlight fill my eyes the instant I enter the church – almost, but not quite, drenching the glow from the many burning candles. There are few people here yet, but the place echoes gently with the movements and whisperings of arriving worshippers who cross themselves as they face the white Madonna, before finding a place.

Altars shimmer in white linen edged with lace.

I turn around to see who's here, who's not. There are many young girls in pretty colourful dresses – their Sunday best. All seem to be giggling and conferring among themselves, deciding who is the prettiest of them all.

Naturally the older women are in traditional black smocks and scarfs as if at a funeral.

Finally, when the church is nearly full, Don Giovanni at last makes his entrance in his long black cassock topped with a white surplice.

Perhaps because of the glow from the candles he looks younger now. He glances at me – do I imagine a curious smile on that wide mouth of his?

After the first hymn – how refreshing sometimes it is to sing – Don Giovanni mounts the pulpit for his sermon. I thought he looked in good cheer, but the moment he opens his mouth his face reddens, and he stutters with rage, denouncing 'certain people' in the congregation.

'Certain parents,' he shouts, 'do not have any control over their children – this is where the problems begin!'

There follows a denunciation of all sorts of vice that he claims have riddled the soul of Casarsa. Can there be so much sin in such a little place?

Like a volcano about to blow, Don Giovanni grows hotter and noisier, his face purpling now with self-righteousness. I see froth forming on his long, mean lips as he assures other groups of 'certain people' everlasting damnation if they don't mend their ways.

I should have brought an umbrella to protect me from all his spittle raining down on the front pews.

After the service, the congregation file out of the church, led by the impatient young girls. I suppose they all feel they've done their Sunday duty. One thing is for certain: church-going for some is an opportunity to attend a fashion parade and show-off new clothes.

Outside the church, I see that the old women have huddled into little groups, gossiping. Perhaps they're naming all the 'certain sinners' of the week Don Giovanni had in mind.

I am certain that the girls are waiting for me to pass, for as I walk by they make eyes at me and giggle. I smile back at them, thinking that if I were a young man of their age I'd be doing everything to spite Don Giovanni.

On my way home I spot the other Giovanni – the drunk card-player of the other night at the Sabatini – standing outside his huge, barn-like door which has grown rickety with time.

I say, '*Ciao*, Giovanni,' but he barely smiles at me. I'm sure he does not remember me. His house is large, white, made of stone, and must have been quite impressive and stylish when first built. That's true of many of the properties of Casarsa: it's as if the village is dying of indifference.

Then I bump into Kate who says she has just delivered my laundry.

'Thanks. How much do I owe you?' I ask.

'No hurry.'

'Look, come back and have a drink with me and I'll pay you.'

She agrees readily – I could do with the company.

Back at the cottage I open a bottle of vino as Kate tells me she can't stay long because there's lunch to cook. She says, 'Mamma is not hopeless but I feel happier when I am with her.'

I think of Vilma next door and what she may imagine Kate and I are up to together. I'd noticed her curtains twitching on our arrival. I could just make out the figure of Vilma in the window, with her skinny husband standing just behind her, spying on us.

Soon the village will think I am having an affair with Signora Martina's daughter, especially now that Lucia is not to be seen.

As if picking up on my thoughts, Kate asks, 'Is Lucia unwell? I've not seen her recently.'

I tell her Lucia has had to go and look after her sick mother.

'I am very sorry, Marco,' she says with concern. 'I hope it's nothing serious.'

I change the subject. 'Kate, who used to sleep in the west bedroom upstairs?'

She looks surprised. 'Well, my mother. Any reason why you ask?'

'Just curious – no particular reason.'

Then I ask her if she knows how her mother's nephew died.

'I honestly don't know,' she says, furrowing her brow. 'My mother never likes to talk about him. I ask about him from time to time but I get no response.'

What a strange pair – 'What do you talk about all day, you and your mother?'

'Well,' Kate says, uncomfortable at my questions, 'nothing very much. I think she prefers to talk to you!'

'I don't think your mother has said very much to me about anything.'

'My mother is very secretive and she is too old now to be anything else.'

Kate is not her mother, altogether more open – at least with me: her mother would've told me to mind my own business. I think Kate and I are good friends now. She is intelligent, I like to talk to her – 'another glass?'

'No,' she says. 'I'd better not. Mamma will start wondering where I've got to. I must be going now.'

I take her to the door so that Vilma can see us. 'I'll see you again,' I say. 'And give my regards to your mother.'

Chapter Eight

I think of Lucia just as I plan to start work on my novel. I wonder how she is coping. Our last meeting was tense, not very pleasant for her or for me. I know I can be selfish. I have never given much thought to her.

How on earth has she put up with me all those years together?

Since I have known Carmen I have become more aware of my weaknesses. I pray that Elisabeth will one day understand me and what has happened.

God forgive me for devastating their lives.

I must talk again to Lucia and Elisabeth about Carmen, to explain to them how I feel. Perhaps I am being naive: how can they understand? These must be guilty thoughts. If I went back to Lucia I'd be no good, I'd hurt her again . . .

Tomorrow I pray to see Carmen – we must talk. Has Lucia seen a lawyer yet? If I hear nothing by next week I will definitely have to see her again.

I work for hours on the novel. How alive it seems when I feel so dead . . .

Oh God! The Fabrisis!

I suddenly remember my supper date at eight-thirty. Have I mentioned the tub I have to use to bath in? It's just a wine barrel sawn in half, and I heave it into the kitchen. Only the wealthy people like the Fabrisis actually have a bathroom in a town like Casarsa.

Yet life as a primitive gives a sense of freedom. It takes time regulating the water temperature. It's either too hot or too cold if you're not careful.

As I soak, and more fresh water boils in a pot on the stove, I decide I'll wear my casual suit, whether the Fabrisis like it or not.

Before I leave I think again of the west bedroom. I wonder if Kate has locked it this time because of all my questions. I pop upstairs and try the door. It remains unlocked. Maybe there are no secrets.

For the first time I notice a portrait above the fireplace of Signora Martina and her husband as young people. The picture has faded with time, like the furniture, like Signora Martina herself.

In the drawers – two are locked – there are only mothballs to be found. I give up and close the door behind me.

A stiff ten minute walk will get me to the Fabrisis. Vilma and her husband are sitting on their doorstep in the evening sun, like a couple of parcels. They both wave.

'Going anywhere nice?' shouts Vilma.

'Very nice!' I reply, without further explanation. She's shamelessly nosy.

Via Valvasone has been turned into a sort of open-air dance hall tonight as young people step and spin in the streets to gramaphone music while others sip orange juice. Crazy swallows swoop high and low above the dancers' heads, feasting on the wing, to the sounds of tango. At this time of the evening no cars pass (maybe the odd old bike). There is so much life, gaiety, colour and laughter.

A small community alive as one. Later these young

people will drift down to a dance platform, specially erected near the railway station, and continue to love and laugh and live . . .

The Fabrisi house shines with light. All the windows of the long white villa are open. The scent of night flowers, the distant music from Via Valvasone and the peaceful stillness of this district . . . if only Carmen were with me now, the night would be complete.

I am filled with no particular excitement to meet the Fabrisis: but I don't want them to think me unsociable. I approach the black courtyard gate and pull the bell chain to the left.

After a full minute I hear the crunch of someone's approaching footsteps on the gravel drive within. The door opens to a tall, well-built man with a domed, gleaming, almost hairless head. I guess he is the master of the house.

'Signor de Silva?' he asks – he has a deep voice.

'Yes, I am.'

He moves aside as a way of beckoning me in.

'I am Paolo Fabrisi. I am glad you managed to come.'

As he guides me to the house itself he seems to grow ever more in stature – a true giant with hands as large as dinner plates.

We enter a smart portico with terracotta roof tiles. I notice bamboo chairs – unusual for these parts – encircling marble tables. At one of them two women are sipping drinks. They look up at us.

'Come and meet my wife Rita,' says Paolo – we are already on first names, 'and my daughter Eleanora. I have also a son but he couldn't make tonight.'

In contrast to Paolo's casual cottons, Signora Fabrisi – somehow I cannot bring myself to call her Rita – is swathed in a bewitching green silk dress, and for a woman in her forties, she's in youthful shape. Her manner reminds me of some ancient Roman wife – haughty but stylish.

Eleanora shakes my hand and almost curtseys – she looks pretty in her white linen dress. I am struck by her large brown eyes. She's as slender as a wishbone.

'It's a great pleasure meeting you Signor de Silva,' says Signora Fabrisi. 'May I call you Marco? – Paolo! Do get Marco a chair before he collapses in the heat. Marco, how dull Casarsa must seem after life in the city.'

'Not at all—' But already Signora Fabrisi is fussing with the chair, and with one thing and another, and I see who rules the roost in the house of Fabrisi.

'Marco – would you like an aperitif?' asks Paolo.

'Yes, you must have an aperitif,' echoes Signora Fabrisi. And suddenly she brings her tiny hands together like cymbals, clapping for service – 'Lucia! Where are you!' The maid appears from another room. 'There you are. An aperitif for Signor de Silva. Is everything all right in the kitchen? Tell cook to go easy on the tabasco.'

How unfortunate that the maid is called Lucia. I wonder if they know of my Lucia. I am unsettled by the way Signora Fabrisi talks to her maid who appears too used to the snapping at her heels.

'Lucia came with the house,' says Signora Fabrisi. 'We kept her out of pity really. I mean, where would she go if we threw her out. Do you like our portico?'

And for the next ten minutes she talks wildly – with flamboyant gesticulations – about her new veranda, the incompetence of the builders, and the ruinous expense of authentic terracotta.

All the while Paolo and Eleanora sit at the table, still and quiet.

At last Lucia – the maid – returns to announce that supper is ready. Signora Fabrisi rises quickly and leads

365

us to the dining room. No expense has been spared in elegance. Huge pictures are hung on the walls – one looks suspiciously like a portrait of Signora Fabrisi herself – and the table has been laid in the old country way with candelabra, fanned napkins and crystal glass.

I feel truly embarrassed.

Over the *antipasto* – or starter – Paolo tells me he has made his money in property development . . .

'Marco doesn't want to hear about that,' interrupts Signora Fabrisi. 'We hear you are a writer, Marco.'

'Yes, I am in Casarsa to write a novel – a romance.'

'A romance!' she screeches. 'How wonderful! But what a dull place for you to come and write it. What kind of romance could take place in Casarsa – with all these farmers, and their carts and horse dung all over the place! Goodness, Marco, I can't imagine your romance is set in Casarsa. But I suppose your sophisticated readers love a little authentic background – you must sell lots of copies!'

To my relief Eleonora pipes up – 'Is your book a love story, Signor de Silva?'

Her mother tuts – 'Well what else would a romance be if it were not a love story—' Then she catches sight of Lucia – 'These plates are not very warm, are they? What have you been doing with them – sitting on them? Don't just stand there – *please* Lucia . . .'

I ignore Signora Fabrisi and talk to Eleonora. 'Yes, it is a love story of sorts. What do you do Eleanora?'

Signora Fabrisi smiles at her daughter – 'Tell Marco then.'

'I am an assistant to a lawyer. But I have other plans for myself.'

'We'd love to see her married and settled down,' says Paolo.

Eleonora dabs her lips with obvious irritation at this, and I notice colour about her cheeks.

'You must find writing a very profitable pass-time,' says Signora Fabrisi.

'It is my career, Signora Fabrisi.'

'Yes, and one day perhaps you will settle down – mm?'

'Settle down? I am already married. And I have a daughter – younger than Eleanora.'

The smile on Signora Fabrisi's face freezes at this news. I'm astonished she doesn't know I'm a married man – clearly even the gossips avoid her.

At last she says, 'I am very sorry. Had I known I would have invited your wife also.'

She puts the napkin to her forehead. 'Goodness, it's hot in here. What is your wife's name, Marco?'

'Lucia.'

'Lucia!' she repeats, appalled.

At that her maid Lucia re-enters the room, thinking she has been called – 'Yes, Signora. The beans are nearly ready.'

'I didn't call you, you fool!'

'But you called me, Signora.'

'Be silent and fetch Signor de Silva more water.'

Then she claps her hands like thunder, dismissing her servant from our presence.

I tell her that Lucia is not with me because I need to be alone to write my novel – 'I am staying in a property owned by Signora Martina – do you know her?'

Signora Fabrisi quickly recovers her composure. 'Well of course, we know of Signora Martina. I believe she lives in the house she was born in. Can you imagine living in a house all your life?'

Then she pulls a face . . . 'On the other hand I could

be wrong and she may have only lived there since her marriage – or is she a widow? – I do not know. I think she has more money than the usual farming stock around here – though no one is quite sure how she acquired it.'

'Her properties are worth a lot,' says Paolo, who is drinking quite heavily.

'I can't imagine she acquired money by just growing corn,' says Signora Fabrisi tartly. 'Of course, one has heard rumours about certain members of her family – all very tasteless.'

'That's enough Rita,' cautions Paolo. 'Marco maybe a friend of Signora Martina's.'

'What are these rumours?' I ask.

'Oh well, ages ago,' says Signora Fabrisi, recovering herself, 'sometime before we came here – there was a scandal over someone in her family. Some matter to do with crime – the police were involved and whatnot. But don't ask me names or places, I don't know and I don't care. Don Giovanni has a few things to say about Signora Martina. Marco, never tell Don Giovanni anything. He is a terrible gossip and I dread to think what people tell him in the confessional. We hire our own priest from outside Casarsa to hear our sins! But we give Don Giovanni money for the church and that keeps him quiet. Anyway, why should I concern myself with the doings of Signora Martina and the like? Eleanora, you've hardly touched your food. Lucia!'

How frustrating that Signora Fabrisi can't tell me more about Signora Martina . . . I sense the Fabrisis have lost interest in me. Sadly, I am not to be their son-in-law after all!

Back under the cooler portico, Paolo lectures me on the wisdom of buying Signora Martina's cottage.

'One day it will be worth a great deal,' he says. 'Casarsa

won't just be a farming community then. Industry will in time grow in the surrounding towns and our workforce here will earn more in the factories. They'll all be rich because then they will get labourers for their farms and have two incomes. Don't listen to Rita. Casarsa is a goldmine!'

I stifle a yawn. He is very proud of himself, of his villa, his belongings. He is what we say in Italy *mezza calsa* – a 'half-stocking'. All money and no class.

When I announce I must be going Signora Fabrisi looks almost relieved. Only Eleanora has the good grace to say what a pleasure it was to meet me and wishes me luck with the book.

Paolo sees me out.

I don't think there'll be another supper date with the Fabrisis. Despite their wealth and airs they're a lot less interesting than some farmers I have got to know.

Out in the fresh, warm air I realise I've drunk too much and try to straighten up. The village is quieter now, the dancers are in their beds. But as I pass a drinking house I hear some talking and laughter. The street lights along Via Valvasone are dim.

I know I am near home because now I can hear Vilma's harsh voice directed at her shrimp husband. Drunk again?

What a day. First Don Giovanni. Then the Fabrisis. What a people!

The next day I work on my novel till midday. After a light lunch and some wine I go for my usual walk and once again find myself on the way to San Lorenzo, almost in a dream.

Before I reach the village I experience *deja vu*. I encounter a woman in a black dress – the same woman, I think, who had handed me Carmen's note days ago near this spot.

369

As she approaches she quickly takes out an envelope from her pocket and hands it to me. Then she rushes off without saying a word, disappearing into the fields as before. Why all this ridiculous mystery? Is it to do with Carmen's aunt?

The old woman is nowhere to be seen now. Nor do I recall seeing her approach me in the distance. I'd think I'd imagined her were it not for the envelope in my hand.

I tear it open, allowing paper to scatter on the dusty road. The note's from Carmen of course. She writes that she has only just returned this morning and that she's looking forward to seeing me again tonight at six.

'And I will explain everything to you,' she promises. 'Always my love, Carmen.'

I ought to feel great pleasure and excitement. Instead, there's apprehension, or an anxious feeling hard to describe.

As I walk back to Casarsa I decide that tonight she must tell me everything about her life and what is going on. Her conduct is bizarre. And who is this woman in black?

Near the narrow lane I am filled with the need to weep. What has happened to me? Maybe I am ill . . .

Back home I pour wine and open Carmen's diary. Marcus is still at her family home . . .:

> Marcus grabbed hold of me and kissed me passionately. I knew he would have liked to make love to me. But gently I pushed him away. He understood nothing was going to happen in my parents' house that night.
>
> After breakfast he explained to mamma why he wanted to take a hotel room. I could tell she was surprised but papa said that Marcus was doing the right thing and told him not to worry about offending them.
>
> I took a week off work to be with Marcus and to

make arrangements for our wedding. One day he asked me whether I'd like to go up to his hotel room.

'I am not married to you yet Marcus,' I said. 'This is my home town and it would not be respectable for me to go with you.'

Marcus asked me if I loved him. I told him that I loved him very much but it would not be dignified for an engaged couple to be seen in the hotel together. 'If you didn't know that then I forgive you,' I said, teasing him a little.

He apologised but added that I had him wrong if I presumed that he wanted something from me by inviting me up.

Then with a mischievous grin he said: 'I understand that I can't make love to you again until we're married. But what you can do is dance for me before I return to Rome. The flamenco.'

Poor Marcus. How I teased him. I said I'd dance for him but not till our wedding night. He pretended to be tired with me and said, 'Do I have to agree to no pleasure at all till after our wedding?'

When the moment came for his return to Rome he said it had not been easy for him to control his feelings.

'But I love you,' I said. 'And I control my feelings.'

After I saw him off I returned home. Mamma was in the kitchen — she wanted to talk to me. 'I don't feel happy about you living in Rome after the wedding,' she said.

When I asked her why she said, 'I don't know. But I have this feeling that Marcus is not for you. I can see he's handsome and all that business but there is something about him that troubles me and I can't help worrying about you Carmen. You will be lonely in Rome.'

I told her not to get carried away with her imagination . . . 'The trouble is,' I said, 'you don't see what I see in him.'

'Of course not,' she said. 'I am not in love with him and

371

therefore I can see more. Love is blind. Never were these words more true. It takes more than loving a man – one day you will remember these words.'

'Please mamma, try to be happy for me and don't say anything more about Marcus.'

I was sitting by the kitchen window when papa came in. He said to me: 'Do you think Marcus has arrived back in Rome by now?'

'Definitely.'

Papa said there was still much to do for the wedding – 'Are you sure Marcus will be back in two weeks' time?' he asked.

I was honest and said that I could not be certain. It depended on his work.

Then he asked whether I was sure I wanted to marry Marcus. I had never been more certain of anything and I looked at my father in a hard way – I had never looked at him like that before – 'Of course I am sure. In fact when I first met him I knew right away – this is the man I want to marry.'

Papa was taken aback by my vehemence – 'Well then, I hope you will be very happy with him.'

Two weeks later a telegram arrived from Marcus to say that he would not be in Spain for another week because of work commitments. I realised then that life with Marcus would always be like this. I would have to get used to it. I knew it wouldn't be easy. But I loved him so much that I was prepared to put up with anything.

Mamma was disappointed by the news but said that at least we had another welcome week to plan the wedding. I recalled what she had said earlier that if I married Marcus I would know what true loneliness is – particularly in a strange country. But she had added that there was nothing she could do about it and she hoped with all her heart that she was wrong about Marcus.

In the next week Marcus suddenly turned up unexpectedly at the house when only mamma was in. He had apologised to her for not letting us know he was on his way. Apparently it was a sudden decision.

Mamma, typically, had asked him whether he always behaved this way. Then she had forgiven him and made him a cup of coffee after asking him if he wanted something stronger.

Dear mamma, the kindest heart she has. But Marcus told me he sensed her unease with him and he thought she'd only been kind to him because of me. Yet she invited him to stay in the house — he decided to return to the hotel.

'She only asked to be polite,' he explained to me later.

That afternoon Marcus came to my office to collect me — I was over-joyed to see him and we arrived home shortly before papa. We told we wanted to marry by the end of the week.

So the marriage will go ahead. As I read I forget that this is the same Carmen I love. Why would she want me to read about the love of her life? I suppose I must read on . . .:

Naturally I asked my friends to help me with the wedding dress and everything else. The dress was traditional white with lace trimmings, a veil made up like a montilla — lace to match the dress.

Everyone said I looked so beautiful in the dress that it took their breath away — it seems boastful to repeat this here, but their words added to my incredible excitement.

My two maids wore satin blue, and it must be a trick of memory that I now think the church bells rang all day and night.

Shortly before the ceremony in the local church Marcus introduced me to his mother and step-father. They were clearly not used to being in a foreign place. I couldn't imagine what Marcus had in common with his mother who seemed grim.

After we had exchanged vows Marcus whispered that I looked angelic. My mother wept as we walked down the aisle – I had heard her snuffles behind me throughout the ceremony.

The reception was held in a local hotel. As we drove there I told Marcus again that he looked very handsome.

'Not handsome enough for you,' he grinned.

Outside the hotel we stood gazing at each other for several moments as if we had said everything we ever wanted to say to each other.

My parents came over to wish us happiness. Then Marcus said to me, 'I want to see you dance tonight – you promised you would on our wedding night.'

I said I always keep my promises – I would dance for him later.

What he didn't know was I had already hired a flamenco guitarist – a friend of mine – and towards eveningtime I left to change costumes.

It was magical to step into my beautiful quilted satin red dress, layered to fan out on spins, and with many frills. I pinned a fresh red rose in my hair, and then put on my half-heel black shoes. In the mirror I saw the other Carmen of my fantasies.

When I made my entrance at the reception all the guests cheered and clapped.

Marcus could hardly speak – he said later I looked like a vision of fire. The guitar strummed to life and I was instantly the dancer – it was as if another soul had *entered me with the music and I was no longer myself.*

The stamping of my feet filled the room with Spain, but this was my secret language to Marcus; I could not expect him to understand the codes of flamenco, my special expression of love for him.

I spun and stamped and tapped, and struck wild poses like a peacock. I think in these moments a crazy gypsy took possession of me, at the mercy of a violent guitar. When I had finished, guests applauded me like thunder, while I gasped for breath.

Everyone was shouting for more. Marcus rushed up to me, his face full of amazement. He said that he had always sensed a fire in me but had only seen it come to life on the dance floor – 'I will have to learn more of this new Carmen,' he half-shouted.

Then he took me in his arms and in front of everyone kissed me on the lips with great passion – with as much passion as I had danced for him.

Desperately we wanted to be alone, and we said goodnight to everybody.

The next day we would leave for Rome but that night was for us, for love and for passion.

Every word is terrible to me. Carmen married . . . yet she's so young. When could this have been? Is it real? Or the fantasies of a young girl? – perhaps this is not a diary at all but a story, like the stories I write. More terrible is the strength of her love . . .

But she called it a diary, it reads like one . . . I must suppose she is married. I assume it's not her aunt she lives with but her husband . . . Carmen and I are the same, married to different people. This must be what Carmen wanted me to understand through her diary – this would surely explain her elusiveness.

It's getting late now, nearly seven . . . she said she would be here at six . . . and no sign of her . . .

Just when I think she will never come I hear a noise from upstairs. It sounds like someone walking across the floor. I get to my feet, alert for more sounds of movement, but there is nothing.

I run up the staircase to investigate. From the landing I see nothing. I enter the unlocked west bedroom – nothing. For no reason I can think of, I turn to look out of the window . . . and there, in the distance, I spot the unmistakable flame figure of Carmen.

My heart beats fast, I feel elated; I daren't move from the window in case she disappears. I watch her in a trance as she approaches. Close to the house she looks up, sees me and waves. She couldn't possibly disappear now. I rush downstairs – and to my amazement she's already there, standing in the living room . . .

She could be the flamenco dancer of her diary in her white lace blouse and red skirt. How could I have not known she danced?

And her eyes seem even darker than I remember.

'Carmen—'

I embrace her – she says quietly, 'Please forgive me for not coming sooner.'

'Oh God, you're here now – I know your secret, about Marcus . . .'

'Don't say anything more,' she says quickly, breaking away from me. 'Read the whole diary and then we can talk.'

'What has happened since you married him? You're living with him—'

'No – I can't tell you – read the diary.'

'But you're still together— ?'

'No – it's in the diary. I will not talk about it until you have read every page of the diary.'

I feel irritated, though I should be pleased she's no longer with Marcus – 'Don't you think it's time we talked about *us*,' I say. 'If you're free of Marcus we have no reason to delay being together.'

'Give me time Marco.'

'Time for what? Why all this mystery? Why didn't you just talk to me about Marcus? And who is that strange woman who gives me your notes? – she says nothing to me.'

'She is just a woman I know from the village.'

'I want us to be together always.'

Carmen strokes my head – 'But we will be together one day.'

'What one day? What about now?'

Carmen does not answer me. Instead she says: 'When you have finished reading my diary and you have completed your novel, then we can talk about what we are going to do.'

Then she adds, 'One day you will understand.'

'Understand? All I know is I want to spend my life with you.'

I tell her about the separation from Lucia. How Lucia is meant to be seeing a lawyer. I say I'm going to Lucia soon to find where we stand.

'Don't worry so much,' Carmen says. She is so calm, so self-possessed. 'Everything will fall into place. See Lucia but be kind to her.'

I'm infuriated by her maturity, her lack of longing to be with me – 'Of course I'm kind to her – how can you be so relaxed about this? It's as if everything is going to be easy when I'll be losing everything for you.'

She caresses me as if I were a child. 'I want you to know,' she says, 'that I truly love you. And I have never felt so deeply for any man as I do for you.'

Her words should reassure me. But they don't reach me. Instead I suddenly think of her mother, I remember she has been unwell. I feel a pang of guilt – how selfish of me. Not once have I thought of Carmen's recent problems – perhaps the thought of her mother's illness prevents her from being with me . . .

I ask about her health.

'She is much better,' Carmen says. 'That's why I am back here in Italy now. Do you think I will leave you tonight? Because I will not. Tonight I will stay with you.'

I kiss her and ask her to forgive me for my selfishness. I open a bottle of wine – 'To celebrate our second night together. To us, darling,' I say.

Chapter Nine

Very early next morning I am awoken by the sounds of a heavy scratching sound from downstairs – as if nails are being drawn across wood. Carmen is not in bed with me – I must believe it's her aunt she returns to – or does she lie about Marcus?

I must read the diary.

I conclude the sounds are of Carmen letting herself out. But downstairs I see nothing, and there's no sight of her outside.

I should visit Signora Martina again to discuss these disturbing noises – it would be pointless talking to Kate. I don't think she would understand.

Back in bed I wonder seriously about the possibility of a haunting. Ghosts – or scurrying rats! That would make more sense. Signora Martina says she never experienced any supernatural happening here . . .

But what about the noises I heard out in the countryside? Nothing makes sense to me. Nothing about the noises or about Carmen, Marcus, or anything. I bury my head in the pillow as my tired mind whirls with theories and terrors.

At seven I get up and make myself a strong coffee *nero* to wake me up – I feel fatigued.

I light an oil stove – I can't be bothered to chop wood for the cooker. How Signora Fabrisi would mock me if she saw how the glamorous writer lives! Most of the families here still cook as their ancestors did – over wood – but the Fabrisis have gone one better and had gas installed.

I prefer the old ways. Modern life is so tedious – too neat and impersonal.

Just as I prepare to work I notice a sheaf of paper tucked under my typewriter. This has to be from Carmen. I feel she is still with me – at once there is something scary and beautiful about her.

I unfold the note. It's Carmen. She promises to return soon. 'I will let you have my address. All my love, Carmen.'

At last! Will the day arrive when I can visit her, and her aunt? I cannot imagine what it is like just to drop in on Carmen, to be ordinary with her . . .

I can't work now. I am too full of thoughts. So I dress and decide to see Signora Martina.

To my surprise the old lady answers the door, shaking somewhat on her stick.

'*Buongiorno*, Signora. How are you?'

'Very well, considering my age. Come in young man. What brings you here? Whatever it is I am always pleased to see you.'

She sits me down next to her in the kitchen – 'And have you had another encounter with the unknown since the last time we met?' she says with a smile.

'How did you guess Signora?'

'So, it has happened again.' I spot humour in her eyes.

'Yes, it has happened again. And I don't know what to make of it anymore.'

'So long as these occurrences do not harm you . . .'

'I am more annoyed than anything else.' I say, probably

with a frown. 'I don't like it when noises wake me up in the early hours of the morning.'

'So what do you intend to do?'

'What can I do? Nothing. I like the cottage as it is. And whatever is in it nothing's going to shift me out. I may yet buy the place from you, Signora, if it's still on the market.'

'Would you really?' She almost sparkles with excitement.

'Quite possibly, if my book takes off, which I think it will. I know that I've never written a book like this before.'

She leans closer. 'And what is so special about your book?'

What a question! Impossible to answer.

'It's, er, about emotional fulfilment – I will give you a copy of the book when it's published. I shall always be grateful to you for letting me your house, Signora. It has done so much for me.'

The old lady smiles – 'And another thing interests me. Lucia – how is she?'

A note in her voice puts me on alert. It's as if she has sensed a change in me, or my life.

'She is very well – where's Kate?'

'Oh, she's out shopping. She should be back any moment now.'

Out of the blue, and anxious not to talk about Lucia, I remember the one crucial question I have been meaning to ask Signora Martina. Why is Casarsa's full name Casarsa Della Delizia – 'Delightful Casarsa'?

The old lady laughs. 'Well, I'm sure you won't believe me!' she says, catching her breath.

'But I'd like to hear it.'

She leans back in her chair. 'So this is the story. One

day Napoleon Bonaparte – this was before even I was born! – Napoleon Bonaparte was passing through Casarsa with his troops. Naturally he was on his horse, and Napoleon was not in the best of health. His digestive system was – how can I put it delicately? – blocked. Word had already reached the people of Casarsa of the little French Emperor's great discomfort, and so as he rode through, down Via Valvasone I'm sure, the peasants offered him some of their finest grapes.

'Napoleon was game for anything – there was a real fear he might explode – and even before he had finished eating ten grapes he was seen to dismount his horse and rush off into the bushes for his call of nature.

'Well what can I say? Nature did indeed take its course. And when later, much relieved, he emerged from the bushes, he was heard to say to his soldiers . . . "Ahh, Casarsa has cured me . . . delightful Casarsa."

'And so was born our new name: Casarsa Della Delizia.'

We both laugh. What a character Signora Martina is. It hardly matters if the story is true or not. She is herself delightful, like Casarsa.

'You will forget all about the disturbing noises in the house,' she says. 'Mind you, I don't disbelieve you, and I think you know that otherwise I wouldn't be listening to you. I think there is a force in the cottage—'

At this moment we hear Kate struggling into the house with her shopping. She is surprised and pleased to see me.

'I thought it was time to come and see you and your mother.'

'Well, mamma is always pleased to see you and she loves your company—'

The old lady coughs at Kate's words – but she is not cross.

'Would you like a drink?' offers Kate.

382

'Sure. A quick coffee if that's not too much trouble.'

After Kate has left the room Signora Martina leans over and says she will try to visit me. 'I'll ask Kate to help me there, and I'd like to have another look at the cottage if I may.'

'I would be very happy if you could manage that. I've got the car so if you told me which day—'

'No! That's very kind of you but I prefer to walk as it is good exercise for me. I don't mind even if it takes half-an-hour.'

I wonder what it is she wishes to see. How I wish I could read minds. Perhaps she hopes to make contact with my supernatural friend or just to make a sentimental journey.

I finish my coffee and return home.

After a small lunch and some wine I'm suddenly gripped with the idea of seeing that little bridge again where I first met Carmen.

The air is hot and there is thunder in the air. I feel the odd spit of rain on my face – carried long from clouds yet to be seen in the sky, perhaps from as far away as the glorious Dolomites.

We need a downpour – everything looks so dry and I know the farmers are praying for it.

If it rains I can always shelter under a tree.

I sit on the bridge and think of Carmen, of the weird circumstances of our first meeting. I have yet to make myself comfortable when I see someone walking towards me from a nearby field . . . the figure is familiar to me, it's Carmen's strange messenger, the woman in black. She has the gift of a bloodhound for tracking me down!

Perhaps she has another note for me.

She stops a few metres away. I see no sign of another

letter. She fixes an odd smile on me; it's a curious spiteful expression, almost of triumph − as if she has beaten me in a game.

'I want to talk to you,' I say.

I get up and walk towards her. But she takes off and disappears into a nearby shrubbery. I follow her but she is nowhere to be seen.

Like a magician's rabbit she is simply no longer.

I run around, searching here and there. A stranger might think me mad.

More hallucinations? Like the noises in the house? I must pull myself together before I lose my mind − I return home.

I pour a glass of wine. The typewriter cannot entice me to work on my novel. Not for now.

I get out Carmen's diary instead. I have dreaded reading of their marriage − it's a comfort to think they are no longer together . . .:

After our wedding night Marcus and I prepared for our midday flight to Rome. Before that we went to my parents to say goodbye. Mamma became very emotional when she saw me arrive with Marcus. Tears welled in her eyes. Maybe she suddenly realised she was finally losing me.

She said to me 'Don't leave it too long to come and see me.'

'I won't, mamma,' I said.

Marcus said to her: 'I promise I will look after your daughter and take good care of her.'

'Make sure you do,' said papa, 'and I hope to see you both not before long.'

On the flight Marcus gazed at me lovingly as if he had captured something he had always dreamt of.

'At last we are alone again,' he said, 'after all that wedding fuss.'

At the time I didn't think that was a strange thing to say. For me the wedding ceremony was not a 'fuss' but something sacred. It meant we would love and care for each other forever.

I said it was not very nice of his mother and step-father not to come and wave us off.

'I'm sorry darling,' he said, 'but I forgot to tell you that my step-father has been unwell, and my mother phoned while you were in the bath to say they would visit us in Rome sometime in the next few days.'

'Well I'll be pleased to see them both.'

We arrived in my favourite city on time and went straight to Marcus' flat. I was not prepared for its elegance or luxury.

The shiny parquet floors, the expensive rugs and antiques, a sea of mirrors in all the rooms, telephones everywhere, an eighteenth century chaise-longue in the hallway – I hadn't suspected he had so much money.

If only mamma could see this, I thought at the time.

'What a beautiful place your flat is,' I said.

'Our flat,' he said quickly. 'Get used to enjoying good things. I'm relieved you like it – I want to spoil you.'

I held him in my arms. 'My darling, you don't have to spoil me. I am happy just being with you.'

'But I can afford to spoil you,' he laughed, 'and give you everything you've ever wanted.'

We embraced tightly for a full minute. Then I felt him relax, and I had a sudden intuition he had something else on his mind.

'Carmen, I have another important phone call to make.'

I giggled innocently, 'Well, you have all these phones here.'

385

'This is business.'

'So? Can't you make business calls from here?'

'It's business,' he repeated.

Immediately I understood that his 'phone call' was another way of saying that he had 'business' to attend to.

'But we have just got here,' I said crossly. 'I expected you to stay with me at least for today—'

'Darling, you will have to get used to my comings and goings, that's my job.'

I knew there was no point in arguing with him. If I had tried to, it would have spoiled everything. I could feel his determination to get on with his 'business'.

At least he did make one phone call from the flat – upstairs. When he came down he told me what I expected to hear – that he had to leave for a while.

I gave in. 'If it's that important,' I said, 'then don't worry about me. I will find plenty to do here. Besides, I have dinner to think about.'

'Don't worry about that,' he said throwing on his jacket. 'Quite probably we'll be going out.'

'Then I'll unpack the cases. That will take my mind off you while you're out.'

I said this sharply to make him feel guilty.

I couldn't believe how much space there was in the flat. I wished I had ten times as many clothes to fill the racks and drawers.

The doorbell rang. I assumed it was Marcus – perhaps he had forgotten his doorkey. Instead there was a glamorous young-ish woman at the door – no more than twenty-eight – with a severely made-up face and reddish hair.

'I am Giulia,' she said, 'your next door neighbour. I don't know if Marcus mentioned me but I'm a friend of his – I take it you're Carmen – he told me about you, and he said I was to keep an eye on you!'

She laughed at this point, but I didn't know if she was joking.

She added: 'I hope I haven't come too soon to meet you. But I saw Marcus leaving, and since it's my day off I thought to call on you.'

I wasn't sure what to say. I wasn't accustomed to the direct manner of the Romans — they speak to you as if you're a life-long friend after two seconds.

'I can't ask you in,' I told her. 'I'm just unpacking and the place is a mess and I have so many things to sort out — shall we make it another time?'

'Sure!' She seemed quite excited. 'It's nice to meet you Carmen.' Then she said: 'You must think of Marcus and I as just good friends.' She winked and laughed.

I wondered what she was trying to say. I think she picked up on my unease because then she said: 'I must tell you that Marcus is very much in love with you.'

Obviously Marcus and she were good enough friends to have discussed me.

'Look Giulia, I am pleased to have met you but now I have to go — I will give you a phone call. We'll have supper. My in-laws are coming soon and when they're gone we'll meet up . . .'

Not long afterwards Marcus returned with a wonderful bouquet of red roses. 'This is for you,' he said, 'with all my love.'

I forgot everything at the sight of these beautiful flowers — they represented our love and flamenco and all the things that were life to me.

I put my arms around him and kissed him. Even now I relive that wonderful moment, the happiest moment of my life.

Then the moment ended.

'Darling,' he began, 'we are going out to dinner tonight.

387

My friends have invited us. They all want to meet this beautiful Carmen they have heard about. I'd love you to wear that fabulous red dress – it suits you so well. We don't have to stay late if you don't want to.'

'Well,' I said, disappointed that he didn't want to spend this precious time alone with me, 'that depends on how the evening goes.'

I stop for a rest. She writes of the happiest moment of her life. Happier than anything with me?

My mind drifts back to the woman in black. I wonder if she and Carmen are related in some way. I see the woman's face again in my mind's eye, it's unpleasantness. Nothing makes sense . . .

I just pray Carmen will show up soon.

After reading Carmen's diary I usually want to write more of my novel, as I do now. Then I think of Lucia: Why have I not heard from her lawyer yet? I wll have to see her.

I think of Elisabeth. She will not have forgiven me.

Early next morning I drive to see Lucia. The wheat in the passing fields has grown tall. So preoccupied am I with my life I've failed to notice that nature moves on regardless – I feel I've been in Casarsa forever.

I recall the excitement when I first arrived here. I must have known I was about to meet Carmen.

At the family home I park the car in the drive. As before I'm reluctant to use my key – it would seem like trespassing just to walk in. This is no longer my home.

I ring the doorbell instead.

Nobody answers so I'm forced to let myself in. There's an eerie sense of emptiness. Lucia is not about. I'm relieved to get out.

In the past she would have been in at this time. One could always track her movements by the clock.

I go to the school to see Elisabeth. I wait outside for lessons to end – I can hear children chanting numbers and phrases all in a jumble – then suddenly the school bell peals and there is an audible sigh of relief from the pupils.

They stream out of the buildings for lunch. I spot my daughter and call her name.

She turns with a surprised look on her face. She is frozen to the spot, unsure what to do – whether to talk to me or turn her back on me.

Thank God she doesn't run away when I get to her.

'How are you Elisabeth?'

'Fine,' she says curtly. She doesn't ask me how I am.

'How's school?'

'Very well . . . considering.'

She said the very same thing before.

'What do you mean, darling, by that?'

'You know! Why bother to come here?' Her face once again is creased with hostility.

'I am here to see you, because I care about you—'

'If you cared you wouldn't have left mother.'

I see it is hopeless to talk to her so I ask her where Lucia is.

'Don't you know?' she snaps. 'She has gone back to work as a secretary in a big company and she's much happier.'

'Well,' I say, 'I am very pleased to hear it. I must see her because I have important matters to discuss with her.'

Elisabeth takes a piece of paper out of her satchel and scribbles something on it. She hands it to me, then walks off without another word.

I call her but she is deaf to me. Can I blame her?

On the paper is the address of Lucia's employers – a short drive from the school.

At Lucia's company offices a receptionist asks me my name. I must identify myself to talk to my own wife. I'm told I can't just walk into her office.

When I insist that I must talk to Lucia, the woman at the desk phones up.

'Your wife will be a few minutes,' she says, once she has replaced the receiver.

In fact Lucia keeps me waiting half-an-hour.

I'm not prepared for what I see when she finally comes down to reception. She's wearing a dark business-like suit – a waist-length jacket and a tight long grey skirt, with a jewel pinned to her collar.

'What do you want?' she asks calmly.

'You know why I am here. Can we talk somewhere else where we won't be disturbed?'

'Very well,' she says. Even her speech has become business-like.

We drive back home.

'I can't stay long,' she says as we enter the house. 'I will have to return to work pronto.'

'I'm pleased you've found a job,' I say. 'It's better than staying indoors all day.'

'I feel better for it,' she says, taking her jacket off.

'Have you seen a lawyer?'

'I haven't got round to it yet.'

I see signs of the old Lucia, the hurt as she looks away from me.

'Are you trying to avoid what has to be done?'

'I don't have to do anything,' she says sharply. 'Have you ever told me the truth about anything?'

'I have never tried to hide anything from you, Lucia. Don't you think it would be better for both of us if we separated.'

'We're already separated! I have not had a moment to think about lawyers.'

'Don't make excuses Lucia. You know it has to be done. If necessary I shall see a lawyer first.'

'There's no need for that. I can see that woman has really turned your head, hasn't she.'

'Enough of that! These things happen and for a reason.'

Perhaps Lucia feels she's said too much. She apologises but says she is still very hurt. She says she does not deserve such pain. I feel sorry for her.

'I saw Elisabeth at the school. She still hates me for what I have done to you.'

Lucia nods without comment. Then says: 'You have changed so much. There is no way I can reach you.'

'You agreed last time that we should separate – have you changed your mind since then?'

'The truth is I don't want a separation. But I have no other option but to give into you.'

'I'm sorry Lucia, it's for the best.'

She sits at the kitchen table and gazes out of the window.

'I suppose it is in a way,' she says quietly. 'But I have to find a moment of strength to go to a lawyer. Just give me a little time.'

At last I have got through to her. I tell her to think harder and sensibly and she will come to see the wisdom of our parting.

'Shall we remain friends?' I ask her, sitting by her side now.

She turns to me and nods.

'Would you like some lunch somewhere?' I ask.

'I don't feel I want anything. I'd like you to take me back to work.' She puts on her jacket.

'Sure.'

She still knows how to make me feel guilty with her little ways. Not wanting to eat. Asking me to do something I would do anyway – like take her back to work.

But I suppose I deserve it.

It's a ten minute run to her office. As she opens the car door to leave Lucia says, 'Don't worry too much about Elisabeth. She will come round to the situation eventually.'

Driving back to Casarsa I feel relieved to be away from all the tension. The thunder in the air grows heavier so that by the time I've reached Via Valvasone the sky is dark – coal-coloured clouds edged sinister whitish-grey.

The bells of Don Giovanni's church ring out. Someone told me this was a local superstition – that the bell ringing will help break the storm.

As I enter the cottage the rain begins to bucket down with terrible force – I cannot help but feel God is punishing me.

I rush about the place closing windows. Above the rumbles I hear Vilma making greater noise outside as she chases her chickens and geese into a shed. I struggle with the shutters in the kitchen whose hinges are stiff with rust.

Then I glimpse poor old sodden Vilma in her yard. She's chasing her husband around in the mud, not her livestock as I assumed, and cursing him – 'You good for nothing!' she's screaming.

Hunger pangs remind I've not eaten today. I make a ham roll and open a bottle of wine – this will help me to relax a little. I sip . . . and think of Carmen. I wonder when I'll see her again. She has sent no note . . . perhaps she'll call unexpectedly.

What a relationship!

I open her diary where Marcus has asked her to wear her green dress:

While I got ready I told Marcus that his friend Giulia had called soon after he'd left.

'Really!' he said, intrigued. 'So you have met her. What do you think of her?'

I thought she seemed a nice person, and pretty. I couldn't resist asking him if he'd had an affair with her. At that his tie knot fell apart in his hands.

He stared at me hard and said: 'How could you think such a thing? I never had any affair with Giulia. We have always been good friends from the start and when you know her better you will understand.'

'Sorry,' I said. I was happy with that answer. 'It was just a joke, a silly thought.'

Marcus knotted his tie and asked me if I was ready. 'We must go now.'

We arrived at a huge mansion on the outskirts of the city.

'Your friends must be very rich,' I said. He said they were — 'One day we will live in a place just like this,' he added with feeling.

I said nothing. He couldn't know how such things as big houses and wealth meant so little to me. Only our love mattered.

We were let into the house by a thin woman in a long, black diamanté cocktail dress — and immediately I was intimidated by everything I saw. There seemed something wicked about the splendour and sumptuousness — all those horrible animal skins on the wall, the strange paintings of contorted naked figures . . .

A couple approached us – they were in fancy dress. He wore a toga with a laurel crown on his head. She looked like Tarzan's Jane – I wished Marcus had told me this was a fancy dress.

'These are my best friends,' Marcus said pointing at the couple. 'Alfredo and Clorinda.'

They made a great show of welcoming us, and as they led us into another room there were cries of 'Bella! Bella!' directed at me – much to my embarrassment.

I could see Marcus was very proud. I felt uneasy.

At once I knew I did not fit in with his friends. Everything about them seemed alien. The way they bellowed at each other, the constant touching of each other, the coarse innuendo – my eyes were constantly drawn to the skins on the wall.

Everything seemed gross and cruel.

When finally Clorinda had got everyone to the table she sat next to me and asked me what I had done for a living before marrying Marcus. I told her, and then she pursed her lips and remarked, 'Well, my dear Carmen, you can do much better things with your life now that you are in Rome. Marcus won't be having you in any lawyer's office, that's for sure!'

At that the table exploded with laughter, as if they were sharing a joke at my expense.

Then to my horror Marcus announced I was a brilliant flamenco dancer. I looked at him disapprovingly but now Alfredo and Clorinda were clapping their hands demanding that I dance and soon the whole table was shouting 'Gypsy! Gypsy!', insisting I put on a show.

I turned to Marcus and asked him to take me home because I was not enjoying the evening. He said that I must not take too much notice of his friends – 'They mean well,' he whispered.

I decided to stay a bit longer to please him but refused to dance. His friends didn't bother to disguise their disappointment. I felt I had let down Marcus in their eyes. I said I did not feel well.

When a bit later they asked me again to perform I said to their face, 'I did not come here to dance the flamenco.' I then demanded Marcus take me home.

I felt hurt because I had expected Marcus to understand that my dance is an expression of my love and joy. And though I had danced at our wedding reception, it had really been just for him.

But to him it was a performance.

Back home Marcus asked me why I was so hostile to his friends.

'You should know,' I shouted. 'If you don't then I wonder what we have in common.'

'Carmen, I know they asked you silly questions but you have to try to rise above it.'

I said goodnight to him — I felt very tired.

The next morning I was hurt again when he told me suddenly that he was going to have to leave me for a little while. He hoped I felt a bit better after last night.

'Remember Carmen that I am in business with my friends and we have to try to be civilised with them.'

I reminded him that his parents were due anytime now. 'I will be back by then,' he promised.

But of course he wasn't and I had to see to them alone. I didn't much care for his parents who never had anything to say, and were as much put out that Marcus was not there as I was.

But they tried to be nicer to me. And it was a relief when they made an excuse that they would have to return to Florence sooner than expected because of the step-father's business.

As they prepared to leave his mother asked me — 'Are you getting used to Marcus' strange little habits?' Since I didn't get her meaning, I just smiled. I couldn't be bothered to ask her what she meant.

I was alone, a woman in a foreign country with no friends and nothing to do. I decided to call Giulia in the evening. But just as I thought of her, Marcus phoned and asked me if his parents were still with me. He was sorry he had missed them. He promised to be back tomorrow and said he loved me very much.

The moment I replaced the receiver the phone rang again — it was Giulia.

'How are you?' she asked.

'I'm all right,' I said.

'Need some company? Fancy supper?'

She assumed I was alone — how well she knew Marcus. I was more than happy to say yes, but asked her to come round as there was so much food in the flat. She turned up smartly dressed within an hour.

As we ate I asked her if she'd noticed in the past whether Marcus was always away.

'I should say so!' she said, rolling pasta on her fork against a spoon. 'You really do have to get used to it.'

Without thinking I confided my doubts about his work. 'Is it tobacco?' I wondered aloud. I couldn't understand what his job involved exactly.

Giulia was quiet for a while and then she said with a giggle — 'Perhaps he's a spy!'

'Is his business in tobacco, Giulia?'

'He's only a friend, Carmen. I know nothing more than you — and you're his wife!'

Then she said I should make lots of friends as she had who invite her to parties — 'Why not come to one.'

396

I thanked her and said I might just do that when Marcus was away.

I don't believe Marcus is in tobacco. No wonder they've separated. How could Carmen become involved with such people? I read on:

In fact Marcus was more away on business than at home with me. I never imagined the situation could be so bad as this. I kept on hoping it couldn't get worse.

I finally accepted Giulia's invitation and went to one of her parties. It was terrible mistake. I met a man called Gino who was immediately infatuated with me.

I had too much to drink and he took advantage of me. He offered to take me home and I accepted. Once indoors he put his hands all over me. I tried to push him away but he was very strong. In the end I let him do what he wanted. I can't recall how long he stayed — I can only recall some moments.

In the morning I woke up naked — and remembered what had happened. Now I felt dirty and disgusted with myself. I must try to forget it, even now.

When later in the morning Giulia called round and asked me how I had got on with Gino, I said casually, 'OK' — then added that her parties were not for me. I said I'd prefer to join a flamenco dance club.

I couldn't help but wonder what she got up to at these parties — I hadn't seen her for much of the evening.

The next day Marcus returned. We embraced for ages.

'I'm joining a flamenco dance group,' I said.

'Good idea. You're such a good dancer already.' Then he added that it would not always be necessary for him to go away. He kissed me passionately as I tried to forget the foolish night with Gino.

Two days with me and then he was off again. At least he phoned me in the evenings.

My darling Carmen, how long will you go on like this? I feel tired but, I must read on . . .:

A few days after Marcus left me the police called at the flat, asking me where he was. 'Just a routine enquiry,' they said. 'We just want to ask him a few questions.'

'What is he supposed to have done?' I asked naively. I felt apprehensive. Then a terrible fear overcame me.

When the police left I called Giulia in a panic. I told her that I feared for Marcus.

'I'm sure the police have made a mistake,' Giulia said. 'Try not to worry about it.'

I felt a little better. When Marcus did finally return home he said he had no idea why the police would want to talk to him. But he became agitated and I knew something was very wrong.

He tried to act calm.

He tried to reassure me that it was all a misunderstanding — 'I will go to the police now,' he said. 'I haven't the slightest idea what they want me for. I'll be back soon.'

My unease grew. I knew instinctively that it was his 'business' which interested the police. He had always hidden that side of his life.

He did not return home as he promised. I couldn't sleep.

In the early hours of the morning I phoned the city police station and asked them if my husband was being held. The police said no one of Marcus' name had called in that day.

Oddly the policeman who took my call guessed who I was — 'We'll let you know when we've tracked down your husband, Signora Fiore.'

I was tired with worry. I made a cup of coffee. Just as I took my first sip the doorbell rang. I opened the door. The first person I saw was a large man in a suit. Then I spotted a group of uniformed policemen behind him — I was terrified now.

He asked me if I was Signora Fiore. He said he was a police inspector and that he had a difficult task to perform. I understood him immediately.

'This is to do with your husband,' he said.

'What has happened to him?' My voice trembled.

'I'd like you to get dressed and come with us. I am sorry to tell you this but we need you to identify a body.'

I asked him what he was talking about — did he mean Marcus was dead? The inspector did not answer my question but repeated that I must get dressed and go with him.

I can't remember dressing, or the moments before I was taken to the mortuary. I wanted to scream, I wanted my mother . . . I prayed that it wasn't Marcus.

Then I saw his body lying on a table. At that moment I knew my life was over. He had been so full of vitality, life itself to me, and now . . . this. I kept thinking that he would spring to life any moment — I began to feel faint, I couldn't feel my legs, and one of the policemen had to support me.

I can remember the inspector asking me if there was anyone he could contact to come and collect me. I could only think of one person — Giulia. I had to know what had happened to Marcus, I shouted at the inspector demanding to know.

He suggested we leave the mortuary and drive the short distance to his office.

There, he wondered if I was strong enough to talk about the circumstances of Marcus' death.

'I want to know now!' I demanded.

After a pause he said, 'We think your husband was

murdered. We found him in the street, lying in a pool of blood. At first we didn't know who he was. Then we found his driver's licence. We had been watching your husband for sometime. He was suspected of supplying illegal drugs. We suspect his life was taken by another dealer or a client – we don't know at this stage.'

I gripped the chair rests – I couldn't cry.

What flashed in mind was my terrible dream of Marcus' death before we married – it must have been a premonition.

'Did you know any of your husband's business colleagues or friends?' asked the inspector. 'He travelled widely. Where did he go?'

I had no idea – I knew nothing of the travelling, though that would explain his absences. I told him what I could – of his awful friends at the party he had taken me to.

The inspector was nice to me – I think he sensed my innocence. He thanked me for my help.

There was a knock on his office door. A policeman led in Giulia. I was so relieved to see her.

Before I left the inspector said he wanted to ask me one last question: 'Did you know of your husband's activities? I know you are in shock . . .'

Marcus had only said he was in tobacco – and I accepted that. I did not tell the inspector of my doubts. At the back of my mind there had always been doubts.

'You can go now, Signora Fiore,' he said. 'I may need to talk to you again.'

In the next few days Giulia took care of me. She was very supportive. The police were satisfied that I was not an accomplice in Marcus' drug-running. Giulia nagged me to tell my parents . . . but first I had to tell Marcus' parents.

They couldn't understand what I was saying – it was a

terrible moment, especially when I had to tell them I still
had no idea when the funeral could take place.

   My plans were to return to Spain — then I would tell
mamma and papa.

   I felt dead when I finally flew out of Rome forever. I was
no longer the woman of fire.

   And this is the end of my diary.

I close the diary. Now I understand her refusal to discuss
Marcus. She said I would understand. I do now. What a
terrible ordeal. And how remarkable that she wants me to
use her life story for my novel . . . a story I could not have
imagined. It was obvious Marcus was up to no good but I
will say this of him: he loved Carmen, I have no doubt.
His downfall was greed.

But when did this all happen? There are no dates, and
the diary itself is undated . . . I will make up to Carmen
for my doubting her. I will try to be the man Marcus
was not.

The rain has stopped now.

I open the shutters and some of the windows. I can smell
the air, cooler and fresher. On the doormat I spot a letter —
the postman couldn't have delivered it during the storm.

It's from Carmen.

'Please come to San Lorenzo tomorrow afternoon,' she
writes. There is an address. 'I hope you will come. All my
love, Carmen.'

Chapter Ten

The next day I walk to San Lorenzo. On the way I again spot the odd woman in black. This time I shout out at her, 'What's your name?'

As before she slips out of sight, like a cat, into the fields.

Perhaps she is just simple.

In the rundown village I soon track down Carmen's home.

I can hardly believe it.

It's an ancient little house, quite ramshackle, almost in ruins I should say. The roof tiles are displaced, and the paintless front door is shot with rotting holes so you can spy within if you wish.

The little front garden though is tended with vegetables and flowers.

I knock on the door and nobody answers. I knock again – at last I hear some movement inside. For some reason I feel nervous . . .

The door creaks open as if shut for years. It reveals a very old woman in the usual black peasant clothes, bowed and white-haired.

'Yes?' she asks.

She has the native manner and doesn't bother with the social graces. Could this be Carmen's aunt?

'I'd like to see Carmen if I may.'

'Carmen? I don't know . . . who is this Carmen?'

'I understand she lives here,' I say. 'I know she lives here with her aunt and uncle. She is Spanish.'

I get out Carmen's letter – 'Here, she wrote to me yesterday, and invited me to visit.'

She takes the letter and, deep in thought, turns it about in her gnarled hands before passing it back to me, unread. I have no idea whether she can read, but now she looks alarmed and flustered.

'Is this a jest?' she says. 'A dare?'

'Sorry Signora?'

'I think you should go away now.'

'But—'

'I don't know who you are, Signore, but I tell you this Carmen stayed with her aunt here a long time ago. I remember Carmen – she was a Spanish girl – I saw her only twice. She married a local man she met in Rome—'

'Marcus?'

'Yes, bless his soul. So you know the story?'

'But she couldn't have married him years ago – how long ago?'

'Many, many years ago, Signore. Someone's played a cruel joke on you. They lived in Rome. His aunt is still alive, she must be older than me. We used to be friends but we lost touch. She will explain to you. Someone has played a cruel joke on you. She is called Signora Martina – she lives near the church in the next village south, Casarsa. Just ask the way.'

'I know her,' I say.

'If you know her then go see her and she will tell you everything.'

'But . . . you're thinking of someone else,' I say with some exasperation. 'Carmen is a girl, no more than

403

twenty . . . I've seen her – as I see you now.'

The old woman shudders.

'Sorry,' she says briskly, 'but I cannot help you any-more.'

Then she shuts the door quickly.

I am shocked and confused. The old woman must be senile. The elderly often lose sense of time. But she was certain, and knew of Marcus . . . Or she's lying – if she's Carmen's aunt she would see off any male caller perhaps. I don't know what to think.

I don't walk straight to Signora Martina's. I need to think everything through first. I return to my little bridge in the fields and sit in the grass.

A terrible thought returns: perhaps I did imagine Carmen – but what about the letters? our love? the diary? There was always something unreal about our relationship; the mystery, the unanswered questions. But she *is* real. Even now I can feel and sense her.

Instinctively I kneel and pray: 'God, please help me. It cannot be true.'

I must see Signora Martina – she is sure to be in.

I run down Via Valvasone and knock on her door.

I am so beside myself that Kate's first words are, 'You look in a state – you're white. What has happened to you? Come in – let me get you a brandy.'

'May I see your mother, Kate?'

'She's still upstairs but I'll tell her you're here.'

After a minute I hear them both coming down.

'You look as if you've seen a ghost,' says Signora Martina, smiling.

'Signora Martina – there is something I must talk to you about.'

Kate doesn't leave the room as she would normally but sits next to me.

'Now what is it?' says the old lady as she lowers herself into her chair.

I don't bother to prepare her. I tell her everything in a great rush, about Carmen and Marcus, about Carmen and me. And about the diary, the old woman who brought me Carmen's notes, and what the other old woman in San Lorenzo told me.

Signora Martina is quiet throughout, deadly serious, and shakes her head every moment or so, as if doubting my sanity.

When I have finished she orders Kate to fetch her a brandy and then to leave the room.

'I'll stay here this time, mamma.'

The old lady is surprised at her daughter's defiance, then relents.

'Very well, provided Marco does not mind.'

I nod.

She gazes at her daughter, 'What are we to make of this, Kate?'

Then she turns to me and sighs heavily before she continues: 'Your story makes no sense to me, but I know you are a truthful young man. Otherwise I would think you mad or wicked and I would have you thrown out of Casarsa. Yes, my late nephew was called Marcus and he did marry a young Spanish girl called Carmen. He was murdered in Rome. He was a good boy but he was weak and became involved with bad people – it was they who murdered him.'

'When was this?' I ask.

'Maybe twenty years ago.'

I cannot believe it.

I tell Signora Martina again that I saw Carmen, she is a young woman, I love her, have felt her. I talk of her diary, her letters . . .

'Where is Carmen?' I ask.

She shakes her head and for a moment is lost for words.

Then she says: 'This *is* the truth. Carmen is dead. She has been dead twenty years. Carmen could not live without Marcus. When she returned to Spain she could not come to terms with what had happened. Shortly afterwards she took her own life – an overdose. It broke her parents' heart.'

I can barely hold the tiny glass of brandy that somehow Kate has put into my hand. It is inconceivable to me that Carmen – *my* Carmen – is dead. She would never kill herself. Her strength. Her self-possession.

Signora Martina is talking about another Carmen. It is all a fantastic joke.

This claim alone convinces me that the old woman has lost her head—

'The only reason why I am prepared to listen to your story,' says Signora Martina, 'is because a number of years ago I thought I saw something in the fields which I have never forgotten. For a moment I thought I saw the figure of Carmen as I looked out from this room. This was long after her suicide. I did not imagine this – no one will convince me I imagined it though I know the mind can play tricks.'

'You never told me,' Kate says.

'There's much I have not told you. She was moving through young wheat. It *was* Carmen. She was wearing her red dress – it was an apparition or whatever you call it. That is what you saw, Marco. An apparition.'

I cannot accept this.

'It could easily have been another girl from the village – anyone!' I say.

'No!' Signora Martina is adamant. 'No one in Casarsa

looks like Carmen. It was she. She seemed lost. I prayed for her to find her way—'

'What of the woman in black?' I say. 'The woman who brought me Carmen's letters.'

'From what you say of her,' says the old lady, 'I think that is Carmen's aunt – she died sometime ago. She behaved in the manner you have described—'

'All ghosts then, illusions?' I interrupt desperately. 'Nothing real! What about the noises in the cottage?'

Signora Martina shrugs her shoulders. 'Who knows,' she says. 'Maybe the spirit does not die. Perhaps it was Carmen herself who made those noises which so disturbed you. Perhaps she came to you because of your likeness to my nephew Marcus. I do see him in you. Maybe there's more to it. Maybe her soul came to you to fulfil her love. You are so like him. It is uncanny. I do not know.'

To me it is fantasy. I repeat to the old lady that Carmen was real, a ghost could never do all this . . . 'We love each other very deeply. She can't disappear just like that—'

I sound mad to her, I know it.

I turn to Kate. She looks stunned – as if her mother and I are both crazed.

'Did you know of Carmen and Marcus?' I ask her.

Kate nods her head. 'I swore to mamma not to tell – we don't talk about them. It was a scandal. What you've told us is incredible . . .'

'I believe we go to some place from here when we die,' says Signora Martina, ignoring her daughter. 'We cannot understand all this but I suppose we will one day and all this will make sense.'

I have heard enough.

I tell them that I must go now.

As I get up to leave Kate calls out that she'd like to walk back with me and stay with me for a while.

407

Kate says, 'I would like to see her diary – if I see it I will believe you Marco—'

'It doesn't matter what you believe—'

I feel her concern for me, she means well . . . I tell her to stay with her mother. I shall be all right.

I return dazed by the brandy, by everything. I drink more than I know. There must be a rational explanation for what I have experienced . . .

I open a bottle of wine. I want oblivion. I touch Carmen's diary. This is the proof she is real. I look at my novel – suddenly, what does it matter? It is nearly finished, but how can I end it if I am not to see Carmen again?

Nothing Signora Martina said makes sense. I made love to Carmen – she was so warm and vibrant. It is unthinkable that she could only have been a ghost.

It is absolutely absurd.

I decide I cannot finish my novel until I see Carmen again. I wrote it because of her and for her. I am certain she will show herself any moment now.

I go upstairs and lie on my bed and drift in and out of sleep. I am exhausted with thinking, with not believing. I want to be lost in nothingness and never wake up – that's what I want to happen to me.

Because without Carmen my life is nothing.

That is my last thought as my mind slips away; I do not know whether I sleep now. I feel I have drifted into another world, into a world of dreams and vivid colours, and somewhere in these bands of colours I catch sight of the image of Carmen.

She moves close to me – I see that she is real. I knew she was real. She is talking to me but I can't tell whether she calls me Marco or Marcus.

Am I Marcus?

She tells me I must finish my novel. She has come to say I am her true love, and one day we will be together for eternity.

'Your book will give me joy,' she says. 'One day everything will be clear. Remember, that book is about us.'

She smiles. She is so beautiful.

Then as I become aware of Carmen's aunt standing behind her – the woman in black – I wake up, calling out Carmen's name, imploring her to come back to me.

It is three in the morning. The time, in the past, of those strange sounds in the house which I know will disturb me no more.

I get up and know what I must do now.

I must complete my book.

Because I know that her love is real. And one day Carmen and I will be reunited.

Epilogue

Many years have passed since I wrote those words. I am much older now but my love for Carmen is unfaded by time. It is as alive as the first time I saw her in Casarsa.

I feel she is always near me even though I do not see her. She waits for me.

I remain certain that one day, when the time comes for me to leave this life, I will see her again and we will be together.

I did go back to Lucia because we needed each other. But of course our marriage was never the same again.

I love Lucia always as a great friend.

My daughter Elisabeth is married with grown-up children. Thank God she has forgiven me; we are close now.

And my novel was a great success. I have written more books and I continue to write.

I returned to Casarsa only recently. The place has changed out of recognition. Hardly anything is as I remember it. Signora Martina's little cottage where I stayed has been demolished, but the little bridge amid the Casarsa fields still stands.

I know because I walked across it one more time, and through the country lanes, where once I met the true love of my life.